MYTHOLOGY

THE ETERNAL

BOOK 3 OF THE MYTHOLOGY SERIES

Helen Boswell

An Artemathene Book

Copyright

MYTHOLOGY: THE ETERNAL
Helen Boswell

This book is a work of fiction. References to actual locations are intended only to provide a sense of place and authenticity. All other characters, places, and incidents are products of the author's imagination and should not be construed as real.

ISBN: 1512097438
ISBN-13: 978-1512097436

To everyone who believes.

To anyone who snuggles with demons.

To all of the slugs and demon cougars too.

Contents

MYTHOLOGY

———✦———

THE ETERNAL

Amiens, France
500 years ago

Jonathan

The old church had been crumbling for decades, but I liked it. I liked how the structure was still so resilient after multiple attacks during the worst of the *guerres de religion*. I liked how the cracks in the walls allowed the moonlight and the smell of autumn to enter. It was the perfect place for me to marry Adrienne. Marriages were arranged and not thought to be based on love in that time, but we were one of the exceptions. I swore I'd never let anything short of death separate us.

I waited by the pulpit as the priest paced by the entrance, muttering prayers under his breath and casting nervous glances to the door. Adrienne knew him through her connections, but he'd been hesitant to help until I'd persuaded him he wouldn't be in danger. Getting people to bend to my will was easy, something I'd been able to do since I was a young boy. The harder part was always dealing with the repercussions.

The only convincing I had to do with Adrienne that night was to talk her into waiting until it was dark. She was the one to insist that war shouldn't be a factor in whether or not we got married, and she was right. Out of all of the forces conspiring to keep us apart, war was definitely the least of them.

Adrienne's family would gravely disapprove of our union. She was adopted by aristocracy and raised to be like her sisters, but Adrienne possessed a rebellious streak. She completely defied her parents to be with me. Adrienne Dufort, the daughter of a noble family who chose to secretly wed a spy.

She slipped in through the church doors as the bell in town rang midnight, the priest rushing to bar it behind her. He hurried to take his place at the pulpit, but my sole focus was on Adrienne as she walked toward me. Her auburn hair, usually done intricately, was loose beneath her veil. A single wild rose was in her hand, and she wore her best dress. So beautiful, but it was the way her eyes lit up when she stood by my side that made my heart swell.

She could have had so much more than this. An extravagant wedding, a husband of noble status, but she insisted that all she needed was me, a priest, and God as her witness.

"*Bonsoir*, my wife-to-be," I whispered as I took her hand.

Her cheeks, already pink from having hurried there, flamed with color. "*Bonsoir*, my husband-to-be." Her words were spoken too quickly, and before I could say anything else to her, she turned to address the priest. "Please be quick, *mon père*. We need to leave the province immediately."

"Adrienne, what's wrong?" I gently turned her to face me. I could read her better than I could read anyone, and her tone was frightened. "Are you having second thoughts?"

"No, my love. Of course not." Her worry seemed to ease a fraction as she looked into my eyes, her bow-shaped mouth curving into a smile. "I'm only anxious to start our new life together."

The priest didn't need any more encouragement than that, and he led us in saying our vows. Adrienne hung on his every word, repeating him with solemnity. But to me, his words were only prompts, and they faded into the background in comparison to her. For over a year, she and I had kept our meetings secret from her family, our moments together stolen and brief. The notion of having that new life and all the time in the world with her was more than I ever could have hoped for.

I kissed her as soon as the priest blessed the union. Her mouth smiled against mine, her lips warm and sweet. I worried about asking her to leave everything and everyone behind, and I still feared for my own mother's safety. But in that moment, it didn't matter because all I needed was her.

But then she pulled away from me, worry again etched on her brow. "We must leave now."

I nodded and drew out of my pocket a handful of coins to give to the priest. I'd stolen them from the camp that night, and the post horses waiting out back for us as well. I knew we had to ride for a good two hours or more until we got out of the province, and then we'd have to keep heading south until we were out of France. I reasoned that Adrienne's family would assume she'd run off for adventure's sake, as she was apt to do, and weren't likely to come looking for her right away. The Huguenots would assume I was one of many on the list of casualties of war.

Adrienne and I ran hand-in-hand to the horses, and I pulled out a set of man's clothes from a bag I'd earlier stashed behind a tree. I waited until she put the breeches on under the dress before I used my sword to cut away the skirt.

She lamented as she put on the shirt, "My best dress."

I drew back her hair and tucked it into the collar. "I will buy you an entire bureau full of new dresses one day," I said solemnly as I placed a fitted cap on her head and fastened a cape over her shoulders.

Her eyes shone. "Oh, I don't know about that. These clothes suit me, don't you think?"

She mounted the smaller horse, and I grabbed the bag of rations and money before mounting the other. "You could make anything suit you. You chose to marry me of all unsuitable people, didn't you?"

"Oh yes." She kicked her horse into a trot, rolling her eyes to the sky. "In choosing you, this noblewoman may as well have married the devil."

I grinned at her as I started my horse into a gallop. I knew that if her father ever found out what we just did, that would be his exact thought right before he sent me to hell.

"The road ahead may be perilous. May God be on your side," the priest called quietly from the door of the church as we passed.

"Thank you, *mon père*," I said.

Adrienne called back to him. "May God be with you."

She tossed him her rose before spurring on her horse.

<hr />

I had vivid dreams that night. Of interrogation rooms and screams. Of broken spirits and lies. Of everything that I'd made my life into since I'd left my home in search of my father. I could never know for sure, but I imagined he died in a prison cell just like the ones where I spent my days working.

"*Réveille-toi*, my love." *Wake up.*

Adrienne. I opened my eyes to find her propped up on an elbow and gazing down at me, and the memory of dark dreams immediately slipped away. She lay under the wool blanket next to me, her warm skin against mine. In that moment, I knew that all would be right in the world.

"Is this real?" I reached up and removed a small piece of straw from her hair. She smiled a little sleepily at me, and shifted positions as though she was stiff.

The crude straw mattress was just as good as anything I'd ever slept on, but I felt bad about having to treat her to such meager accommodations. We'd ridden the horses for just over an hour the night before when mine had stepped into a hole. The horse had broken its leg, and I'd told Adrienne to ride on ahead while I put it down with my sword.

We found a place that the priest had told us about beforehand in case we needed a closer stopover point. It was a farmhouse right outside Amiens, and I'd given the owner a good share of our money for his silence. He gave us a place to sleep in what he called his guesthouse but what was really a barn. With Adrienne by my side, I didn't dare try to convince him in other ways to give us something better.

It wasn't a pleasant thing to watch, when I used my powers of persuasion.

"I'm very real," she whispered. "But I know what you mean. Everything since last night has been like such a lovely dream."

"I see. Such as our dreamy, luxurious room." I chuckled, and she lightly slapped my arm.

"Do you think of me as being spoiled, Jonathan Drapier?" she scolded. "I told you once, and I'll tell you as many times as you need to hear. I don't require all of those wasteful, material items that my parents were so fond of accumulating. It's disgusting, the way my mother mourns over the loss of some of those meaningless trinkets as though she lost a daughter." Her eyes held mischief as she traced a fingertip across my chest. "I only need you, or was last night not enough of a reminder of this?"

"You have me," I countered as I caressed her hair, my other hand moving over her hip and drawing her closer. "But you're welcome to remind me of how much you need me."

She breathed against my ear, "I shall be happy to. Every morning for the rest of my life."

I took her face in my hands and looked into her eyes, my entire body and soul yearning for that reminder. Despite all of my planning and precautions, I knew it wasn't safe for us to stay here for too long. I needed to get the horse ready, and I had to figure out how to get another one or we wouldn't make good time out of the province. But as I kissed Adrienne and the warmth of her body melded into mine, I thought that we didn't need to rush at all.

The wooden door suddenly splintered, an axe breaking through to let the sun in through a gash. Adrienne sat up and screamed. I was out of bed in the next instant, grabbing my pants and my sword.

"Adrienne!" a voice bellowed.

"Edmond," she whispered, her face going ghostly white. Her older brother.

The crashing blow hit the door again, the door creaking on its hinges. I knew it wouldn't hold for long, and I turned to Adrienne, who was clutching the wool blanket to her chest and petrified with fear.

"Get dressed and wait for me outside," I commanded in a low voice. "Get the horse ready. Hurry."

She blinked and then nodded, slipping her chemise over her head and running barefoot away from the door. It wasn't a second too soon because it caved in with Edmond's next strike. The wood and metal crashed to the floor, the explosion of debris paving the way for Adrienne's older brother, a brute wielding a monstrosity of a battle axe. Both he and his weapon had a definite size advantage over me, but his emotions were single-tracked. Bloodthirsty. I knew that if I could get close enough to touch him without being crushed, I would be able to get Adrienne out of here.

"You," he spat, "have dishonored my family and desecrated my sister."

He charged at me like an angry bull, battle axe raised, and I lifted the sword as though I was going to deflect him. Only when he swung, I lunged to the side instead and stepped so I was behind him. He pivoted around with surprising swiftness given his size, but I leapt onto his back and took his neck in a chokehold.

I drew upon the strength from the worst possible moment of my life.

"Step aside, boy. We're here to take your father."

"What? No. This is a mistake! What do you believe he's done?"

Maman ran over, demanding answers. Her hands were covered in flour and flailed in the air as she spoke, but they covered her face after the officer struck her across the cheek. She fell to the floor and I jumped up, my fists clenched and ready to strike back in her defense. But a single hand gesture from Papa stopped me. He wanted me to wait to act. No, he wanted me to not act at all.

"He committed an act of thievery against the court," the officer declared. He took Papa by the arm, and Papa didn't resist.

No, it was me. I was the thief.

I knew in that moment. Papa somehow guessed it was me that stole the money from the court, and he took the blame. I wanted to scream the truth, but Papa shot me another warning look and said softly to my mother and me that he loved us.

"Take care of your mother, Jonathan."

Maman lifted her head, the tears sliding down already-wet cheeks as the officer took him away. I rushed to her side, sinking down next to her with a heart full of despair.

An eleven-year old boy who just found out he needed to be a man.

Edmond fought for air while I fully engaged the memory. The residual emotions from my past were the key to my power of persuasion, and I shuddered as the despair threatened to incapacitate me. But it was merely an illusion, a way for me to tap into my own anguish from six years prior, and I transferred the same illusion over to Edmond with a mental shove.

He clutched at his chest, the shock to his system bringing him down to his knees with a thud. It's what I did – or what I'd been doing – when I interrogated prisoners of war. Sometimes it was enough to stop their hearts, but in Edmond's case, I didn't push very hard.

The axe landed heavily next to him, and I kicked it away before grabbing my shirt from the foot of the bed and slipping it on.

I crouched down next to him and looked him in the eye. "How did you find us?" I demanded.

He stared at me and made a choked laugh. I stared back, his reaction unexpected. True, I hadn't used my full force on him, but I tensed up, suddenly knowing I'd been a fool. Adrienne. I'd sent her out back by herself without checking to see if there was any danger.

In the next heartbeat, I heard a horse's whinny, and then the sound of hooves moving hard and fast. Panic welling in my chest, I ran to the back of the guesthouse in time to see her father on his black steed leading another horse away. Adrienne was tied to the other horse, her limbs limp, her head lolling with every hoof beat. I rushed to follow, but our horse lay under a tree, its throat slit.

"*Adrienne!*" I screamed to the wind, because they were already gone.

I rushed back into the house and grabbed my sword. I tried to rationalize with myself. That I wasn't too late. That if they tracked us here, I could find them too. I could get her back. I could get her back…

"You won't find her," Edmond called from behind me. He had the battle axe again, and he lumbered toward me with a sneer. "He'll exile her to prevent this from disgracing the family name."

I pivoted around, my sword pointed at him. "Where is he taking her?"

His eyes shifted to the side, and I knew he was about to feed me a lie. "I don't know. I only know that I'm supposed to kill you."

"Liar." His threat barely registered with me. "Tell me where he's taking her. You cannot seriously be part of this plan. She's your sister!"

He shrugged, his fat lips widening in a smirk. "She was adopted."

Edmond charged again, and I dodged his swing. He spun around to come after me once more but was moving clumsily this time, and he stumbled.

Adrienne had been fond of him. It was my last thought as I watched him trip on his own feet and pitch forward, his arm holding the axe thrusting out as he tried to catch himself. He landed with a grunt and a horrible crunching sound as he fell squarely on his own axe.

"Edmond?" I approached slowly, the utter horror of the present moment replacing my despair from the past.

He wheezed, his cheek pressed against the floor. With some effort, I rolled him onto his back, trying not to look at the axe buried in his chest. His lips moved silently at first, but then I barely heard his words.

"He told me only… he'll send her away…to marry another… already arranged."

His hand fumbled and reached into his pocket to take out Adrienne's rose. The rose she was holding the previous night when I married her, the rose she gave to the priest. If he was the one who betrayed us, the only ones who could vouch for Adrienne and I being married were the two of us and God.

I stared down at Edmond's body as it twitched at my feet, at his chest as he drew his last breath. I knew in my heart right then that I was all alone in this. That God could not save us now.

Edmond's arm fell to the floor with a thud, and the blood-red petals of the rose scattered like the pieces of my heart.

1

Jonathan

Black rage fills me as I crouch down by the dead guardian.

He's sprawled out on the back step of my art gallery, his neck twisted unnaturally and from the looks of it, his legs broken beyond repair. I can feel from him that his soul was decimated by something unnatural and dark – the obvious work of a demon. But to blatantly violate my territory and place his body here in such a defiled state doesn't speak to the work of the Impiorum demons.

It speaks to something much worse.

This is the third guardian death of the week, and like the other two, this one's face is slashed beyond recognition. The only difference is that the others hadn't been dumped on my doorstep in what's obviously a message. I draw back his blood-soaked collar, taking in the lacerations that continue down to his neck and upper chest. He's not breathing, his skin colder than death, but I can feel the last lingering traces of his *lumen* – his light and power – as it struggles to return home. I place my hand over his heart and draw upon the collective *lumen* of guardians to help him.

I release you.

The guardian's soul breaks free, intense sorrow ripping through me as I feel his last remnant of light rejoin the guardian collective. But the sensation is merely instinctual, and it's gone within two breaths like his shortened existence.

I straighten to a standing position when I hear a gasp from the other end of the alley. Raleigh, my second-in-command, has just arrived and must have felt his departure too. She travels the length of the alley like a breeze and crouches down next to the other guardian's body while I take a moment to hide my anger. As the director of the guardians in my sector, I show only certain faces to my constituents. The more controlled I am, the better control I have over situations. I've noticed that even Raleigh is more at ease when my emotions are measured, and we've known each other for decades.

"Jonathan." She looks up at me through her long tawny locks, her expression a mixture of anger and sadness. "Who could have done this?"

I don't reply right away, instead studying what's left of his face. I recognize him after all – a young guardian from my sector with a mere two hundred seventy years under his belt as an immortal. But now he's no more, and the way his body lies stirs up long-ago memories of deliberate bloodshed. The cuts themselves start on his forehead, and they crisscross themselves in an unusual pattern, almost as if... I tilt my head at an angle as the red lines connect to form letters, and then the words.

your eternal end

Revulsion creeps down my spine as the words sink in. I've seen this exact phrase once before in the past five centuries, and the individuals responsible embodied the very definition of nightmarish. They once wreaked havoc in this realm, and if they've returned, both guardians and humans are in huge trouble.

"I think the *Seraphim* might be back," I mutter. It's an ironic usage of the term, the name of a group of angels for the very worst demons to ever walk this realm, but it's no joke.

"The who?" Raleigh frowns at the word, her eyes suddenly widening in alarm as she recognizes the name. "No." Her horror flows out toward me like waves of energy. "You told me they were banished from our realm over four hundred years ago. Isn't it more likely to be the work of the Impiorum?"

"Could be. However, no living Impiorum member would have had memory of how the *Seraphim* operated." I gesture down to the guardian's body. "But that exact phrase…. I've seen it firsthand."

I bend down to drag the guardian's body inside, and she storms after me.

"Did he leave you his wishes?"

"Yes, he wanted to be buried along his descendants. His family has a plot in Rochester."

There will be no memorial service, no loved ones attending. He doesn't have any living relatives left. Not all of my constituents have reached that point in their existence where they've left provisions for when they meet their ends. Raleigh hasn't, but then again she's spent less than a century as a guardian. Losses are consequently harder on her, and sure enough, as I lay the body in the corridor of the gallery, I can feel the grief pouring out from her.

I turn to her and place my hand on her shoulder, but she jumps away from me, her eyes narrowed in suspicion. "Jonathan Draper, don't you dare manipulate my emotions. It's perfectly normal for people to grieve."

"I beg your pardon," I say with unwarranted innocence. "I wasn't necessarily going to manipulate anything. But now that you mention it, I do need you to do some work."

I walk toward my office, and she protests, "We can't leave him lying here."

"He's already gone. We'll take care of his body later," I shoot back. "Right now I need you to look up the most recent assignments of the three guardians that were destroyed this week. Examine their locations relative to each other and see if you can come up with a pattern. The message they left us tonight was deliberate, and with three, we might be able to triangulate their position."

"All right." I feel her concentration sharpen, and I can tell she's already considering which of her custom-made macros to use. "I'll also check police and campus incident reports for anything suspicious and throw that into the formula."

I nod in agreement, but Raleigh's already gone in a blur of speed. She's accessing my workstation when I get to my office, and I stand back against the wall and watch her work. Raleigh built the secure database from the ground up and maintained it for the guardian that preceded me as director of the region. When I took over as director last year, she — thankfully — took on the same role as second-in-command with me.

Some days I think she'd be more effective at being in charge than me but while Raleigh reigns in efficiency, she's also too quick to let passion cloud her judgment. According to her, I'm the exact opposite. Logical and centered, but less efficient.

"South campus of UB," she says after a few minutes. "If there's any sort of pattern to their activity, that has to be where they're based."

"Are you certain?" I walk around the desk and peer over her shoulder at the three intersecting lines on the map. There are other points scattered within the triangle, and they all converge on an area directly south of the older campus of University at Buffalo.

"I'm sure," she says firmly.

"Dispatch four teams to monitor the perimeter here." I tap the four locations on the screen. "I'll run through to see if I can flush anything out. If they are indeed *Seraphim*, they'll be drawn out by our collective signal, but we need to fall back as soon as we confirm what they are. Do not engage. This is solely reconnaissance."

Her lips press together. "I agree that if they are in fact here, we need to know, but shouldn't we also act to destroy them?"

"The Praxidikai were the ones to originally banish the *Seraphim*," I say calmly. "If we find them, we report them and that is all."

Raleigh stares at me for several seconds longer, the conflict evident in the green of her eyes before she bows her head. She hits several quick commands on the keyboard, the screen going black when she's done.

"The teams are already on their way."

"Thank you, my dear."

I put my jacket back on and grab my keys for the BMW, gesturing for her to accompany me, and she walks with me toward the back door of the gallery. "You keep track of the teams. Have them report directly to you about any suspicious activity. I'll communicate with them via phone if I need to."

She draws out a small transparent earpiece from her jacket pocket. "Try this. It's a communicator. It's secure and…more modern."

I take it from her, turning it over in my hand. "Are you sure they're secure?" I see her raised eyebrows and immediately put it in my ear. "I see. You designed it, did you not? Of course it's secure."

"It taps into the collective energy, so you only have to think and you'll be able to communicate telepathically," she instructs me. "Those devices on matching frequencies will be able to hear your thoughts and respond accordingly. I'll be on your frequency and direct the others on a second one."

"You'll be able to hear all of my thoughts?" I say lightly.

"Are you afraid of spilling all of you secrets?" She smiles. "No, you must touch it with a fingertip to activate it."

I test it out, lightly tapping it with my finger and thinking something about Raleigh.

Her smile broadens, her hands smoothing over the front of her blue tunic dress. "I'm glad you like it. It's new." She steps outside, and we hurry through the alley. "Drive separately or together?"

"Separate." I'm still marveling over the ingenuity of the device when reach the street. I can see her Jaguar parked a block away, and I disengage the security system of my BMW in front of the gallery and turn to her. "What do you call it?" I ask out of curiosity.

She cocks her head. "Sorry?"

"What do you call it?" I repeat. "If you invented it, it must have a name."

"Oh! Well...." Her eyes widen, as if hadn't considered this. "It's a telepathic communicator device, so perhaps we should call it that."

"A Pathicomm," I say decidedly. "It's quite remarkable."

Her hand trails through her hair, her expression pleased. "Thank you. And now that that's settled, where would you like us to start?"

"You stay on the perimeter with one of the teams. I'll conduct the sweep through the area."

I sense her mood flattening. "Forgive me, Jonathan, but if it's truly *Seraphim* we're dealing with, perhaps it's a better idea if I help you search for the threat."

I come to a stop by my BMW. "Hope will help me search."

Her eyebrows arch in surprise. "Really? Is that well-advised, considering?"

"We need Hope to confirm what they are, and that is all. She won't be in any danger."

"I'm just saying," she persists. "Hope is more focused on the fact that she doesn't have a boyfriend anymore than on her guardian duties."

"Raleigh," I say sharply. "That is hardly a fair assessment."

"You know what I mean," she says. The glint in her eye tells me she's holding firm, but so am I. I know Hope has been in pain since Micah left, but she's capable of this and much more.

"My decision is final."

Raleigh opens her mouth to say something else but thinks better of it. I know her stance on this issue. She's made it perfectly clear on numerous occasions what she thinks about my protégé's emotional state these days.

I give her a grim smile as I get into my car.

"Besides, pain is a stronger motivating force than joy."

"Do what you absolutely must to survive. We'll bring you out as soon as we can."

The first statement was like a repeating mantra in my head for two years. The second was my superior's promise to me, spoken one year before Adrienne was taken from me on our wedding night. The Massacre in the nearby commune of Vassy occurred in the previous month, but the repercussions of it still affected the citizens in my city of Amiens on a daily basis. I was no exception – I was still stationed with the enemy as a double-agent. My primary task was to feed intelligence to the rebel forces, which I dutifully completed when I could get away. I'd been working for the revolutionists to get information that would help the Huguenots. On the side of religious freedom but in a pretense of working for the other.

As time went on, I was able to sneak away less and less because the enemy put me to good use once they figured out how persuasive I could be. Night after night, I manipulated emotions of prisoners of war to get them to release their secrets.

My own emotions I kept carefully locked away. Ever since I lost Adrienne, I had no use for them.

That night started out much like the others, and the viscount's beady-eyed stare bore into me as I entered the holding cell. He was a greedy and deplorable man, and he curled his lips in a sneer as I took in the scene before me. The prisoner's emotions felt raw and desperate and devoid of all hope. I knew only the essentials — that he was one of theirs that was caught sneaking away from the camp earlier in the day. He was crouched down on the floor in a submissive posture in the shadows of a third.

I didn't recognize this third individual from my time at the prison, but he stood as though he had a right to be there. He wore a tattered black uniform, his cheeks still showing the signs of youth beneath greasy and unkempt blond hair. I approached him with confidence. He was perhaps sixteen or seventeen, no older than I was, but when his eyes locked with mine, the amount of malice in them was enough to give me pause.

"Jonathan, this is Cyril," the viscount said in an oily voice. "I have placed him in charge of things here from now on."

From now on. Not only for this interrogation session. I camouflaged my dismay behind a frown. Being under someone else's charge would limit my ability to direct the interrogations. I started to protest, but one look from the viscount was enough to silence me. He was a naturally suspicious man, and I sensed that he was even more so that night. But he was also prickling with the edgy taste of fear, and that in itself was enough to pique my interest.

I inclined my head. "Of course, Lord Viscount."

He nodded curtly, looking away. I knew he thought I needed direct eye contact to read the emotions my subjects, but that merely provided me with a focal point. I'd always been able to tune into the subtleties of body language, could detect in a scent the faintest changes in body chemistry. Reading people was most of what I did — the rest was merely persuasion. Luckily the viscount couldn't read me, or he would have known how insincere my efforts were.

He cast a quick glance over his shoulder at Cyril before hastening his pace out of the room. His mannerisms departed from the norm, and as soon as the door slammed behind him, I turned my attention on Cyril with interest.

I could feel that he was guarded, with walls of his own that he'd constructed to shield his emotions, but my gifts allowed me to see through them. I don't know what I expected from him, but it wasn't the poison that flowed over to me. The darkest sort of hatred. Heart-pounding madness. He smiled at me, but it was more like a leer, and as I watched, his eyes transformed from a dark brown to black pits.

The prisoner began to cough, blood tinting the sputum that hit the stone, and I realized that Cyril had already inflicted torture upon him before my arrival. Cyril completely ignored the prisoner at his feet, approaching me instead.

"You have quite the reputation here. I have heard that you can manipulate the will of men." He was trying to provoke me, but he presented it in a voice that was smooth and almost hypnotic. I shrugged off its effects, still curious about the reason he was brought here.

"As you say," I say simply. The intensity of his emotions roiled and crested beneath his calm facade and unsettled me. I shut off my senses, mustering up the nerve to challenge him. "I am in charge of this block. Why did the viscount bring you here?"

"Don't worry. He still values your abilities, but he felt you were not as effective as you could be."

Only then did he look down at the prisoner. He swung his leg without warning, his heavy black boot connecting squarely with the jaw of the man. The prisoner fell backward with a grunt, his head striking the stone floor. He struggled to get up, but Cyril was already crouched down next to him with his hands clamped on either side of his head.

"Look at me," Cyril growled.

The prisoner's eyes squeezed shut but Cyril held on, and as soon as his eyes opened a crack, his body began to rack with convulsions. It was as though Cyril was tearing the soul away from the man, and I was too horrified to act or do anything but watch this devil in black administer his torture.

Abruptly, Cyril stood, countering my look of shock with a sly smile. "I already got the information we needed from this one. You're in charge of clean up."

He brushed off his hands and strode out of the room, leaving a trail of hatred in his wake.

I dashed over to the prisoner, who lay on the floor with a hand clutching his chest. I didn't know exactly what Cyril did to him, but judging from how weak he felt, he didn't have much time left in this world.

I placed my hand on his forehead and funneled a sense of calmness into him. He trembled beneath my touch and opened his eyes. "You can't stop him," he rasped. "He said he couldn't die."

I shook my head, my own fears building. "How is this possible?"

He didn't answer, his trembling slowly ceasing and eyes closing as I murmured a prayer for him. A chill crept into my bones after he drew his last breath, as if his soul took with it all of the warmth in the room upon its departure.

The front of the prisoner's coat fell open, and I noticed for the first time the fresh blood on his shirt and the cuts that were seeping through in red lines.

I jumped up, my legs weak and body drenched in sweat. My own despair leaked through my defenses as I stared at the words forming on the prisoner's shirt. For that's what they were. Deliberate cuts in the skin of this unlucky soul.

votre fin éternelle

your eternal end

2

Micah

Fifty-nine days.

Fifty-nine days since I left behind everyone I love. Since I walked away from my family, my friends, my life. From Hope. I'm counting down the days until I can go back to her, determined in the meantime to make every day that we're apart count. And I'm almost done. Two months of training with the alliance, and they'll give me the choice of staying for another month or putting in for a transfer.

Despite missing everyone and everything from home, I haven't made my decision on what I'm going to do yet, for reasons out of my control.

It's just past midnight, and Jehoel and I work our way through the outskirts of Seattle. We've been chasing leads throughout the Pacific Northwest for three days with no luck, and I keep telling myself to be patient.

Our intelligence unit back at the stronghold detected a sharp drop in Impiorum membership this past week in Seattle, and Jehoel and I came out here with hopes that some of them fled and weren't just killed outright. He and I make up one of the scouting teams for the alliance, and our sole job is to recruit other Impiorum defectors.

He parks the car in front of a homeless shelter in one of the poorer neighborhoods, and I can tell even before getting out that we won't find anyone but humans inside. "I'm not picking up anything," I say impatiently. "I know we're supposed to sweep a radius, but I say screw that. We need to go into the city. C'mon, J.T."

He carefully adjusts his glasses, a gesture he always uses when he's irritated, and I kick myself for my slip. As soon as he joined the alliance, Jehoel started going by his given name instead of J.T. I think it's symbolic of him finally being able to be himself, of being accepted amongst the brotherhood of demons. Or maybe he's annoyed because I want to do something different. He's like a rock on these missions. An overly cautious rock that does the same thing every time.

I glance at his profile, at the literal battle scars standing out in relief on his skin. They make him look a lot older, but I also think part of it is because he's so serious all of the time. Back in Buffalo, he was the keyboardist in a band, but I can't imagine him ever letting himself go and having fun. Since getting out here, he's been one-hundred-and-twenty percent committed to the alliance, and that's been about it.

He doesn't reply until after we're climbing the steps. "It's never smart to head directly into the storm."

"We'd stand a better chance of finding anyone who wanted to defect if we were closer to the source," I argue.

"The demons in the Seattle Impiorum make the ones in Buffalo look almost civil," he informs me before yanking open the door. "We don't want to risk invading their territory, trust me."

"What, you're afraid we'll get caught, and that they'll torture us? There's risks in everything we do," I say flatly.

"We follow procedure," he retorts.

The demon alliance is less than a year old, and I don't know which of the things we do I'd even call "procedure." But I do know that Jehoel views our job as looking for demons that have already defected from the Impiorum. To me it's no better than a fishing expedition, but to Jehoel, it minimizes the risk to the alliance.

I'm not one to blindly run into danger. I'm also not the most knowledgeable one in the group, and I'm definitely not in charge of anything. Honestly, most of the other guys in the group stay away from me. But I do know that up until two months ago, I used to struggle to not take souls on a daily basis. On an hourly basis. Pretty much whenever people got too close to me. There have to be others in the Impiorum who might feel just as lost and afraid to take a chance, and I know that heading straight to the source would be better than this.

We walk inside the building, and a woman looks up to greet us.

"Hello. Do you need lodging tonight?" Her voice is monotone, tired.

Jehoel goes over to talk to her, while I stuff my hands in my jacket pockets and hang back. We've been moving nonstop for three days, sleeping minimally and probably looking like hell.

I follow Jehoel to a room set up with rows of cots and blankets. There's a handful of people in there, all homeless. All humans. I stamp down my impatience and go with him as he walks up the row. He pauses now and then to check a newspaper that was left behind or to poke his foot at a piece of forgotten clothing beneath a cot. It's like he's sleuthing for clues, but I never know what he's looking for, and he never tells me.

"Not the Hilton, but it's not so bad." A woman with frizzy hair and wearing layers of sweatshirts grins at us from her cot. She has a newspaper folded on her lap with a crossword puzzle facing up. "You guys staying for a while?"

Jehoel ignores her, but I manage a smile and shake my head.

She's probably in her mid-twenties, about the same age as my older sister Lina…before she died. I wish I could give the woman something to help but don't have a penny on me.

"I ain't like the others," she says, rocking back and forth a little. "My boyfriend ripped me off. Stole all my money and burnt my stuff before kicking me out. I'm just here until I can figure out what to do."

"I'm sorry," I say honestly. "Do you have any family?"

"No, love." Her eyes shift over to Jehoel, who's almost at the end of the row now. "That your brother?" Jehoel has short, red hair and mine is blond and in my face half the time. But we're roughly the same height and build, and maybe we could be mistaken for relatives.

"No. I don't have any family either."

She nods and leans forward, whispering confidentially, "The kitchen's supposed to be locked. But the outside door don't lock so good anymore. I think someone jimmied it open last week. In case you're hungry." She looks me up and down. "A big guy like you has gotta eat."

"Thanks."

I glance over at Jehoel, who looks frozen in place. He was stony-faced already, but demon hearing is super-sensitive, and I know by his reaction that he had to have heard her. Maybe he's hungry. Or maybe it's something else. Before he lived in Buffalo, he was a pastor and like me, lived among the general human population. I know he can't be completely unaffected by being around so many people with tragic stories.

"I'm checking it out," he says vaguely.

He heads out of the room, and I follow, catching up to him when he's outside. We walk around the building until we get to the dumpsters next to an outside door. It's locked when we try it, but it jerks open when I pull on it a second time. Jehoel peers at the locking mechanism – it's obviously messed up, like someone's broken into it before but wanted it to stay closed. I follow him into the kitchen, my nerves prickling. I half-expect someone to jump at us or to find the place ransacked, but when Jehoel flips on the lights, it's bright and clean.

I glance at him as he stares at the cupboards. "What are you thinking?"

"Just start looking."

"For what?"

He doesn't answer, just starts opening drawers. I join in, frustrated because he's not sharing his thoughts. As always.

We make the rounds through the kitchen, but I don't see anything out of place. He heads into what looks like a walk-in pantry as I crouch down to look into a low cabinet. There's a backpack stuffed into the far back, and I give the strap a yank to pull it out.

"Hey, Jehoel," I call to him. "Check this out."

He comes over as I unzip it to reveal a t-shirt and baseball cap wadded up on top. I stand back as he goes through the rest of it – mostly clothing and bathroom stuff. He pulls out a dog-eared copy of an Edgar Allen Poe collection from the outside zippered pocket before stuffing it back in.

"Why would someone risk hiding out in here instead of staying with the others?" I muse more to myself than to him.

Jehoel is silent, placing everything back into the backpack the way it was. He gestures for me to follow him back outside and closes the door, also making sure the locking mechanism was the way we found it.

"I'm going to wait here for a while to see if he comes back. Do you feel like sweeping the area from above?"

This is a first. Jehoel asking me instead of just giving me orders.

"Sure." I hold up my wrist. "I'll activate the tracker if I pick up anything." The tech guys at the compound made these tracking bracelets custom. They only allow for a specific location to be sent between scouting partners.

He gives me a curt nod, his sign of approval. "Good. Check in with me in thirty minutes, whether you pick up something or not."

"Will do. And thanks," I add as an afterthought. I call up my *deimos*, my power emerging as invisible wings, and run down the steps before he can change his mind. My natural camouflage and a sense of relief both settle over me as soon as I take to the air. I haven't flown all week, and it's good to get up here.

I miss so many things about being home. Hope and my family. My old friends. Even school. But I miss the little things too, like my morning flights and how I didn't use to need the buddy system to go everywhere. Prior to joining the alliance, I'd been on my own so much that having to take orders all of the time now grates on me.

Not that it's any worse than taking the orders of the Praxidikai.

If the thought of eventually going back home to Hope is what's keeping me going these days, having the power of the fire goddess of the Underworld in my blood is just the opposite. She's like a harbinger of doom, always there as a constant reminder of the curse I'm carrying. When I'm out scouting for defectors, her presence is even stronger. Probably because she didn't just give me the power to set things on fire at will, but she also gave me the ability to create the mark – the power that I'm supposed to use to send the defectors' souls to the literal version of Hell.

Given that I'm one of the defectors now, I obviously haven't done the job I was tasked with. While I don't have a specific deadline, it's still like a ticking time bomb in my blood, tracking me wherever I go. It's the main reason that I can't go home yet. Not until I make sure that the bomb won't explode around the people I love.

I circle the neighborhood until I come to a house with a subwoofer that's loud enough to rattle the windows. The energy from souls is easy to tap into when the owners' wills are weak, and from the amount of revelry that's likely at this party, it makes a perfect demon watering hole.

I touch down on the roof of the house across the street, surveying the party from the shadows. There's definitely another demon in there, brief and sporadic pulses of his *deimos* hitting me like small shocks of electricity. But it doesn't feel like a full-fledged effort. It's like he's feeding but also trying his hardest not to.

As if on cue, Vahni's power surges, flames erupting from my hands. I duck down low on the rooftop, my head pounding with each beat of my heart. Anyone who happens to look up right now will probably think the house is on fire and will call 911. My hands ball into fists, my mind waging the internal war until I'm able to bring the fire back inside me. But I know I didn't win forever.

I should probably call Jehoel. But I wait and watch as the front door to the house opens, and couple of college-aged looking girls stumble outside and fall onto the lawn in a giggling heap. They start pointing at the stars, and I duck down a little lower so they won't see me.

The front door opens again, three guys coming out of the house this time. My sense of recognition prickles as I hone in on one of them, a tall, lanky kid with messy dark hair. His hands are jammed into the front pockets of a gray hoodie, and he runs down the steps and stops short when he sees the girls on the grass. The other guys are drinking beer and seem oblivious to most of everything, but the guy in the hoodie – it's him. I can feel his signature, and his *deimos* erupts just as I think it. I tense up, preparing to intervene if I need to, but instead of acting on his obvious need to feed, he stares at the tangled bodies on the lawn and backs away.

I know that look of torment on his face. I've totally been there, not even that long ago. Jehoel taught me how to take energy without stealing the day after I left Buffalo, but prior to that, I was a mess.

One of the girls twists her head to look up at him. "Hey, Ben," she slurs. "It's Ben, right? Hey, come look at the stars with us."

Ben looks around wildly as though for help, and I wish I could send him a telepathic thought. Not sure what I'd say, but I just want to tell him it'll get better.

I press my finger firmly on the metal of my bracelet to send Jehoel my location, hoping he doesn't teleport into a swimming pool. The tracker is a prototype and a little glitchy. Sometimes the location is off by a few meters. Sometimes if you accidentally activate it if you're too close to the other person, it feels like you're getting electrocuted. But it's secure, and that's what matters most.

I sense the heat from him teleporting in right before he materializes. He teeters a little on the sloped roof, and I pull him down to lie flat next to me until he can shake it off. Teleporting has its fair share of side effects, disorientation being the most common one.

"Guy in the gray hoodie," I whisper.

We've been working together long enough that I know what to expect now. We'll keep an eye on Ben until we can get him alone, Jehoel will do most of the talking, and I'll chime in and vouch for the alliance.

Ben's literally turning in circles on the lawn right now, looking indecisive as hell. The girls on the lawn must have gotten impatient waiting for Ben to join them because now they're laughing and pointing at the stars again.

"Did he feed?" Jehoel murmurs.

I shrug. "He's been holding himself in check pretty well since he got outside."

He throws me a cutting glance. "You mean he fed when he was inside?"

"A little, yeah. That's how I was able to pick him up."

Jehoel frowns. "Then we put him down as someone to track. We'll check back on him at a later date. You know procedure."

He's staring straight ahead, the stubborn set to his jaw mirrored by my own feelings. Yeah, I know procedure, but that doesn't mean that I agree with it.

"We can't just leave him here," I argue. "He's obviously alone, and he's struggling."

"Too risky. He's not an ideal candidate." Jehoel's face darkens, and he looks ready to go the rounds with me on this.

"I wasn't an ideal candidate when you first found me," I point out. "But you took me with you anyway. Isn't the reason the alliance exists in the first place? So we can have a second chance?"

"Yes, but now that we're more established, we need to minimize risks. The whole of the alliance is greater than its parts," he says firmly. "I'm not bringing anyone risky back to the stronghold."

"Ben's an ideal candidate because of the very fact that he's trying *not* to feed," I argue.

Maybe I say it too loudly because Ben whips up his head, his eyes narrowing as he stares at our rooftop. Jehoel and I were both keeping our voices down, but obviously not enough. Ben starts running toward the back of the house, and I shoot a meaningful look at Jehoel.

"I'm going after him," I say. "Call it instinct or whatever, but I gotta do it."

I push out my wings and give chase before Jehoel can respond. No guarantee Ben will even want to come with us, but he deserves a chance. That's the whole point of the alliance's existence, and Cael, the leader of the Alaskan stronghold and founder of the entire movement, is always reminding us of this. If he were here with us right now, I know he'd back me.

The thought spurs me on as I follow Ben through the side yard and into the back yard of the neighboring house. He runs full-speed, leaping over the fence to hit the street, and keeps on running. But Jehoel materializes right in his path to intercept him, and Ben crashes into him and brings both of them down to

28

the ground. He lashes out with his fist, and Jehoel grabs hold of him and teleports both of them away. They reappear just a few feet away, and Ben drops like a stone.

He reels and scrambles to his feet before falling to one knee. I know exactly how he feels – fighting off the disorientation and probably nauseous from the jump – and I swoop down but stay in a hover, my flight camouflage still in effect.

Teleporting isn't one of the most common gifts for demons, but when Ben manages to get back on his feet, he doesn't look even remotely surprised that Jehoel just appeared out of thin air and dropped him out of it. He scowls, the lines on his face sharp and angular. Now that I'm closer, I can see that the hoodie is practically hanging on his frame. The guy looks like he's practically starving, and not just in terms of souls.

"We're not here from the Impiorum." Jehoel's palms are facing out in a surrender gesture. It's his standard greeting for this situation, and it always makes me think of chiming in a little, "We come in peace."

"The hell you're not," Ben spits. He turns around and starts to run again, and suddenly he's gone. I scan the area for him, catching a flash of light gray as he briefly makes contact with the ground. He disappears again, and I catch another glimpse as he catapults off a rooftop three houses away. He zigzags all over the neighborhood, almost like he knows about Jehoel's limitations. Teleporters have to either know the exact physical coordinates or be able to see and then visualize their targets to land somewhere specific. Ben's movements are so erratic that there's no way Jehoel could intercept him.

I fly up a little higher and keep an eye on the neighborhood, watching as he keeps bounding off rooftops. My head pounds every time he disappears and then reappears, like Vahni's subconsciously telling me she wants me to go after him.

I see movement in the back parking lot of the homeless shelter, and then he's gone.

Gotcha.

I can see Jehoel waiting by a street corner below – probably trying to look inconspicuous but with his bright red hair and all of his scars, he never really does – and I dive down to get him. He burns out a lot of energy each time he jumps, and I know he's probably recharging.

"Incoming. Target acquired," I say as a warning right before I grab him. I hit the skies again, holding him under his arms.

I can't see his face, but I know he's rolling his eyes. "You play too many war games."

Guilty as charged, though by "too many," it's still way less than most people's gaming standards.

"What else is there to do in the middle of Alaska?" I say lightly as we touch down by the back of the building. The "games" at the stronghold aren't actually video games but fight simulation software for training purposes.

"You could try sleeping now and then." He steps away and rakes a hand through his hair, darkness under his eyes as evidence of his own fatigue.

I shrug. "Sleep is for the weak."

He pauses outside the kitchen door. "You still sure about this one?"

"Yeah, I am." Ben reaction in trying to get away from us was a classic scared-rabbit response. I can tell he's been running, that the guy is desperate but doesn't know where to turn. Even now I can feel his presence like a magnet pulling me inside.

"All right." He gestures for me to go in first. "I'll follow your lead."

I pause before entering. "Since when?"

"Since you're so sure of yourself." He gives me a rare smile. "Besides, your instincts are usually right."

I'm surprised by the compliment. The alliance is still so new to me, and most of the time I feel like I'm floundering to figure out what I'm doing from day to day. Not to say that I'm not as committed as the rest of them, but Jehoel and the stronghold leader Cael are definitely more tuned into what's going on, both at home base and with the Impiorum.

We're silent as we step inside the kitchen, the only light coming from the emergency lights in the corner. My ears pick up the faintest sound from out in the hallway, like the scraping of metal against metal. Even before we get there, I think I know what it is.

"Out there," I whisper. "Let's go."

There's no one in the hallway when we get there, but there's an empty can of beef stew with a spoon sitting in a small alcove by the bathroom. I turn around and look, the hackles on my neck rising as I face the front of the building.

"He's that way," I whisper. "Can you sense him?"

"Not yet, but you're always better at this than I am."

Two compliments in a row. I glance at Jehoel, wondering whether he's feeling all right, but he's standing there with a calm expression like he's waiting for me to make my move.

I take us down the main hallway and eventually back to the room with the cots. The lights are dim in the room now, but I spot Ben right away. He's sitting on one of the far cots, rubbing his face and looking like he's about ready to crash hard.

He should have been able to sense our approach, but his face registers shock when Jehoel starts to walk over. He scrambles to his feet and bolts for the emergency exit, but Jehoel anticipates his move and takes the leap to intercept him outside. I hurry down the row of cots, the frizzy-haired woman I'd spoken to jumping up as I approach. She moves unexpectedly fast to intercept me and grabs my arm.

"You don't belong here," she hisses. "You're s'posed to go *home*." Her dark eyes are creepily vacant now, mouth angry and twisted. Her fingernails dig into my arm before letting go, and she sits heavily on the nearest cot.

She's probably a little crazy, but I have to ask, just in case. "What do you mean?"

She blinks, staring up at me like a frightened owl. "What? Do I know you from somewhere?"

Crazy. Though she'd seemed lucid when we spoke before. Her fingertips rub her temples as she starts humming, and I dismiss her as I run to the emergency exit. Only not completely. That interaction vaguely reminds me of something else, but it's out of my reach, and I need to cover Jehoel's back right now. I reach the outside to find the two facing off.

Cornered now, Ben snarls at us, his head whipping back and forth and alternating glares between Jehoel and me. I expect him to throw out a strike at one or both of us, but he doesn't. His eyes are sunken in hallowed sockets, the gauntness of his frame even more apparent now that I'm standing only a few feet away from him. He's tired, too weak to fight, and I bet all that teleporting he just did all over the neighborhood to get away from us took a lot out of him.

Not to mention that his *deimos* feels like it's shot to hell.

I project the thought into his head the second we make eye contact.

We come in peace.

3

Jonathan

South campus appears to be outwardly peaceful when Hope and I pull into the parking lot, but I can feel the currents of unrest in the air. Hope is even quieter than usual, and I glance over at her as I park by the athletic fields. She's hunched down low in the passenger seat, one of her hands fiddling incessantly with her long ponytail.

Troy Russo sits in the middle of the BMW's back seat like a loyal puppy. Ever since Micah left to join the alliance, he's been taking it upon himself to be something akin to Hope's bodyguard. Troy is Micah's best friend, and I suppose this might be somewhat natural. Only I happen to find it very annoying.

"So what's the plan?" Troy asks as I turn off the ignition.

I ignore him, a fraction of Raleigh's earlier doubts creeping into my thoughts. "Hope, if you're not feeling up to this, you need to tell me."

"I'm always up for hunting the bad guys." Her voice has no inflection, her jaw too tight, and I reach over and put my hand over hers to still it. She draws her hand back and turns her head to look out of the window, the wall between us almost palpable.

For the past two months, Hope has done everything that's required of her, whether it be for school, for her family and friends, or for me. But it's also felt like she's closed off a big part of herself to the world. It hasn't helped one bit that Micah also cut off all communications with her, with no word whatsoever, not even indirect. My own ire rises as I think about how every day she doesn't hear from him, she turns a little bit darker.

Tonight Hope feels even more melancholy than usual.

"If you're sure you're fine...." I prompt.

"I'm totally fine." Hope sits up straighter and gives me a tight-lipped smile. "Had a bad day at school, so this will be perfect."

"What happened?" I shoot her a concerned look, and she releases her breath in a sigh.

"Nothing. It's stupid."

"Hope," I say. "Nothing that is bothering you qualifies as being stupid."

"Oh, some girls made some crap comment about Micah. Or the fact that he left me high and dry right before prom." She shrugs, still looking sullen. "See? Just gossip. Stupid. Just like prom."

"Told her to let her demon loose on those girls," Troy mutters from the back seat.

She smiles a little at him, something she rarely does anymore. "It was tempting, but I probably would have gotten in trouble."

"The way I see it," I half-joke, "that *deimos* of your serves no other purpose than to exact your revenge upon bullies. Especially if they were being mean to you."

She turns to me, a genuine smile on her face, and it's almost like I'm seeing the old Hope again.

"I will happily take you to your prom," I offer. Troy bristles, emanating an air of defensiveness on behalf of his best friend, and I add, "As your mentor and friend."

"It's okay," she says, still smiling. "I honestly have zero desire to go." She finally stretches out in the seat so she actually looks comfortable. "So...tell us about the bad guys."

I try to stem my irritation over the fact that she's including Troy in any of this. "All right. Some background about these demons. They were once immortal, born from the darkness of the Underworld, and they were allowed to roam this realm for approximately a century. The Praxidikai banished them back to Asphodel because they wreaked too much havoc upon this realm. I saw firsthand the harm they caused during the wars of religion in Europe."

"Whoa." She gapes at me. "I sure didn't learn about them in Dr. Halverson's English class."

"Or in European History," Troy adds.

"Brian Halverson had to fight them off once," I reflect. "As did I. It's actually how he and I first met, during those *guerres de religion*."

Her cheeks pale. "So, in addition to the crash history lesson, we're here to…"

"Look for something out of the ordinary," I say quickly. "Something dark. They have the ability to harvest the energy from a soul and send it straight to Asphodel. So refrain from using your guardian or demon powers, if you would. I don't want them to know what you are."

"I don't want them to know what I am either." She nods, some of the color coming back to her cheeks. "Okay, let's do this. My brother may be pretty understanding about me going out with you, but tonight I actually promised him I'd be home early." She and Troy open the door to the BMW before I can say anything else, and I get out of the car and press the button on my key to secure it.

"If you find one, we leave immediately," I remind her. "And you…" I look at Troy. To his credit, he's had his uses on various small jobs in the past, but I don't want him tagging along on this one. "…stay here and watch over my car."

Troy folds his arms across his chest. "I'm pretty sure your fancy schmancy security system does that for you." He touches Hope's shoulder, "Call me if you need some legit muscle, 'kay?"

"Don't hold your breath. Or lean on the car, lest its fancy schmancy security system electrocute you." I hold out my hand to Hope. "Shall we?"

"Can't you try to make an effort to be nice to him?" Hope shakes her head as we walk away. "You're as bad with Troy as you were with Micah." She clamps her mouth shut, averting her eyes.

I don't bother to reply. Micah. Always Micah. But I refuse to entertain the notion that Raleigh is right about Hope's state of mine.

We leave the Rotary Fields at full speed, first heading for the Bailey Avenue neighborhood south of campus. I know the area well – despite community efforts to clean up the neighborhood, it's shady and filled with petty criminal activity.

The passersby don't notice us as we blur past them. My empathic senses are able to pick up on Hope's emotions – excitement, a healthy dose of fear, an unexpected amount of anger. Whatever doubts I had in her abilities fade, especially as I feel the others converging around the perimeter of the area. Combined, their guardian power is like an uplifting force. But Hope's *lumen* isn't part of the group. She may be one of us, but she possesses both the guardian *lumen* and the demon *deimos*, which means she's a chimera and not a pure guardian.

Since her transformation, Hope's been accepted into the guardian community as one of us, but I've taken great precautions to keep hidden the fact that she's part-demon. Aside from myself, only Raleigh knows. Given the universal hatred of demons in my sector, I fear the others would not be very understanding.

It's late-spring, and the air feels heavy with humidity. I guide Hope through a route that winds through the side streets but let her set the pace. Two blocks and she's still going full-bore, which means she's not picking up on anything out of the ordinary.

I do pick up something unexpected, and it's coming from the other guardians. They feel much too close now, and my concern rises as they converge on our position. I grit my teeth at the flagrant disobedience, but knowing Raleigh, she's angry over having to miss out on the fun of being on the frontlines of a hunt. They need to fall back, and I need them to do it now.

I concentrate on sending my emotions into the collective, and Hope stops in her tracks. By the time I stop and turn around, she's standing more than fifty meters behind me. I rush over, worry flooding me until realize that I must have inadvertently sent Hope the same message of caution.

"What did you do to me?" She wraps her arms around herself. "I just went from feeling like I was on my game to wanting to crawl back into bed."

"I apologize. I didn't think it would affect you." I think about the fact that we were holding hands, adding, "But of course it would."

I look up as a college-aged boy exits the nearest house and take Hope's hand again, leading her away at a regular pace. I glance at him a second time, but he's carrying a large black garbage bag and only looks like he's taking out the trash. "I was trying to use the collective to get the other guardians to fall back," I say in a low voice.

"Oh." She swipes a loose strand of hair back behind her ear. "Well, I think I might have picked up on something nearby, but it was right when *that,*"she waves her hand over me like she's casting a magic spell or voodoo, "whole thing happened."

"Let's keep going. We can circle around again if needed."

A beep sounds behind us, and I glance back as the boy with the garbage bag opens the trunk of a Honda Civic parked on the street. I notice that there's no trash can nearby.

Hope suddenly draws in a sharp breath, apprehension spiking out of her.

The garbage bag hits the inside of the trunk with a heavy, sick thud and the boy turns to look at us. His gaze flicks from Hope to me, and I stare back as he starts to levitate.

"*Run!*"

I don't wait for Hope to respond before tugging her into a sprint, immediately thinking better of it and scooping her up in my arms. Hope is undetectable by both guardians and demons unless she emits her destructive powers or unless they see what she can do. I take the leap onto the nearest rooftop, wanting to avoid Bailey Avenue because of the foot traffic.

"It's a demon. But he doesn't feel like the others." Hope's voice is like the wind because of our speed. "He feels so much worse."

Seraphim. Bloodthirsty, devious, and responsible for over a century of misery, chaos, and destruction. It was five hundred years ago, but I'd been alive at the time, a mortal trying to living my life in the darkest of times. One of them was also the immediate reason for the demise of Adrienne.

I keep scanning the skies for the demon as I continue jumping from rooftop to rooftop. South campus is one street away, and I briefly let go of Hope and touch my finger to the Pathicomm right as we land on the sidewalk across the street from the athletic field.

"Identity confirmed. Tell everyone to fall back. *Now!*" I forget that I don't need to speak my thoughts, my voice coming out as more of a roar.

The explosion hits me before I can hear Raleigh's reply. My legs give way as the demon's power jolts up my spine, and Hope screams as her hand is torn away from mine. I push my *lumen* out to fight off the oncoming paralysis, leaping back up to my feet. Hope is crouching on the ground not ten feet away, and if I use my full force of my powers right next to her, I'll hurt her too.

The demon floats right above the ground just beyond her, the light from a nearby streetlamp hitting the lower part of his face and illuminating a wide grin. I leap forward to stand next to Hope, rapidly weighing our options. It's no use trying to run from a demon who has the ability to fly, and I feel Hope's posture stiffen as she takes in the fact that he's inches above the ground.

"That didn't take long," he sneers. "If you were looking for another dead body, I was just disposing of one. I'll be glad to add your pieces to the mix."

"Are there others like you?" I bait him. "*Seraphim?*" Out of the corner of my eye, I see Hope start, as though the name strikes a chord of recognition, but I don't have time to question it.

His lips peel back over his teeth like a wolf that scents something in the air. "Not as you knew them. Consider us new and improved."

Hope makes a disgusted sound under her breath, and his attention shifts to her. He moves toward her with a greedy glimmer in his eye, like he's about to have her for dinner.

Not a chance. I pluck some of his recklessness out of the air and absorb it, charging forward at full speed with my *lumen* concentrated in my fingertips. The demon raises a wall of *deimos* to deflect me, but not until after I get my hands around his neck and force my power into him. He tries to knock me away, but I hang on until his breath sputters in his throat. His *deimos* flares outward, but I bear it and infuse even more of my *lumen* straight into his soul. His power bursts out in retaliatory strikes against me, but they're weak and briefly jolt through my body like small surges of electricity before they die.

He shoots straight up into the air with me in an attempt to get away from me, exactly what I was waiting for. Micah has the power to fly, and Hope told me once that it's like being swept away in a hurricane, especially when he loses control of it… which gives me an idea on how to fight off this one. I keep my grip tight on the demon's neck and keep pummeling him, feeling him weaken more and more the higher we go.

Self-preservation, above all.

I let go of his neck, pushing out my power to slow the impending freefall. But his hands suddenly clamp like iron restraints around my arms, his power shooting into me with the impetus of a storm, and I realize my mistake. He's been playing with me up until now, biding his time until he could do real damage.

I stare up at him, his ice-blue eyes blazing back at me with fury but absolutely no fear, and for the first time I notice the scars on his face, wounds that no true immortal would bear.

My muscles seize up as he draws my *lumen* out with his *deimos,* my nerves crackling in agony as I realize what he's doing. He's not destroying my guardian power. He's taking it for himself because he has *lumen* within him too. He's like Samael, the Impiorum demon who killed our guardian healer before Micah sent him back to Asphodel.

He's like Hope.

"You're a chimera," I say in surprise.

"And you can't fly," he grunts before letting go of my arms.

My senses flood with panic that's purely my own. I clasp onto the chimera's hands before he can completely shake me off, and he gnashes his teeth at me and he zigzags through the air. But I hold on as tight as I can, not throwing a strike because I know he'll only subsume my power into his own.

But I can hurt him in other ways. I draw up one of my worst memories of my life, channeling the pain straight into his soul.

If my heart had still been capable, it would have shattered.

I saw Hope from a distance, lying on the cracked asphalt within the alcove. The faint glint of her auburn hair shone in the light, her body still as if in sleep, her head turned so she was facing the sky. I ran to her as fast as my powers let me, but I already knew that I was powerless to save her.

The ache in my chest spread to my limbs as I fell to her side, her chill spreading through my skin when I touched her cheek. She was the reason for my existence, the last of my line. The one who insisted on me being involved in her life, even though she didn't know who I really was.

She was gone. Life extinguished, like all of the others, only I'd never grown to love any of the others like I loved Hope.

Micah lay on the ground beside her, his arms covered in the same lacerations that slashed through Hope's tender hands. For her sake, I'd grown to accept the fact that they were together. I found out for myself that Micah wasn't like the Impiorum demons. But when I saw them lying there like star-crossed lovers that finally met their fates, it hit me with utter certainty that Hope died for Micah, and I hated him for it.

"Hope..."

I looked at him in astonishment as he sucked in a breath and choked out her name.

Micah lived, while Hope lay there broken, and my sorrow twisted into a dark knot in my heart.

Hatred. Agony. Loss. The demon stiffens as he takes on every ounce of my pain from that day. He loses control, and panic registers in his eyes as we both spiral out of control.

"I'm here. I'll catch you."

It's Raleigh's voice coming through the Pathicomm, her presence strong and directly beneath me now. My power is momentarily tapped out, but I'll happily rely on hers. I knew she would come. She has a certain knack of knowing when she shouldn't follow direct orders.

I let go of the demon and drop straight into a freefall, the world slowing to a stop as Raleigh sends her *lumen* spiraling up to capture me. I latch onto her energy, pushing it out around me to slow my descent. The demon drops to the earth like a stone, and I watch helplessly as he smashes straight into my car.

My BMW's roof crumples, the reinforced glass windows splitting and shattering, and his body seizes up as the security system sends enough electricity through him to fry him.

Damn it all.

I'm still about a hundred meters up, and I hear a door slam shut from one of the nearby houses. It's dark enough outside that I don't think anyone would see me, but I release Raleigh's power and fall to the ground the rest of the way.

Hope and Raleigh are standing by the athletic track, and they run over to me at full speed when I touch down in the parking lot. Troy is already by my car, looking fascinated at the electric charges that the security system's spitting out. We all start as the murderer's clothes catch on fire.

My lips curled in disgust, I deactivate the security system and walk forward to dispose of the body. I reach for him when the demon opens his eyes and leers at me.

"Nice ride," he sneers.

"It was a nice ride, but it's evidently time for me to upgrade." I grab his head and give a sharp twist to break his neck before he can say anything more.

He won't be able to destroy any one else, but if any sort of justice was served tonight, it wasn't equal. One chimera's life exchanged for the lives of three guardians. Not to mention the life of my car.

Troy drags the body from the roof and grabs a blanket from my trunk, laying it over the body to smother the fire while I storm back over to the others.

"Send some of the others on damage control," I order Raleigh. I add as an important afterthought. "And thank you for your help."

Raleigh touches her fingertip to the Pathicomm in her ear as she puts out the message, turning to me to report. "Done. Damage control teams are sweeping through a three block radius out from here in case anyone saw. And I called for cleanup to assist with your poor car. Although," she adds with a cocked eyebrow, "Troy seems to be doing just fine so far."

"Gah." Hope makes a strangled sound from the back of her throat. "Calling for cleanup. Like in a grocery store?"

We both turn to look at her, my anger subduing slightly when I see how pale she is. I reach to put my arm around her, and she shudders.

I turn to Raleigh. "I need to take Hope home."

"Of course. Troy and I will get a ride with one of the others." She tosses me the keys to her Jaguar. "You can keep it until you get another."

I nod, too furious to respond. And worried now too. The demon used the word "*we*," which means there are others like him.

"That guy wasn't a regular demon," Hope says as we get into Raleigh's car. It's not a question.

"No."

"He used the word *Seraphim*." She grabs her seatbelt, turning to me before fastening it. "That's what the Impiorum demons call the demon-guardian hybrids."

"The *Seraphim* are also the demons I described to you earlier." My stomach turns as the connection solidifies in my mind, and Hope doesn't look like she's feeling any better. "It appears that the ones I knew from long ago and these new have the same essence, which is not good for us at all." I peer at her before starting the car. "Did you feel anything from him?"

"Yes, but at the time I didn't know what he was. But now that you pointed it out, yeah…he felt like Samael Richter, the chimera that killed Ms. Salazar and Micah's sister," she mumbles. "A chimera," she repeats as if in shock. "Like me."

Her eyes are downcast, and I reach over and gently lift her chin. "Not like you." I give her a stern look. "These chimera are inhuman. You are not."

"None of us are really human, Jonathan. Not anymore." She gives me a small smile, but there's no humor in it. "I know you don't consider demons human, or you wouldn't be able to destroy them so easily."

The ride back to her house is shadowed by silence. Hope stares out of the window with a frown while I ponder over repercussions that are bound to result from this incident. When the guardians find out exactly what was responsible for the death of our own, they'll cry for retribution.

"What did the *Seraphim* do during the wars of religion?" Hope asks quietly.

I hesitate. "They were used as instruments of torture."

I don't bother to mention that so was I.

4

Micah

The stronghold is housed in an old juvenile detention center, the building abandoned by humans over fifty years ago. Pretty fitting considering how all of us abandoned our human lives by coming here to live in the middle of the Alaskan boreal forest. As far as location goes, it's perfect for the alliance. We're all a bunch of delinquents from the Impiorum anyway, or at least that's the running joke around here.

Ben is the most recent delinquent to join the group. It was a week ago when we first brought him in, and tonight was the first time we took him out to feed.

Cael meets us as soon as we step into the foyer of the now-renovated building, his teeth flashing white against his dark skin as he smiles. He's not only the stronghold leader but is also one of the founders of the alliance.

"Jehoel, Micah, Ben. Welcome home." He nods at Ben, who's standing stiffly between us. "How did it go?"

"It didn't," Ben grumbles. "Jehoel had to stop me from hurting someone."

His hands ball up into fists as he blows out a breath in frustration. Cael picks up on it and moves to stand right in front of him, and Ben's posture visibly relaxes. Cael has the ability to either calm or incite situations, which comes in handy.

"I'll take him out again later," Jehoel says to Cael. "The first time's always difficult."

"You mean impossible." Ben glares at his sneakers with a sullen expression.

"It'll get easier," I chime in.

"Go on, Ben. Go get some breakfast," Cael orders.

Ben nods, his face lighting up slightly before he heads down the hall.

I start for the stairs so I can go up to my room, but Cael holds up a hand to stop me. "Micah, wait." I turn to him as he says in a quiet voice. "Ben's current rooming situation is not...ideal, shall we say. I'd like him to switch to the empty bunk in your room."

"Okay." I hesitate. "Is he rooming with me permanently?"

Cael cocks an eyebrow. "If he does, is there a problem with that?"

"No," I say. "I'll get it ready for him."

I walk upstairs, spotting a few of the guys from different scouting teams talking and goofing around in the small TV lounge on my floor. As soon as they see me coming, they shut up and pretend to stare at the TV.

Same crap, different day.

It's a few minutes past midnight, and the facility is buzzing with activity. Our days are mixed up here, with our workdays starting in the evening and ending late morning. The rationale is that the scouting teams work at night so we draw less attention to ourselves. The rest of the guys are essentially like our support units and work the same hours as us. In addition to the scouts, there are guys that run security, technology, intelligence, training, and others who take care of the daily functions of the compound. We each have a job here, a role to fill. They haven't given Ben an official assignment, and I wonder where they'll wind up putting him. He's young and a little volatile, but from what I've seen so far, he really wants to do well.

I stay in the room and work on homework while I wait for Ben to be done with dinner. Cael isn't only the founder of the alliance, he also used to be a high school teacher, and he insisted on having those of us who came to the alliance homeschooled so we could graduate high school. For me, that means that I'll be able to go to college in the fall, which was my original plan from back when life was semi-normal. There are a handful of us who fall in that category, but going on these scouting missions all of the time means I always have to play catch up whenever I get back.

I log onto the laptop in the room and access my assignments. Ben comes in about an hour after I start and crashes on the empty bunk without a word. He thrashes around a lot in his sleep while I work. The guy has a lot of nightmares.

It's dawn before I take a break. I still have to write an English essay before I'm all caught up, but I can't concentrate on homework anymore. I climb out of the window onto the flat rooftop, the silence striking me like it always does. There's no civilization for miles, so different from the noise of the city back home.

When it's quiet like this, I feel Hope's presence most of all.

My eyes close, concentrating until my senses fill with her. Until I can almost hear the sound of her soft voice. Until I can imagine the feel of her skin, the scent of her hair. Until it hurts too much. I'm on the other side of the country from her, but it might as well be in a different realm. It can't be any other way, not while I'm still like this.

I clench and release my hand, watching as the flame effortlessly flickers to the surface. It shoots straight up before landing back in my palm with a flash of intense blue and heat, and I wince a little as the high from the borrowed power replaces the pain. It feels a little too good, like the extreme rush I used to get when I free-fall on purpose so I'm out of control. I can still call up the fire at will, but sometimes Vahni makes her presence known without any prompting on my part, like last week when I first picked up on Ben.

Carrying this power is the main reason I'm on the fence about transferring or staying. Jehoel's already told me he's going to stay here, and he keeps telling me that if I stay for another month, he has ideas on how to help me control it better.

It hasn't done much to win friends here, that's for sure. Most of the guys started avoiding me after the first time they saw me do it. I've kept my distance since. Except for me, the group is pretty tight-knit, and the sounds from inside the residence hall prove it. Voices, clatter from the kitchen as the staff prepares dinner, and laughter. A wave of homesickness rides through me like nausea as I make myself sit and listen to it.

The window behind me slides open, and Ben steps out and sits next to me on the rooftop. I glance over at him as he shoves a hand through his dark hair and frowns down at his sneakers.

"It'll get better," I say. "Being here, I mean. I had a hard time at first, too." I still do have a hard time, but I don't bother telling him that.

He stifles a yawn. "I've been here barely a week. It's already better than it was when you found me."

His voice is quiet, understated, but I can pick up how pained it is. New recruits are usually pretty quiet when they first get here. Totally understandable after all of the stuff that they've gone through to make the break with the Impiorum.

"Good."

He yawns again. "Hey, can I ask you something?"

"Sure."

He hesitates, like he's having second thoughts about asking, but then blows out a breath and asks, "How did you get away?"

Getting away... Getting away had been a simple matter of Jehoel teleporting me out of Buffalo, but I have trouble saying it out loud because my pain from that night is still too fresh. That was the night I left the girl I love and anyone who's ever meant anything to me. That was the night my sister was killed right in front of me. The worst night of my life.

I can feel Ben's eyes focused on me, but I need a few seconds to get a grip. Instead I stare out into the trees that come almost right up to the rooftop – that's how secluded we are from civilization. I'm tempted to walk to the edge and touch the branches of the closest tree, to make sure all of this is really real.

"That bad, huh?" Ben says.

I watch my breath form clouds of mist that linger and then fade. "Jehoel took me away. Teleported me out of the city like he did with you when we found you. I got a chance to say goodbye to my girlfriend and best friend at least. Guess I was lucky in that way."

"Oh. Yeah." His voice is unsteady. "I only got away because my half-brother helped me. I escaped, barely. But he got caught."

I give him a sharp look. "You have a half-brother still in the Impiorum? Have you told Cael? He can send a team to find him."

Ben looks out into the trees too. "They destroyed him."

The gravity of his words hit me like a physical strike. I know this pain, I've felt his loss. I still feel it whenever I think about my sister and how she died, and I think about telling Ben about it. But I can't because the agony is still too fresh.

"I'm sorry. I lost someone too." I don't know what else to say, so I veer the topic back to where it was. "The way you jump from place to place? I don't think I've seen anything quite like it. Do you teleport, or is it something else?"

"It's kind of a mixture between teleporting and flight, I guess. I can do these quick jumps, but that's about it." He shrugs. "My half-brother can teleport. Or at least he used to be able to."

He falls silent again, and we both sit without speaking for a while until Ben's stomach makes an audible rumble. He's been perpetually hungry since he got here.

"They're making dinner downstairs," I say. "You should go and get some."

He nods but doesn't move. "What about you?"

"Already ate," I lie.

"You don't ever eat with the rest of the guys, do you? Because they're afraid of you." He says it as a statement, not a question.

I glance at him. Despite how dead on his observation was, he's looking down at his Chuck Taylors instead of me.

"What makes you say that?" I cough a laugh, but there's no humor in it. I'm not blind or deaf – far from it. Most of the other guys tense up whenever I walk into the room, the conversation always dying down.

"It's kinda my thing," Ben explains.

"Oh, are you an empath?" Some of the other guys here are empathic and can pick up on emotions. It's similar to what Hope can do with her ability to read negative emotions and energy. She's been really strong and has learned to deal with it, but I still think it pretty much sucks for her.

"Nah." He shrugs. "Maybe it's kinda like being an empath, but I'm just good at reading people. Or demons, as the case may be."

"Yeah?"

"Yeah. This place is generally full of good vibes." He smiles a little as he pushes up to his feet. "In case you weren't sure. I'm going to go get that dinner. See you later?"

"See ya."

He climbs back through the window, and I stay on the rooftop, thinking about last week in Seattle. About what the woman at the shelter had said about me not belonging here. I get along with some of the other guys one-on-one, especially the ones I personally recruited, but they all still treat me a little differently. With distance.

Ben will probably do the same when he finds out about the demon mark thing I can do.

The forest is unusually quiet tonight. It gives me plenty of space to wonder what kind of emotions he'd been able to pick up from me. If he's getting good vibes from the stronghold, that's good. I'm honestly glad for him.

But part of me knows that crazy woman at the shelter from last week was right. I don't quite fit in with the alliance, not like I should.

5

Jonathan

It's just past nightfall, and the guardians in the Buffalo sector are calling for blood. It's been one week since the incident with the *Seraphim*, but rumors reached all of the guardians under my directorship within a day. Since then, I've been putting out fires all over my sector.

The bright red Ducati Streetfighter bike pulls up to the curb. Raleigh's dressed in a splendid scarlet jumpsuit to match. She holds out a black helmet to me, but I make no move to take it.

"Well, this is nice." I gesture both to the motorcycle and Raleigh. "But given the nature of what we're about to do, perhaps we should take your car instead."

"This isn't a rescue mission." She tosses the helmet at me, a smirk beneath hers. "What's wrong? Is it too twenty-first century for you to ride behind a woman?"

"Not at all," I say, getting on behind her. I can feel her custom-made blade beneath her jacket, an affirmation to her words that this isn't going to be a rescue mission. "You drive."

"Well, that was the plan all along," she retorts. "Hang on."

With my hand resting on her waist, I can feel a mixture of apprehension and excitement emanating from her. I'm briefly tempted to send a pulse of *lumen* through her to calm her nerves, but we may need that spark of hers tonight.

Ever since the death of the healer Gail Salazar, the guardians in my sector have been restless. Many of their actions have been careless, their efforts doing nothing but draw the attention of the human population to us. Raleigh's informant messaged her twenty minutes ago, reporting that a small, angry mob of guardians captured two demons from the dormitories at Buffalo State and took them to the grain mills in the old industrial sector of the city.

Normally I would trust my constituents enough to stay out of their dealings, but not if they're going to take risks in plain view of humans. They have gone too far this time.

Raleigh drives us to the site, hitting no resistance from traffic and opting for side streets as we get closer. The warehouse is in a run-down section of the city, abandoned and falling apart to the human eye and protected by magic that disorients the rare human that trespasses. By coming to formal guardian territory, the guardians have the protection that was granted from the shamans of Asphodel, which means the demons won't be able to use their destructive powers here.

She pulls into the cracked asphalt and gravel lot by the wooden barricades and cuts the engine.

"Strategy?" she asks as I get off the bike. She takes off her helmet, shaking her long tawny hair free. Her green-eyed gaze is steady, and I can tell she's ready for battle mode, as always.

"I don't have one, yet." I hand her my helmet and start walking with her toward the building. There's no point in keeping too low of a profile – I can already feel the collective presence of the guardians inside, which means they can also feel ours. The energy signature is a larger one than I'd expect from a "small" mob. "Not until we see exactly who and what we're dealing with. I'll go in and talk to them. You stay outside and stand by for my signal –"

A woman's scream sounds from within the building, and we exchange glances. Most definitely human. So much for this not being a rescue mission.

"And that," I say drily, "would appear to be the signal. Let's go."

We move quickly, heading toward the side entrance of the warehouse. The scream doesn't repeat itself, but I can hear shouts inside and the unmistakable sound of crying. Raleigh breathes out a low hiss by my side, her cheeks flushed pink and her normally delicate jaw stiff with anger.

"I take it your informant didn't tell you a human was here?"

"No," she bites out. "He most certainly did not."

I glance up at the low roof of the building, which slopes upward to a horizontal row of windows before rising to another level. Her gaze follows mine, and she moves to quickly scale the fire escape before I can suggest it. It's one of the benefits that comes from working closely with someone for over half a century – Raleigh and I are practically empathic when it comes to each other.

She looks a bit like a cat burglar as she hangs from the top of the fire escape. "Be careful, Jonathan," she whispers.

I give her a curt nod and walk up to the warehouse door. The iron handle is cold to the touch when I slide it back, and a guardian immediately blocks the space in front of me. I recognize the physically imposing individual named Corbin. His eyes narrow upon seeing me, and he draws out a long-bladed knife from under his jacket.

"That's no way to welcome your director."

"I have my orders."

"From whom?" I retort.

He hesitates, indecision flashing across his expression. His grip tightens on the hilt of the knife as though firming his own resolve, but I'm already done with this banter.

"You'd better step aside." He doesn't move, and I suppress my irritation at this entire situation. I need to harness more useful emotions right now. The blackest sort of dread should do it, and I call on the specific memory from five hundred years ago.

I arrived at the upper castle rooms ten minutes late. I'd spent the better part of the day in the dungeons interrogating prisoners of war, and I was grateful to leave behind the stench of despair and desperation. I knew that the fact that I was summoned to come upstairs meant they wanted me to use my particular brand of persuasion on a prisoner of nobility.

The guard was waiting for me, and he briefed me as he unlocked the door. "This one was caught sneaking out of the war room with papers that belonged to the duke. She has so far refused to talk."

Interesting. A woman likely meant a spy or messenger of some sort. And one of nobility with apparent mental fortitude.

The cell was a far cry from the stark cells of the dungeon, decorated and furnished as it were a guest room in the regular part of the castle. The elegance was a lie, a farce, obscene in its contrast to the amount of suffering that happened within those walls. Suffering that in many cases was delegated by my hand. It didn't matter that I'd done those things to get information for the cause. I'd made people suffer and in some cases die, and I would have that forever branded on my soul.

When I saw who was inside the cell, my heart seized.

There was a woman sitting on the floor with her knees drawn to her chin. Tears flowed down her cheeks when she lifted her head to look at me, but my full attention was on the other woman in the room. She had long auburn locks and cool gray eyes amidst delicate features.

Adrienne. My Adrienne. But it couldn't be. I'd tried to hunt her down for months after she was taken from me, and I even found her gravesite...

She turned to face me, her expression mirroring my feelings of shock.

"Madame Thibault very kindly turned in this prisoner for spying on the government."

The viscount spoke from the corner. He was looking at Adrienne with something like admiration, and it took a Herculean effort on my part to hide the fact that I recognized her. The Madame title meant she was married now, and if her surname was now Thibault... I needed answers, but we were in a veritable fortress, and if I tried anything, the viscount would kill both of us.

He was waiting impatiently for my response, and I murmured something to Adrienne about how grateful we were for her loyalty to the monarchy. Still, the viscount stood as though he was waiting for me to do more.

Dear God, he wanted me to interrogate the prisoner in front of my wife, the woman I loved.

The door swung open, and Cyril walked into the room. I'd been forced to work with him for weeks now, and he was a ruthless killer, pure and simple. His sights landed on Adrienne and the woman prisoner huddled on the floor, and feelings of lust radiated from him like heat.

Adrienne's cheeks reddened slightly, though she kept her composure while I stood there like a deer in the headlights. It took every ounce of my willpower not to take my wife and run.

Dread, panic, confusion, despair. I've kept my emotions from that moment locked away, but I use them now to get past Corbin. I lunge forward and catch hold of his arm, funneling everything into him until his jaw goes slack. His eyes become mirrors to my own agony from that day, and when they glaze over, I know he's incapacitated. I let him go, and he drops to the floor, twitching and groaning.

My head clear again, I step over his body and walk inside to face what awaits me.

6

Micah

"I'm waiting for you..."

I'm out on the roof waiting for Ben to be done eating with the rest of the guys when I hear the voice in the forest.

The property immediately surrounding the building is under 24-hour surveillance, and I know someone will come and check it out if someone's actually trespassing. I step to the edge of the roof anyway, casting my senses out and hearing it in the next moment. Someone living, breathing, with a slow, steady heartbeat. Moving through the underbrush, footsteps light but cracking occasional branches as she heads straight toward the detention center.

I focus on the shadows beyond the trees and let my deepest instincts take over, something Jehoel taught me to do to make a connection with the energy of others. It's essentially a milder form of what I have to do to feed my *deimos* these days, but serving more for I.D. purposes, to find targets and distinguish friend from enemy. The heat pours into me and slides away in my next breath as I get a better sense of who's out there. Not human. Not pure demon or pure guardian, either. Something in between. Like a chimera maybe... like Hope.

I try my best to keep my own hope tempered, but it's possible that she could have found me. Jehoel is somehow able to give me weekly reports on her and my family, and if he's having someone keep tabs on them, there's a chance that someone could be tracking us. Granted, we've been extremely careful, Jehoel insisting that we move by teleporting from place to place instead of by foot or flight, but still –

"*Micah.*"

It's nothing more than a whisper, but it makes my heart clench up like a fist. To heck with waiting for compound security to show up. I gotta check it out.

Everything silences as I comb through the forest, like the wildlife just got spooked by something dark and foreboding in its boundaries. Maybe it's me.

My *deimos* gives me silent wings, my body experiencing a rush as I quickly weave through the trees. There are acres of land within the compound to search through, and I remember the first few times I'd ever tried flying through. The trees had seemed intent on clipping me, and I'd even met a few head on. But Cael insists on all of us being comfortable with the property, and navigating it comes much more naturally to me now. Whatever else is out here definitely doesn't feel natural.

I get an even better sense of it when I'm on the far north perimeter. I veer to the east to close the distance, my sights landing on a figure standing among the trees about a hundred meters out. Judging from the long hair, height, and slightness of build, I'm guessing female. The sun's rays are filtered and hazy through the trees, but I think I see a flash of auburn.

Long, auburn hair. My internal alarm screams at me that what I can sense from her doesn't feel like Hope, but there's no way I can turn back now.

I land way too hard in my haste, hitting the ground in a crouch. My camouflage slips away as soon as I straighten, and I know I made a mistake in coming out here by myself as soon as the smell hits me.

The stench of death and decomposition rises from the ground along with something else that's foreign but all too familiar – the smell of brine that surrounds me like a vapor. I narrow my eyes, my muscles tensed and ready for action. I stare at the dark form that steps out from the trees. She's wearing a dark cloak with a hood to conceal her face, her head bowed and long auburn hair spilling past her shoulders. But I can tell that it's not Hope, only a crude imitation of her. Whoever's playing these parlor tricks obviously knows me and how to feed on my emotions. A current of fear slices through me as I realize they must know Hope, too, enough to at least roughly replicate what she looks like.

"Who are you? What do you want from me?" I reply.

One second she's over by the trees, and in the next she grabs hold of me and pitches me forward. I catch myself on my hands and knees, stuck in time and space as the leaves and branches split apart in front of me. The dread settles hard in my chest as I stare down at dark and murky waters that shouldn't be there.

"*You've forgotten them, Micah.*"

No. Hell, no. The voice isn't completely feminine anymore. It's raspy and almost mocking, entering my head like an echo. And it belongs to Vahni.

The goddess hasn't made her presence so apparent like this since I left her domain, only in terms of me feeling her power inside. But now she's showing me the Sea of the Dead, the place where souls go to rest after their physical forms die. It's like when Vahni gave me the special tour of her domain, only it's worse this time because I recognize more of the souls. They swim over and around each other, looking like ghosts of the people they left behind.

Jack Williamson. Gail Salazar. And oh, God. My sister Lina. For a minute, I spiral through the same heart-shattering loss and anger that I felt when I held her lifeless body in my arms.

No. Mind games. These are just mind games.

I force myself off the ground and stagger to my feet, telling myself that Vahni's just messing with me and putting the visions in my head, that what's down there isn't real, but it's too late. I can't *not* see what's down there. Jack wasn't just my boss – he was like a father figure to me, and more than that, he was my mentor and friend. Gail was more than a teacher and healer – she put herself at risk to save Hope and got destroyed in the process. And Lina… My older sister's death will weigh on me for all eternity.

The cloaked figure is standing in front of me as still as the trees, and I take a step forward. "I haven't forgotten them. Why are you showing them to me?" A threatening growl rumbles in my chest. "I've already lost them. You can't use them as bartering tools."

"They are here with me, Micah."

No. I'm already carrying around too much guilt for this. I don't want to listen, but it's like she's inserting her thoughts straight into my head.

"Why are you here?" I demand.

Her head lifts so I can see her face, and my stomach twists in revulsion. It's a corpse, its hair changing to become dull and brittle as I watch. One of its eyes is gray like Hope's, the other one is missing, and as I watch in morbid fascination, a black tongue darts out to lick half-eaten lips.

I'm suddenly glad I didn't have any dinner. But if Vahni's here – sort of in the flesh – she's within a mile of the compound. She could destroy that and everyone in it too, but I'm gambling on the fact that she hasn't already killed me and that she sent some corpse to come and talk to me instead.

"You have forsaken the task that my son requires of you."

Interesting. Raphael's throwing a fit over me not killing the big, bad defectors on his behalf, is he? Maybe I'm just irreverent, but I don't trust him or the other two of the trio. Raphael came off to me as a power-hungry ass, and Arete was more of a blind idealist. I'd gotten the feeling that Vahni was more impartial than the other two members of the Praxidikai, but I'm still far from at ease talking to this…thing. Vahni could have sent a memo instead of appearing here in my realm in the guise of my girlfriend. Hiding her face, like a coward.

She shifts positions like she heard my thoughts. Yeah, I knew she would. We're bound together by soul and power like that, unfortunately.

"I refuse to send anyone to Asphodel," I manage to say in a level voice. "I won't send anyone to his death."

It's a bold move on my part, considering that Vahni's a freaking goddess and could kill me with a snap of her rotten fingers. But she can just march her puppet of a dead body right back to Buffalo and finish the job herself. If she wants to.

"That was Raphael's assignment. I do not require this of you."

She hinted to me in Asphodel that she wasn't exactly into Raphael's agenda, so I'm not that surprised to hear it. But I'm even more wary now over the fact that she came all this way to tell me. It means she wants something else.

"There are very dark times coming for us all. I need you to return home."

No way. I'm not leaving until I'm done here. I've put in my two months, and I'll admit that I've been a little envious of others that have left. But I still don't feel totally confident that I can do all of this on my own, not yet.

"Nice. What, is that supposed to be some sort of prophecy? Am I *the one?*" I say bitterly. "I'm just supposed to go back to Buffalo, and then what? These so-called dark times won't happen?"

She blinks, one of her eyelids sticking to whatever congealed goo is her eye socket. Her other eye is milky and stares back at me, and I shudder and step back.

"Not to Buffalo. I need you to return home to me," those dead lips grate out.

"No," I whisper in horror. "Why?"

"You are my ward, and I have my own task for you to complete. Return to me, and in exchange, I shall release you from your obligation to

Raphael." The corpse takes a rattling breath. "*You do not belong to him.*"

I don't belong to her either. I shake my head, unable to look away from the dead eye of the corpse, which is turning muddier and darker by the second. My hand balls up in a fist, but a brief flicker of fire licks my fingertips as if she's trying to show me that I'm under her control.

"What do you want me to do?"

"*I need your assistance to purge a dark element from Asphodel. It is for the good of both races.*"

She needs *my* assistance? Now I know I'm hallucinating. "You're a goddess. Why can't you take care of it?"

"*I am too close to this element to purge it. Our powers are too interconnected for me to fight off this evil.*"

Okay, assuming I even understand what she's getting at, that would explain that. But me? Go after something as powerful as Vahni. Sounds like a suicide mission if I ever heard one. "What if I say no?"

"*It is ultimately your choice.*"

Doubt that, and I'm sure that's the standard thing she says to all of her pawns.

The corpse moves closer again, rapidly and before I can get away. I don't feel it strike me, but I'm suddenly on the ground, the leaves bursting into flames all around me. The heat of Vahni's power erupts from within me at the same time, more intense than ever, and I scream but no sound comes out. My palms blister as I struggle to get up, as I fight to get it under control. But I know my efforts are useless, and I can almost feel Vahni's satisfaction seep out through the corpse that's watching me burn.

My own desperation and fear inflame. I'm going to spontaneously combust, become black ash like the leaves and litter around me before I have a chance to see Hope again. She'll never know what happened to me. She'll never know the real reason I left. She'll never know how much I wanted a life with her.

The internal fire suddenly dies, and I collapse to the ground, the breath rushing out of my lungs. I look to the side, watching in revulsion as the corpse shrugs off the cloak to reveal its rotting, naked form. The cloak disintegrates into cinders as its body melts like wax straight into the Sea of the Dead, the leaves and pine needles stirring and fluttering across the ground to cover it like nothing was ever there.

An owl calls right before it swoops overhead, the other sounds of the forest breaking the silence. It's like something horribly unnatural wasn't just here. I stare at my hands, but they're not blistered at all. I check out my arm and the leaves I'm lying on. Unmarred, not burnt in the slightest. It was all an illusion. Or a hallucination.

But I hear Vahni's voice in my head again just before I pass out, and it's like she's right next to me.

"You shall return home to me, one way or another."

The sun is low in the forest. No idea what time it is. My lips are dry, my throat feels like I just took a nap in a sandstorm, my brain is foggy and heavy.

Talking to Vahni is always like listening to a bad fortune teller – I remember never getting a straight answer from her, but at least I'm still alive. And not in Asphodel.

I get to my feet, aching from head to toe and feeling like the entire Sweet Home High football team tackled me and left me for dead. My entire body feels draggy, like seeing that *thing* left me feeling a little bit like death as a reminder of its visit. I take a second to get my balance and slowly walk back to the detention center.

As I pass through the forest this time, the animals ignore me. I could try to dismiss Vahni and her visit too, but I know that would be a mistake.

The good of both races… Vahni could have meant demons and guardians, or possibly humans and the rest of us. But from former experience, her idea of "good" is questionable at best. A small part of me was tempted to take her offer for protection, not gonna lie, but if there's anything I learned from the first time around, making a deal with the Praxidikai is like making a deal with the devil.

That's been the hardest part of all of this, of what I'm doing with the alliance. Balancing my worry of Hope and the people I care about with the need of what I'm doing with Jehoel and the others.

Besides, I'm pretty sure that Jonathan is keeping a close eye on Hope. I trust her, and I at least trust him to keep her safe from The Impiorum. Less so in other ways.

The heat inadvertently builds in my palm until I realize what I'm doing. I quash the flame just in time, but it burns me in a completely different way to think about Hope and Jonathan together. I can't think like that, not when I disappeared off the grid like I did – a move that *was* ultimately my choice. I can't let jealousy get the best of me. I have to let it go like I have a thousand times before or I know the fire will consume me until I'm ash.

No. That corpse-thing is the only thing that's going down in flames, not me.

7

Jonathan

The air is thick and buzzing with anticipation. I make my way through the warehouse to the center room, the murmur of excited chatter steadily becoming louder. Either they're having a cocktail party, or the small mob inside is waiting to burn someone.

I face no more obstacles, and my guard goes up like an alarm. Corbin had been almost too easy for me to bypass. A bit of physical intimidation, a flash of a weapon, but he hadn't really done anything to prevent me from entering.

They want me to be here.

I enter the main room and take in the scene before me. This is no small mob. It looks like almost all of the guardians from the Buffalo sector and even some of the ones from Chicago are gathered here.

In the middle are two young males. One fair-haired, one dark, both shackled to a post in the center of the room. I can't be sure until I get closer, but the dark one looks maybe fourteen or fifteen, not nearly old enough to be a full demon. One female human is chained alongside them.

The guardians form a loose circle in the middle of the room, two of them standing in the center near the hostages. I recognize the short female with the long black braid and wide brown eyes as a guardian from Toronto named Tricia Han, but I'm surprised to recognize the male that's with her. He's one of my oldest associates, also currently stationed in Toronto, Rowan O'Connelly. This entire situation is disturbing enough. Every guardian in this room – including Rowan – is ignoring the pleas of the human hostage. This goes against our entire directive.

"Jonathan." I pick up only the slightest hint of strain leaking out of his native Scottish accent. "We've been expecting you."

"If you needed to summon me, there are much easier ways."

I walk in a circular path around the perimeter of the room, holding my own emotions in check. Rowan slips in and out of my view as I pass guardian after guardian. I recognize all of them as my constituents. They all avert their eyes, but not Rowan, who keeps me in his line of sight the entire time.

"What crimes have these individuals committed?" I demand.

"Specifically? Co-mingling with humans. Sharing a bed with this unfortunate human." He nudges the female with the toe of his boot, and she whimpers and shuffles as far away as the chain will let her. He pins me with his gaze before adding, "Associating with the demons that killed our comrades."

"So you kidnapped them and brought them here?" I raise my eyebrows. "Are you trying to lure the *Impiorum* right to our territory?"

"Dude, we didn't do nothin'!" the fair-haired demon protests. Tricia stalks over to him, clamping down on his neck with her hand, and he howls in pain as her *lumen* spears him.

Rowan completely ignores the exchange, folding his arms across his chest and fixing me with a steely glare. "They were consorting with known murderers. We were justified in removing them from the dorms."

"Whoa, wait. We don't know anyone like that!" the one with dark hair protests. He struggles against his restraints, his gaze flicking over to the young woman. "We were just there for a party last night!"

I watch Rowan for his reaction, and there's no surprise or indignation in his expression. We've known each other for over two centuries. He's perfectly aware of my ability to pick up on emotional states, and in this moment, I know. He'd known these boys hadn't done anything, but he took them anyway. He used his powers in plain view of the public. He kidnapped an innocent human with no regard for her well-being or of the greater consequences. And he assembled all of these guardians as witnesses to this. Or had he brought them here for something else?

"You had no due cause to take them, did you?" For the sake of the human prisoner, I don't outwardly voice the accusation – that Rowan had *not* in fact caught the two demons stealing souls. He stares back, his posture defiant, but I know he understands my meaning. The Impiorum has every right to retaliate now. And as director of the guardianship, *I* have every right to punish him.

"In general, their very existence is a crime against humanity."

"Not your judgment to make. Let them go," I say darkly.

I'm very aware of Raleigh above us on the roof. Despite there being dozens of other guardians here, I'm attuned to her signal well enough to sense that she's moving closer. She's still out of sight for the time being, but I have a feeling that it won't be for long.

"If we don't stop The Impiorum from making more chimera, they'll destroy us, too." Rowan's tone is full of derision, his words stirring some of the others to murmur their assent.

This. This is the central theme of all of the recent unrest.

I raise an eyebrow. "You suspect these boys are chimera themselves?"

"I imagine they are well on their way."

Before Rowan can react, I insert myself through a break in the crowd in one rapid move, stopping in a crouch in front of the prisoners. I cast out my *lumen* to measure the power of the older-looking boy, his expression immediately contorting with pain as his *deimos* reflects back to me. His power is undeveloped but not far from the level of darkness indicative of a full demon.

While I've never been one to root for Team Demon, I can't condone this.

"You would punish them because the Impiorum *might* attempt to turn them into chimera?" I straighten, an accusation in my stare. "My friend, I thought you were more reasonable than this."

He smiles. "No, *my friend.* I don't plan on killing them. We want to experiment on them, steal their *deimos* to infuse with our *lumen.* If we were chimera ourselves, we'd be protected against the Seraphim. As it is, we are helpless to defend ourselves."

"This is pure madness," I protest. "There is a better way than this."

"It's the only option left," he replies calmly. "Your constituents are not happy with you, Jonathan. Your attempts to negotiate with The Impiorum got thrown back in your face. You have been too civil in seeking for a resolution, but in the meantime, the Impiorum is slowly destroying us, one by one."

"Your actions are as unjust as the Impiorum's," I argue. "These boys haven't done anything."

He cants his head slightly to the side. "I've known you for centuries, Jonathan, and so forgive me if I find your stance most interesting. Quite the change of heart from your usual no-tolerance policy for demons."

I'm aware of all eyes turning to me, a hush falling over the witnesses as they watch my response to this accusation. *As they judge me.* The realization hits me, my adrenaline surging as I realize I was baited. This was more than a mere abduction of some students at a college dorm. It was an attempt to cast out a net and lure me in.

Rowan obviously wants something specific from me, but I'll be damned if he gets it.

"What are you asking of me?" I snap.

He shrugs, affecting that same bored tone as he strolls around the prisoners. "My sources tell me there was a chimera present the night that the UB Center for the Arts burnt down. And that this chimera was with you."

His gaze pierces through me, and my unbeating heart clenches like a cold fist in my chest. He could mean Samael Richter. Samael was the chimera that destroyed Gail Salazar, one of the most powerful guardians in existence. But if they suspected that I had been in any way consorting with him, they would have questioned me by now.

Or he could mean Hope. She's a chimera, and she saved dozens of people trapped in the Center for the Arts before it burnt to the ground. It's true that she used her *deimos*, but besides myself and her, only humans were present in the burning building.

Even if they suspect her, I have no intention of giving up Hope's identity to anyone, certainly not to a madman on an obvious fishing expedition.

"Is this so?" I pin him with my gaze. "Because this is news to me."

His ruddy complexion becomes flushed. "My source was very clear about what transpired."

"Let this so-called source come forth and make these allegations then," I counter. I sweep the room with a glance. "Even if you did find a chimera who was willing to speak with you, who's to say whether or not the transformation process could be replicated? According to our intelligence, the Impiorum's attempts to make chimera resulted in the death of countless demons." I gesture to the captives. "You do not need to add to those numbers."

"Necessary casualties," he barks. "As are these two, if you refuse to turn over his identity."

The room breaks out into deafening accusations.

"Who is he?"

"We heard you sent him away after he killed Samael Richter!"

"Why would you send someone away who could help us?"

I stand in puzzled silence. They must think the chimera is Micah, not Hope. And so be it. Micah fled the city, and as long as he stays out of the picture, he'll serve as the perfect red herring. It's not that I don't understand the guardian's fears. I do. With Gail Salazar gone, there's no one on this side of the world who can heal us. Her destruction leaves us vulnerable. If there's anything we need as a defense, it's another healer.

"Stop!" I hold up my hand. "This plan of Rowan's is as misguided as the efforts of the Impiorum. Surely you all cannot be on board with this."

I survey the faces, feeling some who are conflicted and some who are thirsty for revenge. All of these guardians are technically my responsibility. And maybe I have failed them so far, but not like Rowan will do if he convinces them that his way is the best way.

"Please, old friend," I implore. "What you suggest goes against our directive and everything we stand for."

He barks a laugh. "I'm doing this for the guardians. That's what I choose to stand for."

Rowan's perfectly serious. Hell-bent on following through with this plan. I don't need to be an empath to see this, and I need to shift tactics. Need to make the witnesses understand what they're in for if they side with him. "Tell me," I retort. "What guardian in his or her right mind would volunteer for your 'experiment'?"

He slowly pivots around, his gaze seeking out certain guardians in the circle. They step forward slowly, one by one, my heart slowly sinking. Rowan's certainly found a way to play on everyone's emotions.

"As you can see, I have secured volunteers. And enough backers that if I were to call for a vote right now, it would be enough to remove you as director."

Rowan's words are like ice water, and I try to shake off the shock induced by them. Honestly, I never wanted to be director. It only fell to me after my predecessor met with his demise earlier this year. But Rowan's declaration still comes as a blow. If they vote for my "removal," it means I'm ousted from the sector forever. It means I'd have to leave Hope. And Raleigh.

This is not happening.

"Tell us where the chimera is," he says in a firm voice.

"Not on my life," I say through my teeth.

A burst of power suddenly enters me in a torrent, melds into my own light, burns to my core. Before I can retaliate, Rowan rushes into me and throws me across the room. I push out my *lumen*, flipping over to right myself before landing. My power is readied to retaliate, but Rowan is now behind a group of guardians who moved to form a physical shield.

I'd just gotten a strong sense of his emotions when he grabbed me, and he'd felt… smug. Satisfied. Not like his usual self.

I rush the group of guardians as Tricia runs forward to intercept me. I leap over her, throwing a brief pulse of my power upward, but Raleigh is already exploding through the glass, undoubtedly having heard everything. She lands and immediately comes to my side.

"Now, Tricia!" Rowan roars.

Out of the corner of my eye, I see Tricia pull out a black device.

"Do it! Now!"

Uncertainty flashes across Tricia's expression, but then she points it at me and Raleigh.

"No!" I shout.

My warning barely hits the air when Rowan hits me with a strike of *lumen*. It knocks me flat on my back at the same time that something akin to a supersonic blast goes off. Time seems to slow to a crawl as I wait for the windows of the building to blow out, the lights explode and plunge us into darkness, but the explosion is only in my head. I hear the muted shouts of the human and some of the guardians. I can't think, can only react, and I scramble to my feet as Raleigh does the same.

My head sears with blinding pain as I get hit, but it's a physical hit and not a strike of power. I try to retaliate, but my *lumen* feels thick, immobilized.

The guardian that attacked me falls to the side as Raleigh delivers a kick. She pulls me up to my feet, her emotions a whirlwind of anger and relief.

"She used a disrupter!" Raleigh shouts at me, her sword poised in front of her. "You won't be able to use your *lumen* to fight them."

Guardians aren't supposed to fight each other. We're supposed to be modeled after Arete, the Eternal guardian. A unified light. Not supposed to kill each other. Raleigh stands by my side and deflects the attack of a guardian that charges us with a dagger. I see now that they're prepared for this, as most of them are wielding weapons. I can see remorse on some of the faces closest to me. These are guardians whom I thought of as my friends. And they're intent on destroying me.

I have nothing but myself when they rush us. I dodge a swing from one of my former friends and sink down in crouch, grabbing his leg and throwing him back. His head strikes the floor and knocks him out, but I know it won't be for long.

The guardians drive a greater wedge between Raleigh and me, cornering me until there's nowhere to go. I deflect assaults left and right, and Raleigh has her hands full defending herself against those guardians that attack with steel. The ones we knock down rise back up again, and I know it's only a matter of time before we exhaust ourselves.

I look up toward the shadows of rafters. The effects of the disrupter are starting to wear off now, and I direct all of my concentration into my legs and leap. I barely make it, one hand coming into contact with the girded beam, but it's enough to grip onto. Shouts come from beneath me, and I use the split-second of confusion to swing myself up and start running. Another leap and I make it to the row of windows that Raleigh burst through.

Self-preservation, above all. It's been my mantra since I ultimately lost Adrienne. But something stops me this time.

Raleigh. I have to evade them, just long enough to recharge, and then go back and help her.

I lie flat on the sloped roof, knowing I have mere seconds to act before they find me. Guardians can't use their power to hurt someone who's unconscious, only to protect, and I concentrate on making a completely different sort of leap. I pick up the same memory I'd used against Stephen before, only this time it's to alter my own state of being.

Adrienne was alive and standing in the same room as me, and my world as I knew it flipped upside-down. With both Cyril and the viscount watching, there were far many questions I would never have the opportunity to ask: how Adrienne had escaped her exile, if she had indeed been forced to marry another man, why she was here now.

The last time I saw her was the morning after we'd been wed, when she had been aglow with passion and our lives had been full of hope. She looked far too wary now, the shadows under her eyes evidence of exhaustion. Her initial shock was gone, her face completely expressionless as I walked up to her. She adopted a mask just as I did.

"Madame Thibault. A pleasure to make your acquaintance, but you may not wish to remain in the room during the interrogation." I took her hand and bowed over it, fighting the urge to take her into my arms instead. But then a dark swirl of emotions flooded me upon the physical contact. She was enormously relieved to see me, but overshadowing her love was her fear of the viscount and something else I couldn't quite read, something much darker. I withdrew from her, wondering what it was.

"I have in fact received permission from Lord Viscount to be here for the beginning of the interrogation." She kept her voice steady. "I have always been curious over these sorts of proceedings."

I glanced at the viscount. He was busy conferring with Cyril, who was boasting rather loudly about what he had done to the last prisoner. Cyril wanted to be the one to interrogate the woman that Adrienne had brought in, but the viscount expressed concern that he would kill her too quickly.

"How did you find me? Why are you here?" I said quickly. My voice was low so only she would hear it.

"You were easy to find. Your reputation precedes you. I came here to help you," she whispered back, and there was sadness intermingling with her storm of emotions. "They keep you under lock and key. This was the only way for me to get in."

It was true. I was a prisoner myself. It had been weeks since I'd been able to escape to report to my superiors with information. Before I could protest, Adrienne reached out and clasped my hand again, this time pressing something into it. "A mixture of deadly nightshade and opiates. Just a 'touch of death,' to protect her," she whispered, her gaze flicking to the woman on the floor, "and to protect other prisoners from your powers. I know you are not like Cyril."

I stared at her, my feelings of horror multiplying. I had never told Adrienne about what I could do, but she seemed to know exactly what damage I was capable of inflicting to this prisoner if I manipulated her will. If my reputation preceded me to such an extent, I had truly lost my way. I was here to help the cause, not to harm the people held within these walls.

Adrienne withdrew, leaving the vial of powder in the palm of my hand. She'd always been fascinated by forbidden things and had once told me about different plants and how they could be used to provide the illusion of death. Or in larger doses, death itself.

The viscount cleared his throat and called over, "Monsieur Drapier? You heard Madame Thibault. There is no need for concern. You may begin now. Cyril, I'll oversee this one."

Cyril stared at him in disbelief. But he backed down with much show, growling as he stormed out of the room, and the viscount's shoulders sagged out of relief.

"If you're absolutely sure," I said to Adrienne, ignoring the viscount.

"Oui, Monsieur." Her gray eyes were wide as they flicked to my hand, and I understood the meaning of her gift.

If I gave the prisoners the Touch of Death before the interrogations began, I wouldn't be able to hurt them, and neither would Cyril. She was here to help the prisoners. And in showing me how to help them, she was saving me as well.

My breathing becomes shallower, my temperature dropping even lower than normal for me. What's left of my *lumen* dims in intensity. Ironic to think of it, but I learned this trick from the very people I was supposed to hurt. From that night forth since Adrienne found me at the prison, I secretly administered the anesthetic to the prisoners before every interrogation — just enough to protect them from any long-lasting effects of Cyril or even my powers. It was one good thing that came out of Adrienne finding me at the prison.

I've only utilized this trick on myself on one other occasion long ago, but I'm relieved to find it works just the same. My own power fades to match the near-blackness of the night. A streak of energy bursts toward me, and I recognize Raleigh's signature. She calls for me, and I hear tussling in the rafters, the sound of the metal striking metal. I'm shrouded in my illusion of death but I can still hear and am relieved to know she's intact.

I feel my *lumen* rejuvenate, but I'm too far into the process to bring myself out of it yet. Seconds pass, and Raleigh is by my side and shaking me. I hear her snarling at the other guardians who followed her. I once told her of my ability to feign death, though she's never seen me do it. Out of anyone in this realm, she knows me the best, and I'm confident she'll connect what she sees with that memory.

She's suddenly gone, and I feel the guardians' emotions roil in a mass of chaos. Seconds tick by, and my chest suddenly feels like a void. One of the guardians was just destroyed.

Oh dear God. Please don't let it be Raleigh.

I think I hear the sound of approaching cars and struggle to draw myself out of the trance. My *lumen* slowly flickers and strengthens, and I look into the center of the building. It's dark except for a streak of light filtering into the space from the partial moon.

"The *Impiorum* is approaching!"

The shout comes from one of the guardians outside, and everyone scatters. Rowan gathering so many of us together in one location must have produced a collective signal too large for the Impiorum to resist. And the fact that we have two of theirs in captivity undoubtedly means they're coming to destroy us.

The guardians still inside shove each other to exit the building, but it's like watching a silent movie. I feel none of their panic or fear, can register absolutely nothing from them.

I scan the space for Raleigh, my vision muddy or perhaps as a human can see things. Squinting into the darkness, I see a form land in the middle of the guardians with a battle cry.

It's Raleigh, and she's holding her custom-made short sword in one hand and Rowan's head in the other.

8

Micah

Something doesn't feel right in the world tonight. I'm supposed to meet Jehoel out in the forest to do property rounds, but I'm on edge, everything I hear sounding irregular, every shift of shadow looking like someone's stepping out from the trees.

It's been three days since the incident with Vahni, and I'd filled in Cael and Jehoel on the bare essentials of what had happened, leaving out the details about the corpse and Sea of the Dead. I'm pretty sure those things were just to torment me, not to share.

In retrospect, I suppose it could have all been in my head. I could be that crazy.

Jehoel's ten minutes late, and I turn to head back inside to the dorms when the temperature shoots up. He shimmers into view in my path a few seconds after that, his face bright and excited and his lips moving even before he fully materializes.

"...need to head out right now." His tone is brusque, his expression indecipherable through his glasses.

I lift my eyebrows in surprise. "I know. We were supposed to start rounds ten minutes ago."

"It can wait. Let's go before it's too late."

My frustration builds like it always does when he pulls this crap. I doubt he's intentionally hiding something from me, but sometimes he's so committed to the alliance that he forgets that some of us need guidance now and then.

"What's going on?" I rack my brain for possibilities. "Did intel find out something about Ben's brother?"

Confusion briefly clouds Jehoel's expression. "Who? No, nothing from intel."

"Wait. Then why...."

My words are left behind as he grabs hold of my shoulder and teleports us out of there.

⟫⟨

A floodlight blinds me, and I brace myself against the nearest structure. Brick wall. I concentrate on the texture of it for a minute while I shake it off. Teleporting with Jehoel is always like blazing through a wall of fire, only the burn is inside instead of out. My least favorite way to travel, but Jehoel is convinced it's more efficient and safer than flying.

My vision clears, and I gather we're in parking lot behind a building – a restaurant from the sounds of it and a seafood one from the smell of it. Given how disoriented I am, I'm betting we're still in Alaska. The farther he leaps, the worse the aftermath, and if we'd gone out of state lines, I'd be puking out my guts right now. The stench from the dumpster back here has the same effect, and I almost heave anyway.

"This way." Jehoel's already walking toward the back door to the restaurant. "We're just in time."

"Hold on!" Just in time for *what?* I bite down my irritation, but this is just how Jehoel operates, that he's used to working alone and in his head. Before he can open the door all the way, I speed around him and shut it again. "What are we doing here? Are we cleared for this, because I didn't even know we had plans to go out this week?"

Jehoel adjusts his glasses. "I informed Cael that I've been following this lead, but I don't have time to brief you right now."

I used to think that Jehoel was quick to judge, but he's usually pretty dead-on in his assessments. I feel a little bit of my tension dissipate as I follow him into the restaurant, but I'm still disturbed by the fact that I haven't been in the know about this so-called lead this entire time. Jehoel may be my mentor, but we're also supposed to be partners.

We walk through the kitchen, the staff ignoring us as Jehoel stops to speak to one of the chefs, a woman with short brown hair and a wary expression. Sharp blue eyes briefly scrutinize him but bypass me as he hands her money, and she pockets it discreetly.

"Where are we?" I ask under my breath.

He doesn't say anything until the woman leads us to a stockroom in the very back of the kitchen and walks away. The whole setup is weird, with the workers at this place pretending we're not here. And now Jehoel's holding open the door and grinning like we're about to embark on a huge adventure.

"Fairbanks." His smile fades a degree. "We might need to fight."

I'd assumed we were here on one of our usual demon recruitment missions, but maybe not. His instructions are still vague, but at least I can understand this. "I'm always ready to fight if I have to."

He nods. "As you should be."

The door opens into a short corridor with a single bare bulb lighting the way, and I follow him to another door made of steel.

"Be prepared for anything," Jehoel warns me as he pulls it open.

I don't answer, my *deimos* surging as I pick up the scent of blood.

The shouts fill the cramped stairwell, the scene abruptly coming into view in a burst of color. Two guys in the middle of the lit basement, attacking each other with their bare hands with a crowd of about thirty or so cheering them on. It's unregulated violence, and the crowd looks rough and just as rowdy.

"Stay in the back," Jehoel advises.

Gladly. I still don't know what we're doing here, but I nod, my gaze drawn to the fight. The guys look about my age, and they look like they've been going at it for a while. One of them is dark-skinned and huge, like pro wrestler size. He definitely has an advantage in terms of pure mass, and I watch in half-disgust, half-awe as he slams his forehead into the other guy's nose.

"What is this?" I mutter to Jehoel. "Some sort of fight club?"

His smirk tells me he gets the reference. "Actually, yes. One of the originals."

"Like… a demon fight club?"

He shrugs. "Some nights."

I cast out my senses, aware of Jehoel because he's right next to me but familiar enough with his signature that it fades to background noise within seconds. The smaller guy who's in the fight is definitely demon. Everyone else in the room besides those two feels human. I watch for a while, waiting to see if the guy will use his *deimos* or not, but so far he's keeping it in check.

Lewd insults fly all around us, money passing hands with almost every move. This is totally not the kind of scene I'd expect Jehoel to be into. He's no saint, and with all of the scars on his face, he actually blends in pretty well with the crowd. But considering he was once active in the Impiorum, he leads a pretty peaceful life.

"You ever gonna tell me what we're doing here?"

"We're looking for somebody." He takes off his glasses and wipes the lenses. Probably got sweat or spit on them. "In the meantime, why don't you feed?"

I shoot him a look, but his expression is carefully closed. There's no point in pressing him for an explanation before he's ready. Jehoel may be a pain in the but about certain things, but he's also more of a mentor to me than anyone's ever been, and I trust him. He's been teaching me the way of the alliance, the directive for our actions simple – seek out other ways to live without hurting souls.

On the night I left Hope, she tried to tell me that she could teach me how to feed off of the residual energy of souls. That was the night she told me she was part-demon, but I don't think I quite believed her in that moment. Everything had been so crazy, and I had just lost my sister… Sometimes I wonder if I should have brought Hope here with me or if I can ask to send for her even now, but then I think about how her brother needs her there.

And whenever I think about some of the places that Jehoel's taken me, I think twice about that. Case in point being tonight. I'd never want Hope to come to a place like this to feed. Yeah, I still can't picture her having to *feed*.

The mood of the room is chaotic, dark, violent. Perfect for me to tap into. My demon senses magnify while my human ones dim, and I feel the same rush that I always do. The general noise of the room fades, but I can pick out the energy from the hostility and greed of the crowd.

I'm aware of everything around me more viscerally, the shouts and jostling bodies of the crowd, the punches and kicks of the fighters. The energy from the noise and action burns through me and shifts to something else, something more pure. The harder I concentrate, the more intense the sensation gets, and I breathe in as I make the connection. Hold my breath. Exhale as the residual energy enters my body and incorporates into my *deimos*.

There's a momentary lull in the activity in the room, as if everyone just got hit by a small wave of calm. Jehoel nods his head slightly, subtly expressing his approval when I glance at him.

But it's only seconds before the crowd goes even more nuts, the shouts becoming louder, the gestures and jostling more furious. I direct my attention to the center of the room and see that the fighting came to a stop. The bigger guy is still standing, his fists at the ready, but the demon is staring out into the crowd. Staring at me like he knows what I just did.

He beckons to an older guy on the sidelines, never tearing his eyes from me, and two burly guys start pushing their way through the masses. Also headed straight for me.

"New challenger!" someone roars. This couldn't be what Jehoel wanted to happen. Could it?

"Uh, Jehoel? What's going on?"

Panic fills my chest as he edges away. *Trust me*, he mouths.

No. I was just thinking about how I do trust him, but still… I stare at him incredulously as he takes out his wallet and hands a sizable wad of cash to the guy taking bets. What the heck is going on?

His earlier warning echoes in my head. *Be prepared for anything.*

But I'm obviously not prepared, because I'm clinging to the notion that this can't be happening. That Jehoel wouldn't set me up like this. I'm in too much shock to react when the two guys grab me on either side. They push me through the crowd, jeers and catcalls filling my ears, and that about does it for me.

I'm not playing this game.

I call up my *deimos*, my jaw tight and senses sharp as I summon the power to throw a quick strike. I took a vow to never hurt a human soul, but the demon in the fight circle is a completely different matter. I saw enough of the previous fight to know that directive or not, I need to act or I'm gonna be this guy's punching bag.

I get shoved into the middle of the fighting circle. Cursing out Jehoel in my head, I turn to face the other demon. Pretty sure I underestimated this guy's size before because of the sheer mass of the other one. I'm six foot two, but this guy has to be at least that, plus he's way stronger-looking than me.

No use of powers here. His voice sounds in my head, commanding and stark.

Telepath. I almost feel a sense of relief at this, only because I can communicate back to him and not risk anyone overhearing. Not that anyone could hear us in this mess.

Sorry if there was any misunderstanding. I didn't come here to fight.

His lips curl in sneer, but I can almost hear it in my head. His thoughts follow a second later.

Shoulda thought of that before you fed in my club then.

There's no referee, no moderator of the fight. The telepath charges me without warning, and I lunge to the side. He's going at human speed, but his hand extends – way more than human speed – as he passes.

He whips around before he gets to the edge of the humans watching the show, and I stare down at the blood on my side. Telepath evidently has claws, but I'm not that hurt – my blood is already slowing its flow. I'm more pissed off at the fact that he ripped my shirt. I had to leave Buffalo with literally only the clothes on my back, and my shirt is one of the only things I have from back home. I face telepath again, a low growl coming from my throat, and he bares his teeth in a grin.

I can't pick up on much of his *deimos* now. He said no powers, but he had no problem using his inhuman speed. I bet he brings out the big guns when he really needs it. I remember guys like him from school. They'd toy with someone smaller than them with taunts and shoves, but if they ever felt remotely threatened, they'd beat on the other guy full on until one of the teachers intervened. Freaking bullies. Like Samael Richter.

Sam intrudes into my memories like a bad dream. I took care of him, though, and I can take care of myself now.

Whatsa matter, kid? You afraid of the big bad demon?

Telepath is glaring at me, like I'm breaking one of the unwritten rules here by not engaging him. But I'm not sure what I'm supposed to do, other than defend myself. He rushes me again just as I have the thought, and I leap out of the way. His movement follows mine, and to anyone in the crowd, it probably looks like he tripped and fell. But I see it like it's in slow motion, his shift to tackle me occurring mid-stride. We both crash to the ground, the wind knocked out of me as I hit the concrete. The sicko laughs as he punches me right in the kidneys, his legs pinning me down and making it impossible to for me to move.

I ignore his directions and grab onto him, the energy from my *deimos* pulsing in my hand. But my strike meets with resistance and packs no punch. There's something surrounding him that repels my power, and it makes my hand feel like it's full of sludge instead of energy.

He laughs again, his eyes shining with a twisted sort of enjoyment as he leans closer.

You got problems listening to directions.

He jumps off from me and throws a kick, but I roll out of the way and keep rolling as he pursues me. His feet come down hard on the concrete, over and over as he tries to stomp on me. My vision turns red, and I stop rolling and grab onto his closest leg to shove back.

Vahni's fire roars to life. Telepath howls and kicks away from me right as the flames swallow him.

No. Not again. I'd only meant to defend myself, not burn the guy.

The air fills with the stench of burnt fabric and skin, and I scramble backward and away. Someone runs up to telepath with a fire extinguisher and douses the flames, but the legs of his pants are already falling away in shreds. The room clears in seconds, the entrance to the stairwell filling as people shove and push to get out of here. The telepath is rushed upstairs in the chaos, the guy who'd been collecting money running past me. I stagger to my feet, scanning for Jehoel, and the guy with the money jumps away from me, wide-eyed and looking at me like I have some sort of disease.

Diseased. Cursed. Same thing. I stumble toward the steps, feeling like walking death, like I was back out in the forest when that equally dead thing came after me to deliver its message. My blood feels like it's on the verge of boiling right beneath my skin. Like the fire goddess is itching to come out and play.

9

Jonathan

It's been centuries since I've had to come back from a death-like state. I don't remember it being this terrible.

There was a moment of stunned silence following Rowan's death, but with the arrival of the Impiorum, now all hell is upon us. The demons come running through the doors, their destructive powers suppressed because they're in our domain but more than making up for it with physical violence.

These aren't run-of-the-mill Impiorum demons either. They are more of the *Seraphim*.

Raleigh escapes out of one of the windows, at least a half dozen guardians right on her tail. I think I hear her yell at me to follow, but my equilibrium is off as I totter to the edge of the rooftop.

The prisoners. They're still in the center of the room amidst the chaos. I climb back through the window and balance on the nearest rafter, ignoring the slash of pain as I land on broken glass. Tricia is already freeing the human when I get to her, and I grab her by her shoulder. I'm momentarily stunned by the intensity of grief pouring from her. She must have loved Rowan or at least cared deeply for him.

Her eyes shine with tears, her lips curling back in disgust. "You! I thought you were dead. You *should be dead,*" she hisses, throwing my hand off her shoulder.

"I'm afraid not. I cannot allow you to take the human."

"I'm taking her to safety," she spits at me.

"You expect me to believe you'll keep the human safe after abducting her in the first place?"

The girl, free now, scrambles away from both of us and the demons on the floor. They're still shackled and not going anywhere.

"Fine," she snaps. She throws a glance at the stampede of panicking guardians. "I have to see to the safety of *Rowan's* constituents."

She's already off to join the tail end of the mass exodus. Ridiculous. Rowan had no constituents, and despite the shift in loyalty tonight, they are still mine. I peel the girl off the floor, but she screams and kicks at me. I attempt to channel a sense of peace into the girl, but she yanks her arm away and starts running.

Not exactly the response I was expecting. I give chase, indecision pinning me to the spot when I get outside. The last of the vehicles are just leaving the lot, Raleigh nowhere in sight, and my sights land on the cars in the distance. The girl is still running, and she throws a frightened glance over her shoulder before frantically waving her arms in an attempt to flag down the approaching cars.

I push out my energy into my legs so I can get to her, but my *lumen* feels thick and doesn't come through. Not surprising after the guardians attacked me. I'll need time to recover, but we have no time right now. The girl is on a collision course with the *Seraphim,* and there will be nothing I can do to save her if they get to her first.

Her death was imminent.

The thought worms its way into my head, the darkest sort of despair surging through my veins.

Her death was imminent. Her death was imminent…

An unfamiliar dark brown sedan suddenly tears around the building and barrels toward me. Raleigh's shout brings me back as the car screeches to a stop next to me.

"Good lord, what are you doing just standing there? Come on!"

I climb into the back seat, Raleigh hitting the gas before I'm all the way in. She races toward the running girl, slowing as we get close enough. I jump out and grab the girl, drawing her into the back seat with me as Raleigh kicks the car into gear again.

Raleigh drives expertly through the labyrinth of streets while I try my best to quiet the girl.

"I am here. Everything will be all right," I say.

The words are automatic, words from a memory that I'd spoken in another time and in another life. But I'm barely clinging to my own sense of calm, and she's acting immune to what little I have. She struggles until her will seems to give out, and she sags against the seat and sobs.

"Do you need help with her?" Raleigh glances back at me, her forehead pinched in a frown.

"If you wouldn't mind."

Given my state of being, it would be foolish for me to object. We're in a residential area in the city now, and Raleigh pulls over, throwing the car into neutral and reaching back to place her hand on the girl's arm. Her head whips up, her eyes wide and full of terror as she stares into Raleigh's bright green ones.

"Go to sleep," Raleigh purrs. "You'll wake up at the hospital with no memory of anything except for having one drink too many."

The girl slumps back, the car falling quiet except for the sound of the idling engine and the occasional hiccups from the girl. Raleigh turns around again and stares straight ahead, her voice brittle when she finally speaks.

"So…I'm very glad that you are intact."

"Likewise," I say. "Where did you get the car?"

She sighs. "It's Rowan's. He didn't need it anymore."

⌇

Raleigh drops off the girl at the emergency room at Buffalo General. It's the only thing we have that even remotely resembles a plan, and silence immediately falls over us when we pull away from the hospital.

Our options are limited. I refuse to leave the city, but I'm afraid for what the guardians will do to Raleigh once they regroup. The only retaliation tonight had been on Raleigh's part because she'd believed me to be destroyed. This is my fault, and I need to make things right again.

She navigates the car through the city streets, heading away from either of our places in the city. My hand tightens into a fist as she tears up Elmwood Avenue.

"We cannot go to the gallery," I protest.

"We're not," she throws over her shoulder after a moment. She keeps driving past Delaware Park, pulling into a parking lot between a church and apartment complex. "I need to dispose of this car." She keeps her eyes averted from me. "You can't run, can you?"

"No," I admit.

She takes a key from her pocket and holds it out to me. "This will let you into the church. I'll be back in no more than ten minutes."

I take the key from her, taking her hand as well. "I am very sorry about what happened. I will do everything in my power to fix this."

She stares at her hand in mine, her mouth opening to reply but shutting again as she bites back the obvious, that I might as well not have any power.

When she lifts her eyes to look at me, there's no doubt in her expression, only trust.

"I know you will," she says with conviction.

Raleigh is so loyal, unfalteringly so in all of the time I've known her. I squeeze her hand before getting out of the car, still feeling wracked but also filled with gratitude.

My senses are dull as I look around, but I head straight for the church as Raleigh instructed. It's one of the older houses of worship, some of the windows cracked and the rest dark except for where the sun strikes one of the stained glass windows. I head for the back door, each step I take through the lot like I'm walking through water. The keys fall out of my hand as I try to unlock the door, and I curse myself under my breath. I haven't felt this uncoordinated, not even when I was a human.

Even worse is the fact that I couldn't get a sense of what Raleigh was feeling back in the car, not even when I'd touched her hand. The physical aftermath of the attack I've encountered before, but not the silencing of my senses.

The old wooden doors creak loudly in protest as I enter, the air heavy and stagnant as I walk into the vestibule. The interior of the church also lies in disrepair and neglect, some pews missing, others tipped over, dust lying in a film over most everything. I don't know why Raleigh chose this place, but in this city, things are not always as they appear.

I sit in one of the intact pews, the quiet finally allowing me to think.

Rowan must have been behind some of the other smaller uprisings in the last few months. He was obviously taking the time to build supporters, but I'm certain that the trouble will continue with someone new at the helm. Now that he's gone, I wouldn't be surprised if Tricia emerged as the new challenger.

While he didn't formally call for the vote to oust me from the directorship, it doesn't matter. The guardians *attacked* me tonight, and my second-in-command committed an unforgivable crime.

She did it because of me, and I need to make sure I'm the one to make it right.

As if on cue, Raleigh strides into the church, her breath making clouds in the air. She locks the door behind her, and I look at her closely for the first time since we left the warehouse. Her hands are covered in dried blood, a bloom of color on her side that's shades darker than her red jacket.

"You're injured?"

She shakes her head. Her brow is clouded with worry, but I still can't feel anything from her. "I'm fine. What about you? You look like a lump. Can you move?"

"Not too well at the moment, no."

She's by my side in an instant, pulling me to my feet. "You feel like deadweight."

"It feels that way on my end as well," I mutter.

Raleigh walks with purpose as she leads me through a row and to the east wall. She runs her fingers over the impenetrable looking surface until she reaches a small fissure. When she pulls, the seams of a doorway appear.

I peer inside, surprised to see the start of a curved stairwell. "What is this place?"

"My sanctuary."

She gives me a strained smile, and I can't tell if it's because she's bearing some my weight or because she's giving me access to her sanctuary. Every guardian has a place they use to connect with the light of the collective. We have to do it every hundred days or so, many opting to do it more frequently than that. But sanctuaries are sacred, and Raleigh bringing me here is unprecedented.

"Raleigh, you don't have to –"

She shakes her head, her grip tightening on my arm. "Do not object. We need somewhere safe to regroup."

That may be the case, but being here feels like I'm violating her privacy, and given everything, I'd rather be the one to make the sacrifice. "Then let's go to my sanctuary."

"No time."

She closes the door and tugs at me again, and I hesitate for a second before making my sluggish legs follow. The dark corridor leads to a stairwell that illuminates as we enter, the modern light fixtures in contrast to the stone walls. They come alive as we descend and extinguish as we pass.

"Nice touch."

"Thanks. This entire structure is protected by *sanctuarium* magic," she informs me as we continue to spiral down. "Other guardians won't be able to find us here. Demons either. The building itself was designated as having historical status, which means that any extensive renovations are strictly prohibited."

"Good thinking." Knowing Raleigh and her resourcefulness, she personally made sure that the building earned historical status and is probably low on the list for city renovation projects.

We go through a small round antechamber that leads to the main one, and I stop in the entryway in surprise.

"Make yourself at home," Raleigh says quietly.

She moves in a burst of speed to stand at a computer station that's against one of the walls of the large rectangular room. The room is fully functional, more like a studio apartment than merely a place for meditation. There's a kitchenette off to one side and a door leading to a bathroom, a comfortable-looking sofa, lots of cushions in a pile on the floor, and a low table holding an assortment of thick candles in one corner. More of the same light fixtures are glowing around the perimeter. The room is full of bright colors that might have clashed in any other context but somehow come together to make it feel peaceful.

Only I can tell from Raleigh's unsteady breaths that she's far from feeling peaceful right now. I couldn't get a good read on her on the drive because I'd been too stunned, and she was guarded when she came into the church. I'm feeling slightly more centered now, and I move to stand behind her, placing a hand on her arm.

She freezes. "What am I feeling? Tell me," she asks without looking up.

"I can't tell." I withdraw and walk over to the sofa, sinking down and resting my head on my hands. I'd literally felt nothing from her. It's as though my special senses are on mute, and I don't like it.

I hear her move away from the computer and see her boots come to a stop in front of me.

"Jonathan...."

I don't need my senses to hear the fear in her voice. I look up, the expression on her face striking me almost senseless. Raleigh Peyton is a warrior, someone who's not afraid to take on the challenges that this world throws at her, but in this moment she looks afraid.

"What you did earlier?" She hesitates, her eyes like troubled green waters. "You've attempted faking your ultimate death before, and with success?"

"Yes, I told you this once."

She releases a sigh before crouching down to be level with me. "And it was my fault for not remembering."

I still can't pinpoint how she's feeling, but my own unease spreads through my chest. "Why do you ask?"

"I cannot feel your *lumen*. At all."

I stare at her, the meaning of her words slowly settling over me. Raleigh knows me and my signature more than anyone, and if she of all guardians can't feel my power....

Her eyes search mine as though looking for answers, but I have none. Feigning death was for self-preservation, a ruse to throw the guardians off track so I could escape their attack. These aftereffects – what I'm feeling and what Raleigh cannot – must be an artifact of that trick.

"Give it time," I finally say. "I will be fine, just as you will be."

I reach for her jacket to see the extent of her injury, but she stands abruptly and walks over to the table with candles. She lights all of them without saying another word, the fixtures on the wall automatically dimming.

"I'll be back by ten," she announces. "Don't go anywhere until I do."

I move to get up. "Raleigh, I am not going into hiding. If they want to come for me, they will come for me."

"Fine." Her tone is brisk. "But in the meantime, somebody has filed a report to Buffalo State Public Safety about an incident at the dorms early this morning. I must tend to damage control. Given the state of affairs this morning, I doubt any of the others have bothered." She hesitates. "You need to stay here and trust me to take care of things."

Her tone is still curt, but I hear the tremor in her voice. I walk up to her and take her hand in mine. Raleigh gives me a look of pure exasperation. She's obviously in a hurry, but I have the sudden need to say it.

"You know you are my dearest friend and that I do trust you. More than anyone."

Her gaze drops to our linked hands. She looks up again, blinking rapidly to fight back her tears, and I lift my eyebrows in surprise. I've only ever seen Raleigh cry once in the sixty plus years that I've known her. The first time was when her beloved Charlie was destroyed by the Impiorum. This time is solely on me.

"I know," Raleigh finally says, her voice uncharacteristically quiet. "Use the Pathicomm if you need me. I collected the others from the teams the other night, so only I will hear you as long as you're in range. I shouldn't be far." She takes her hand back and heads for the exit.

"Raleigh. Be careful," I call to her.

Still facing away, she hesitates by the door. "Work on getting your *lumen* back while I'm gone. I'm not averse to working with you if you're mortal, but it will make things more complicated."

She disappears from the chamber in a blur, leaving me speechless.

Mortality. It's not possible. I never intended to live forever, but I almost have a harder time considering being mortal.

The urge to rid myself of all of this morning's stress is overwhelming now, and I focus on the flames from the candles in the center of the room. Guardians have to periodically purge ourselves of the weight we take on from the humans. It's like a cleansing rite, and if we don't take the time to do it, we function as well as a person that goes without sleep for too long.

I fall into a trance and let myself dream, thinking about Raleigh's assessment. She can't be right about my *lumen* being extinguished. If this were true, I wouldn't be breathing right now.

✷

For two months, Adrienne showed up at the prison every week, sometimes twice in a week. She had both the viscount and Cyril wrapped around her little finger, and they allowed her to attend the beginnings of some of the interrogations before we actually extracted the confidential information from the prisoners.

Her excuse was that she was naturally curious about death. I don't think it was a lie.

She brought me more of her carefully concocted touch of death powder each time. I slowly learned more about her life in our year that we'd spent apart.

Adrienne told me she had been sent away to another province and arranged to marry a Lord Thibault, but he was trampled to death by a horse on their wedding day. The two families had lied and said that the accident occurred after the marriage was consummated in order to forge a relationship between the two, and Adrienne was branded for life as not suitable for marriage. I didn't press the matter for obvious reasons, first and foremost that she was still my wife in my eyes.

"So I became a widow at the old age of seventeen," she declared one day.

"And I became a widower at the same age," I told her. "I found your gravesite."

"They did that to throw you off track should you ever try to find me." She hesitated. "I believed you were dead at first too. My father lied and told me that Edmond had mortally wounded you before you delivered the strike that killed him."

I don't know why we kept up the madness of our ruse. Numerous times, I tried to persuade her that we should run away together, but Adrienne always insisted that we could not. She told me that I was the only thing standing in the way of Cyril torturing innocents. Despite the darkness of my world, she was like my light every time she walked into one of the prison cells.

I used my abilities to distract guards, and we snuck into empty cells together whenever we could. We found time to laugh. We dared to talk about our dreams of a life together someday, after the war and when it was safer. We stole kisses and brief moments together, like we used to before we were married. I thought often of our wedding night, when she told me that she only needed me.

She wanted to know more about my ability to manipulate the wills of men. I was at first too ashamed to tell her, but I eventually told her everything. I confessed everything about what happened to her brother, Edmond, on the morning after we were wed.

She listened until I was done. I waited for her to become angry or show her disgust, but instead of judgment, she gave me a soft kiss on my lips.

"Do not let your abilities define you. You are a good person, Jonathan. Trust in yourself."

10

Jonathan

I wake to the sound of approaching footsteps that are quick and light. The cleansing ritual had worked, and I feel better by leaps and bounds. It takes me a moment to remember where I am. And what century it is.

"Jonathan?" Hope bursts into the chamber. I hear her approach more slowly, as though not sure whether I'm asleep or awake.

I open my eyes. "What are you doing here, my dear?"

She rushes to my side, her auburn hair flying. "Raleigh let me in. She told me everything. What are we going to do?" She's out of breath, her cheeks spotted with color as if she'd sprinted here all the way from her house in the suburbs.

I wish Raleigh hadn't told Hope anything at all, and it takes me a moment to suppress my annoyance. "Business as usual."

"But —"

"Rowan has been destroyed," I say firmly. "If the others vote me out of the directorship, so be it. But we have a new element to worry about with the *Seraphim*, and my directive will still be to protect the souls in this city."

"Can you still do that? Raleigh said that if they vote you out, you have to leave." She worries her bottom lip, her eyes filled with concern.

"Raleigh told you far too much." I frown. "Where is she?"

"She told me she had to go to her office to plug up the media leaks of what happened this morning. She said it might take a while."

"So she sent you to babysit me. Well, as you can see, I am intact. And you should be in school."

She snorts. "How could I possibly go to school when one of my best friends is hurt?"

"Hope, your existence cannot be all related to being a guardian. Or chimera," I add. "We all have our normal lives to lead."

"Some people don't."

Her bitter declaration hits the air like a sting, but I know she doesn't mean me. Micah walked away from her, and in doing so, he walked away from everything normal.

I reach out and pat her hand, her pain flowing into me. Her skin is hot to the touch, much hotter than a typical guardian's.

I keep my tone light. "You recharged today?"

"I fed my *deimos* last night." She throws me a sideways glance. "If that's what you mean."

"I suppose I meant fed," I say back. "If you must call it that."

"It is what it is, Jonathan. Sylvia dragged me to this party with the drama club students last night. There were so many people there that it was easy to feed off of them." She grimaces. "Okay, I see your point. That just made me sound like a vampire."

"Well, technically we are members of the undead," I say reasonably. "Though you're not sucking their blood, just tapping into their energy."

"Right." Her smile fades, and she sighs and leans back again. "I wish Micah could have let me show him how to do it instead of having to go off with the alliance." She mumbles down at the floor. "Sorry, that's selfish of me, I know."

"He had other reasons for leaving," I point out. "And as being a guardian is inherently selfless, it is perfectly forgivable to have selfish desires in other aspects of our lives, especially when it comes to those we love." I give her a grim smile. "I'm sorry, my dear. I could use my powers to alleviate your pain, but it would only be an illusion."

"Yeah, don't do that. Besides, what's happening with you is way more important than my little life right now."

"I appreciate you thinking so, but your life is more important."

She rolls her eyes. "Seriously, I hate it when you say things like that."

I smile despite the gravity of the topic. Hope reminds me so much of Adrienne at times. Independent and spirited. Outspoken and blunt. It reminds me of someone else from my past…

"Did I ever tell you about Colette?" The name rolls off my tongue, the thought of her sending a sharp pang through my heart.

Hope's brows scrunch together. "Oh no. If she's another girlfriend of yours like Christianna, I kind of don't want to hear about it."

"No." I stare at the candles that are now halfway gone. "Colette was merely a human I knew long ago, after I first transformed into a guardian. She was born during wartime and orphaned soon after. She lost her mother when she was a baby."

I hesitate, deliberating over my next words. "Her father died around the same time."

"Oh." Empathy replaces the doubt in Hope's expression. Her parents had died too, though Hope had been significantly older. "And you protected her?"

"For as long as I could." The words linger on my tongue like an old sorrow. "But back then, I thought it would be dangerous for her to know what I really was. I filled a role as her caretaker as best as I could for as long as I could, but things became…complicated. I had to orphan her all over again so she wouldn't suspect what I was."

Hope sits very still, looking entranced by my story. I know she's waiting for what's coming next.

"Even after I left her, I kept watch over her from a distance until she died." I glance at Hope, and it takes me a moment to collect myself enough to say it. "Her mortal life was more important than my immortal one. I would have given everything back if I could have spent my days with her."

"Oh, I see," she breathes, and a silence falls over us as she considers this. "Could you ever do that? Give up your immortality to become human again?"

It's an ironic question considering Raleigh's earlier concerns about my state of being. "Not that I'm aware of, though earlier this morning certainly felt like it." I look at her more closely, but her expression is unreadable. "Why do you ask?"

"Just curious, I guess. Sometimes eternity feels like an awfully long time." She laughs a little. "Which of course, it is."

I nod. "Indeed it is," I say gravely. "But you know immortals in this realm can be destroyed. There are very few entities in existence who are true Eternals."

"Really?" She leans forward, her eyes shining. "Who are they?"

I smile at her enthusiasm. "I've already made you even later for school with my storytelling. Next time."

"School." She appears to deflate again. "Being there these days…Ugh. You sure you're feeling well enough for me to go?"

"Certainly." It's true, though I'm not yet at one hundred percent. "You skipped school yesterday to do guardian service," I say sternly as I rise. "I refuse to let you do it again on my account."

She follows me to the stairwell, her phone going off as we start climbing. "Troy," she says, rolling her eyes. "He's all worried because I missed homeroom. I swear, I can't breathe with the two of you coddling me. And Davis too."

"We love you," I point out.

"Yeah, well. I love you guys too. But just so you know, it's perfectly acceptable for me to play hooky," she mutters as I walk her upstairs to the main part of the church. "Senioritis is normal."

"Senioritis?" I keep my tone deliberately light. "Is this some sort of disease?"

She shoots me a suspicious look. "You'd better not be shutting me out or trying to do something noble like 'protecting me.' You, me, and Raleigh. We're a team now."

I usher her through the side door, scanning the overgrown parking lot for anyone lurking nearby. Nothing. I might not be able to read Hope's emotions like I usually do, but I can hear the anger in her tone. I know it's how she's always thought of herself and Micah – the two of them as a team.

"You will help. Later, but right now I have to deal with guardian politics, and it would be best if you didn't involve yourself in this one." I lock the church door behind us and check my watch. "You can still make it in time for second period if we hurry. Where did you park?"

She sighs and points. "Three blocks that way."

"All right. Let's keep to human speed."

We walk down the street together, and I feel a flicker of nostalgia that's purely my own. Not so long ago she and I used to have time to train, time to spar, but those times have taken a back seat to recent developments. I scan for any signs of trouble as we pass side streets, alleys, empty storefronts, but nothing pops out to me as being overtly suspicious. Although with all of my senses on mute, I wouldn't be able to pick up any guardians that might be nearby.

She says suddenly, "Can I ask you something?"

"Always."

"Why didn't you ever go back to Colette?"

I have no immediate response to this. Not one I can verbalize, anyway. I say after a while, "Because it was the best thing for us both."

"Oh." She frowns down at her sidewalk.

We turn the corner, and I spot Hope's Mazda 6, an early eighteenth birthday present from her brother that was secretly financed by me. Davis simply has trouble remembering that part. She takes out her keys as I give a passing glance to a nearby bakery that's bustling with activity.

"I need you to be around other humans today, Hope," I say as she unlocks the door.

She pauses, her hands clenched around her keys. "Why? Why are you worried about me being conspicuous?"

"Because the guardians in this city aren't feeling very tolerant of anyone different today."

"Huh. Just like high school." Hope shakes her head as she gets into the car, and I'm relieved she doesn't ask any more questions. She'll be on her guard now, and that's what counts. She lowers the passenger-side window and leans over to speak to me. "Don't worry. I'll play human. I'm supposed to go to the movies with Sylvia and Troy after school anyway."

"That sounds fun," I say with approval. "Do that."

"I will do that," she mimics. "But promise me you'll check in with me later."

I smile as she drives away, but as they say, my heart isn't in it.

My own emotions feel in flux today, perhaps because the ones around me are still so inaccessible. But my relief is real as her car turns the corner. Ordinarily, I wouldn't object to Hope playing hooky, but the main reason I can't have her with me is because she'd have major objections with what I'm about to do.

I glance at my watch. Just before nine. I haven't heard from Raleigh, but she said she would be back by ten.

Hands in my pockets, I walk in the opposite direction of the church. It irks me to no end that I can't tell if there are guardians around, but maybe I can use the collective energy of guardians to my advantage. Any one of them in close proximity will be able to pick up *my* signal, and I might just be able to throw them a bit of a false trail so I can slip away undetected. But first I have to make sure I have enough *lumen* to pull it off.

I double back to the bakery Hope and I passed. It's packed this morning, full of people stopping in on the way to work. My appearance is a little worse for wear after this morning but I probably fit in as well as anyone else, and I join the flow of traffic and head inside. There's one free table in the far corner, and I spot a young woman juggling a cup of coffee, pastry, and a laptop making her way over. I arrive at the table just as she does.

She frowns. "Sorry, but this is my table."

"I do believe it was open. Perhaps we could share." I smile and pull out the seat closest to her. Her cheeks flush, her plate rattling on the table as she sets it down.

"Okay, fine. But just so you know, I'm not interested in small talk or anything else." She puts her laptop down with a clatter.

"I wouldn't dream of it," I say.

The color gradually leaves her face as she gets to work, and I take a seat opposite her and wait. The woman is dressed in a flannel shirt, her hair in a messy topknot. She's taking multi-tasking to new levels, switching back and forth between looking at her phone and doing something on her computer at the same time as she tries to eat her breakfast. None of it very effectively, either. I give her thirty seconds until she fails miserably at whatever she's trying to do.

It takes less time than that before she spills coffee on her computer. She jumps up, her pastry rolling to the floor. "Goddammit!"

I grimace inwardly at her blasphemy but reach over with a handful of napkins. "Allow me."

She looks up at me as she grabs the stack to mop up the mess, and I finally measure her soul. Every guardian perceives it differently – Hope sees colors, Raleigh attains a sense of someone's well-being – and I feel their brand of pain. From the outside, this one looks like she has everything together, but she's full of so much bitterness that I can almost taste it. Sometimes I encounter people like this, ones who can no longer see the light. She could definitely use a little bit of mine.

As I get up to leave, I summon my power of protection and cast it over her. She's still grumbling over the state of her laptop, but I pick up the change in her mood as my *lumen* settles over her like a security blanket, see her shoulders relax and the lines on her forehead smooth out.

I move through the room, casting my protection over the people at the next table and then through the queue, a little bit of my *lumen* jumping from me each time. When I'm done, the souls of everyone in the coffee shop are protected.

I slip out of the front door and walk away. The pedestrian traffic is thick this morning with people on their way to work, and I cast out more of my protection as I go until the area is saturated with my signal. To any passing guardian, the coffee shop and surrounding area will be like a beacon with my signature, and the people leaving will be emitting fresh signal as well. It won't fool the others for long, but it might be enough to bide me the time that I need. I duck into the nearest alleyway, scaling the fire escape and running as soon as my feet hit the roof. I want to keep my trail to a minimum, and I use the least amount of energy I need to get up to the speed I need to jump to the next rooftop. Within minutes, I reach the financial district of downtown Buffalo, and I quickly scan the alleyway below before taking the last leap.

A knife whips through the air from above, striking me in the chest. I grab the hilt and look up. If it had penetrated through my jacket, it would have caused some damage, but luckily it struck my phone.

Tricia jumps down from the rooftop, and I leap straight up to intercept her mid-air. I grab hold of her arms, but before I can immobilize her, a surge of electricity jolts through my arm and stuns me. My vision explodes with white as I hit the ground, the burst of light diffusing into stars as Tricia moves into my line of sight. I don't know how she'd been able to follow me. I'd been periodically checking behind me along the route and hadn't seen her. My inability to sense other guardians is proving to be extremely inconvenient.

"Very clever, Jonathan, dropping your signature throughout the city like that. But I've been onto you ever since you walked your little friend to her car."

Hope had made some quip about her not wanting me to be protective, but Tricia's comment inflames my temper. Her knife is on the ground by my foot, and I grab it and lunge for her. She falls but rolls away before jumping up. I'm already on my feet and in her path when she comes for me again, and this time I manage to grab her wrist as she throws a punch, my other hand bracing her own knife against her jugular.

As soon as we make physical contact, I get a sense of her emotions. Grief, so deep and intense, that it momentarily stuns me. It hits me like a flash but then disappears, her expression hardening. She shoves away from me, and in the next second, she's standing at the end of the alley.

"Where is she?" she challenges.

I don't know if she means Raleigh or Hope, but I'm glad that Tricia doesn't know the answer to the question, whomever she means.

"You had no problem locating me. Find her yourself."

"Call her and tell her I need to speak to her," she grinds out. "Now."

I pat my shredded jacket pocket, taking out my phone. "I'm sorry. But this took a knife to it and does not look to be in working condition. Incidentally, you also owe me a new suit."

Her eyes narrow. "Where is she? I've had half of the guardians searching the entire city for her since we left the warehouse."

I've spent centuries tempering my emotions, but I'm sure my face reveals my surprise.

This can't be. If I had been easy for Tricia to find, Raleigh should have been even easier. She told me she was going to the college campus and told Hope she was going to her office at The Buffalo News. The guardians would have easily found her at these places. Unless she withheld the truth from both of us and went somewhere completely different. I have the Pathicomm in my other pocket, but I can't use it with Tricia watching.

"I have absolutely no idea where she is."

Tricia blinks at my honest reaction but quickly recovers. "You don't expect me to believe that you'd abandon your precious second-in-command."

"It depends on your propensity to accept the truth."

Her face turns a shade of crimson, and even though my empath abilities are still limited right now, I can tell by how she's worrying her lip that she's conflicted.

"Very well." She finally lifts her chin. "Then you will deliver the message to her. Raleigh will face judgment for the destruction of Rowan O'Connelly in three week's time. I have already sent for the tribunal."

I knew this was coming, but my heart still feels like a rock in my chest. The Praxidikai rule over both their realm and ours to establish overall guiding principles, but each sector of guardians has a local tribunal that has power to take care of local matters. They are summoned rarely, and only for grave offenses. Of course, beheading Rowan counts. If Raleigh had done it in self-defense, it would have been one thing. But she did it in defense of me.

I advance on Tricia, and she flinches – it's the slightest reaction, but it's enough.

"You are not the director of this sector. You have no power to summon the tribunal."

She folds her arms across her chest. "And neither do you, as you were present and therefore implicated in the incident."

"Every guardian in the sector was there," I retort. "The vast majority of those were under the influence of Rowan. There is no way that the tribunal would be fair, and you know this as well as I do. Try again."

"All right." Her face brightens, as though this was what she was waiting for. "I'll cut you a deal. We'll bring the matter to an outside tribunal if you turn over the identity of the chimera."

"No." I glower at her. "That's not an equivalent exchange. We're talking about the fairness of a trial, not Rowan's twisted plan. You still have no authority to do this."

"Actually, I do, under these unusual circumstances. That's my final offer. You said it – Raleigh doesn't stand a chance against the tribunal here, regardless of who's in charge." She folds her arms over her chest, and I can see that this was the card she was hoping to play this entire time. "All I need is a name. You have my word that we won't harm the chimera."

I'm not completely delusional. I know my chances of staying as director are slim right now. The guardians settled on the chimera as their magic bullet and are looking to Tricia for leadership. If I throw her a bone, I can still execute my plan, even if I'm ousted.

I think quickly, knowing I have to do what's best for Raleigh but also for Hope.

"If I tell you a name, you must vow that you shall not harm him."

"You have my word. I only want to speak to the chimera." She moves closer, her eyes brighter as she holds out her hand. "If the identity checks out, you and Raleigh will have the full three weeks to prepare for the trial. My constituents will leave you in peace."

Her constituents. Tricia definitely has gall. But I also know that she's managed to get control over the guardians when I've failed.

She steps back, her eyes still alight as she waits for the name. I take a deep breath and release it, knowing I need to give her something plausible. For Raleigh's sake I need to buy us some time.

I steel myself to say the lie. Thank God that Hope isn't here to witness this.

"His name is Micah Condie."

11

Micah

Betrayed. I was betrayed by my mentor and so-called friend Jehoel, to whom I simply handed over my trust and left behind everyone I cared about. And I don't even know why he did it.

I'm still reeling from what happened back in the basement of the restaurant. I'd waited for the place to be completely empty before I'd ventured upstairs. By the time I'd gotten up to the kitchen, the restaurant was closed and no one was around. Not even Jehoel. Telepath joined the mass exodus too. I know he'll heal, but that's not why I'm really upset. I lost control of Vahni's power again, and this time I hurt someone.

I haven't gone back to the compound since leaving the restaurant. It's almost dawn now, and I fly so hard that I hurt. A voice in my head tells me that I could easily say screw it and go home to Buffalo right now. Except that I know better, that running won't solve anything.

Still, right now the only thing I want is to be away from everyone and everything. I head for the coastline, trying to clear my head. I don't know exactly where I am, only that I'm passing over occasional cities and towns and am therefore still on the grid. I push myself to go even faster until everything blurs together. The stars in the night sky. The lights from the towns beneath me. My dreams of going home. The stark reality of not being able to leave.

I don't get it. Jehoel and I are a team. From day one, I've worked hard to prove myself to him to show him I'm committed to the alliance. Everything had gone to hell so quickly my last night in Buffalo, and I'd suddenly had this huge decision to make – leave with Jehoel and establish a better way of life or stay behind and keep running from the Impiorum. Hope had trusted Jehoel enough to bring him to me, and that was a big part of why I went with him. I've done everything he's asked of me, gone on countless recruiting missions to seek out others like us, and tonight he threw me to that pack of wolves like I was nothing.

Just like Jonathan handed me over to the Praxidikai in the first place.

I can feel Jehoel tracking me from the ground, his signal brief and sporadic as he teleports from city to city. Part of me is glad he's following me. That he's burning off more of his precious energy with every jump he makes. I hope he's suffering at the very least from that, if not the remorse from what he just made me do.

I adjust my flight path and head west toward the Pacific. There's no way Jehoel will be able to follow me if I take a route mostly over the water. I'm raging only slightly less by the time I hit the coastline and keep on going until I pass the fishing boats doing night surveys. I hone in on where the ocean looks black and as pure as the night sky.

The air whips around me like a mini-tornado, the temperature penetrating my invisible shield. The blazing heat hits me right before Jehoel does. His arms pin me, his *deimos* shocking my system, and we plummet toward the water.

I'm paralyzed and can't get free. Can't even open my mouth to shout at him. Can't concentrate enough to send him my thoughts. My thoughts are too raging to be coherent anyway. We pick up velocity, the speed of our descent making it hard to breathe. Maybe this is how Icarus felt, only he didn't have someone dragging him down. I'm more pissed at Jehoel than I am worried that we'll hit the water. He'll teleport us to land before we do.

We smash into the surface of the water, the impact knocking the breath out of me. My back ribs feel crushed, the pain white-hot against the icy cold water. I go under, only vaguely aware that Jehoel's not hanging onto me anymore. My need for air overrides everything, but the ocean is spiraling and churning around me like it's alive and determined to drag me under.

The panic builds up in me like pressure until Vahni's power explodes. My body jerks from the propulsion of the blast, and I burst through the surface of the water, my lungs stinging as I fight for air. Jehoel latches onto me even before I can see him. I thrash and try to throw him off from me, but he holds on tight.

"I'm sorry, Micah." He sounds waterlogged too, but I can't bring myself to feel bad about that. "I didn't have enough energy…to make another leap…after I grabbed you."

I open my mouth to shout at him, but I get a mouthful of sea water. I gag and spit out the water. "Why did you do that tonight?"

"I understand your confusion." He's calmer now, his voice quiet, his teeth devoid of the chattering like mine are beginning to do. "I owe you more than I'll ever be able to repay."

I splutter out an almost-laugh. "You owe me. Funny way of showing it."

But his comment makes me curious, despite everything. From day one, I'd trusted Jehoel because Hope had been the one to bring him to me. He's never given me reason not to. Until now.

His mouth turns down as if in remorse or regret, and he shuts his eyes, still hanging onto me. I can feel how weak he is right now, and I'm not feeling too powerful right now either. Don't think I could fly out of here if I tried. Even Vahni's immortal power is quiet, as though the energy required to send me to the surface of the water tapped it out for the time being.

I have to work harder to stay afloat, Jehoel weighing on me more and more heavily. My limbs are numb and becoming more sluggish, and I'm suddenly afraid that this – a misfired attempt of a teleporter to get me to come back to land – is going to be my ultimate downfall.

What am I thinking? My brain must be frozen. After all I've gone through and with everything I still have to do, I refuse to let this be the end. I shove away my earlier fears too, that I'm burning out, that my time is limited.

No way can this be my fate. I refuse to accept it if it is.

I start kicking as hard as I can, trying to get feeling back in my legs. "Work with me, man." I grit my teeth. "You owe me, remember?"

He starts moving too, and the water begins to bubble and churn as it warms up. I have pins and needles in my fingers and toes now, but the sensation of needles suddenly becomes a thousand times worse as Jehoel utters a grunt and teleports us out of the ocean.

The outside wall of the juvenile detention center wavers in my view right before we hit the ground. I hunch over and dry heave, but I manage to keep it together until I hear Jehoel puking out his guts next to me.

I stagger away, my body wracked with chills. Jehoel's crouched close to the ground, pale as a sheet. Given the number of leaps he had to make tonight to track me, it's no wonder. Looks like he lost his glasses somewhere in the ocean too. He raises his head to look up at me, and I read agony in his eyes.

He straightens and takes a step toward me, and I take one back, my posture as rigid as I can make it. Right now all I want is answers.

"Why did you put me in that fight?" I demand.

He glances up at the security cameras on the outer wall. Instead of answering, he rubs his hand along the scar on his neck, the one that's always looked to me like someone tried to decapitate him. I've always wanted to ask about it, but right now I can't bring myself to care. I glower at him, my *deimos* heating me up until the water leaves my clothes as steam.

"You were never in real danger." Jehoel says quietly, his *deimos* doing the same thing as mine.

"Could have fooled me."

He glances up toward the cameras again. "I'm looking for someone. I should have told you this from the start, but I was afraid that if you knew the plan, your display would have been less effective in drawing out this individual."

"Who?" I frown. "It wasn't that guy I was fighting, was it?"

"No. But it's someone the alliance has been waiting for."

"And you can't tell me anything more than that?"

"Not yet."

Even though I'm warm again, a shudder rips through me. "You know what? You can take someone else on your scouting 'missions' of yours. I put my two months in."

He sighs. "You can't leave yet. It would be detrimental to the alliance."

"I lost control. If I can't get a grip on Vahni's power, keeping me here doesn't make sense," I argue. "I could send every one of you to Asphodel."

He starts shaking his head even before I'm finished. "Your lack of control over her power is the issue, not the ability to use the mark. You're less likely to accidentally harm anyone out here than you would in a more populated area." He lifts his hand as though to adjust his glasses, dropping it again when he remembers he's not wearing any. "I'm trying to help you."

"Help me *how?*" I snap.

Jehoel suddenly lifts his hand in the air, pointing to the roof. We both listen as something softly scuffs against the shingles.

"We have company," Jehoel says in a low voice. His tone is curt and authoritative again in the next breath. "Meet me inside later. I'll speak to you then."

I open my mouth to object, but he runs off, going for the front door this time instead of teleporting. I look up and push out my wings, the ascent to the roof to join Ben more like a short leap than flight. My camouflage slips away as I land in front of him, and he jumps, his breath coming out in a rush.

"Geez. My brother used to do that all the time, and it always scared the crap outta me. You a teleporter too?"

"No. Cloaked flight, and yeah, it used to scare my girlfriend."

Ben's expression is pained as he thinks about his brother, and my chest aches at the thought of Hope. I fold my arms and look out into the trees, quickly changing the subject. "So did they give you an assignment yet?"

"Yep. Guess I'm gonna work under Daniel. I'm kind of good with that techy stuff." He shrugs, but I can tell by the way his face lights up that he's being modest.

Glad he's excited about it. Daniel's in charge of technology, which means he spends a lot of time geeking out and testing out all sorts of new devices. He's the one who made the secure tracking comms that we use in the field. I think he designed the fight simulation system also.

"That's great." I move toward the window, happy that Ben's more comfortable here now. But that doesn't mean I'm in a great mood to talk. "Well, I'm gonna get something to eat."

"Micah?" There's worry in Ben's tone, and I look over my shoulder. He's staring at me, his expression serious. "I was up here when you and Jehoel were talking and kinda heard everything. Sorry, but not sorry. Things didn't go well tonight, huh?"

I manage a rueful smile. "What gave you that idea?"

"I picked up a lotta anger… and distrust."

His assessment is pretty dead on, and I'm sorry he had to tune into all of that. Not the greatest thing for a new recruit to pick up on, especially not from the guys that brought him here.

My head has been hurting all night, actually pretty constantly since that night in Seattle when we found Ben. Or maybe it's been since the fight. Either way, I have to take a second to get my focus back.

"It's nothing, okay? Jehoel and I work with each other all of the time and I think we just got on each other's nerves tonight. But just so you know," I blow out a breath, try to put aside my anger for Ben's sake, "I still trust him. He's my mentor. Friend too."

"Yeah, okay." He runs his hand through his hair, making his curls stand up on end. "But just so you know… the lack of trust wasn't coming from you. Jehoel is totally hiding something from you."

12

Jonathan

Tricia doesn't trust me, and nor should she. Her posture is tense, her eyes frequently flicking in my direction as we sprint to the waterfront. Her condo is on the top floor of a small complex, the decor sparse and simple. She insisted on me coming with her to confirm Micah's identity, and I need to play along for a little while longer. Though what I really want to do is throw both Tricia and my sense of diplomacy out the window.

"I'll be right back. Don't try to do anything stupid like escaping," she says.

I resist the urge to say something just as condescending and walk to the window. Her place offers a city view, and I can see the financial district below. The building where Davis works is right there, in plain view but completely out of my reach. Hopefully Raleigh is not.

I take the Pathicomm device from my jacket pocket – the one that's still intact after Tricia's attack – and put it in my ear. The energy of the collective condenses around me as I focus on my thoughts. No idea how Raleigh figured out the technology for this type of communication, but it's ingenious.

"Raleigh. I need some assistance. Where are you?"

Her translated voice comes through my earpiece. *"The better question is where are you? I'm at the sanctuary, where you should be."*

I can hear Tricia doing something in the kitchen, and I hurry. *"If you have access to a computer, I need you to make Micah Condie a defector."*

An excruciatingly long pause, then, *"He already is. Do you mean you need me to create a computer trail?"*

"Yes."

"I'm on it."

Tricia heads back into the room holding a tray with two steaming cups. I turn to face her, my hands clasped behind my back.

She extends a cup. "Tea?"

I don't move to take it. "I'll pass."

She throws me a cutting glance as she sets one cup down on her coffee table. "The tea won't kill you, and neither would being civil. Ultimately we're fighting for the same cause."

"I hardly think that creation of chimera is justifiable in any sort of cause," I snap.

"I understand that you feel this way." She takes a sip from her cup, dark brown eyes appraising me over the rim. "Rowan was convinced it's what we need to fight off the *Seraphim*."

"And what about you? Are you convinced?"

She hesitates, briefly but enough for me to see, and I jump at the chance.

"You've undoubtedly heard how unpredictable and violent the *Seraphim* were centuries ago, and the modern ones are no better. Whatever the Impiorum has done to create them, they are nothing but mad dogs with complete disregard for the rules, even Impiorum rules. How do you know a chimera created from a guardian wouldn't yield the same results?"

Tricia's eyes narrow. "You are merely speculating."

"And what if I'm not? What if the creation of the chimera yields disastrous results? Or fails?"

"It will not fail," she shoots back, but the way her eyes drop to the floor belies her uncertainty.

"If it does fail, you will look the fool."

She sets down her tea at her desk with a sharp clatter and pins me with a stare. "Cut to the chase, Jonathan. What do you want?"

"Only what's fair," I say grimly. "This entire situation occurred because of Rowan's conviction that the chimera are the solution. And now you're willing to put someone else's existence on the line to test this."

"How so?" she barks, but her expression doesn't match her tone. She looks scared now, and I know I have the advantage of knowledge.

"In order to create a new life like you propose, you must first take a life away," I say. "Think about how all of the guardians are here. We had to die first. What if this volunteer of yours doesn't come back?"

Her face remains stony as she contemplates this. "All right," she says stiffly. "So what you're saying is that if I fail…."

"*When* you fail, you will have a guardian's blood on your hands."

She opens her mouth and shuts it again, and I prepare myself to deliver the final punch.

"I will provide proof to the guardians that the creation of a chimera in this way is impossible. That will remove you from any fault that lies with Rowan's decisions, and in exchange you will pardon Raleigh's actions."

"How will you prove this?" she retorts.

"I will ask Arete herself to provide the proof."

"Arete," Tricia repeats in a flat tone. "The mother of all guardians."

"Yes."

Tricia narrows her eyes at me, and I feel her *lumen* connect with mine as though it's probing me for the truth. I keep both my emotions and any thoughts about Hope carefully sequestered.

"I believe you," Tricia says curtly. "Or at least I believe that you're convinced this is the truth. I'll grant you the three weeks until the trial to produce such proof."

"And in return you will pardon Raleigh for her crime."

She picks up her tea again and sips it slowly. "A crime of passion is still a crime. But yes, I will pardon her *if* you meet your conditions," she says. "How you'll convince Arete to intervene is beyond me."

My hackles rise. Tricia's tone is dubious, and it's obvious that she doesn't think I can fulfill my end of the bargain. As for the crime of passion accusation, Raleigh did what she did out of loyalty to me, yes, but I hardly think I need to address this.

"Then we have an accord," I bite out, heading to the door. "I'll let myself out. I have other things to do today."

"I still need to verify Micah Condie's identity," she calls after me, and my blood turns to ice.

"That won't be necessary given what we just agreed upon."

"You have three weeks to produce Arete's testimony. I need something in the meantime to placate a legion of angry guardians." Her expression is smug. "Or have you forgotten about our original deal?"

I stay by the corridor that leads to the door, and she walks over to her workstation on the other side of the room. I hope that Raleigh had enough time to leave enough of a trail, but I also don't doubt her abilities. It's only a matter of minutes before Tricia starts quizzing me about Micah — reason number ninety-three why I'm glad Hope is at school and not witnessing this right now.

Technically, Micah's powers could pass for a chimera's. His powers certainly don't qualify as being purely demon. More importantly, the fact that he's not exactly what they're looking for won't matter because they'll never find him.

"Micah was registered with The Impiorum earlier this spring. A bit late considering his age."

"If you say so."

She glowers at me, evidently another reminder to be civil. "According to this, he defected almost immediately afterward. Why would they let a chimera slip away from them like that?"

I shrug. "Defection does not exactly sound like something that they 'let' members do. Unless you've heard otherwise."

She ignores my quip, tapping the screen again. "Interesting," she says more to herself than to me. "He was reprimanded for disobeying orders and seeing his adoptive family after he joined them." She cocks an eyebrow. "His apartment burnt down the day after he defected. The Impiorum burying evidence? Or perhaps he was attempting to fake his death?"

Raleigh was thorough, as I knew she would be. And evidently she also had fun doing her job. I told her about that fire, how I was the impetus for it when I went and confronted Micah at his apartment building. But that happened before he defected and left with the alliance, not after.

Tricia looks up at me with a frown. "You never said, but what were you doing with him at UB that night?"

She sounds genuinely curious, but I smell a trap. "I wasn't *with* him," I say truthfully. "We were both there trying to accomplish different things, which now apparently winds up being a lucky coincidence for you."

"He destroyed another demon that night," she prompts, peering again at the computer.

"Yes," I say. "I am aware of this."

"Did you see how?"

"With fire." I have no way of knowing what Raleigh planted into the databases, but in case I'm being tested, I'm going with my gut and speaking the truth. "Same as his apartment building."

She steps away from the computer, her gaze locking with mine. I must have passed the test because a sense of relief flows out from her and into me.

"His story seems to check out. The Impiorum's records on his are deliberately vague unlike with their other members, and the fire means he has unusual powers." She presses her lips together. "Terribly inconvenient that his current whereabouts are unknown."

I shrug. "You have sufficient resources to track people. Find him yourself."

Tricia lifts an eyebrow. "Oh, believe me. We shall. Consider today the beginning of three week's of reprieve from us."

"Yes, because a reprieve is exactly what someone should seek from one's constituents," I say sardonically. I stalk toward the door. "Enjoy your time with them."

She follows me. "I'll have collected enough votes by the time of the trial to oust you as director."

I hesitate with my hand on the doorknob. "They aren't necessarily going to choose you now that Rowan's gone," I counter.

"Who else is there? Everyone in this sector is terrified of Raleigh. And now you, by association…." She trails off, her eyes fixed on the door. "You had someone tail us here."

I don't sense anyone's approach, but then again I can't even pick up Tricia's signature when she's standing five feet away from me. I hear a door in the corridor quietly click shut, soft footsteps approaching. Tricia rushes past me and out into the hallway, and I move at lightning speed to grab Tricia's knife out of its sheath on her belt.

Raleigh stops short in the hallway, looking a bit like a female rendition of Robin Hood in a hooded dark green outfit with green leggings. The two women stare at each other, the confined space filling with so much tension the air feels thick.

"Why did you take him?" she snaps at Tricia. "It's me you have the quarrel with."

"She didn't *take* me," I bark. I'm glad to know she's all right, though, and I soften my tone just slightly. "I came of my own accord."

Her eyes narrow when she sees the knife in my hand. "I see." She turns her attention to Tricia. "I heard your ridiculous plan," she spits. "You're trying to take over the directorship? How dare you do this? I should take your head as well."

Tricia appraises her steadily, without a sign of fear despite her earlier declaration that all of the guardians are terrified of Raleigh. "You won't destroy me. You and I have too much history."

"History is only as good as the people that create it." Raleigh fixes her with a steely glare, and I move to stand by her side before she can prove Tricia wrong. "You don't have what it takes to be director."

Tricia bows her head. "Your current director was just on his way out. He'll fill you in on what you need to know, but it seems like you've heard enough."

I step out with Raleigh, and Tricia becomes a wisp as she beats a hasty retreat back into her condo. The door slams, and Raleigh slips me a wary glance as we walk to the stairwell together. "You don't need to brief me about the trial. She's right. I heard enough."

I look her over. Raleigh looks completely worn out, her hair unusually messy, her eyes tired.

"Despite what just transpired, I'm happy that you found me. I suppose me leaving a false trail was predictable."

"It wasn't. After I didn't find you at the sanctuary, I checked your apartment and gallery. I only came here to see if I could scare the information out of Tricia." She gives me a sideways glance. "I knew the trial was impending and thought I could talk her out of it, which was pure stupidity on my part...." She trails off and sighs.

"To talk her out of the trial?" I push open the door to the stairwell, and we climb the first flight in silence.

"Yes. Stupidity, I said," she reiterates when we get to the landing. "I suppose I thought I could appeal to her emotions. She and I used to be good friends."

I catch a heaviness in her tone, a sadness that touches me. "I didn't know this. What happened?"

"We had a falling out. It was right after Charlie was killed. Tricia said some things I can never forgive, and we fought. But never mind. It's not important now."

This is news to me. I was friends with Raleigh's partner Charlie long before Raleigh was even a guardian. I was the one that made introductions between the two. But I had no idea that Tricia and Raleigh had even talked to each other outside of regular guardian duties, let alone fought.

It strikes me that while I've known Raleigh for over half of a century, I know very little about her private life, her friendships, or anything aside from what we do for guardian business.

We reach the roof access door, and I turn to her before opening it.

"Do you need to talk about it? I can listen if you do."

She looks at me with widening eyes, her hand flying to her mouth. It's my turn to look at her in surprise as she stifles a giggle.

"I'm sorry." She lowers her hand to reveal a grin. "That was just, um… unexpected of you. No, I don't want to talk about it. But thanks for offering."

I smile back, the tension from the day broken. It's just for the smallest of moments, but I'm grateful for it. The wind whips through the door as we walk through, and I lead her to the edge of the flat rooftop while she tucks her long hair into her hood.

"So," she says more seriously. "Now that my life's on the line, what are we going to do?"

"Your life is not on the line, but we do need to head to the financial district to retrieve something that will help with matters," I say. "Come with me?"

"Of course, director." Her eyes shine momentarily before they close, and I know she's summoning the power to fly. Not flight in the literal sense because guardian angels don't have wings, ironically enough. We walk to the ledge, and she reaches out her hand and squeezes mine.

Everything from her releases like a flood.

Her emotions are vivid and passionate, her love intense as it flows through me. If my heart weren't already dead, it would stop right now.

I have no idea if it's intentional, her letting me feel her like this, but she's never let me have access to these sorts of emotions before. Maybe it's because of the impending trial. Or because I tried to get her to open up to me. But in this moment I know that her love is solely for me.

She takes the leap, running and bounding between the rooftops, and I manage to shake myself out of my stupor long enough to run and overtake her. But my mind is whirling because of this new development, and it takes me at least ten buildings until I can make sense of my own feelings.

I can handle standing by her in the impending trial. I can even handle taking a journey to the treacherous realm of Asphodel if I absolutely needed to. I would do any of those things for Raleigh.

But I don't know how to handle this.

Things could have been different. I should have insisted that Adrienne and I escape from the prison.

But our plan to save the prisoners of war from the viscount and Cyril was working. We took our original measures to the extreme, anesthetizing the captives with the touch of death to the point that the viscount was convinced that Cyril had killed them. The bodies were dumped outside the camp, and Adrienne would use the antidote to revive them and then help them to safety.

The danger of it all was like a drug to Adrienne. The higher the risks, the more passionate she was toward me when we were alone. I don't know exactly what she went through for the past year and two months, but it had changed her, and I fed her addiction to fuel that passion.

It was a Tuesday, and I knew Adrienne would not be coming inside the prison that day. My mood was black as a result, and Cyril was more irritating to me than usual. His habit of leaving his signature mark on the flesh of his victims was becoming problematic. He carved up some prisoners to such an extent that I had no choice but to use the touch of death to put them out of their misery. There was nothing else I could do.

I walked out of a cell where this exact thing had happened, my nerves frayed and temper on a short fuse. I wasn't prepared for Adrienne to burst out from one of the cells, and I jumped out of my skin. She smiled at me and dragged me back inside.

"What are you doing here?" I blurted out.

She shut the door behind us, feigning offense. "Are you not pleased to see your wife?"

My surprise escalated to shock. Adrienne did not refer to herself as my wife these days, not anymore. She was Lady Thibault, or simply Adrienne, and that had to be enough for me. But that day her eyes were full of passion, and she stood on her toes and pressed her lips to mine before I could respond. Her ardor increased, her mouth parting and a soft sigh escaping her lips.

We would be killed if anyone found us here. Rather, she would be killed, and I would be tortured and then killed. But I didn't care. Her breath quickened as I kissed her with increasing urgency. Her hands clutched my arms as I pressed her body against the wall, and dammit. She was my wife, and no other woman would ever take her place in my soul or in my heart. I was tired of these facades, the pretenses we went through. I just wanted her and nothing else.

She broke off the kiss, staring at me with a gleam in her eye. "I think you should try it on Cyril."

I stared at her, my heartbeat at a gallop and my body aching from desire. "What?"

"The touch of death. See if you can slip it into a drink or food. Use twice as much as you give to the prisoners when we help them."

"Adrienne." I gripped her arms and took a half-step back so I could see her face. "I don't think that's a wise course of action."

Her brows knitted together while I struggled to find the words to explain. Cyril was different. He was a monster, inhuman, and I didn't know if the touch of death would work on him like it did other humans. If the touch of death worked to kill him, it would be a benefit to all. But if it failed, he would be even more of a monster, and he would naturally suspect me. Or Adrienne. I'd caught him scrutinizing her like she was a petty thief the last time she was in the room with both of us. He didn't like the fact that the viscount let her into the interrogations, not at all.

"Why not?" Adrienne's face fell, and she dropped her hands from my arms. "You aren't actually friends with Cyril, are you?"

"Absolutely not." I shudder. "But I'm just not positive it would work, given Cyril's constitution. I'm not sure it's worth the risk."

Adrienne stepped away from me, her eyes tight with anger. "Tell me. What's worth the risk to you, if saving the lives of innocents is not?"

"You are," I say without hesitation. "I would do anything for you."

"Then prove it to me." Her lips push out a little in a pout. "I want you to show me. If you would do anything for me, then use the touch of death on Cyril."

She was acting petulant. I would not do what she asked.

"We will handle Cyril differently, in a way that won't implicate either of us," I say firmly. "Trust me."

13

Micah

I trusted Jehoel. Until now.

Ben's revelation that he felt Jehoel's mistrust directed at me shakes my confidence to the core. I was already pissed off at him for everything that happened at the fights, but to find out that he doesn't trust *me* is almost enough to push me over the edge. I need some answers from him now, or things are going to come to a head.

It's just past dawn, and the compound is at its height of activity. I comb the inside for Jehoel and don't find him. Not that I'm surprised. After all of those jumps he took to follow me all the way to the ocean and back, he probably needs to feed. It's something I should think about doing too, but it can wait until tomorrow night. I don't feel like venturing back out again, and even though I'm cloaked when I fly, we're always supposed to wait for a teleporter to leave the compound for security reasons.

I head down to the surveillance team's domain in the basement instead. There's always at least one guy on duty, and this morning I hear Cael talking to whoever it is.

"...we should be able to improve upon the boundary spell first thing tomorrow if the witch shows up at the rendezvous," Cael says.

I hear the other demon scoff. He's younger than Cael and a regular on surveillance. "I hope this witch is legit. Or if she's not a real witch, maybe she'll be hotter than the last one."

Cael chuckles. "You're so shallow, your reflection is see-through."

"Hey, can't blame me for wanting at least a little bit of action now and then. This life of solitude is for the dogs."

They both fall silent, and I know they sense me coming. The guy on surveillance flinches when I walk through the doorway and shrinks back into his chair, directing all of his attention on one of the computer monitors. In complete contrast, Cael gives me an easygoing smile and nods at me.

"Hey, Micah. What's up?"

"Can you keep an eye out for Jehoel and let me know when he's back on the property?" I catch the two exchanging quick glances, knowing that they're probably wondering why I'm asking them to spy on my own mentor and team leader. "You know teleporters," I say lightly. "Can't keep track of him. Sorry, I need to talk to him about something important."

His gaze is suddenly sharp. "Is there a problem that I should be aware of?"

I like Cael all right. He's one of the few demons here that doesn't treat me like I have the plague. I should probably tell him everything because he's technically my superior, but I hesitate. Cael glances over at the other demon on duty, who seems to be wholly concentrating on the monitors or just doing a really good job at faking it.

He points to the hallway, and I follow him out and toward the end.

"What's this all about?" he asks in a low voice.

"Actually, I'm not totally sure," I admit. "Jehoel's out doing something, looking for someone and I don't know who. He didn't say anything to you?"

"Jehoel beats to his own drum, which I'm sure you've noticed."

"And you trust him enough to do that?" I hear the bitterness in my own tone.

"Of course. He hasn't failed the alliance in finding people with talents that round out the needs for the group as a whole." Cael looks at me thoughtfully. "He found you and brought you and your gifts to us, didn't he?"

I shrug, not knowing what possible talent he could mean aside from being good at scouting for Impiorum defectors. That's not a talent, though. It's more luck, being in the right place at the right time. Or maybe he means my ability to accidentally cause things to go up in flames. Yeah, that's it.

"You're required to report anything you feel compromises the safety of the group. Do you feel this is the case?" Cael's tone is ultra-smooth. His particular gift is to calm situations, and I feel the effects of his power settle over me, my shoulders relaxing, my mind easing.

"No," I admit. My problem is with Jehoel's methods, but it's not anything I can complain about to Cael. Jehoel put me into a fight, but it's in the nature of this business to be prepared to fight. He's looking for someone he says will help the alliance, but I don't have any evidence to the contrary.

Cael nods, seemingly satisfied. "All right. I'll let you know when he's back. You'll be up in your room?" He hesitates. "You doing okay, man? You look like crap."

"I'm okay," I lie. Thanks."

He smiles and heads back to the surveillance room. I think about wishing him luck with the whole witch's spell thing but don't want to let on that I was eavesdropping. I was aware of the protective magic but didn't know real witches existed. There's probably a whole list of things going on here that would be eye-opening.

I drag myself back upstairs, avoiding eye contact with the others along the way. I get into a near-collision with one of the other guys hurrying through the foyer, and he stops, does an about-face, and books back to the kitchen. I watch his retreat, suddenly tired. Tired of everyone avoiding me. Tired of constantly fighting off Vahni's power and feeling like I'm always on the brink of losing control. Tired of secrets and hidden agendas.

Ben's not in the room when I get back, and I'm glad. I need the alone time to clear my head, and I crash on my bunk and think about my next move. Jehoel and I are supposed to head out again in two nights to scout the northern Canadian provinces, which will be majorly awkward unless I clear the air between us.

The alliance as a whole has been making progress over the past year, and the numbers have been building and new strongholds steadily popping up throughout the developed world. This one here is the main one in North America, and there are three other primary ones, in Japan, France, and Argentina with lots of other secondary places that serve as pockets of alliance activity. Right now we mostly use those secondary cities as stopping points when we work through an area, but I've heard Jehoel and Cael talking about how they could serve as seeds for new strongholds. One of the smaller seeds is somewhere back in New York.

I think every day about how I'd eventually balance this life and my old one once I go back home. Reconnecting with my adoptive family is daunting – I don't know if they'll ever forgive me for leaving after Lina died. Reconnecting with Hope is something that keeps me going every minute of the day. I get up and take out my notebook that I keep hidden between my mattresses. Communication is regulated here, which means correspondence isn't supposed to leave unless it's official business. I still write letters to Hope in here on an almost daily basis, and Jehoel's been able to sneak batches out for me when he can.

I hear the swift footsteps coming down the hall, the nape of my neck prickling as I get out of bed. My room is separated from the others, at the end of the corridor. Whoever's coming, he's coming for me.

I open the door before Cael can knock. He's wearing his wireless comm and looks all-business, no smiles.

"Jehoel's back. Sort of. Just barely picked him up past the south boundary."

I frown. The perimeter is protected by one of those spells he and D. J. were talking about. I was warned on my first day here that if I were to walk through the boundaries of the compound, I'd feel so disoriented I wouldn't be able to find my way back to the building. I haven't personally tested that, but that's another reason we always use the teleporters to get out and back inside.

"Past the boundary? Couldn't he teleport in?"

"No. Maybe he accidentally crossed over and can't. He's just wandering around like he can't find his way in." His finger touches the wireless comm in his ear. "Copy that." When he turns his attention to me again, his brow is creased with a frown. "Go and guide him back in. Be careful you don't overstep the boundaries either, or we'll have to send out someone for both of you."

"No problem."

He leaves, and I go for my window.

Walking and not teleporting in, huh? I thought Jehoel might be out feeding because of all the jumps he made tonight, but maybe not. I shove open the window, climbing onto the roof and taking the leap to the ground below. The sun's rays spot the trees, twigs exploding beneath my feet as I bullet toward the perimeter. Usually the forest is full of songs and calls of birds at this time of day, but there's an audible hush as I pass through. I ignore the sting of branches that occasionally whip me and keep going.

Sure enough, Jehoel's standing outside the edge of the trees that mark the outer boundaries of the compound. He turns around to face me, calmly as though he's expecting me. If I look like crap, he looks like death warmed over. His face is pale except for the dark circles under his eyes, his expression drawn and pained. Definitely wasn't out feeding.

"Micah." He sounds relieved. "I'm glad you're here."

I feel my temper flare, but I work to keep it in check for now. I still have questions that he needs to answer. "What's going on, Jehoel? You told me to come find you, but then you left?"

"Sorry about that. I've been following a lead."

For once, Jehoel lets down his guard, his eyes glimmering with excitement. I almost let my curiosity get the better of me but stamp it back down again, the memory of what Ben told me burning. Distrust. Jehoel doesn't trust me.

"What kind of lead?"

"You'll see soon enough." He gives me a rare smile. "I have to thank you. She came to me only because of you."

I open my mouth to argue again, but shut it again when I realize what he just said. *She.* I try to keep my reaction locked down, but my heart leaps in my chest. While I know he can't possibly mean Hope, a small, irrational part of me wonders at the possibility. But everything else – the way Jehoel's been acting, the warning from Ben – acts to quash that faint hope.

Things were a lot simpler when I was the cynical Micah who never wanted to believe in anything.

"This better not be another trick," I say, my voice flat. "I'll request another partner. Or I'll request a transfer. This isn't the only alliance stronghold in the world."

"You can't leave here yet."

"Why not?" I counter. "You haven't exactly given me a good reason to stay. Why do you want to keep me here so badly?"

I stalk toward him, stopping short when I realize I'm about to cross the perimeter. Jehoel is still standing right outside of it, though now that he knows which way is in, he could come in any time. It's like he's waiting for something, and my newfound suspicion for both him and his motives make me turn away. I'm going back to the juvie hall. Maybe kill something on the fight simulator.

"Micah!" he calls out. "You have a gift. We need you here."

I bristle at his words, but they have the effect he wanted because I turn around and stalk back. "You and Cael both seem to think I have this 'gift' for scouting. Why? Why is what I do different than anything you do out there?"

He hesitates, and I see it. The knowledge in his eyes that he's been holding back from me.

Jehoel is totally hiding something from you.

Ben's words sound off in my head like a warning. Jehoel looks so far away standing there just outside the compound boundaries. He's been my mentor, and I thought for the past two months that he was also my friend, but I don't know about that anymore.

"You don't know why you're drawn to the defectors in the field?" he prompts. "Why you have more luck than the rest of us?"

I have no idea what he's talking about, but I do know how thin my patience is getting. I've always hated how he's so vague like this.

"Luck. Like you just said," I retort.

"Poor choice of words on my part." He points to my hand. "Your power to make the mark. It leads you right to the defectors."

I stare at him as his meaning sinks in, and he looks back at me with a knowing expression, like this was the answer to understanding my propensity to burst into flames all along. But I have to admit it makes sense. How many times have I been out when I thought Vahni was urging me on? And the same thing with the vibes I've been getting off the defectors that lead me straight to them.

"How long have you suspected this?"

"For some time."

I grit my teeth, almost crossing that physical boundary and invisible one. He's my superior, my team leader, and the hierarchy means that I'm supposed to defer to his judgment unless he says otherwise. But this is different. This is about me.

"Why did you keep this from me?"

"It wasn't the right time for you to know." He's so calm it's infuriating.

And he still seems like he's waiting for something from me, like he's baiting me for some reaction aside from being irritated. And yeah, I could go there if I wanted, but I don't want to give him the satisfaction. It infuriates me that I didn't tune into how he was before now.

It makes me wonder why he even bothered, what his agenda really was in asking me to join the alliance in the first place. If he knew the mark would help the group boost its recruits like he said, then his promise to help me find a way to get rid of Vahni's power was a lie.

I can taste my own bitterness, and without another word, I turn around and push out my wings.

He lunges for me, grabbing hold of my arm before my feet can leave the ground, and I whip around, resentment roiling in my gut. Vahni's fire bursts from my hands, flames licking out toward Jehoel. He steps back, something almost like satisfaction in his expression.

"You've been fighting that power the entire time you've been here. Don't you want to learn to control it?"

I close my eyes as I push Vahni's power back, but it doesn't completely submerge. Never does.

"You keep too much of your pain internalized," he adds quietly.

"I don't know where else to put it," I retort. My guts turn at how calm and almost smug he looks. "Why did you really take me with you when you left Buffalo?"

Jehoel's façade slips away again and he looks away, his silence saying it all. I'd always assumed his intentions were true, but I never really had justification to think that.

"Why did you take me with you? What were you planning to do with me?" I feel shaky from Vahni's latest outburst but am too angry to stop this line of questioning. "Use me or destroy me?"

"Destroy you." He looks at me evenly this time, not even a hint of remorse in his expression.

No. I've been so blind. So naïve. I gave up so much of my life to be here. I left the Condies behind, everything and everyone that made my life meaningful, and I did it because I thought I'd eventually be able to give something back. And the worst part of it is that his confession is a betrayal of Hope's trust in him too.

I don't need Ben's empathic power to see that he feels no remorse or regret about this, and I shut my eyes and turn away, my hand shoving through my hair. My mind in turmoil. My heart in my throat.

"Seriously, why?" I don't know if I'm saying this to him or to the powers that be. "Why go through all the trouble of teaching me how to live if you were just going to kill me?"

"I took you with me that night in Buffalo because I'd seen what you were capable of. I spent much of the first few weeks trying to figure out how to destroy you, yes. But later when it became apparent you would not use the mark against us and that it was in fact useful for scouting, I became curious about you and took to studying Vahni's power instead."

He's so calm that it's infuriating. And what he'd said — is he expecting me to say "thanks" for not killing me those first few weeks?

"This whole time, you've been keeping me under observation to see what I could do?" I spit out. "Like some animal under study with a trigger ready in case I turned out to be a threat? How does that make you any better than the Impiorum demons?"

That finally gets a response from him, but it doesn't shake him like I want. He looks genuinely amused. "I treated you no differently than anyone else, Micah. Everybody contributes something here. Your friend Ben shows an aptitude for technology, and once we train him, he'll probably be dispatched to another stronghold that can use him. If anyone we take in proves to be a danger or liability, we destroy him to remove the risk."

I blanch. I don't get it. I thought I did, but maybe I don't after all. Who decides these things? Jehoel? Cael? Maybe it's never happened in this group since I joined, but destroying anyone sure isn't up for any sort of vote.

"You used to be a pastor, right? And you had human friends. So what about the human side of things?"

He scrutinizes me, as if suddenly noticing my head is on backwards. "Yes, I was once a pastor and had human friends. But we left our human lives behind us when we decided to come out here and fight for the alliance. This is war, Micah."

His words hit me like a punch in the face. I suppose this is war and that we're fighting for a place in the world that won't get trumped by the Impiorum. But he's wrong about one thing. I left my human life behind, but that doesn't mean I can't ever get my life back.

He's shaking his head as though he can follow my train of thought. "You walked away from all of that. I fabricated those weekly updates on Hope and your family."

No.

"The correspondence you thought I was sending to Hope was never sent either. Regular communication between groups is far too risky at this time, but I knew you wouldn't stay unless you were sure they were safe."

NO.

I press the heels of my hands to my eyes as if it can keep me from losing it. I can't…I can't function unless I know they're safe – Hope most of all – and Jehoel had exploited that. Lied to me.

I don't know if they're safe. And Hope hasn't gotten a single one of my letters and doesn't know if I'm even alive.

Rage takes over reason, and I strike.

Vahni's power and my *deimos* merge together and tear out of me like a firestorm, and I fight it, trying to pull back and reign in the power, but I can't. He was right about one thing. I was fooling myself if I thought that I ever had control over Vahni's power. The underbrush and layers of dry pine needles on the ground ignite, and I stagger back in horror as the fire explodes around Jehoel.

"Jehoel!"

Not again. I hadn't wanted to do this. I search wildly through the fire for him, but the fire leaps higher and higher, and I can't see him.

"*Jehoel!*"

I barely hear shouts from the juvie center. Help is on the way, only it's too late. I vowed to never again use my power to harm anyone.

Too late. Too late.

I grip my head and spin. I thought I could carry this. I don't think I can anymore…

The fire burns hotter and hotter, and I can actually feel the heat of the flames this time. Vahni had warned me about this once, that the power would consume me if I used it too much. I'd seen it happen to another ward of Vahni's, watched with my own two eyes as she turned to ash.

I can see faces through the fire. It's like what I saw in the Sea of the Dead except it's everyone this time and it's from my own head. Like the memories they sometimes say you see right before you die. Everyone I've loved, lost, or left. Lina, my adoptive mom and dad, my brother and sister. My best friend Troy. Hope.

14

Jonathan

When I buried the location of the *clavis* within the mind of a safekeeper, I vowed that I would only unearth the secret if it was a matter of life or death. I didn't expect an occasion to arise right away, but with both Hope's identity and Raleigh's existence in jeopardy, I believe this qualifies.

The black stone guardian key to Asphodel had been Christianna's, one of the few people I've allowed myself to get close to for centuries. An odd coincidence considering she was also the guardian who saved Micah from his demon father after his death.

"Do you feel anything?" I'm within inches of Raleigh, and I'm careful not to touch her.

Raleigh looks pensive, maybe even a little pale as we both look down at the fifty foot drop to the alcove below. Despite Tricia's promise of a reprieve, I'm still concerned that guardians might be watching.

"Hmmm?" Her head jerks up. "No, I'd tell you if I sensed any guardians."

"Good."

I make the jump, my adrenaline leaping at first as the air rushes past. But then my light takes over to still space and slow time, giving me time to appreciate the fall. Raleigh is just above me, and she does a flip mid-air before landing gracefully next to me. I start walking to the service entrance, but stop when I see Raleigh's feet are planted firmly on the asphalt.

"This is where Hope's brother works," she points out.

"I know. I need to unlock his memories. It won't take but a moment." A moment that will be traumatic and excruciating for him, but this is why safekeepers are only trusted with the most important secrets.

"What on earth does that mean? Unlock his memories of *what?*"

"Davis is a safekeeper. In this particular case he's keeping a secret safe in his mind." Anxious to get on our way, I lift an eyebrow as she appears to digest this. "You'll be able to see what I mean for yourself."

I pick up the pace once we get into the building, and Raleigh hurries to match my stride. It's not unusual for her to turn heads, but today my nerves prickle because of the distraction. I suppress a growl as a middle-aged man in a business suit gives her an obvious head-to-toe visual examination, and Raleigh casts a quick glance in my direction.

She flicks out small fragments of her *lumen* as we walk to the elevator, and no one else bothers her the rest of the way. It's one of her guardian gifts, useful in making herself less memorable to others in the vicinity. My edginess dissolves by the time an elevator becomes available. I'm irritable because of what I'll need to do and how I need to do it, that's all.

Raleigh finally turns to me once the doors close.

"Will you explain this safekeeper concept to me? Because I've never heard of such a thing. And exactly what is it you're seeking?"

"It's something specific to my lineage, not to guardians in general." I frown at the elevator buttons until I remember what floor, and turn to her after pressing the button. "My male descendants have always had a gift for safeguarding secrets. In this case, Davis is holding the knowledge of where he hid the guardian *clavis*."

I hear her sharp intake of breath as the elevator doors open. A woman and man enter, but bits of Raleigh's *lumen* continue to sprinkle off of her like fairy dust, and the man begins to complain loudly about a meeting as though they're alone in the elevator.

"Why do you need the key to Asphodel?" she demands. "Are you going to go there?"

"Not necessarily. I'm going to petition Arete for her help." I watch the doubt flood her expression, and add, "Christianna used the key to directly communicate with Arete, and I'm betting I can do the same."

"That's a pretty risky bet."

"Yes, but it's one worth taking."

Raleigh worries her lip, her expression displaying her apprehension, but I don't share in this. I may have lost some of my faith in divine forces when I lost Adrienne to dark forces, but the guardian Arete is not divine – she's powerful and ancient, and if anyone has the best interests of the guardians at heart, it's her. She's one of the originals that existed long before the demon-guardian lineage split and she knows that the fate of both races rely upon a balance of light and dark. There's no way that she would condone a plan to make chimera.

"I see…." Raleigh swallows, as though she's holding back her full commentary. "And pray tell, what exactly are you going to ask for?"

I glance at our company in the elevator, but they're still under Raleigh's influence, the woman now sharing some piece of gossip with the man.

"I'm going to petition her to bind the *lumen* and the *deimos* as separate energies so that no more chimera can be made."

The elevator doors open again to let someone else in, and we all shuffle positions while Raleigh drops more of her *lumen*. She and I wind up standing close in one of the corners, and her chin lifts to look me in the eye.

"If they bind the powers that sustain us, then we won't be able to heal. And not that I even give a damn, but that also means demons won't be able to replenish their *deimos.*"

"I meant 'bind' in the sense that the powers are restricted by magic to each lineage," I clarify.

"You don't think they already know about the new *Seraphim?*" She frowns. "They must, with the amount of energy returning from all of the failed attempts to create them."

"Why would they assume it's from that?" I counter. "No one's ever attempted anything like this in our history. The original ones were created by the Praxidikai in the first place until they realized their mistake. No, I'm positive Arete wouldn't approve."

The elevator stops for the second time, and we follow the man and two women as they also get out on the twentieth floor. They walk past the receptionist and through a set of glass doors that lead into the offices, and Raleigh and I step up to the receptionist. The frazzled-looking young woman continues to type furiously and ignores us.

"Raleigh," I hiss. "You're still emanating." Being invisible was convenient when we were in the elevator, but right now we need to be noticed.

She flushes at her oversight and closes her eyes, drawing her *lumen* back into herself, and the woman looks up at us, startled. "Oh! Welcome to Stanley and Associates. How may I help you?"

"I need to see Davis Gentry."

"Oh!" Evidently this is how she begins her sentences. She scrolls through something on her computer screen. "I'm sorry, but he just went into a meeting. It's expected to last for an hour if you'd like to come back then." Her gaze shifts from me to Raleigh. "Or you could also leave a business card."

Raleigh draws herself up to her full five-foot-ten height as she prepares to intervene, but I put my hand on her elbow to stop her. I draw out one of my business cards from my jacket pocket, touching the receptionist's hand as she reaches for it.

"This can't wait." I lean forward and take her hand more firmly. "It's a matter of great importance."

The receptionist blinks at me as I take my hand away, her brow breaking out in a sweat. She fumbles with the phone at her desk.

"Please send Davis Gentry out front. Right away," she says briskly. "Yes, I know he's in the staff meeting, but it's very important."

Raleigh and I step away from the receptionist's desk to wait.

"Does Hope know about Davis? Or what you're doing right now?" she murmurs.

"No."

She frowns. "Hmm…I suppose that's for the best. Perhaps the better question is if *Davis* knows that he's holding the secret?"

"He knows. But he doesn't remember."

She arches an eyebrow. "That seems awfully risky, entrusting the secret to a single mortal. What if he's hit by a bus?"

"That's happened before, but never because of a bus." The last time it occurred was in the eighteenth century and because of cholera. "The secret doesn't die. It passes to the nearest person as a phrase, who serves as a vessel of sorts until I can retrieve it."

She shakes her head. "So much trouble for a phrase."

I smile at her. "It's usually a very good phrase."

Davis hurries out of the glass doors, his anxiety levels spiking as soon as he sees me. He swipes a hand through his auburn hair and rushes over.

"Jon, what are you doing here?" He glances over at the receptionist, but if she's eavesdropping, she's also back to typing. "Is it Hope?" he adds in a lower voice.

"Not exactly. But we need to talk. Do you have a private office?"

"Uh, sure. Come on back."

I follow, pushing my *lumen* over to him in a quick burst to ease his mind, Raleigh doing the same to the receptionist after she looks up in alarm. The concern in Davis' brow smooths out, and he wavers in indecision as he navigates through the main part of the office. I may have pushed my power a bit harder than I needed to just now, but I wasn't sure if I could access my full set of abilities yet.

Davis stops short at his office door, doing a double-take when he notices Raleigh for the first time. She's smiling at him, still in her hooded green outfit and leggings, and I honestly don't know how he could have missed her.

"Who are you?"

"Raleigh Peyton." She extends her hand. "I've heard so much about you."

His face colors as he shakes her hand. "Do I know you from somewhere?"

"I'm sure it's possible we've crossed paths before, though I think I would have remembered," she purrs. "I work for the Buffalo News."

"In advertising?"

"No. I'm one of the contributing editors."

He lifts his eyebrows, impressed. "Nice. Where did you go to college?"

I clear my throat. "While I am sincerely glad you two have common interests, I'm afraid we do have slightly more urgent matters to address."

Davis blinks, looking like he might have momentarily forgotten that I told him I needed to speak with him. "Right. Sorry. Come in."

He shuts the door and holds out a chair for Raleigh, and she gives him a coquettish look while preening the ends of her hair. I slant her a look as I take the other chair, and she folds her hands demurely in her lap. Davis sits across the desk from us, finally giving me his full attention.

In the long line of my descendants, we've all shown predispositions to having certain powers. Hope displayed her gifts for almost her entire life, and from the moment I met Davis, I looked for the qualities I've seen in the other men descending from me and Adrienne. He's loyal and headstrong, just like the other safekeepers in my lineage, and that's exactly why I'd given him the task of protecting the location of the *clavis*. Only his deepest subconscious holds the memory of hiding it.

The trick to releasing it is getting him to remember the event I linked to that memory.

I look him straight in the eye. "How did your parents die?" I ask.

His face turns a shade paler. "Excuse me?"

"Your parents," I repeat. "They died in a fire when you were twenty-two. What caused the fire?"

"Nobody knows that."

"You actually do know. You were there." I keep my tone soothing, ignoring Raleigh's questioning stare. The more traumatic the event is, the deeper in the mind the safekeeper will bury the secret. Davis hadn't actually been there when his parents died, but I recreated the events for him as though he had.

"No. I was away at college when it happened." He rubs his forehead, as though trying to erase the frown on his brow. When he looks back at me, his agony is almost palpable. He swallows hard. "They died in a fire. They were looking at a house with a realtor when it exploded in flames."

"Yes," I prompt. "Go on."

"The police thought there was a gas leak, but any evidence they had turned out to be inconclusive. And even if that had been the case, they had no idea what could have ignited it..." He squeezes his eyes shut. "But there was someone there that day, standing outside of the house. Watching them." His eyes snap open, and he gapes at me. "How did I just see this?"

"What else do you see?" I urge. I'm vaguely aware of a shift in Raleigh's position as she leans forward, her lips parted expectantly.

Beads of sweat break out on his forehead, his angst building as his words pour out of him. "I just walked up to the side of the house. I can see my parents and realtor through the kitchen window."

I sit up straighter in my chair as he switches his tense to be in the present. He's reliving the moment, as he needs to be. A storm of emotions surges from him – anger, indignation, a resurgence of grief. It won't be long now, but he has to go further.

"This person outside. I can't really see what he looks like." His eyes narrow, like he's trying to see better in real time. "He's like a shadow, but I can see something bright in his hand. It's…it's fire. He's holding a lighter or something."

Footsteps sound in the hallway, and Raleigh gets up swiftly to lock the door to the office. Neither Davis nor I budge as he accesses the memories that aren't really his, and I feel his pain increase with his level of understanding. We're almost there.

His pallor goes completely white. "He's staring right at my parents," he whispers. "He's making the sign of the cross.…"

Raleigh starts as Davis jumps out of his chair, tears flowing down his cheeks. I place my hand on her arm, and she tenses up but stays seated. This is what I've been waiting for.

"Davis," I say firmly. "Tell me where it is."

"Holy shit. They were *murdered*." He breaks eye contact with me, his gaze wild as he looks around his office. "I need to call the police."

I rise from my chair, startled. This *isn't* what should be happening right now. Davis shouldn't be connecting the memory of those events with what's happening now.

"I'll tell them to open the case. They have to. Maybe if I can remember more, I can I.D. him." His hand closes around his car keys on his way to the door. "I have to tell Hope."

I step in front of the door, grabbing him by his shoulders. My *lumen* courses out through my fingertips and into him. "Davis. I'm sorry. You can't do anything about this." I keep my voice steady and controlled. "They're gone."

"No." He shakes his head from side to side, trying to throw my hands from him, but I hold on as he protests. "They're gone, but whoever did this has to pay."

I send a stronger stream of *lumen* into him, and he stops struggling and stares at me, stricken. So much heartbreak, loss, unresolved anger. It all wells up to the surface, and I momentarily connect with it like it's mine. I need to end this. Now.

"Tell me," I command. "Where did you hide the *clavis?*"

He tilts his head back and away from me, his eyes rolling back in their sockets. In a snap, the space we're in becomes a vacuum, all emotion sucked away to leave only emptiness.

"Where Sarah lies," he whispers.

It's the key phrase, and I know exactly what it means. I guide Davis to the chair I'd just vacated and release him, and he sinks to a sitting position. That was the absolute worst of it, but he'll break out of his stupor any second. The memory will fade and take the trauma of the event with it.

The memory had been real, and it had been Christianna's. When I released her soul and light back to Asphodel, she released some of her memories to me. They'd been in a flash and like what Davis described, the person responsible had only been in shadows, but I was able to put it together.

Christianna had been there that day when Hope and Davis' parents died. Or she'd been given the memories of someone who had.

"Jonathan," Raleigh says in a low voice. Her face is pale, shocked. "That was rather awful. Was that all necessary?"

"Yes," I admit. "The mind shuts down when it's forced to remember a traumatic event. I linked his memory of where he hid the *clavis* with Christianna's memories of seeing this happen. He naturally buried the trauma, but I had to trigger it again to unlock it."

She looks at Davis with sympathy and concern, and I add. "The memory will be buried again. Thankfully he won't remember it."

Her hand reaches out to rest on Davis' arm. He doesn't seem to register it, blinking down at the keys in his hands instead.

"And what if he wants to remember it?"

I don't answer, but it's something I've been grappling with ever since I saw how their parents died. There have been several times when I've come close to telling Hope and Davis the truth, but the time has never been right.

Davis gives a visible shudder and rests his head in his hand, and I know his mind is working to purge the traumatic memory.

"Go get the *clavis* then," Raleigh says. "I'll stay here with him for a little while longer to make sure he's all right."

"He'll be okay," I assure her. "Are you sure, my dear? I'm going to have to leave the city for this, but I'll be back by tomorrow." I add after a moment, "And kindly check on our favorite chimera for me as well?"

"I'll do that," she says curtly. "You should go now, Jonathan. I'd hate for all of this to be for naught."

I know when arguing with Raleigh is futile, and now is one of those times. There's always a heavy price to pay for unlocking a secret, and I need to draw upon the collective power of guardians before I go.

I don't say anything else before I make my escape.

Time for me to pay a visit to the gravesite. Where Sarah lies.

15

Micah

I'm helpless to escape, frozen in place and in time for what feels like hours. Can't move. Can't scream as the fingers from the strange woman feel like they're extending into my head. My *deimos* churns in response, but she probes even deeper. Red-hot pain rends me from the inside out, and I don't know if it's because of what she's doing or if it's Vahni's power acting in retaliation.

I feel like I'm encased in a grave.

The woman burrows into my soul even more, and my vision swims with lines and spots as the pain intensifies. I wonder how many screams have sounded between these walls. I wonder why Jehoel is letting this happen to me. And if I'm going to survive this.

As suddenly as it starts, it stops.

I would have fallen if I weren't already lying on the floor. The pain is completely gone, but my muscles feel like jelly. Gradually, the ability to move trickles through my body, and I lift my head to see Jehoel and the woman conferring. All of the accusations I want to unleash on him crash through my head. Whatever she just did to me was obviously part of Jehoel's plan. Maybe he couldn't bring himself to destroy me. Maybe he tried to use her to disable me.

"Isabela?" Jehoel says, "What's wrong? Did it work?"

"I…I'm not sure," the woman – Isabela – gasps. She sounds about as stunned as I feel.

"Are you all right?"

At first I think he's talking to me, but he addresses the question to her. I almost laugh. I'm the one lying on the concrete floor feeling like I just went through a shredder, and he's asking her if she's all right.

The fight. The ocean. The lies. The torture Jehoel just put me through. I should be furious right now. Raging mad. The Micah from the past two months would have burst into flames and lashed out. But instead I feel completely together. Centered.

"I'm fine," Isabela says, and it's like an echo of my own thoughts. "But something happened when I tried to heal him."

Heal me? Demon healers don't exist, or at least that's one of the things I was led to believe. Though right about now, almost anything seems possible. I manage to get up on my knees, making sure I'm steady before getting up to my feet. Both of them keep talking as if they're oblivious to the fact that I'm here.

I'm not sure what I was expecting. Given the torture she just tried to execute, maybe I thought she'd have an evil leer on her face or something else indicating sadistic tendencies. But when Isabela faces me, she looks so normal. Peaceful, even gentle. She's wearing a fleece hoodie and jeans, and if I didn't pick up that something about her was different, she could totally pass for the mom of someone from my old school. It's almost enough to bring me off the defensive. Almost.

"What did you just do to me?" I demand. "Did Vahni send you?"

Jehoel walks over to the side of the room to turn on the light, and I blink to adjust to the change. We're not in some dungeon or even a modern rendition of a torture chamber. It looks like an unfinished basement in someone's house. Lots of junk piled in boxes against one cement wall. An old washer and dryer against another. A staircase heading up to a door. I know I could fight off Jehoel and make a run for it without even breaking a sweat, but I have plenty of things to say to him right now too. And from the way he's staring at Isabela with something like reverence, he's not going to vanish anytime soon.

Isabela looks at me with undisguised interest, and I stare back and try to figure her out. My *deimos* is reacting to her a little bit like she's human, but the characteristic prickling just under my skin makes me think she might be partly demon too. I don't know what that means, unless she's like Hope and a mixture of things.

And we're not alone. There's a young girl crouching next to the steps leading to the door. She looks maybe about six or seven, the same age as my adoptive sister Dani, and the way her big brown eyes fix on me makes my heart twinge.

Amazingly, she flashes me a smile.

I turn my attention back to Isabela. "What did you do?" I repeat.

"I tried to draw out the power of the *ignis* – the fire power bestowed upon you." Her dark-eyed gaze is steady, thoughtful.

"Vahni didn't send you," I state as a fact. I don't know how I know this, but I do.

"No one sent for me," she says calmly. "I'm a reservoir."

"A *what?*" A reservoir for what? For excessive pain?

"She's an energy reservoir," Jehoel replies. I expect him to meet me with that overly smug expression like when we were just barely out on the edge of the compound, but his eyes seem to be only for Isabela. "She's been helping small groups throughout the world, but she's been very careful to keep her existence a secret from the Impiorum. If they were to find out about her, they would want to use her for their own purposes."

Ironic considering I'm betting Jehoel wants to use Isabela for the alliance's purposes. I'm still waiting for Vahni's power to explode, but it doesn't come.

I address her and not him. "I don't know what that means."

"It means that I store energy. I can take energy from one and give it to another. I use my power to heal souls, to replenish the energy of those in need. After I received word about what you did at the fight last night, I spoke to your overlord." She glances at Jehoel. "He told me about the goddess' power and also that he's been seeking out a way to heal you."

Consent. Evidently these people haven't ever heard of asking for someone's consent before going ahead and messing around with someone's life force. Jehoel stays silent, not confirming or denying what Isabela says.

"He's not my overlord," I grind out.

Her eyebrows pinch together. "I'm truly sorry that I had to use the factor of surprise. The most effective way for me to access someone's energy is if it's in its most potent form."

I don't acknowledge the apology. I'm still too angry with Jehoel for everything he'd done and said before he took me here – also without my consent. I haven't even skimmed the surface with how I feel about him fabricating all of the reports about Hope and my family. Or taking my letters.

"So you're a demon healer?" I ask. "I didn't think demons could be healed. I thought that's why we have to feed our *deimos*."

"I can heal anyone as long as I have an excess of energy," she says simply. "Which is exactly why I was hoping that I could take the *ignis* from you. The potential to heal others would have been…." She holds out her hands palms up, as if to say it would be limitless. Or maybe that she doesn't know.

"This is one power that you don't want," I say bitterly.

I close my eyes and breathe in, noting again how centered I feel. Jehoel was dead on earlier when he said that I've been battling for control over Vahni's fire. From day one, she could erupt and take over at any time, and I've left enough damage in my wake because of it. I'd burnt down my apartment building. Almost killed Jonathan because of it. Just barely caused Jehoel to go up in smoke. Vahni's power has been right underneath the control that I fight for, but now it feels like it's gone.

"Thank you," I say to her, my jaw feeling stiff. "For taking away the goddess' power."

Isabela blinks rapidly, suddenly looking unsure of herself. "But I didn't. I'm afraid I was unable to draw it out from you. Your *deimos* warded off my attempts."

I frown. She must have done *something,* because I feel like my old self again. No, not quite. I feel better.

"Is that normal?" Jehoel's tone is concerned, and the derision in my gut rises like bile.

"Normal in this case. My power only works one time for each individual," she answers slowly. "And I think I've encountered Micah's soul before."

"What?" Jehoel interjects before I have the chance to say anything. "You told me you've never met him."

She faces me, certainty in her expression, but I'm positive I've never seen her before. The only time I ever needed to be "replenished" was the day my *deimos* took a serious hit, the day that Hope saved me by giving me her soul. But that was all Hope, not the work of some energy reservoir. And what Isabela just did to me – there's no way I would have forgotten *that.*

"I don't know you," I say in a flat tone.

"You were too young to have remembered, but I never forget. And technically, it wasn't your soul." She's speaking in riddles, and I come close to interrupting her when she adds, "A demon's soul is always the same as his mother's."

Her words make my heart seize up. My mother. I never knew my mother because she died during childbirth. Because of me. But what is she saying – that she recognized my mother's soul?

I swallow hard. "You knew my mother?"

"Yes. I was there when you were born," she says.

She means she was there when my mother died, but I can't bring myself to say it out loud. "Why?"

"I was trying to help her," she says in the same quiet, calm tone.

It makes me want to yell. Punch the wall. This is another one of Jehoel's ruses to trick me into flying off the handle. Or maybe this is what she needs to sink her claws into my power. They're baiting me, trying to get me to lose my temper and burst into flames.

I can't hope for the impossible. Still, I need to know.

"Help her how?" I say just as quietly.

"Your mother was pregnant with you and in the process of losing her soul to you." She says it in that same matter-of-fact way as before. "Your father came to me and begged me to save her life."

My hands close into fists at my sides. Now I know she's lying. I have no good memories of my father. Never did. He wasn't good to me – more like terrible and abusive – and I have a hard time imagining that he would do anything to save anyone.

"He wouldn't have done that." My lips move to say it, but my voice doesn't sound like my own.

She tilts her head slightly to the side, as if trying to balance what I'm telling her with what she's saying. "But he did. He was friends with a guardian named Christianna. She was a social worker, and I was working at a women's shelter. When she saw how I was helping the women there, she suspected what I was really doing and brought your father to me."

My head is starting to pound now, hearing Christianna's name in the mix. The guardian from Asphodel who also took it upon herself to meddle in my life. She'd told me things during the short time I'd known her, and I remember her telling me that my father was once a good person, that it was my mother's death that made him lose all hope and turn into an agent of darkness. Maybe so, but I've never been able to accept that he actually loved her.

I grit my teeth, telling myself that this new information about my father doesn't matter, not in the big scheme of things. I've lived with the guilt of having stolen the soul of my mother since the day I learned of my heritage. Whether I shift the blame to my father or carry it myself, the fact remains that my life was only possible because I took my mother's.

I'd been gravitating back to Isabela as we were talking, but now I stalk away again to the other side of the basement, my mind reeling. I never even thought of the possibility that my mother might have been saved – because *it's not possible* – but now that the moment's here, I need to know.

"Did you?" I whisper. "Save her life?"

Isabela casts a glance over her shoulder at the girl still sitting on the steps. They don't speak, but the girl flashes that same smile at me as before. She gives Isabela a tiny nod, and Isabela touches her chin and then bumps her wrists together like she's saying something back in sign language.

Isabela gives me a warm smile and reaches her hand out to me.

"You're welcome to see for yourself. She lives in New York City."

16

Micah

My mother lives in New York. Everything has changed. With just one sentence. The news makes me feel like Jehoel just teleported me and dumped me into another dimension.

She *lives*. It's a so-called impossibility, but my world already feels upside-down so what's one more?

I wait outside the war room for Cael, my insides hot and my skin freezing cold. Gradually, the heat ebbs and I'm left feeling numb inside.

The "war room" is what used to be the common room of the detention center, but it has the right feel for the name. Smaller rooms extending off the main one for the intelligence and technology groups. The combat simulator is on one side, a conference table for planning purposes on the other. I know that Cael's inside negotiating with Isabela the terms under which she's willing to help the alliance. She'd taken the little girl in with her too, which struck me as odd. Not sure what bringing a kid so young in with her during negotiations might accomplish, though I think the girl might have some power of her own.

I'm waiting my turn so I can ask for a transfer.

I don't want to sever ties with the alliance. The Alaskan stronghold is the most established and has the most influence. I'd have to essentially start from scratch if I transferred, but I was eventually going to leave anyway. And now I have too many issues with Jehoel for me to stay.

The door opens and Cael steps out, his face brightening when he sees me pacing the hallway.

"Micah, Isabela has agreed to be an advocate to the alliance. She'll be on call to heal new recruits."

This will be a huge help to the alliance, and I'm honestly glad to hear it. Some of the guys we've been able to bring in from the Impiorum were just like Ben when we found them, with their *deimos* in bad shape. Some of them didn't survive after getting here.

"That's great," I say.

Jehoel filled me in about everything you did to make it happen." He holds out his hand. "This is a huge triumph for us, and it's thanks to you."

"It was all Jehoel. He's the one who found Isabela." I haven't made the mark appear on my hand for months, but I reflexively check to make sure my palm is clear before shaking Cael's hand. "I didn't have anything to do with it –"

He starts shaking his head before I can finish. "That's not my understanding. Isabela wouldn't have approached Jehoel if she hadn't been intrigued by you."

"Okay, well, whatever. I'm happy for you guys."

He cocks an eyebrow. "You sounded like you weren't including yourself in that statement. Any particular reason?"

I bite the bullet, figuring there's not going to be a good time for this. "I'd like to request a transfer. To one of the alliance branches in New York."

His face falls, and I have a momentary flash of panic. I told myself that I'd leave regardless of Cael's decision, but I'd definitely rather go as part of the alliance.

"Come inside." He gestures to the door of the war room. "We'll talk."

When we step in to the room, Isabela is hooked up to the simulation set-up and battling it out opponent-style with Jehoel. The little girl is sitting on the couch, watching them with a smile and eating a cheeseburger and fries that they must have sent from the kitchen. Cael takes me over to sit at the conference table on the other side of the room. His earlier jubilation is gone, his expression grave. I try to brace myself to hear the worst, but I have no clue what that could even be.

"Micah, if you're hoping to go back to Buffalo, there's not a branch in that city. You and Jehoel were there and know the Impiorum has too large of a presence there," Cael says in a grave tone. "The closest branch is in Albany, but the entire group took a hard hit last week from a group of demon mercenaries. Have you heard of them?"

I haven't, but Cael's tone says it all. An entire group, almost destroyed. He rubs his forehead before going on. "They're a relatively new and very unfortunate phenomenon. Picture the most violent members of our kind. Bloodthirsty and without restraint. The Impiorum's been using them to do the dirty work that no one else wants to do. Torturing humans to get the most energy out of them before killing them. Doing the same to their own kind if they catch them trying to defect. Or in Albany's case, punishing them for defecting." He glances over toward Isabela and Jehoel, but they're plugged into the system and can't hear us. "Isabela's seen their handiwork in Seattle, which is part of why she's so willing to help us out here."

I feel sick to my stomach. Ben said his half-brother was caught and killed trying to escape Seattle, surely by these sickos that Cael's talking about. And going after an entire group of alliance members out in Albany… I'm struck with a horrible thought.

"Are these mercenaries coming from Buffalo?"

"Honestly, we don't know. If so, the Impiorum don't know what they're getting into, using these mad dogs. The demons in the Seattle branch have managed to control them, at least to an extent. But our intel still picks up occasional reports of random acts of violence within their group, and we think it's because of them." He shakes his head. "The Albany group needs help to rebuild. I've been thinking of heading out there for a while."

"Then I need to go back. I still request the transfer," I say without hesitation. It's only a two-hour flight for me between the two cities, and if it's possible that the mercenaries are running rampant at home, I need to be there too.

He raises his eyebrows. "The alliance there is unstable. Things will be in flux. They won't train you there. You wouldn't have a mentor. Are you sure?"

My glance shifts to Jehoel, who's making slicing motions in the air as part of the fight simulation. I wouldn't have a mentor if I stayed, either.

"Yeah, maybe I can help them out." Before he can say anything else, I add, "Everyone deserves a second chance. Isn't that what you always say?"

Cael still seems tense, but my comment makes him smile. "Indeed." But his smile quickly fades, his eyes shrewd. "Why do you really want to leave, Micah? Is it because you and Jehoel had an altercation? I'm not blind to things that go on in my own compound."

"No," I say. Cael doesn't tolerate anything less than the truth, and I know his decision largely depends on my answer. "Honestly, I need to find my mom. And now that I'm sure I won't burn things down in my sleep, I was thinking now would be a good time. I'll help out the alliance no matter where I'll be. You've taught me here that self-redemption is possible, and I promise I'll teach others too."

He regards me seriously for a few seconds then nods. "Okay, give me a couple of minutes to establish a secure channel through intel, and I'll talk to the people there. We'll see what we can do." He walks me out of the room, adding. "You'll be back in New

York, which means you'll go and see her, won't you? Your girlfriend."

"Yes," I say truthfully. That's pretty much a given.

"I hope it works out for you two," he says simply. I gape at him, and he winks. "We're demons, but we're human too. Don't forget that when you're out there, Micah."

He gives me his easy-going grin that he uses to put people at ease, but his words have almost the opposite effect on me. He disappears, and I stay frozen in place. I honestly don't know how it's all going to work when I get back together with Hope.

I hear light footsteps behind me.

"Micah? Isabela wanted me to give you something."

I turn to face the little girl, who's holding a piece of paper out to me. She's smiling a big smile and twirling one of her braids like Dani always used to do, and there's something about her that's so innocent yet also somehow wise beyond her years.

"Thank you…" I look at her quizzically. "I'm sorry. What's your name?"

"Shandra." She steps forward, still clutching the note. "This is your mom's address."

Shandra's words steal my breath, making my legs turn into jelly. "Are you sure you want me to have this?" I whisper.

"Yes, we're sure." She beams at me. "You're one of the good ones. I can tell. But you have to promise that you keep Isabela a secret. You can't tell anyone about her and who she really is. Isabela said it would be dangerous if people found out the truth."

"I promise," I choke out. "I won't tell anyone about her."

"I know." She says it like Dani used to say she knew things, with total conviction. There's no doubt or fear in her eyes when she presses the piece of paper into my hand. "She changed her name to Elizabeth Jakobs."

"Thank you," I manage. "Please tell Isabela thank you too."

"You're welcome," she says brightly. "You're lucky. My mother's dead, but Isabela's kind of like my mom now, so I guess I'm lucky too."

I watch Shandra run back to the war room, my heart in my throat. When she's gone, I look at the paper, staring at the name that's written in block letters. Elizabeth Jakobs. Beneath it is her address in New York.

I head upstairs, clinging to the paper like my deepest hope.

———

Ben watches me silently from his bunk as I pack my few belongings. All I'm taking with me are a few changes of clothes and the small notebook that I used as a journal and to write my letters to Hope, the ones that never made it to her. I haven't bothered keeping anything else even remotely personal in the past two months because I knew it could all go up in flames.

"Where are you going?" Ben asks.

"I decided to put in for my transfer," I say simply.

"This is all because of what I told you about Jehoel, right?" Ben's voice is tinged with desperation, and I know I have to make him understand, at least enough so he won't blame himself.

"No. It's not because of that." Admittedly, I would be more conflicted about leaving if Jehoel hadn't done everything he did. I like Ben, but this doesn't involve him, and I don't want to leave him with a worse taste in his mouth than he might already have.

He swings his legs over the edge of the bunk and fixes me with a stare. "Can I come with you?"

I pause with my shirts balled up in my hand. "Dude, no. I have a lot of baggage that you want no part of."

"I've seen some messed up things in Seattle," he challenges. "I can handle whatever it is."

If the mercenaries in Seattle are as vicious as Cael says, I believe him. But Ben's barely coming out of his own hell, and he doesn't deserve to be part of mine.

"Ben, I know you'll have a good thing here working with the others. I can't offer you anything like that. Things in New York will be different. Things are unstable there right now."

His eyes flash with anger. "This is bullshit. If you think things are good here, you'd be staying."

I turn away, pacing the small space and thinking hard. I need to say something more to reassure Ben that he'll be okay here with the others. Given the hard feelings that I have for Jehoel, it's a little hard right now.

"Whatever you do is ultimately up to you," I finally say. "But you already know that the Impiorum way isn't for you. Me wanting to take off from this place doesn't mean it's bad. This group is all about individuals standing up for a peaceful way to live. I just have some personal things to take care of back in New York."

Ben looks so glum, and I feel sorry that I had to dump all of this on him. First week here. Not a great way to start out. He's a good kid – I could see this right away about him.

He stands up, and I can tell he's trying hard to accept this. "Can I ask you something before you go?"

"Sure."

"Can you show me why some of the other guys are afraid of you?"

He wants me to show him, meaning that he heard about what I can do. Not so surprising really. He keeps staring at me with total trust in his expression, and I figure why not. "Okay," I finally say. "You might want to stand by the window, just in case."

He goes to the window, and I stand against the far wall and call up my *deimos*. The heat flows to the surface at the same time, like it's more part of me than it's ever been. Ben jumps a little when the flames first lick out of my hands, but then leans back and watches in interest. I flatten out my palm, the fire condensing and forming a torrent that spirals upward. Impulsively, I push it so it tumbles over my arms. The fire blazes across my shoulders and back down the other arm, landing as a fireball in my other hand. Ben laughs out loud, and feeling encouraged, I flick my palm so it shoots into the air before landing in my other hand.

I internalize it even as the mark burns itself into my hand. It's easier than it's ever been.

"Whoa. I didn't know any of us could do that. That's awesome," Ben says with enthusiasm. "But why would the guys be afraid just because of that? Seems like the power would be a strength."

"Because demons *can't* normally do this. The power's borrowed, and it's linked to this." I hold up my hand to show Ben the blackened char on my palm, but it's not there.

He tilts his head. "It's linked to what? The ability to high-five?"

I clench and release my hand, staring at my bare palm in disbelief. No way. Maybe it's just a fluke with the mark not showing up this one time. Only I know I felt it burn into my hand. Was *sure* that it was there.

"Micah?" Ben clears his throat. "What's the whole fire thing linked to?"

"It, uh…" I force a quick flame out of my palm, make a fist and draw it back in, and wait for the mark to burn itself into my hand. I let Ben stay in suspense, this time waiting for a good ten seconds more before checking.

Nothing. Clear as an angel's conscience.

Okay, bad comparison.

I rack my brain for possibilities and only come up with two. Either Vahni stripped me of the mark when she paid a visit to me as the zombie-in-training, or whatever Isabela did uncoupled the fire from the mark.

"The fire is linked to the power to make the demon mark," I explain. "Or at least it used to be."

His eyes become almost comically huge. "Whaaaat? No way. I thought that was just a myth. Or like a...I don't know, an urban legend that the older demons used to scare the younger ones."

"Nope." I shrug. I hadn't ever heard anything about the mark before Vahni herself stuck me with it, but it's not like I really hung out with other demons before joining the alliance.

Ben shakes his head, his gaze a little sharper as he also shakes off the initial shock. "But just because someone has the power doesn't mean they'll use it. It's a choice. Is the mark why you've been avoiding everyone too?"

I raise my eyebrows, surprised at the question. I never really thought about it in terms of me avoiding anyone, but maybe this is true.

Ben's pretty perceptive, and I can maybe see his point. But the memory of sending an innocent soul to Asphodel isn't something I can really forget, either. "Could be. I've used it before."

"Yeah, but you feel guilty because of it." He steps closer, like he's trying to get an even better fix on my emotions. "And that's exactly why you'd never use it against any of us."

I smile a little, glad that he included himself within the group. "You sure you want to go into tech? I think you'd do pretty good at working with people. Talking guys down from the ledge and stuff."

"I actually like the tech stuff though. Though," he says with a little smile, "I gotta admit. My hack psychoanalysis skills come in handy now and then."

"Yeah. I can see that." I grab my backpack and step toward the door. "Good luck, Ben. You'll do well here."

His face falls. "Yeah. Okay. Thanks for everything."

I half expect him to look down at his sneakers like he usually does, but he steps forward and holds out his hand. I glance at my palm out of habit and fist-bump him instead.

"When you're done training here and if you feel like it, ask Cael to transfer you to Albany. I'll be there."

He gives me a tentative smile, but it fades. We both look to the door at the same time, each of us having sensed someone coming. I open it and step out into the hallway, bristling when I see Jehoel walking down the hallway. He's holding a package in his hands, and he looks about as happy as I feel.

"Cael's waiting downstairs for you with a teleporter to take you out of the compound, and then you can manage your own travel from there," he says, stopping several feet away. "Your transfer's been approved."

"Cool."

At least Jehoel isn't delusional enough to think that I'll teleport anywhere with him again. He doesn't move from where he's blocking my path, and I can't go anywhere else unless I want to go back to my room and out the window. I heft my backpack on my shoulder and walk past him, but Jehoel puts his hand on my arm to stop me. I stiffen, but I don't move away either.

I stare on the stairs at the end of the hallway. "You could have confided in me. I would have helped."

"Isabela might not have surfaced if she knew we were intentionally trying to bait her. You may have noticed, but her companion has a special sense where she can pick up how sincere people are."

"It's called trust," I grind out. "But you wouldn't know about that, would you?"

His hand lifts to adjust his glasses. It's the same gesture that he always makes when he's irritated, or at least that's how I've always interpreted it. Only he doesn't look irritated this time, just uncomfortable. Maybe it's been that the entire time and I've been so desperate for his approval that I haven't noticed.

"I don't blame you for being angry with me." He hesitates, his brow furrowing. "And yes, I know you would have helped."

He didn't apologize, but if the little girl approved of him enough to let Isabela play wargames with Jehoel, maybe I should take that as a sign. Still, I don't want to stay here, and I'm glad that I don't have to.

"Here." He hands me the big envelope. "All of your letters to Hope, unopened. I didn't fabricate all of the reports. I do hear from my contacts back in Buffalo sporadically, but times are tenuous there and regular communication is considered unsafe. Hope and your family are alive and well."

Thank God. I take a deep breath for what feels like the first time all week, saying a silent prayer of gratitude. I should be man enough to say thanks to Jehoel for everything he's taught me. For bringing me to the alliance in the first place and showing me how to help others just like me. I learned a lot while I was here, enough that I think I can move on and feel decent about what I can bring to the table in Albany. But I also know that if I ever get to the point that I'm able to mentor anyone, I'll go about it differently than Jehoel did. I'll be honest.

"Make sure someone takes care of Ben," I say.

"I will. Take your tracker with you," he says. "In case you ever need me."

The tracker is in my jacket pocket, and I almost give it back. But I don't want to make a big deal of anything anymore. I tuck the envelope into my backpack and start to walk away.

"I'm sorry you aren't staying," he calls after me. "Now that you have better control over Vahni's power, you could offer a lot to us."

I glance over my shoulder at him, and he's staring at me just like he looks at Cael. With respect.

Too little. Too late. Jehoel doesn't get to measure my value or worth like that, not anymore.

"You'll be fine without me," I say as I walk away. "Just buy yourself a flamethrower."

17

Jonathan

A part of me died the day that I walked into a prison cell and saw that Adrienne was the prisoner.

Cyril was crouched next to her, and he shot me a wolfish grin as soon as he saw it was me. He didn't step away from her. Instead he grabbed her roughly by her hair and peeled back her eyelids. As soon as I saw her eyes roll back in her head, I knew she'd taken the touch of death to protect herself.

"What are you doing?" I roared. I charged across the room, and Cyril pushed Adrienne's body away as he jumped up to face me. Her head fell back and hit the stone floor.

"Interrogating our newest prisoner. I caught her trying to poison me, so I ran a little experiment on her."

The sight of the vial in his hand sent my heart plummeting. His black gaze burnt through me with suspicion, and my rage boiled just below the surface but out of reach for the time being. My only mission at that moment was to get Adrienne out of there.

"I only gave her a little bit to see what it would do to her. Do you know what this is?"

Cyril held up the vial, waiting for me to respond. When I didn't, he shifted on the balls of his feet, his mood becoming darker and his eyes blacker. Aside from observing how much he was prone to violence, I'd grown to suspect he wasn't quite like other people, that he must be suffering from some sort of emotional deficiency. He derived pleasure from inflicting harm to others and would have turned on me at least thirty times if I hadn't been watching my back. I was the centered and logical one of the pair, and I know that the viscount regretted the decision to make this monster the one in charge.

My face felt like stone when I strode up to Cyril. He looked surprised at my advance, and I saw the surge of emotions in his eyes, angry and murderous. He shifted on his feet in preparation to hit me but hesitated. That hesitation was his mistake.

I thought only of how much I loved Adrienne, how desperate I was to get her to safety, and I struck him right in the face with my fist. The impact was like an electric storm, and we both staggered back from each other. Cyril fell to the floor, twitching just like his victims.

Knowing I only had seconds, I fell to my knees beside Adrienne.

"I'm here. Everything will be all right."

I actually believed those words. I would fight every single guard in our way if that's what it took to get her out of there. I would never again set foot in an interrogation room. I would take her to a province that was safe. I scooped up Adrienne to carry her out of the cell. We were halfway down the corridor when she moaned and opened her eyes.

"Jonathan." Her voice was thick. "Leave me here."

My heart fractured at her words. "No. I'm getting you out of here. I should have done that the first day I saw you in this place. I should not have ever stopped looking for you when I thought you were dead —"

"You're speaking nonsense. Shhh…" She put her fingertip on my mouth, her own lips working urgently to form the words. "You cannot possibly take me out of here safely. But you can leave. You have to leave. You have to find Colette and save her."

I didn't know who she meant, and I shook my head, nothing that she said making sense to me. "I just barely found you again."

"Jonathan, you must. My father has her, and you must get her away from him. I need time to recover from what Cyril did. Find an empty cell for me, and I will be all right there until you return."

I fought to keep my patience. The only thing of importance was getting Adrienne out of there. But the way her eyes beseeched me to understand made me hesitate.

"Who is this Colette you speak of?"

"She is our child, Jonathan. Yours and mine..."

I stared down at Adrienne, the meaning of her words sinking in.

"She has gifts," she insisted. "Already at such a young age, she can read motivations of those around her with just a touch. You cannot let my father kill her abilities. If she were to stay with him, this is what would happen."

Adrienne struggled to say more, but slumped against my chest in exhaustion. I understood what I needed to do. I would come back. I raised Adrienne's hand to my lips and kissed it. She was expending all of her energy in speaking to me of this, and she needed to conserve it.

We had a child.

The beginning of our legacy of darkly gifted daughters. Of our family.

Where Sarah lies.

The sun is just dropping over the horizon when I get to Albany, the scent of late spring wafting in through my windows. I'm full of an unusual amount of optimism when I pull into the property of Glenwood cemetery. A sign posted by the gated entrance announces that it's been closed for two hours, but just in case anyone is still around, I keep driving past and park Raleigh's car on the side of the road about a kilometer away. The road to the north side of the cemetery is deserted, and I run across the cracked and dusty asphalt until I get to a familiar grove of trees. I've been here just once before, but I remember exactly where I need to go. I jump over the fence and head for the small grassy hill nearby.

I've walked over more than my fair share of graves over the years, but for far different reasons than this.

Her headstone sits next to her husband's, and it looks likes someone's been coming here to pay their respects. But it hasn't been recent, as the silk flowers in the sunken vases are faded and tattered.

I kneel next to the headstone and touch my fingertips to the etched stone with Sarah Gentry's name.

> *Loving daughter, sister, wife, and mother.*
> *Eternal rest and peace....*

The air is light and full of energy tonight, as if Sarah's spirit is restless and wishes it could speak of her death. All of the women in my lineage expressed darker gifts, some of them even persecuted because of it. Hope's human gift had been to see someone's worst memory. Sarah's sister and Hope's aunt's had been to see someone's worst possible potential. As far as I could tell, Sarah hadn't expressed any specific abilities in her lifetime, but I always wondered if that was because she figured out a way to deny her magic.

Suppressed magic doesn't ever stay contained for very long, but in Sarah's case, she died before anything ever manifested.

No one was ever able to figure out the cause of the explosion that led to the deaths of Hope and Davis' parents. They'd gone up in the equivalent of a fiery inferno, but the police reports indicated there was no gas or other fuel going into the house and no identified source of the flame. But Christianna had been there, a notion that I still haven't been able to reconcile. As a resident of Asphodel, she was privy to Arete's predictions, so she could have gone there to prevent what Arete had seen would happen. And the other possibility is much more painful for me to think about, but I have to consider everything.

She could have been the direct cause of the fire. Christianna was a ward of Vahni, and the goddess of the Underworld had bestowed to her the gift of fire, the source of her ultimate demise. It would certainly explain the level of remorse she felt over Sarah's death. But to knowingly kill her? My hands are not free from blood, but I can't fathom Christianna – someone I genuinely cared for – doing this.

In the distance, I hear the crunch of tires over asphalt as a car comes up the road. I drop down and make myself as flush as I can with the grass as the car makes its way past at a snail's pace. Its headlights sweep across the landscape and miss me by meters. At this hour, it's likely a guard doing a security check, and if they come onto the grounds right now, it won't be very conducive to me searching for the *clavis*. But it won't stop me, either.

I wait until the car passes the northern point of the property and curves back around south before beginning my examination. I pore over the ground by touch, feeling for signs of disturbed earth or differences in the texture of the grass. Everything seems relatively uniform around the headstone, with the exception of maybe…

There.

I run my fingers along the edge of the headstone itself. The soil bordering it feels loose and not uniformly compact, as though someone had recently dug there.

My phone rings – remarkably it's still in working after Tricia's attack – and when I take it out, the display says that it's Raleigh. I frown, wondering if everything's all right. I haven't spoken to her since I left Buffalo almost four hours ago.

I hit answer. "Yes."

"Did you find it?" Raleigh's voice sounds strained, not put-together like she usually is. And with me, she normally at least says hello.

"I just got here. How is Davis?" Considering the difference in her tone, I add as an afterthought, "Can you speak freely, or is someone there?"

"I'm alone *now*," she says with heavy emphasis the last word. "I stayed with Davis for about an hour. He seemed to have forgotten everything, including who I was."

"Good," I say simply.

"And afterward, I went to my apartment, and it was trashed. Interestingly enough, Tricia was waiting for me outside, but she claimed she wasn't responsible."

My hackles immediately rise. I'm disturbed to hear about Raleigh's territory being violated, but more so to hear about Tricia. She had *guaranteed* Raleigh a reprieve as part of the deal. "What did she want?" I say stiffly.

Raleigh snorts. "It seems that she came to renegotiate terms."

This has been a longer day than most. I close my eyes, rubbing the bridge of my nose, the anger slicing through me at the news. "She cannot renegotiate terms with you. I'm the one that made the original deal with her, though she evidently has short-term memory loss. What does she want now?"

"There have been more killings. The *Seraphim* destroyed another guardian from our sector. And two of their own as well – the demons that Rowan had originally taken hostage the night I killed him. Tricia said that the guardians are becoming even more desperate, if you could even imagine this."

I wait for the punchline.

"She wants you to step down from the directorship and hand it over to her. She said that it would allow you to remain in the sector as opposed to if you were voted out." Her voice shakes with anger.

Interesting. Unlike Raleigh, I'm not furious about this newest development. Tricia could have merely called for a vote to oust me, but she must not have the same backing that Rowan did.

"I see," I say calmly. "And what did she offer in return for this generous offer?"

"Nothing," she spits. "Except as she put it, 'the security of knowing you wouldn't be chased out of Buffalo by a lynch mob.'"

I suppress the urge to laugh. "Nothing to worry about, Raleigh. She knows she doesn't stand a chance. I hope your response was appropriate?" I'm almost afraid to know.

"I did not accept upon your behalf," she huffs. "Suffice it to say that Tricia is still intact after all was said and done."

"I'm glad to hear it," I say, and it's no lie. "We'll figure this out when I return. I'll pay her a personal visit. In the meantime, don't stay at your apartment. And kindly tell Hope that she might want to keep an eye on Davis."

She either sighs, or a gust of wind hits her phone. "I already salvaged what I could and brought my things to my sanctuary. And I will let Hope know. You will be back tomorrow?"

"Possibly late tonight if all goes well. And yes, that sounds like the best course of action. Stay safe, my dear." I hesitate. "I promised I wouldn't let anything happen to you."

"I know you did." Her tone is a hair softer. "You too."

She ends the call, and I chew on this new information for a bit as I stare down at Sarah's headstone. Raleigh and Tricia's history remains mysterious to me, but I can tell from seeing them before that Tricia takes advantage of Raleigh's emotions, and I cannot allow this to continue. When I get back to Buffalo, I'll straighten out the guardian myself.

But first I need the *clavis*.

The headstone is sizable, and Davis would have had to exert some fairly serious physical strength if he hid the *clavis* beneath it. But there's no other area here that shows signs of being disturbed, and it can't be in any other area of the cemetery either. The safekeeper phrase is always very specific.

I start to remove my jacket but then think better of it – I'm going to get dirty no matter what and besides, I dressed for the occasion in one of my more casual suits. The wind stirs again and creates that same disruption in energy, as if the spirits here are already none too happy at what I'm about to do.

I hoist up the granite headstone and carefully lay it aside. The underlying concrete is more of a challenge, and I dig my hands beneath one side of the slab and lift, only to find that it gives with little resistance. The soil beneath is compact and uniform-looking as it should be, which means I'm going to have to dig.

"What the hell do you think you're doing?" a voice demands from behind me.

I let go of the slab, and it hits the earth with a resounding thump. I hadn't heard anyone approaching. If it's security, I'll just have to wipe his memory and send him on his way.

Except that when I turn around, it's Davis standing there, and his anger is directed at me like a laser beam.

He charges forward, and I stay relaxed as he throws a punch at me, my powers on a tight leash so I don't hurt him. But I snap my arm up to catch his wrist, and I sense it. He has energy coursing through him like a live wire. It's the same magic that's been present in all of the women in my lineage. Only the women.

We stand in a deadlock, with Davis' strength matching mine, staring at each other in surprise. Adrienne and I were the ones who started this long tradition of dark magic when we had Colette, and the daughters in our bloodline have always shown the prowess for this power. The sons have always shown the fortitude to be safekeepers.

I could end the physical stalemate by manipulating his emotions, but I've already done too much to his mind today. Instead, I push out a brief pulse of *lumen* that should bring him to his knees. Sweat breaks out on his brow, his balance wavering for just a second, and I stare at him in shock.

It can't be.

I'm reliving his memory like it was mine.

Cold. Pissed off.

I woke up in the middle of the night, freezing cold and plenty pissed off. For a full minute, I couldn't remember where I was, but it hit me as soon as I saw the boxes stacked in the middle of the room.

My parents' living room. It got harder to breathe the more I remembered things from my childhood. All of the Christmases we celebrated and family movie nights we spent in here. Mom planting me on the couch with comic books and chicken noodle soup when I was home sick from grade school. The first time I'd ever taken a girl home and how my parents had grilled us with polite questions before we all sat down for dinner. But my parents had been dead and gone for two weeks, all of those good times gone, and my stomach twisted. I just barely said goodbye to them three weeks before that when I left after university break, and I had to do it again at their memorial service earlier that day. For good this time.

And I'd been forced to stand alone.

Dad had been an only child. Mom was estranged from Aunt Catherine who was her only sister. Sure, there were tons of people from the community who'd known them, even some neighbors that I knew by name. But my one and only sister bailed on Mom and Dad's memorial service so she could lock herself in her room and not have to deal with it. She was just fifteen, but to not say goodbye to our parents was un-effing-believable.

And unforgivable.

I heard Hope's footsteps from upstairs, and then the bathroom door shut. I ran my hand over my face, not wanting to deal with my little sister any more than I have to. She was probably on her way downstairs to grab a bite to eat, but the living room was adjoining the kitchen, and I didn't want to get into another yelling match with her like I did when I got home from the services.

I sat up, still dressed from the night before. The clock still sitting on the mantle said it was only two o'clock. Yeah, I'd just go out to the 24-hour diner dive down the street and get some bad coffee or something. I could bring my laptop and get some work done....I'd be back in the morning in time to pack up the rest of the crap in this house.

Hope wasn't the only one who was good at avoidance.

I stood up, feeling a little woozy because I had a couple more beers than I maybe should have had, but I'd needed something to dull the harsh edges that my parents dying had left behind. I was halfway to the door when something heavy hit the floor above.

"Hope?" I called upstairs, but the upstairs was silent.

I rushed for the stairwell, my heart pounding in my chest. The bathroom door was closed when I finally got there, and I pounded on it. I was being paranoid. Hope was just having a hard time dealing with everything, and…Hell, I was such a jerk for yelling at her earlier that day. But she wouldn't do something like hurt herself. I know she wouldn't. But oh, God, what if she did?

"Hope?" I shouted.

Nothing.

I tried the doorknob, but it was locked. The lock always used to be a little jacked up, but I didn't even really think about it — I threw my shoulder into it, and the door crashed in.

Hope was slumped over on the floor by the sink, her head tilted back at a funny angle, and I suddenly couldn't breathe. I ran over to her, sliding on my knees and putting my fingers on her neck to feel for a pulse. It was steady, She was breathing, thank God. I quickly scanned the bathroom floor and tore through the medicine cabinet and garbage can for anything that she could have taken. Painkillers, sleeping pills, any kind of prescription bottle, but there was nothing.

I forced myself back out of the room and called 911, yelling at them to hurry. This was Hope. We might not have been that close growing up, but she was my kid sister.

We were family, and she was the only one I had left.

Davis regains control and yanks his hand away, and I'm left with what he felt that night. Anger. Panic. An overwhelming amount of guilt. His emotions were like a shield, protecting him from my attempt to control him.

He staggers away with me, his face pale as he fights off the reliving of the moment he just shared with me. And judging from the intensity of his emotions, one of the worst moments of his life.

"I want answers," he spits at me.

He isn't the only one who wants answers. Evidently Davis is the major exception to the pattern in my family. On all counts.

18

Micah

Back home to Hope, to my family, to my friends. My heart feels like it might burst.

I might finally get to meet my mother. The paper with her address is tucked away in my backpack, and the possibility of meeting her for the first time blows my mind. My father hadn't even kept any photographs of her, so I don't even know what she looked like. I've always had to live with the guilt over her dying during childbirth, and knowing she's alive lightens that. But it also darkens my thoughts with the possibilities of why she left me.

It'll take me twenty-four hours or so to fly the three thousand plus miles to Albany, and I have plenty of time to think. Jehoel and I made the original trip in one instantaneous jump plus just over a week to track down the general area of the alliance stronghold and make contact with Cael.

As I cross over the Alaskan wilderness with only my wings, I leave with no regrets.

I originally went there thinking I'd watch and learn the ways of the alliance, and that I would also work hard to do my part within the group, and I feel like I've done both of those things. I'd also told myself I would leave only when I was ready – when I had a plan of what to do about my debt to the Praxidikai and when I had Vahni's power under control. Probably too ambitious of me. Still, two out of three isn't bad.

The one major worry I have left is the Praxidikai. Vahni wants me to come home, and I know she didn't have Buffalo in mind when she made the request.

The landscape beneath me rushes by faster than what I'm used to, the specific cities that I planned to use as landmarks passing by sooner than they should. Either I've forgotten what it's like to fly long-distance, or it's a somehow a result of what Isabela tried to do. Vahni's power usually doesn't surface when I'm flying, but now it feels like it's combining with my *deimos* – Isabela called it my *ignis*, and it's pushing me to go harder, faster, with less effort.

It was late morning when I left the stronghold, and I'd calculated that it would be tomorrow afternoon at the earliest by the time I get to New York. But I keep chasing the darkness, the sunrise nowhere in sight. I set down in a big city somewhere in Canada to grab a quick bite to eat, surprised when I see the signs for Winnipeg. There's no way I could be here already, and I check out my map to be sure. I've done ninety percent of the journey in ten and a half hours.

Math was never my favorite subject, but I do the calculations again just to be sure. At my current flight speed, I should be passing over Buffalo in an hour and a half. Even though I'm supposed to go straight to Albany, I know that I won't be able to resist seeing Hope first. Not when I'm this close to her.

When I take off again, I'm fueled by adrenaline and the thought of seeing Hope.

Home. Almost home.

⟋⟍

The instant I pass over Niagara Falls and see the city lights of downtown Buffalo, I forget about how wiped out I am. I don't think about how many miles I just flew, and I push away my worries about Vahni and the Praxidikai. All of the anger I've been harboring toward Jehoel dissolves and is replaced by something much brighter. Even my *deimos is* quiet for now.

The alliance group in Albany is expecting me, and I should at the very least check in. But I can't. I fly straight to her house.

I hone in on Hope's rooftop from the sky and touch down in the back yard, hidden in the trees on the edge of the lawn. It's almost midnight, and her light is still on. All I want to do is to tear through the lawn to see her, but the what-ifs flood my thoughts and pin me to the spot.

I promised Hope that I'd fight for the two of us to have a life together. But now that I'm here, my chest tightens, knowing that it's possible that she might not still want this. She might have moved on, and the thought of it makes the letters that never made it to her feel like deadweight on my back. I take a step back, but then I see movement from behind curtains in her room.

Hope's shadow passes in front of the window, and seeing her there kills all of my fears. I run across the lawn, reaching up and rapping on her window. I wait, reminding myself to breathe, my pulse hammering in time with each second passing. The curtains move back a fraction again, her face partly in shadows but enough for me to see her. Her hair falls over her shoulders, longer than I remember. She looks sadder than I remember too, and it tears at me. She's so beautiful.

Her eyes widen when she sees me, and my heart speeds up when her mouth forms my name. Even if she tells me to go away, I think I'd be able to live knowing that she's okay.

But there's only happiness and relief in her expression. No anger or rejection. She yanks open the window, forcing it past that one sticky spot. When she holds out her arms out to me, all of my lingering doubts die on the spot. I climb through the window and drop my backpack onto the floor, and she flies into my arms.

"Micah. Oh my God. You're really here."

I squeeze my eyes shut and breathe her in.

I've thought of what this moment might be like a million times in my mind over the past ten hours, but this is better than I imagined. Like there's nothing that matters in the world but us, and all I want to do is hang onto her.

"Are you back for good?"

"Yes," I say into her hair.

I draw back and look at her, awed by the way she looks back at me. Her lips part, her hand reaching out to touch my face like she can't believe that I'm real.

I lean down and kiss her. God, I missed her, and I didn't realize how much until now. The softness of her mouth, the way she tastes, the subtle sweet scent that's purely her – everything about her is just as I remembered but a million times better. She sinks into my arms, her skin soft and cool to the touch, and the way she responds as I take the kiss deeper ignites the fire in me. I have to focus, have to make sure my *deimos* doesn't take over like the last time we were together. But I don't feel like I'm out of control this time, and it's like the forces in the universe are finally letting me have her.

She breaks off the kiss before I'm ready for it to end, her hands still clutching my arms and her eyes full of questions. But then she breaks the eye contact too, her gaze landing on my backpack on the floor.

"Where were you? Where have you been this whole time?"

"Alaska." I stroke her hair, remembering how she always used to love it when I did this. How she used to always close her eyes and practically melt against me. But she tenses up at my words, staring at me with eyes as round as saucers.

"And so you're done there. Or…" She swallows hard. "Or do you have to go back?"

"I'm not going back there. I'm supposed to be in Albany, but not until tomorrow." Her breath hitches, and I take her gently by her arms and look into her eyes. "It'll just serve as a home base for me. I promise. And it's probably less than an hour's flight, just like a commute from the suburbs to the city, so I'll be back to see you every day."

Her gaze drops to the floor again, and even though she's still in my arms, I can feel her pulling away. I want to tell her everything. How I've been living for the past two months, how the only things that I own are in that backpack. How the only thing I care about right now is her.

But I can't tell her everything. I can't tell her about Isabela. Don't know how to tell her about my mother. Can't tell her that I didn't come back because of her. The only reason Cael let me leave was so I could help the Albany group, not so I could be here.

"What's in Albany?"

"The alliance group."

"Do you need to go?" Her voice shakes a little. "And do you want to?"

"Yes, to both questions," I say. "I think it would be better for us if I stay active in it."

She frowns, and this suddenly feels a lot more difficult than I thought it would be. We used to be so attuned to each other, but it's like we have to figure each other out all over again.

"Can I come with you?"

The question is so much like what Ben asked me last night before I left, and I automatically tense up because of it. The pain flashes in Hope's eyes as she feels it.

"Hope," I say gently. "Think about all of the people who need you. You can't just leave them. Think about Davis." There's Jonathan too, but I kick the thought of him straight out of my head.

"You left everyone, didn't you?"

Her cheeks flame right after the accusation. She detaches herself from me and walks away, and her rejection hits me squarely in the chest. This isn't how I imagined things would be when we finally got back together, but I can't exactly blame her for being hurt. I'm more frustrated with myself than with anything.

"You can say anything you want to me," I insist. "Look, I haven't even been to Albany to check in yet. I don't know any of them there, and I don't want…" I take a deep breath, unsure of how to finish the sentence.

"You don't want them to know about me?" She stands a few feet away from me, her voice still quiet but now with an edge to it.

"No, no. That's not it." I feel my defenses go up too, and I push my hand through my hair, trying to explain. "I just don't know yet if I should trust them. I don't know any of the guys there."

"You went all the way to Alaska without knowing any of the guys there," she bites out. "I hope you trusted them, or you being gone all of this time would have been pointless, wouldn't it?"

Trust. She's calling me out, and I prickle in irritation at her words. Not because anything she's saying isn't the truth, but because of what just happened between Jehoel and me. I take a step toward her, and she stiffens. There's a fissure between us, and I don't know how to patch it up. For the past two months, I never wanted to think about the possibility of losing her.

I promised her I'd fight for the two of us to have a life together. So now that I'm here, why do I feel like I've broken that promise?

"Hope." I steel myself to say the rest. "Do you…Do you not want me here?"

"Oh, Micah…." I see the battle waging within her eyes, but then her face crumples, and to hell with the walls between us. I close the distance between us and hug her close.

"I'm so sorry," I say.

She makes a little strangled noise against my chest. "I am too. I'm sorry I'm so mad right now." She looks up at me and gives me a shaky smile. "I promise I'm happy you're back. I…I just never heard from you."

I should give her the letters right now, but I don't want to let go of her. Never again.

"You have nothing to apologize for. And believe me, it's what kept me going every day, the thought of coming back to you."

Her lips twitch with the faintest smile. "Promise?"

"Promise. There's only ever you, Hope."

I see the start of a brightening in her expression – it's still cautious, but it's there. My thumb traces the line of her mouth, learning the bow-shaped curve of her lips like it's the very first time I've touched her. She closes her eyes, and I lean down and kiss her, softly at first to test the waters. The tension in her shoulders and arms dissolves, and she steps even closer. Her body presses against mine, her lips parting to let me taste her. I slip my hand under the hem of her shirt, caressing her lower back. Her skin is so soft, her temperature rising to match my own like she's the one with the fire inside her instead of me.

Her touch is tentative at first as her fingers explore the contours of my shoulders, my chest, my stomach. She reaches under my t-shirt and presses against my stomach so we're skin against skin, and it's suddenly like neither of us can get close enough. She grabs the bottom of my shirt and pushes it up, and I break apart from her to help her get it off the rest of the way. Her fingernails graze gently across my back, sending heat down my spine.

"Can you stay here tonight?" she whispers.

"There's nowhere else in the world I'd rather be."

I kiss the soft skin of her neck and run my hands over the silky curve of her shoulders, loving the sigh I coax out of her. I can't stop kissing her, can't stop touching her, not even when her fingers hook a belt loop of my jeans and tug me with her to the other side of the room. We don't stop until we reach her bed, and she breaks away from me and lies down, smiling a little shyly at me. I think I might explode, but at least it won't be into flames.

"You sure this is okay?" I climb into bed next to her, searching her eyes for any lingering doubts. "What about Davis?"

"Davis isn't home right now. But more importantly –" She reaches up and runs her fingers through my hair. "I want you to be here."

I kiss her again, and I can almost taste her *deimos,* like it's hungry to connect with mine. I slowly move the strap of her tank top down her shoulder, planting kisses along the same path. She's so soft and strong and beautiful, and I marvel at the fact that she's mine as I edge her top further and further down. Her hand knots in my hair and exerts gentle pressure, and I shift down in the bed and kiss the swell of her breasts. She arches into me, and all I want is her, just be here with her tonight, to have everything we could possibly have. Only… I break away and stare at her.

Hope searches my face, and I know she can read my hesitation. "Can we do this? Has anything changed?"

"I don't know." I press my lips to hers, hurting because of how much I want her and because I don't want to let her go. She's here, she's happy to see me, she wanted me to stay. I clung to the hope of seeing her every single day when I was gone. But then why – when I'm here in her bed and with her in my arms – why the hell do I feel like this?

The pain starts to intensify, and it centers in my head right between my eyes. I know that feeling.

"Micah? What's wrong?"

One of Hope's hands is still tangled in my hair, the other one clenching my shoulder.

Guardian.

My senses suddenly go through the roof, and I freeze. But the only thing I can hear are the sounds of our breathing and the blood rushing in my ears.

"I thought I heard something outside."

We both stop and listen, and I hold on to her and close my eyes, trying to get a better idea of what's out there. I thought it might be a guardian, but maybe all of my senses are on overload right now because of Hope. The way she's running her palm so slowly down my back right now doesn't exactly help.

"I didn't hear anything," she whispers. "But maybe we should check it out."

She gives me a sweet smile, reaching up to fix her top. God, I hate myself for being so paranoid, but my thoughts flash to what Cael told me about the demon mercenaries, and I know she's right.

I give her a lingering kiss before I get up, the scent of her making me a little dizzy, and I walk over to the window and peel back the curtain to look outside. The trees in the back of the house stare back at me like still, dark sentries, and I scan the shadows for signs of anything unusual. My sights hone in on a flash of movement, but it's just a cat that darts out of the trees and runs across the lawn.

I let the curtain fall back and turn around. Hope's sitting up in bed, her hair in beautiful disarray and a question in her eyes.

"Just a cat," I say.

"Oh. Good." She looks relieved, reaching for me as I sit on the bed next to her. I touch her cheek, her chin, her lips, and her eyes flutter shut as I lean in close.

I'm hit with a stabbing pain between the eyes, and I know it's not her. I look toward the window a second too late. It flies open, a darkly-clad figure diving through, and Hope screams.

I leap out of bed and rush him, but he crouches in the shadows and throws a strike at me from the floor. It's a direct hit that sends me across the room, and I fly back into the edge of Hope's dresser, red-hot agony slicing across my spine.

"*Micah!*"

Hope shouts my name, and I grit my teeth and scramble to my feet, a snarl ripping from my throat as I hone in on the intruder. He's still crouched by the window, but when he sees me coming, he whips across the room like a storm toward Hope.

A torrent of wind flies past me, and I'm hit again. My vision explodes in white, and I hear Hope shout. I shake off the attack, but by the time I can see again, they're gone.

Hope.

I lunge for the window, reaching for Vahni's power as soon as I hit the ground. Hope is strong, and I know she can hold her own, but somehow the guardian got her out of the window. If he does anything to her, I'll break my vow to never use Vahni's power to hurt anyone. I'll burn him to ash. I can barely see them ahead, and I hear Hope's protests echoing as she gets dragged toward the trees. I follow them, running like hell.

I shove out my wings and take to the sky, my sights set on the shadows within the trees below as I swoop forward fast and hard. I get a better view of Hope's captor as I get closer. Tall, slender, and moving with power and grace like a wild animal. From the way the figure moves, I think it's probably a girl and not a guy.

Hope's yelling something at her but not using her *deimos* to fight back, and that alone almost makes me pause. They break through the trees and into a clearing, and I dive over both of them.

Vahni. Help me.

Her power flares to the surface, and my wings burst into flames. I dip down low, one of my feathers grazing the guardian's hood and igniting the fabric like a candle. They stop running, the guardian's arms flying up to put out the flames, and Hope stumbles away as I jet to the ground to land by her side. I throw a cannonball made of *deimos* straight to the guardian, and she staggers back with a shriek.

Her hood falls back and she glares at me. Venom laces the expression in her green eyes, her mouth set in a determined line, and she retaliates with a sharp pulse of light that fractures my head into a million pieces. I stumble back, gritting my teeth and pitching another strike of *deimos* at the same time that she throws out a swath of her light, and the ground trembles as our powers collide.

"Stop!"

Hope's smaller than either of us, but she's standing tall, her expression one of extreme concentration as she places her hands on either side of her head. Her *deimos* bursts forth like a sound wave to cover the clearing, and the guardian cries out and falls to the ground. She shrouds herself in light to protect herself, while my own *deimos* rages to the surface in response.

"Micah?"

Hope stares at me with her mouth open, flames flickering in the reflection of her eyes, and I realize my wings are still out. Usually they're invisible, but the fire blazes up from my shoulders and intertwines comfortably with my *deimos*. I take a deep breath, drawing it inward until it spirals inside.

"Hope, I'm here to protect you!" the guardian wails. She lifts her head, her face pained from beneath the frame of her long tawny hair. My head still kills because of her, but it's finally starting to become more of a dull background ache.

"Protect me?" Hope shouts. "Raleigh, why the hell would you need to protect me from *Micah?*"

Raleigh. Raleigh's the one who first taught Hope how to harness her abilities when she was strictly human. She's Jonathan's second officer or something like that, and she obviously doesn't think much of demons. She straightens slowly to a standing position, her green eyes wide as she stares at me.

"You're Micah. You're back," she says, her expression frozen as though in shock. "Oh, shit."

"What was that all about?" Hope demands, crossing her arms over her chest. She's only in her thin tank top and pajama pants, and I'm just in my jeans. The clearing isn't completely isolated, the windows of a neighbor's house facing us with a solid view. If anyone walks by and looks out, they'll see us.

"Are the guardians coming after me or something?" Hope adds.

"Whoa. Wait. *What?*" I interject.

"No, no. Jonathan told me to check on you." Raleigh completely ignores me. She pushes back her hair, cringing as her fingers touch a singed part. Her cheeks flush as she finally has the decency to be embarrassed. "I didn't know…Quite honestly, I thought you were being attacked."

"Attacked. By my boyfriend." Hope snorts. "Seriously? And where is Jonathan, anyway? He was supposed to check in with me to tell me how he was doing. He promised."

"He had to go out of town," she says vaguely. Hope starts to protest, but Raleigh turns to me instead. "When did you get back?"

"He just barely got back," Hope says impatiently. "And hold on, we're not done. Have you been spying on me every night?"

"No. But tonight…." She walks toward Hope, keeping half an eye trained on me.

"Stay away from her," I interrupt. Maybe it's too possessive of a move, but I put my arm around Hope to make my position crystal clear. "You tried to attack me, but you could have easily hurt Hope with your powers, too. You must have known that."

"Ah, he knows what you really are," Raleigh states.

"Of course he knows what I am," Hope snaps.

The whole talking about me in third person is getting old, and I'm about to interject again when I look down at Hope and see how upset she looks. She hadn't fought off Raleigh, maybe because she actually thought there was something worth worrying about, and I reach for her hand to reassure her. Hope grips my hand tightly, lacing her fingers with mine.

"What's going on?" I ask, looking back and forth between them. "Why would guardians be after you?"

Raleigh shrugs out of her jacket, examining the hood with dismay. "They wouldn't be after Hope," she says smoothly. "They are, however, a little upset with me. It's a long story that I'm sure Hope will tell you if you care."

Don't care. I start to lead Hope back to her house, but Raleigh rushes forward in a blur to intercept us, her eyes shining in interest. "Your powers. They are not uniquely demon, are they? Are you a ward of Asphodel?"

My nerves prickle as I face the tall female guardian, wondering if all of them are so freaking intrusive. "You're Jonathan's henchman. Am I right?"

"Oh…. You guys have never met." Hope sighs, gesturing to each of us half-heartedly. "Raleigh, this is my boyfriend Micah Condie. Micah, this is Raleigh Peyton. She's Jonathan's second-in-command."

Figures that these two would be associated. All of the old feelings of resentment boil to the surface at the mention of Jonathan's name, and Raleigh notices my reaction. She presses her lips together in a grim smile.

"Don't hold my association with Jonathan Draper against me," she says to me. "I've been helping to keep Hope safe while you were gone. Obviously."

"Well, that's good at least," I admit grudgingly.

Hope protests, "Oh no you don't, both of you. I don't need *protection*!"

Raleigh ignores her, giving me a stiff nod. "I know how much you care about Hope. We do as well." She extends her hand to me as Hope rolls her eyes. "A pleasure to finally meet you. And believe me, I'm *not* at all fond of demons, so you should take that as a compliment."

"Yeah. As far as meetings go, I won't forget it." I look the guardian straight in the eye as I shake her hand. I don't necessarily like her either, but if she cares this much about Hope, I guess that's what really counts.

Tell me the truth. Does Hope need to worry about the guardians?

Raleigh's eyebrows lift in surprise as my thoughts sink into her brain. She hesitates but then gives me an almost imperceptible shake of the head as Hope takes my hand and tugs me in the direction of her house.

"Micah and I will be going now. Thanks so much for your 'protection,'" she says sarcastically. "And I'm so glad you two finally got to meet."

"I'm sure Jonathan will be thrilled as well," Raleigh calls to us as we walk away. "And…my apologies for the intrusion."

I shoot her another look before we're out of range.

I've been warned about a faction of demons called mercenaries. Are they here in Buffalo?

The guardian shakes her head again, her brow furrowing out of confusion, and my worry partially eases. She doesn't act like she recognizes the name. But she'd better not be lying to me about the guardians.

I glance down at Hope. She looks exhausted, but her gaze roams up and down my arm.

"Micah," she breathes. "Your wings weren't just *deimos* before. They were fused with fire. Where did you learn how to do that?"

Vahni. Hope hadn't seen what I could do at UB two months ago, back when I couldn't handle the power, but it strikes me now how much in control I feel over it now. Maybe this is what the fire goddess meant when she said she would help me. Maybe this is why I feel like I could fly to the moon and back in half the time and shoot fire out of my eyes. Sort of.

"It's just part of who I am now," I tell her, and I know it's the truth.

We walk hand in hand back to her house. She nestles close to me when we get back into bed, her eyes closing as soon as her head hits the pillow. She used to run a lot colder than I do, and I wonder if the difference now is because her guardian self finally equilibrated or if it's her *deimos.*

I don't sleep much these days, but Hope whispers my name and snuggles even closer to me, and I finally let the exhaustion wash through and over me until I drift to sleep. I'm here with her now, and all I know is that it feels right.

19

Jonathan

I had a daughter.

I never dreamed of such a thing being possible, and the hope of having both her in my life and Adrienne back at the same time seemed almost too much to wish for.

It was evening by the time I arrived at the house where Adrienne's family lived. It was a cottage, meager accommodations by their standards but similar to the one I had arranged for my mother. I took a deep breath before raising my hand to knock on the door. My daughter was inside this house, and I convinced myself I would do whatever it took to get her out.

The door opened, and elderly woman pinched her lips together as she looked me up and down, not even bothering to ask me for my name. I'd snuck into one of the officer's quarters and stolen clothes to wear, but I knew I looked more like a vagrant than aristocratic.

"Lord DuFort is taking a meal with family at the moment."

Adrienne's instructions to me before I left the prison were that Colette would be in the nursery at the back corner of the house with an attendant. I knew perfectly well that Adrienne's father wouldn't see me, but I needed to know he was otherwise preoccupied before trying to get her.

"I will come back at another time then, I'm sorry to bother you and the family." I bowed and stepped back, and the woman harrumphed and closed the door unnecessarily hard.

The air was still as I moved around the edge of the house. According to Adrienne, her parents and sisters moved here just last month after leaving the neighboring province. The nobility especially took to nomadic ways since the start of the war, moving from property to property with only their personal effects and often having minimal furnishings in the house itself. When I got to the small window of the room in the southeast corner like Adrienne said, I saw a small sleeping pad against the far wall. An infant slept soundly on the mat, her wavy hair as black as mine.

Colette. My daughter. My breath died in my lungs, my resolve increasing ten-fold as I stared at her. She would be my priority from that moment forth, and I knew that I'd do absolutely anything, anything, for her.

It took me over an hour to arrive at my next destination, a smaller cottage that stood on the outskirts of Amiens. It had been three years since I saw my mother, and her eyes widened in shock when I let myself through the back door.

"What are you doing here? Hurry and come inside, mon ange." It was her old term of endearment for me, one from my childhood that meant I was her angel. She quickly shut and locked the door shut behind us. Her eyes dropped to the bundle in my coat, and she sucked in a sharp breath. "Whose child is this?"

Miraculously, Colette was asleep. I'd wrapped her in a blanket and held her in my coat for the duration of the hour-long ride. She'd cried at first and I feared someone would notice and stop us, but nobody did, and eventually she slumbered against my chest.

I walked over to the soft armchair and bent down, gently releasing the warm body of the infant from my coat and her swaddling. She stirred and opened her chocolate-brown eyes that were from me, so innocent and pure that it was enough to take my breath away. I rested my hand on the soft downy curls on her head, and Colette smiled.

I thought my love for Adrienne would surpass anything I ever dreamed, but I was wrong.

"Mon dieu, Jonathan. This child," my mother gasped as she came close. "She looks just like you."

"Her name is Colette, and she is my daughter." Mother's eyes widened with alarm, and I added unnecessarily. "And your granddaughter."

The twinkle in my mother's eyes belied her frown. "She is far too filthy to be my granddaughter. She also smells soiled. Let me have her. I must give her a bath and find something clean for her to wear." She stretched out her hands to the baby, and upon touching her, Colette kicked her legs and babbled happily.

"She knows her grandmother is going to take care of her," my mother murmured just as happily. "Louise?" she called, and a girl poked her head around the corner. "Warm up some water. Not too hot."

"Yes, Madam." Louise gave a shallow curtsy and ducked back out.

"Maman, I need your help. I have to go," I said, and my mother gave me only a vague look before turning her attention back to the baby. "But I will be back, hopefully tonight or at the latest until the morning. I need you to promise that you'll keep Colette safe until then."

She picks up the naked baby and holds her to her chest, her dark eyes focused on the hallway.

"Louise has a son who I believe is a little older, but I'm certain we can find something of his that Colette can wear for the night." She patted Colette gently on the back. "I suppose I will have to have Louise feed her as well."

"Maman, did you hear me? I must go."

My mother sighed and walked with Colette toward the kitchen. "I know, mon ange. You never stay."

I set back Sarah's headstone in its rightful place, the *clavis* sitting heavily in my jacket pocket like a weight on my conscience.

Davis watches me sullenly from next to his father's grave, still indignant but his anger tempered with fear. I used that to my advantage when I told him I would explain everything. But only after I retrieved what I came for.

I level the plot with the board I'd earlier retrieved from my car, and Davis grumbles, "You seem like you've done this before."

"I've not made it a practice to rob graves, if that's what you're asking." I grab the shovel and balance the handle on my shoulder, as if to contradict my own point. "But yes, I have laid many people to rest before. In fact, I had to bury a guardian last week," I add off-handedly.

He shakes his head, muttering something under his breath.

I give him a sharp look. "You wanted answers. And I wanted back what I once entrusted you with, and now I have it. So ask away."

We start walking to the fence, but after several meters I look back and Davis isn't with me. He's standing in front of both of his parents' headstones but almost immediately turns away, as if he objects to me watching.

"I'll start. Question for question," I propose when he reaches me. "Why did you come here?"

His expression hardens. "I come here whenever I'm in town, because *I* have the right to be here. But tonight, you mean? I drove here after you pulled that fun little stunt in my office."

Interesting. And unexpected. "You remember everything that happened in your office?"

"Yeah, I remember." Davis glowers at me. "And believe me, I almost told Hope all about it. I even considered taking her with me to come here, but she went to the movies or something with Sylvia after school. Plus, I decided I wanted to know what was going on first without having to subject her to any of *this*." He gestures to the rest of the cemetery.

Incredible that he tricked Raleigh into thinking he didn't remember anything. She's not someone who's easily deceived. I mull over various possibilities for this until we get to the fence.

"Was it real?" he demands. "What I saw about my parents' deaths?"

"You didn't see it. That memory passed to me from another guardian when she died. And yes, she evidently had been there in some capacity, but I had no idea until she shared the memory with me."

He stops walking. "So how did *I* get the memory?"

"You received it from me."

"I don't understand." Davis shakes his head. "How is that even possible? Is that a guardian thing?"

"It is a 'thing' that some of us have a propensity to do, not all guardians." He stares down at the ground, his brow deeply furrowed, and I take a chance and add, "Davis, it wasn't your fault, what happened to Hope that night. She was battling her own abilities at the time, the ones she eventually told you about."

His head whips up, his face draining of color. "How do you know what I was thinking about?"

"Because apparently I'm not the only one who can share memories with others. You showed me your memory of that event when you tried to hit me."

"But…I'm not a guardian. How can I do this?"

I shrug, hesitant to reveal the truth. Davis feels simultaneously confused and tormented, and I need a moment to puzzle over these new developments myself. He has a mixture of Hope's old ability to see people's darkest memories and my current ability to impart to others emotions.

"I have helped people with similar abilities to this," I offer. "I can teach you how to control it."

"This is crazy," he mutters, and he starts walking again.

"Yes," I agree. I can sense the stress pouring out of him, and I know I need to help him come to terms with this. Davis had eventually found out about Hope's ability to see worst memories back when she was human, and the key is the fact that he'd been able to accept it. If he already accepts the improbable in his sister, chances are he may be more easily to accept what's happening to him.

"So…" He frowns. "I still don't know how any of this is possible, but assuming it is, *why* did you share that memory of my parents dying?"

I pick my next words carefully. "Your memory of where you hid the object at Sarah's…your mother's gravesite was linked to the memory of her death. In order to release the location, I had to release the memory of the house fire."

"Hold on." His eyes narrow, his gaze sharpening, and I know he's arriving at the truth of the matter. "But I received that memory from you. Did you make me hide the…whatever that thing was?"

"Yes."

His face reddens. "Have you done this to Hope? Planted some jacked up memory in her head too?"

"No, I haven't. And I won't," I say firmly. "Davis, this may be hard for you to understand at first, but you were born with a propensity to do this."

"Because of what you did to me?" he spits.

"Because of who you are." I steel myself before saying the rest. "You and Hope are descended from a long line of ancestors who possessed the same magic."

I see it in his face, his disbelief combined with his desperation to get answers. But I'm at a crossroads with the direction that we're headed, and if I keep dropping hints like this, he'll figure it out eventually.

"What?" he rasps. "Have you been keeping tabs on our family, like, for however many centuries you've been alive?"

"Not exactly."

His jaw works, and I feel his anger flare out from him like heat. "You know what? I think you should stay away from both Hope and me."

Davis stalks away from me, and the heavy apprehension in the air is strictly my own. I've never told Hope or Davis about their relationship to me. For the past century, I swore to never let any of my descendants get to know me on a personal level. But Hope broke that pattern the day she walked into my art gallery, the same applying to Davis once she introduced him to me. I'm still unwilling to tell them the entire truth, but I can throw him a bone.

"Davis," I call out. "I can explain."

"You can explain to me how you're a manipulative dick?" He picks up the pace, throwing over his shoulder, "Thanks but no thanks. I'm pretty sure I already figured that out for myself."

He storms off, his anger hitting me like a torrent, but this time it's tinged with agony. His pain fills the space between us until he stumbles to a stop. His hands grip his head, his breath coming out as a gasp as the pain becomes too intense.

I've been where Davis is. It was over half a millennium ago, but I still remember struggling to reign in the power that I couldn't comprehend.

I close the distance between us with a single burst of speed. "Let me help you."

He whirls around, throwing a string of curse words at me along with a punch that connects with my jaw. I step around him with another quick movement and pin him. He struggles against me, the same memory of him finding Hope that night flashing violently through my head.

"What happened to Hope wasn't your fault," I say into his ear. "You need to learn to let it go or the guilt will destroy you." I close my eyes and infuse him with all of the calm that I have.

Davis stops struggling, the furious flashes from his worst memory fading out and then disappearing completely. I slowly let him go, and he staggers away.

He stares at me, awestruck. "I should still want to beat the crap out of you, but I don't."

"How long has this been happening to you?"

"Never. I mean, I've always been haunted by that memory of Hope." He shifts positions, looking steadier on his feet and also slightly surer of himself. "But before today, I've never been able to share my memory with anyone or have anything like that happen. It's like it was playing in my head just now like it was on psycho repeat."

"I'm afraid I might have unlocked your abilities when I released the secret. My offer to help you still stands." I walk to his car with him and wait on the driver's side, and he stops in his tracks.

"Wait. What are you doing?"

"I'm not going to let you drive the four-hour long trip back to Buffalo, in case you experience any ill effects. I'll retrieve Raleigh's car later." I hold out my hand for the keys.

He doesn't budge. "Why am I going to let you do this after everything you just did to me?"

"Because you still have questions you need answers. Plus, I'm an excellent driver."

He mutters a curse under his breath as he tosses me the keys, but his storm of emotions from before are finally calm. "Fine. Okay, whatever. But be prepared for a billion questions." He watches as I open the trunk and place the shovel inside. "What was that thing that I'd hidden away do anyhow? It looked like a piece of rock."

"It serves as a key."

He stops short of getting into the car. "For what?"

"Passage to another realm."

His jaw drops, his composure visibly cracking, but then he swallows hard and quickly regains it. "Wait, I think I've seen this movie before. You had me hide the key because if someone were to open the door to this realm, they'd unleash some evil force. But now you think entering this realm will allow you to help humankind."

"Close, but not quite." I smile without humor as I get into the car. "I have no intention of going in unless I absolutely need to."

"Holy crap. You're serious." He sits in the passenger side of his car, his hand rubbing his forehead. "Okay, so what's in this realm?"

"Immortals," I say. We pull away from the cemetery, my mood lifting as we leave the restless spirits behind.

"For real? Un-effing-believable." He blows out a breath. "Assuming I buy into all of this, what do you need the key for if you're not going into this place?"

"I can use it to communicate with the owner." I'd seen Christianna do it once before, and she'd explained the concept to me. It's quite similar to how Raleigh's telepathic communicator works, if not conceptually identical — by tapping into the collective and using it as a conduit for one's thoughts.

"So is this immortal owner like a god or something?" Davis persists.

"No gods exist in this realm, though there is a goddess who rules over the Underworld," I clarify. "She is one of the three immortals that rule there."

"The Underworld? As in Hell?"

"If you wish, though Hell has gained a negative connotation throughout the course of history. The Underworld is neither Heaven nor Hell. Or perhaps it's a bit of both. It's where all souls go to rest, and it's the residence for agents of both light and dark."

He turns in his seat to face me. "Are you insane?"

"Not generally."

I get onto the toll way and speed up until the world and other vehicles blur past us. Assuming no major holdups, we should be back just after midnight.

"Is this the kind of stuff you and my sister talk about?" Davis demands.

"Sometimes, yes. Anything else?"

"Not right now." Despite his declaration that he was going to ask me a plethora of questions, Davis leans back in the seat with his eyes closed, as though he needs to replenish his energy.

"Davis, if I might ask," I say. "What happens at the end of the movie you were talking about?"

He doesn't open his eyes. "Everyone dies, of course," he slurs. "So yeah. Whatever you do, do *not* go into that other realm."

20

Micah

"Return home to me...."

The last time I passed through the gateway to Asphodel, Christianna opened the portal with her clavis. But this time I only have to raise the flames from the palm of my hand to gain entry to the other realm.Vahni's power is part of me, and I know she spoke the truth when she called me her ward.

I walk into the light, surprisingly comforted as the warm mist envelops me. When I can see again, I have to squint against the unnaturally bright sky. I plod through the stark landscape of dead and twisted trees, the dried dirt crumbling with each step I take. I'm in Vahni's realm, but I don't feel afraid. I feel like I'm at home.

The wind kicks up, dust whipping around and stinging my eyes. But I keep walking, my hand shielding my face and my gaze cast down at the ground. I keep waiting for it to split apart and reveal the Sea of the Dead, like it had in the forest in Alaska.

I stop in my tracks, gagging as the stench of death hits me. But then it transforms into something sweet, and I recognize Lina's perfume. I hear feet crunch toward me, and I lower my hand.

She's standing in front of me. My sister. She's wearing the clothes that she was in the night she died, and her sweater and jeans are dripping wet, her dark curls plastered wetly to her head and shoulders. She looks like she just dragged herself out of the Sea of the Dead, and she takes another shuffling step forward.

"Lina," I choke.

She looks up, slowly, her big brown eyes clouded when her gaze locks with mine. Or maybe it's my own tears blinding me. The wind is still blowing and the water continues to drip heavily off of her hair and her clothes, but she doesn't get any drier.

Drip.

Drip.

Oh God…I remember this sound. I know why she looks like that. It's how she looked when I dragged her lifeless body out of the lake.

"I'm home now," I whisper. "I'll make things right." But I don't know how to do that, and the words feel like a lie.

Her lips move like she's trying to say something back, but I can't hear because the water is teeming off her now like a small storm. I feel and see the ground shifting to make a depression, and the water pools around her, submerging her feet and flowing outward. My limbs are full of pins and needles, and I know from the smell of the sea and death that I can't let the water touch me. I stumble back as fast as my legs will let me, reaching out to Lina but knowing I can't save her.

I can't see her face anymore, can only see the water pouring from her hair, can only hear the low rumble of the earth as the landscape shifts to form the Sea of the Dead. Dark forms rise from the water next to Lina and pull on her arms and legs, dragging her down. One of them looks at me, and all I can see are its eyes, luminous and dark with malice.

The edge of water steadily flows toward me, and I'm forced back farther and farther. Helpless to stop its advance. Helpless to save her.

Helpless to do anything but watch my sister drown all over again.

You can put all of your nightmares to rest, if only you open your eyes and really see.

I wake up, my mouth parched and body broken out in a sweat. The sound of rain hits the windowpane, the water dripping from the rain gutter, and I lie in the dark as my heart rate slowly returns to normal. Just a hellish messed-up dream that was probably a welcome home present from Vahni herself. If she's trying to entice me to come "home" to Asphodel, she's not doing a very good job.

My leg is numb from being under Hope's, my arm full of pins and needles because she's asleep with her head on my shoulder. That's all it was. Just the sound of rain and some discomfort triggering a nightmare. Plus my ever-present guilt over Lina's death. This is why I don't sleep much anymore.

The nightmare's raw edge hasn't completely dulled yet, and I look over at the window. The gray of dawn is starting to edge its way through the curtains, but Hope's room is still mostly dark. My imagination twists shadows into physical forms, and I slowly shift so Hope's not lying on top of me anymore. She murmurs something in her sleep before settling back down again.

I get up to use the bathroom and wash up, careful to be quiet in case Davis is home. I actually didn't hear him come home at all last night, but I'm not too worried because it's Saturday morning – sometimes he doesn't come home until noon on weekends. Just to check, I go through the kitchen and open the door leading to the garage, frowning when I see the dark blue Mazda 6. Davis used to drive a newer Toyota.

There's so much I *don't* know after being gone.

I go back to Hope's room and slide back into bed next to her, trying not to wake her. But she rolls over and blindly feels for me, her hand pressing against my chest. My body reacts to the touch of her, this time my *deimos* stirring a little too.

She blinks and gives me a sleepy smile. "I was afraid you were a dream."

"I'm here." I brush back a stray hair from her cheek, not quite believing that I'm with her again either. I touch my fingers to her cheek just to make sure.

"You haven't heard of a group of demons called the mercenaries, have you?" Raleigh hadn't, but I need to make sure.

"Mercenaries?" she repeats, a little more awake now. "You mean like demons being paid to be soldiers?"

"Never mind." I trace my fingers over her bare shoulder, glad that there's enough light to see her by but equally sorry because it means I have to go soon.

I can tell Hope hasn't heard of the faction of demons, and I try to relax and shrug off my worry. Traces of my nightmare linger like a bad taste in my mouth, but the things Hope and I used to see as our biggest obstacles seem less worrisome now. I haven't fed since before leaving Alaska, but my *deimos* seems quiet for now, and I'm glad because it lets my thoughts shift to the girl lying next to me.

"How long can you stay?" A sad smile touches her lips, like she already knows the answer.

"I should go soon," I admit. "But I'll be back later today."

Her brow creases. "An hour to Albany, huh? Since when can you fly that fast?"

"I'm not sure," I admit. "But I made it from Alaska to here in half the time than I thought."

She props herself up on an elbow and faces me. "Are you okay, and I mean, really okay?"

"I'm really okay."

My fingers trace lower, and I follow the same path by kissing her shoulder. She relaxes under my touch, and I murmur against her skin, "What about you? What have you been doing?"

"Keeping busy doing what I'm supposed to be doing. Going to school. Hanging out with Sylvia. Doing guardian service and trying to figure out their rules." She sighs a little as I move to kiss the curve of her neck. "And missing you," she breathes.

I close my eyes, planting kisses on my way up to her earlobe. "I get that. I hated leaving you."

Hope's fingers thread through my hair. "What exactly have you been doing in Alaska?"

"I finished up my high school requirements. Carved out my place in the alliance." I move my hand lower to edge down one strap of her tank top, stopping so I can revel in the softness of her skin. "Tried to figure out how to live."

"And did you figure that out?"

"I did."

"Really?" She pulls back, her gray eyes wide with curiosity. "Tell me about it."

I think about how best to explain it. "I learned how to feed without actively taking souls. I learned how to find others who were struggling just like me. Most of these guys had things way worse than I did."

"And you were able to help them," she says with conviction.

I think about Ben. "Yeah, I helped them."

She smiles widely, a slice of early morning sun peeking through a crack in her curtains and lighting up her face. "I'm really glad. And I can tell that you're not fighting it so hard anymore."

We're lying side-by-side, and her breath catches as I take hold of her waist and pull her closer. "And you?" I ask.

"There's nothing in my life I need to fight."

I lean forward and kiss her, and any lingering wall that was between us from last night crumbles. Her arms wind around me, her body pressing against mine, and I know that nothing else in the world could possibly be better than this.

We both hear the rumbling of the garage door opening at the same time and break away for a breath. But we stay together, still and quiet, her body next to mine, my forehead touching hers. Her eyes search my face like they can find in them all of the answers in the world, and I give her a rueful smile.

"I need to go," I whisper. Davis coming back home is just one of the reasons for this, and we both know it. "I missed you so much."

"I missed you, too. You don't even know." She squeezes me tightly before letting go. "Can I call you later? Just so I know everything's okay there?"

"I don't have a phone." The corners of her lips turn down, and I add, "I don't know what the protocols are there, but they're probably similar to what they were in Alaska. We didn't use phones to communicate. But wait."

She adjusts down her tank top and sits up, hugging her knees to her chest and watching me as I root around in my backpack for one of the tracker bracelets. Cael sent me with a few extras so I could show them to the Albany group. I'm not worried if Jehoel's is still tuned into mine – it probably wouldn't work over such a long distance.

"Here." I hand Hope the bracelet. It's designed for a guy's wrist and way too big for her, but I show her how to activate it anyway. "This will let me find you wherever you are. If you ever need me, just send me a signal, and I'll come back."

She frowns, turning the leather strap over in her hand. "How do you find me with just this?"

"It lets my *deimos* connect with it somehow. It's sort of like a homing device."

"Oh!" She looks up at me, her eyes questioning. "So could I use it to let my *deimos* find you too?"

"We won't know until we try." I put my hand over hers. "But it's a little glitchy, so don't use it when I'm standing right next to you, or it'll give you a migraine."

She nods and places it very gingerly on her nightstand. "I probably won't use it anyway. I mean, I don't want to bother you if you're working."

"You can use it whenever you want," I insist. "I need you to know that."

I feel Hope's eyes on me as I reach into my bag, this time drawing out the big envelope.

She stares at me. "What's that?"

"All of the letters that never got to you." I hold the envelope out to her, and she takes it, her hands shaking just a little.

"I thought you didn't…" She shuts her eyes and takes a deep breath. When she looks at me again, her eyes have tears in them. "Thank you."

"You're welcome. I'm really sorry you never got them in the first place." I curse out Jehoel in my head as I strap on my backpack. Davis' footsteps are slowly plodding up the stairs to his room, and I make my way to the window.

"Micah, wait." Hope scrambles out of her bed, the envelope clutched to her chest. "You need to be sure you go and see your family. And Troy too."

It's not what I expected her to say, and I don't answer right away. Troy's my best friend, and I totally planned on seeing him as soon as things settled down. But I left the Condies without saying goodbye. I completely missed my sister's funeral. I inflicted way too much hurt on the people who took me in and treated me like their real son and brother, and I have no idea how I'll ever make things better between me and them. I think my mother's heart would break even more if I ever told her about Elizabeth Jakobs.

"I was planning on it, eventually," I say truthfully. "I just don't know if they'll forgive me for leaving."

Something flashes in Hope's eyes, and maybe it's anger. "*I* forgave you for leaving." She reaches down and takes my hand. "Your family doesn't understand why you left, but I know they'll forgive you."

A huge lump forms in my throat, and it takes me a second to find my voice. "You've seen them? How are they?"

She nods. "I've been going over there every week to help with things."

"Why?" I work to keep my voice down, but I can also feel my panic rising. "Are they okay? Is my dad...."

Her hand squeezes mine. "He's totally fine. Everyone is doing fine. No, I've been going mostly to help your mom out with your brother and sister. Usually I just wind up helping them with their homework. Sometimes I take them out to the park or to the mall. Sometimes Troy comes with me. He misses you too."

I crush Hope to me in a hug. She equates the mall with the inner circles of Hell, and she and Troy had no obligation to do any of that, but they did. For me. I hear Davis coming back down the stairs, but I can't bring myself to leave just yet.

"Thank you," I say into her hair.

"You're welcome," she says quietly. "It helped me too."

I detach myself and open the window just as a knock sounds on the door, and Davis pokes his head in before either of us can move. He's still dressed for work, but his clothes are wrinkled and dirty, dark circles under his eyes as evidence that he hasn't slept at all. His jaw drops when he sees me standing by the window, and I freeze, unsure of what to do or say.

Hope bites her bottom lip. "Hey, Davis. Micah's back. He was just stopping by to, um...ask me to prom."

Davis' face reddens, but he looks like he's working hard to pull his expression back to neutral. "Oh. Well, that's...something. When did you get back, Micah?"

"Last night. Sorry to bother you so early in the morning."

"Yeah." He rubs his forehead distractedly. "Hope, you'd better get ready for school. Did you get all of your homework done?"

She frowns. "Davis, it's Saturday. Are you okay? Where have you been?"

"Yeah. Everything's fine. I went out for a walk." He averts his gaze. "Had to work through some stuff."

"Anything I can do to help?" The worry lines in Hope's forehead deepen.

"No, just work stuff. I'm cool, just tired." He yawns like he's punctuating the statement. "I'll leave you two to say your goodbyes." He starts to pull the door shut behind him but hesitates before ducking out the entire way. "And Micah? Please don't sneak through her window anymore. You can come and go through the front door from now on."

Hope shakes her head when he's gone. "Well, that was awkward. And completely crazy."

I smile at her. "Which part was crazy?"

"Pretty much the entire night, I think." She looks down at the floor. "I'm sorry I said that about prom. It was the first thing that popped into my head."

"I was planning on asking you for real," I say with some regret. "Unless," I add as an afterthought, "someone else asked you to go."

"No," she says quickly. "I mean, Jonathan offered to take me, but that's just because I didn't have a date."

My hackles rise, and I hate it. Feeling jealous. It's not me.

"Micah, you've got so much going on right now." Hope takes my hand, her cheeks spotting with color. "You flew here straight from Alaska to be with me. I just spent the entire night in your arms and woke up with you. That's way more amazing than any kind of sucky dance where I'd have to wear fancy formal heels."

I laugh a little, but the thought of Jonathan asking Hope to prom still sits under my skin like an irritant. "You could wear sneakers under your fancy formal dress."

She wrinkles her nose. "You really want to go to prom?"

"You'd really say no if I asked you?" I counter, searching her face and seeing that she's serious. But I add anyway, "Promise me you aren't just saying this." I can't bring myself to say the rest, that I hope it's not because she wants to go with *him.*

"Cross my heart. But you're very sweet for not asking."

She smiles and puts her hands on my shoulders, and I pull her close and touch my forehead to hers before breaking away. "Are you going to get in trouble later for me being here?"

"You mean Davis? He seemed too tired to honestly care." She takes my hand and leads me across the room. "I'll walk you to the front door."

We don't make a big deal about me leaving this time – I don't say goodbye because I'll be back soon, and she doesn't either. My camouflage settles over me as I take off, my wings pure *deimos* and not fire this time, and I catch a slight sense of a guardian as I circle low over Hope's house. Even though she can't see me, Raleigh steps out from the shadows, shielding her hand over her eyes as she looks into the sky.

I'm not surprised. Not totally pissed off that she was probably spying on us all night, either. Raleigh told me she's been watching over Hope and Davis, and strangely enough, I feel better knowing that she's there.

21

J'anathan

Raleigh. She's not here. I scour the church for her, my concern ramping up with each room I hit. The main chamber is cluttered with her personal possessions, and I take note of her collection of custom-made swords carefully laid out by the computer station.

She's more than capable of taking care of herself, but I feel like I'm pushing the limits of my emotional control right now. I have too many people to worry about. Raleigh. Hope. Davis. Not to mention my entire constituency.

Davis had dozed off for the first quarter of the ride, but he stayed true to his word and asked me questions about his abilities for the next half. He silently mulled over everything for the last leg of our journey and had me drop him off at his office so he could get his car. In retrospect, I probably should have dropped him off at his house so I could make sure he was all right. And check on Hope.

But first Raleigh, who had promised me she would stay in the sanctuary. I try to call her but it goes straight to her voicemail. I remember the Pathicomm and try that next.

"I am back, but you are not here. Is all well?"

There's no response, and my head fills with improbable explanations. She was abducted. Tricia came back and engaged her in battle. She sought out a guardian ward and went to Asphodel to plead her case.

These thoughts are far from productive. I storm back down the concealed spiral staircase, looking for a message that I overlooked or any clues to where she might have gone. If Tricia again broke our agreement and did something to Raleigh, I will challenge her myself, with or without the backing of the guardians.

I'm in the main chamber of the sanctuary when Raleigh's presence spreads through me like warmth. Her footsteps hurry down the stone steps, and I move to meet her in the antechamber just as she leaps down the last flight.

I catch her by her arms before she collides with me, and she gasps. "Jonathan —"

"Raleigh, you were supposed to wait for me here," I interrupt, peering at her. Her gaze is wild, worry lines creasing her brow. "What happened? Did Tricia do something else?"

"No." She heaves another breath, waving a slender hand to dismiss the notion. "Micah's back."

"What?" I step back, my stomach dropping. "Are you absolutely certain?"

"Yes, I'm sure. I just met him." She hesitates. "At Hope's house."

I hiss under my breath, but it's more of an instinctual reaction than anything. Naturally Micah would go straight to Hope if he was back.

"Impeccably bad timing. Were they out where people could see them?"

She blinks up at me, and I realize I'm still holding onto her arms. I release her and step back, desperately searching for some of that calm.

"No. They were in her house," she replies. "Her bedroom, to be exact."

I close my eyes at this news. Not that this should surprise me either, but picturing this is nearly more disturbing as Micah being back in the first place.

"I'll talk to Hope," I say firmly. "I need to somehow convince her to get him to leave the city again, or the guardians will put him on the dissection table."

"Will you tell her that you gave his name to the guardians in the first place?"

"If I absolutely need to."

"Do you honestly think she'll listen? Or that he will?" She presses her lips together. "I got the distinct impression that he doesn't like you. Less than any demon would like a guardian, I mean."

"I'm not surprised," I say dryly. "Given our history."

"Oh, and about Davis. He wasn't at home for most of the night."

"Yes, he was with me." I finally think I know what I have to do first and foremost, and I head back into the main chamber with Raleigh hot on my heels.

"He was with *you*?" She peels off her coat and perches on the edge of the couch as if waiting for an explanation, but I don't elaborate.

I take out the *clavis* from my jacket, holding it firmly in my palm with equally firm resolve. It's obelisk-shaped and made of a dark metal that's unlike anything I've ever encountered on earth. It's lighter, stronger, incredibly sensitive to the holder's temperature. Small vibrations emanate from it that send a chill up my arm, and I sit down on the floor cross-legged as I'd seen Christianna once do.

Raleigh watches, her green eyes wide as I place the stone in the center of the room within the circle of unlit candles. "What are you doing?"

"Given the newest developments, I'm going to speak with Arete."

"Right now?" She jumps off the couch. "Tell me what I can do to help."

I scan around the room, simultaneously collecting my thoughts. No one except for the wards of Asphodel are supposed to directly communicate with Arete or Raphael – whenever I've had to petition the Praxidikai in the past, I've had to go through one of the other wards. But Christianna shared with me the secret of how to do it.

"I need this place to be devoid of any signal when I do this. Light the candles and power down everything that has electricity running to it."

"Of course."

Raleigh moves briskly around the room, lighting the candles first and then busying herself with the other preparations. I concentrate on the flame, my thoughts centering on the *clavis*. And on the last time I saw Christianna.

"Are you going to work all night or are you going to join me?" Christianna stood in the doorway to my home office, her arms crossed and toe of one of her shoes tapping impatiently.

I ignored her, frowning at my laptop at the latest report that Raleigh sent. Normally we met in person, but Raleigh logged this one into our computer system, meaning that it was urgent. For security purposes, it was written as a news story, using keywords that only she and I would recognize. I worked through the first part of it. A dead body was found in a dumpster outside of a restaurant earlier tonight…

Christianna sidled over and slid her arms over my shoulders, and I hit the button on my monitor to kill the screen.

"Jonathan," she whispered into my ear. "I can't stay in this realm forever. The clavis is anxious for me to return home soon."

I spun the chair around to face her, taking her small hands in mine. Her long brown hair fell like a curtain between us, and I brushed it back from her face. For whatever reason, she was good at hiding her emotions from me, a fact that attracted me to her in the first place. When I was with her, I could enjoy the quiet. But that night her golden eyes were fluid and shifting colors as they did whenever she felt something strong.

"How can an inanimate object be anxious for anything?" I teased.

"When Arete opens a passageway, the clavis responds to the energy of the collective." She sat on my lap, all of her tension releasing as though giving a full-body sigh. "So we'd better make the most of this night."

I leaned in and kissed her just below her ear. "Call up Arete and tell her that you're indisposed," I said against her skin. "And that you shall be indisposed for another century or so."

She laughed, the sound free and lyrical. "One does not merely call up Arete to chat. Besides, there is too much interference in here for me to speak to her."

I drew back and smiled a little, knowing that I was about to get one of her lessons about Asphodel ways. "Interference such as myself?"

"Yes, you are interfering in lovely ways." Her fingers trailed through my hair. "I meant anything remotely modern."

"No one has ever called me modern before," I mused.

"The Praxidikai are bound by tradition." She traced a path with her fingertip to my shirt collar. "By much decorum. This realm has become very different from theirs over time. There's too much interference here. The modern world is so glaring and excessive."

"I've never been called glaring or excessive, either," I added.

"I was excluding you from that description." She leaned forward and kissed me, lightly and sweet at first but then with quickly growing ardor. I vaguely wondered if she ever let go and loved anyone like this in Asphodel.

She broke off the kiss immediately, the shade of her eyes tempestuous. Christianna had the gift of reading thoughts, and I was always careful to keep mine hidden from her. But evidently I let that one slip.

"No," she said somberly. "Physical love has no place in Asphodel. The collective light is all around you when you're there. It becomes you. It is love and all things worth living for."

I used to think love was worth dying for, but I didn't know if I felt that way anymore.

The color of her eyes shifted again as she looked at me with sadness. "You need to learn how to embrace your light, Jonathan. Perhaps you should come with me to Asphodel for a time. It would be good for you."

I didn't answer. My leg suddenly started to heat up because of the clavis that she had strapped to her thigh. She jumped up and cursed, yanking the skirt of her dress high enough to remove the black stone from the holster. "Oh no. This is most unusual. Arete wishes to speak with me."

I stood up too, knowing that if she left, it likely would be another century before I'd see her again. But if I felt anything, it was only mild regret. Christianna was a friend, and perhaps a bit more when we were able to steal a moment or two together. But I never truly let her into my heart, and I doubt that she did for me either.

"I'll leave you then," I say. "I'd hate to be a source of interference."

The gold in her eyes flashed. "Stay. I'll speak with her here. Can you cut the power to your building? And a peaceful place would be best."

"Done." I was already out in the hallway. "Go into my bedroom if you wish for peace."

When I returned after hitting all of the breakers in the building, Christianna was sitting on my bedroom floor with the clavis in hand, the dark room gently punctuated by the flame from one of my candles. The room was full of energy, the light and darkness mixing with the energy of the collective.

"Yes, Arete. I understand what I need to do . . ." I heard her whisper.

For the first time since I met her, I could feel her emotions, and they overwhelmed me. Deep sorrow over whatever task Arete asked her to complete.

I need several moments to shake off the sorrow from that day. I never knew what Arete had said to Christianna, but I suspect that's when she received the orders to destroy the gateway to Asphodel. She was no fool, and she knew that putting out so much energy would lead to her ultimate demise.

When I open my eyes, Raleigh's standing with her arms crossed in the doorway leading to the antechamber, much as Christianna had been in the beginning of my memory. The difference is in how I feel about it. I want Raleigh to be here.

"Do you want me to leave?" she asks softly, and I detect the slightest tremor in her voice.

"No. Come here."

I beckon to her, and she approaches slowly, like she's wary of the *clavis*. Small vibrations make it hum on the stone floor as though it's already receiving a signal from the collective.

"Stay with me," I say. "You should be here when she gives me an answer."

"My trial is over two weeks away." She attempts a smile as she sinks to sit cross-legged opposite me. "But I suppose I might as well receive the ultimate verdict from the one that matters."

I reach out and take her hand, struck again with how much of her emotion she wears on her sleeve. Optimism and anxiety run through her veins simultaneously, vivid and strong, and I catch myself wishing I had that much passion.

I draw on her strength, breathing in and feeling the strength of the collective energy of guardians. It's all around us, and the oblong black stone rattles against the floor.

"Arete, I beseech you. I need to be heard. I need your assistance."

"*Jonathan Drapier. This is most unexpected.*"

Arete's voice is like the echo of a whisper, and Raleigh starts when she hears it. I realize that we're both still wearing the Pathicomm and she can hear the immortal guardian's thoughts too.

"Forgive me, Arete." I bow my head even though she can't see me. "It is of utmost importance that I speak to you."

"*You are in possession of my clavis. You need to deliver it to a ward.*" Her presence begins to fade away, and I panic.

"No!" I protest, and Raleigh jumps again. But my insolence earns Arete's attention again, and my sense of her immediately strengthens. "There is a great danger to the collective occurring on this realm," I say. "It is my duty to report this to the Praxidikai."

A pause, then, "*I am listening.*"

"The Impiorum is creating a new breed of Seraphim, the race of demons that you yourself destroyed centuries ago." I take a mental equivalent of a deep breath. "The guardians in my realm seek to do the converse in retaliation."

There's only silence now, and Raleigh's grip on my hands tightens until we hear Arete speak again.

"*I am aware of the imbalance in Asphodel and am grateful to know the cause. You asked for my help. What do you ask of me in return for this information?*"

The response is cold and detached. Not what I expected. I remember what Christianna said about decorum, and I search for the words that will placate her.

"Arete, mother of all guardians. I ask for your help for guardians and humans alike. Bind the light and the darkness so it can no longer mix. This practice must be stopped, and those chimera restored to their original condition."

I know Arete would never intervene in the actual trial. The only solution is for her to bind the powers that be and keep them pure. This was always Arete's vision, and it would also return Hope to being a guardian. I can feel Raleigh's questioning gaze on me and know she must have picked up on this additional request, but I don't say anything.

We wait for Arete's response, both sitting as still as stone. Her whisper is soft but has the impact of thunder when she finally replies.

"*No. The forces will equilibrate of their own accord.*"

My heart plummets.

"But what of the *Seraphim?*"

"*The Seraphim shall met their appropriate fate when the time comes.*"

"And what of the fate of those guardians in my sector?"

"*Their fate is incidental to the good of the whole. Unless Raphael convinces me otherwise, I shall not intervene in this manner.*"

Raleigh draws her hand away from mine as I throw another plea, "Please, Arete. I beg you to reconsider."

"The key to sustaining all life is harmony, Jonathan Drapier. Believe, and it will ultimately be so."

Arete's presence fades, an echoing emptiness settling in my heart. I lower the *clavis* and look at Raleigh as she simultaneously searches my face. She drops her head before scrambling up and walking away.

I leap up too. "All is not lost. I promise you."

She faces away from me, brushing her fingertips through her hair in a distracted gesture. "You can't promise things out of your control, and this situation is out of your control."

"Raleigh, if I need to go to Asphodel myself to argue my case, I will."

She shoots me a sharp look, but her emotions are carefully sequestered from me for once. "Arete already gave you her answer."

She's moving so quickly I can hardly see her, from her computer station to the light controls, to the center of the room to blow out the candles. She knocks over the table, the candles rolling, and I catch the ones that are still lit and extinguish them. I've stood by her and watched her become such a formidable warrior over the years. Even on the night when she took Rowan's head, she was furious and determined and vengeful, not panicked and out of control like this. Never like this.

I move to intercept her, and she whirls around, stumbling into me in her haste so her hand is braced against my chest. Her eyes widen, her breath leaving her as a gasp, and my arm winds around her waist to steady her. I hold her close and don't let her go.

"It is never pointless to try, not when it comes to you."

Her cheeks flush with heat. "Why? Why not when it comes to me?"

Because she reads me like no one else can. Because I've known her for only a century but I can't imagine a day without her.

"Because you are one of my oldest friends," I say.

Hurt flashes through her, briefly but just enough for me to feel. Her body tenses up, and she pulls away from me, her eyes focused on the wall. "You can't put yourself at risk for me." She slips back into a slight English accent like she sometimes does when she's under duress. "You need to get the directorship back from Tricia."

"Perhaps so." I don't know why she's refusing to look at me. I can't get a good sense of her emotions anymore, as though she's locked everything down.

"I need to go out for a drive, blast my music, drown my thoughts. *Something.*" She heads for the doorway, hesitating only briefly. "Where did you park my car?"

All of my instincts tell me to chase her, but my muscles lock in place. I hear myself say, "It's still in Albany."

She makes a sound in the back of her throat that sounds like a half-sob, half-hiccup.

"Your motorcycle?" I suggest.

She furrows her brow. "I suppose I'll have to."

I try again. "Do you need a sparring session?"

"Don't you have to go speak to Hope?" she counters.

Her emotions may be sequestered, but I still take note of her stiff posture and the strain around her eyes. "You can try to kill me," I offer. "It might help."

The faintest smile touches her lips, and she nods her assent.

"Yes. Trying to kill you might do the trick."

22

Micah

I get to the University at Albany campus by seven-thirty. The only instructions Cael gave me were to go to something called the quad and wait for the scouts, but as I circle around the campus from above, I spot about fifteen different buildings that could be described as being a "quad."

The sun flashes against the glass front of a large building that I'm betting is the library. My camouflage sheds as soon as I touch down on the side of the building, and I head inside and in search of the computers.

"You shall return home to me, one way or another...."

I shudder at the memory of Vahni's words. The library reminds me a little of the temple of the Praxidikai with its chilly interior, high roof, and pretentious pillars. Only they don't have internet access in Asphodel because all they have to do is send Vahni into my head to check things out.

I walk by signs announcing the library's hours during final exam week, and drop my bag at one of the computer stations. The first one I try asks for a login and password. I try my luck with the next one over but get the same thing, earning a curious look from a girl sitting two chairs over. Dumb of me for not thinking about the fact I'd need an account, but I'm out of practice. The only time I'd used a computer in Alaska was when I had to do my homework, and I was limited to using all of the alliance's secure databases for research. Only the intel guys ever had access to the real world.

The girl that's watching me plunks herself down in the chair next to me, flipping back long brown hair and smiling. I ignore her, and she sips from a Starbucks to-go cup I doubt she's supposed to have in here.

"Hey. You get locked out of your account?"

"Something like that."

She lifts an eyebrow as she sets down her coffee. "Okay, so you know you can use the guest login, right?"

"Uh, no."

"Use 'guest' for the login, and try this…" She leans over me to my computer to type in the password, her arm pressing against my arm. My consciousness floods with her scent and her body heat, and I brace myself for it. The urge to feed on souls has gotten better since training with the alliance, but I still feel it when I'm close to people like this. I haven't fed since Alaska, and I know my *deimos* will egg me on, that it'll tempt me to do my worst.

But it doesn't happen this time.

She says something else, probably the password, but I miss it. "Hey. You okay?" she asks, and now she sounds a little annoyed.

"Yeah, sorry. Thanks for your help. Just pulled an all-nighter." It's not even a lie.

She literally bats her eyelashes at me. "Oh really? Good for you. I never could do that."

I have an internet browser open and do my very best to ignore her, but she doesn't go away. Her gaze is like heat as it roams over me, and I tense up. Sorry, wrong guy. This one happens to be taken, and is also tired and irritated as hell.

I clamp my mouth shut before I say something I regret, some of the tension falling from my shoulders when she digs into her backpack for a notebook. The U at Albany's website comes up immediately, and I navigate through until I get to a campus map. Four dormitories that are officially named some sort of "quad," and they're in the corners of the area where all of the academic buildings lie. One more quick search on Google and I'm done.

I push my chair back, and the brunette looks over at me with a smile. "Hey, so if you want to hang out this week, I'll be around. Got to take a final tomorrow. My luck. Last day of finals week."

"Good luck with your final, but I have a girlfriend."

She shrugs, not even missing a beat. "Well, in case you decide you don't want to be exclusive...." She slides a page from her notebook onto the table with her number and name, sliding her hand onto my thigh at the same time, and all of my civility goes straight out the window.

I toss her a sideways glance, throwing her my thoughts while I'm at it.

Get your damned hands off me. I have work to do, and you're the last thing I want to deal with right now.

She yanks her hand back, drawing in a sharp breath. She heard me, and I don't care. I log out of the computer, looking up just in time to see her to stomp off in a huff and mutter a few insults for good measure.

I shake my head and grab my backpack as a low chuckle sounds from behind me.

The skin on the back of my neck pricks in a familiar way, and I look over my shoulder to see the source of the laughter. A muscular black guy with sculpted hair is eyeing me from the archway to the room, and as soon as we make eye contact, his thoughts echo in my head.

You must be one of us.

I stand up and throw back, *What group are you from?*

His jaw tightens, just slightly but enough for me to catch. *You're on my territory. Identify yourself first.*

Micah Condie. I was sent here by Cael Parsons.

His hazel eyes brighten with recognition. *I'm Eli. I've been waiting for you. Come with me.*

Evidently he doesn't need to see my I.D. And there's no code phrase to get in with the group. I half-expected one, but then again my buddy Troy and I used to watch too many espionage movies. Troy, my best friend since fourth grade and on the long list of people I need to see the next time I'm back in Buffalo.

Eli and I walk over to the quad on the northwest part of the campus, and we talk using words for almost the entire way. Even though he'd plucked my thoughts out of the air in the library, he's like me in needing eye contact to speak telepathically.

"You picked me out pretty fast," I say. "How did you know I'd be in the library?"

"Didn't." He shrugs. "I'm a scout. It's what I do."

I nod, understanding this. "I used to be a scout in Cael's group."

He doesn't say anything as we pass a group of women going to their finals. One of them smiles and says hi to Eli by name, and he smiles and nods back.

"College campuses come with their share of challenges," he says with a wink, but then his smile dies. "How much did Cael tell you?"

"He told me you guys took a hit last week or so because of the Impiorum mercenaries?"

He swipes a card into the outside door of the quad, and the door unlocks with a click. "Yeah, that's one way of putting it. Honestly, your timing is...interesting, so don't be shocked."

We step into the lobby of the dorms, and I don't have a chance to ask Eli what he means. It's total chaos with people moving boxes and piles of junk down the two stairwells leading into the main lobby. I move out of the way as two guys barrel past us carrying the frame of a futon and a giant beanbag. I don't know if this is what Eli was talking about, but with finals week almost over, some of the residents are already moving out for the summer.

Eli leads me up the stairs and down the narrow hallway. We have to walk single file to make it through all of the stuff piled outside of the rooms, and despite the noise in the hallway, his silence is stifling.

The farther we go, the worse vibes I have about being here. A warning goes off in my head that he shouldn't be going this way. That there's danger ahead.

"Eli, wait. I have a bad feeling about this place."

He stops at another door that looks like it requires swipe key access, but this time he holds his hand in front of it instead of a card. It opens with a click, and he holds it open for me with a smile.

Or maybe it's a grimace.

"Welcome to Hell," he says.

~✖~

Interesting timing is an understatement. The quad looks like the aftermath of wartime. We pass by room after room, and clothes and other personal belongings are scattered on the floors and hanging out of drawers. It's like the previous residents left in a huge hurry, but some of the other rooms are untouched. There's hardly anyone left. In total, I count twelve guys including Eli.

Some of the carpets have what look like dried blood on them.

"The mercenaries found us last week," he informs me. "The only ones that remain from our group are the guys that happened to be out on scouting missions and a couple of others."

I feel a pit form in my stomach. "So everyone ran? Where did they go?"

He slants me a sharp glance, like I should already know the answer. "Some of them ran, and we don't know where they went or if they're alive. The rest of them I found here when we got back from our last scouting missions. Destroyed."

Meaning dead. Cael hadn't told me that it would be this bad, but maybe they didn't tell him. Why did they even agree to take me if the situation was this messed up?

"So are you in charge?" I frown, biting back my other question for now.

He stops walking by the entrance to a lounge, shifting uncomfortably on his feet. "No. Like I told you, I'm a scout. We don't exactly have a leader at the moment."

He heads into a big TV lounge, and I follow. The lounge is almost as messy as the entire situation with computer equipment and boxes piled throughout the room. A young woman with short, spiky black hair is the only other person in here, and she sits perfectly still on an overstuffed chair with her profile facing us, whispering a string of words that I don't understand. Cael walks over to a table on the other side of the lounge and beckons to me to join him.

"Don't mind all this." He waves his hand to indicate the mess. "We're in the process of reorganizing."

"Who's she?" I keep my voice low despite the fact that the woman doesn't acknowledge our presence.

He leans back in his chair and rubs his hands over his eyes. "Melanie? She's our resident witch. There's a border spell over this part of the quad that deters anyone from crossing unless they have the right imprint." He holds up his palm.

At least that explains why my skin had been crawling on our way over. I should have known that's what it was because Cael had instilled border protection magic too. "So what happened?" I ask. "How did they find you?"

"They were somehow able to break through Melanie's spell." Eli glances over at her again, but she keeps whispering the string of words. "Either they had a more powerful witch than she is –

which I actually doubt – or someone was keeping surveillance on the quad without us knowing."

"Don't you always teleport out? That's what we did in Alaska so no one could follow us back to the stronghold."

"We don't have teleporters. Never have. Hold on." He stands up and grabs his phone from his pocket, walking away to take the call.

Oh man. No leader, no teleporters. Using what look like normal cell phones to communicate. This whole situation is jacked up. But now that I'm here, I can't exactly ditch out on the group. Or what's left of it. They obviously need more people to help them, and I'm guessing this is why Cael sent me here in the first place. Because he knew I would.

Eli comes back to the table after a minute, his leg bouncing under the table with nervous energy. He fixes me with his gaze like he's sizing me up, and this starts to feel like a job interview – a really weird interview with Melanie continually whispering in the background – but I'm not totally sure who's interviewing whom.

"So what can I do?" I ask. "Do you need me to help with scouting?"

He leans forward, a shine in his eyes. "When I spoke to Cael yesterday, he said you have a knack for strategy and that you could help us in our relocation efforts."

"A knack for strategy. Me?" I almost look over my shoulder to make sure that he's not talking to someone behind me. "I just barely finished my high school requirements."

"But you have experience." I must look doubtful, because he adds, "We're sort of a grassroots movement here. We communicate with the Alaska group, but we didn't train with them. You did, and you actually know how they ran things. You lived it. You can help us rebuild."

He doesn't break eye contact, not even when two of the guys I'd noticed earlier walk into the lounge. One of them shoots me an openly curious look, and the other addresses Eli.

"Got the U-Haul downstairs, boss," he says. "It's just like the rest of 'em that are parked by the curb."

Eli presses his lips together in annoyance. "Not the boss. But that's good. Start loading while I finish filling in Micah here, and we'll join you in a minute."

They start grabbing boxes and hauling them out, and I watch them. "Wait. What's going on?"

"We're leaving this place. All of the residents are packing up and moving out this week, so we won't draw undue attention to ourselves if we leave now."

"To go where?"

"The more remote the location, the better," he says. "We're going to head east to a place off the beaten path in Vermont or possibly New Hampshire. The recommendation came from your old partner? Jehoel?"

I bristle at the mention of Jehoel. It's not just because the recommendation is coming from *him* but because this is something I've fundamentally disagreed with from the start. The entire purpose of the alliance is to help demons make the break with the Impiorum. We need to go toward the source, not away from it.

"Sorry, but I disagree about heading east."

It's Eli's turn to look dubious. "Where do you suggest?"

"The Impiorum is in Buffalo. According to my sources there, the mercenaries aren't," I say, thinking of Raleigh specifically. "Our impact will be greater if we're closer to the source, especially if we don't have teleporters to move us in and out. And they wouldn't ever suspect it if we had a spell powerful enough to conceal us. I say we head for Buffalo."

Eli frowns, but I can tell that he's considering everything I'm saying.

"I need to go back there tonight anyway. I'll go ahead and scout for a place," I offer.

"You understand that most of us defected from there," he says. "The guys won't be anxious to return."

"I get that. But the alliance is about helping others like us," I point out.

"I agree, but hmm. I don't know…" He scratches his ear, his expression conflicted. "Melanie, what do you think?"

Melanie turns her head to look at me the first time, her eyes a startling shade of icy blue. The two of them seem to have a moment of silent communication before she slowly rises from her chair and limps over to us. I notice multiple fading bruises and deep but healing gashes on her arms.

"She was here when the raid happened," Eli murmurs before I can ask. "She used her magic to make the mercenaries believe she was dead, and she's damned lucky that they left her in one piece." He pauses and adds, "I'm lucky too."

Melanie comes to a stop in front of him, and Eli takes her hand. "Melanie, this is Micah. Micah, this is Melanie, my wife."

"Your wife?" I blurt out.

How is that possible? I glance back and forth between them, and I see the way he looks at her and the way she looks back at him. Eli reaches out to her, and she takes his hand and smiles.

She's tall, but compared to Eli, she's tiny. She has a small scar on the highest part of her cheekbone, but from the way the skin is stretched over it, it doesn't look new. Her gaze coolly sweeps over me while I try not to stare. I can't even imagine what she went through when the raid happened, but when she reaches out and takes my hand, I pick up a sense of her energy crackling beneath her exterior. She's obviously not someone who should be underestimated.

"Eli? What's she doing?"

"She's just looking to see what kind of powers you have," he explains. "It won't hurt."

Melanie holds onto my hand and scrutinizes me in silence while I try not to freak out. The last time anything like this happened, it was with Isabela, and it felt like she was cutting me apart with a scalpel. But Melanie just stares at me while murmuring something in a different tongue, and she finally drops my hand.

"He has very unusual powers," she says to Eli. "I can tell from his *deimos* that he's like you and the others. He doesn't harm others when he takes what he needs to survive." Her gaze rises to meet mine, and I can read her satisfaction. "He has pure intentions."

"Thanks, babe." He gives her a tight squeeze before releasing her and faces me with an approving smile. Looks like I passed the interview. "All right. We'll postpone our departure until we can figure out a place to locate in Buffalo. But it won't be safe for us to stay here for long."

"Give me til the morning," I say. "I already have some ideas of where we can hide out."

His eyebrows lift in surprise, but he nods once. "Okay. That'll give me time to brief everyone on our change of plans and let everyone recharge. We've been scrambling non-stop since last week."

For the first time, it hits me that I'm saying "we" and also that Eli's including me in all of this. I never felt like I belonged in Alaska, and maybe it was because of my old power to make the mark. Or maybe it was because of me, like Ben said. And this is crazy – all of this is totally crazy – but I already feel more in my skin being here with Eli and Melanie in this destroyed lounge than I ever did with Cael's entire group.

"Sounds good," I agree.

We both look down the hallway as we hear it at the same time. Someone's outside trying the door to the quad, the one that has the border spell. At first I think it's one of the two guys that had been hauling things down to the truck, but then I hear someone call my name.

Melanie draws in a sharp breath, her eyes boring into mine with accusation.

"You allowed someone to follow you here."

Eli swears under his breath, moving to the hallway. "The mercenaries destroyed our outside surveillance cameras. Can't see who it is."

"I didn't —" I start to protest, but I hear a woman cry out, and Eli must have heard it too because he takes off down the hallway in a sprint. I follow on his heels, the sounds of a definite scuffle happening in the hallway beyond the door.

"Melanie had better be wrong about this," he says, glaring at me. "And she rarely is."

I have no idea who could be here that would know me, but I think about all of the Impiorum demons that want me dead. My instincts kick in, Vahni's fire burning just under my skin as I ready myself. If there's one lesson that I ever valued from Jehoel, it was that I should always be prepared to fight. Eli must be of the same mindset because I feel his *deimos* rise right before he yanks open the door.

The two guys that had been loading boxes have a third one in custody with arms bent behind his back.

It's Ben. Isabela's standing farther back in the hallway, and I can just make out the dark hair of Shandra as the little girl clings to her.

Ben gasps for breath, giving me a painful grin as I stare at them in disbelief.

"Hey, Micah. You said to find you if I was ever in town." He winces as one of the guys holding him tightens his grip on his arms. "So, do wanna call off your welcoming crew before they kill me, or what?"

23

Jonathan

Raleigh and I face off from opposite sides of the room, poised to kill each other.

"Light on or off?" she asks.

"Off."

She bends over to unzip her black knee-high boots, and I shrug out of my jacket and remove my shoes. There are faint stress lines around her mouth and eyes, but she moves calmly to the light switches on the far end of the studio. I know her well enough to see that the warrior Raleigh is in control right now, but also that she needs this sparring practice to release some of that stress.

She hits the switch and submerges us in darkness, and I hear her make a sound that might be a sigh. "All right. Let's do this."

"Magic or no?" I ask.

Her voice floats softly into the space. "Use magic at will."

"Weapons or no?"

"Anything goes."

I move silently in a wide semi-circle, sweeping the area with my senses to pick up her *lumen*, but she must have her telltale signal on lockdown just like I do. I revert back to my more basic senses, listening for signs of movement, my fingertips outstretched by my sides to pick up subtle vibrations in the air.

The faint scent of her citrus perfume wafts over to me from the side, but I stay perfectly still. I know she'll take the offensive as she always does, and I bide my time and wait for her to make a slip.

The air to my left shifts, and Raleigh's feet hit the floor a hair too hard. I give chase, projecting her location ahead to intercept her, but she changes directions on me at the last second. The whisper of fabric sounds from behind me instead, and I leap up just as something cuts through the air beneath me. Her knife strikes the wall with a thud a second later.

I reverse directions and follow the line of the knife's trajectory back to where it came from, and I find her. It's far too easy for me to catch her. As soon as I make contact, I can tell how off her concentration is.

My hands close around her shoulders and bring her down to the floor. Her body bucks as she throws me from her, but I use the momentum to flip her. She lands flat on her back with me pinioning her on top, gasping as the wind is knocked out of her. I have the physical advantage, and anticipating that her next move will be magic, I reach into my mind for a memory to quickly incapacitate her.

But her defenses crumble and release a torrent of emotion before I can. Raleigh's regret and despair are so vivid that it makes my heart twist with pain.

"There is no hope for me, is there?" Her breathing is rapid, but her tone is grave.

"Raleigh…" I can't see her, and I need to. I try to get up to turn on the lights, but her hand tightens on my arm and holds me in place.

"Don't. It's all right. I'm merely coming to terms with my ultimate end."

Her emotions are still flooding me, and I fight down the brief swell of panic in my gut at her words. "You do not need to come to terms with it right now. Because you aren't going to die."

She goes on as if I hadn't said anything. "It's really all right, you know. I've lived a much longer life than any mortal."

"There is no need to go through all of this until you know the outcome of the trial," I protest. We aren't sparring anymore, but the direction that this conversation is going feels more perilous.

She's silent for several breaths, and then I feel her release hers as a sigh. "You haven't come to terms with the possibility of your own end, have you, Jonathan? You believe you're going to walk this realm forever, that you need to pay penance for eternity."

She almost sounds like she's sorry for me, and I suppress my irritation. "What I believe about my fate has no bearing on yours," I say evenly.

Her body tenses as though she's affronted by my statement, and even though we can't see each other, I can sense her glaring back at me. "Well, guess what? You aren't an Eternal. You won't be here forever. And regardless of whether my end comes sooner or later, you need to accept that neither will I."

"I'm not going to let you die."

"Why? Because you think you'd be responsible? Like you think you're responsible for what happened to Adrienne?" she shoots back.

Her words finally work their way under my skin, slicing through me with a bitter edge and inflaming my temper. "This is has nothing to do with Adrienne," I snap.

"Then why, Jonathan? Because I'm so good at running reports for you? Or because we're such congenial work associates that you decided to consider me a friend?"

Her words are meant to be hurtful, but I bite my tongue before a quick rebuttal spills from my lips. The truth is…the truth is that I'm battling with the thought of losing her. The truth is that Raleigh is much more than a friend or associate. My reasons are purely selfish and more than I've ever admitted to her. More than I've admitted to myself.

"Because I need you," I say quietly.

"Yes, well. There are plenty of capable guardians that could fill my role –"

"No," I interrupt. "I do not mean any of that. I need *you*, Raleigh."

As soon as I say it, my anger subsides. I'm still braced on top of her, and her grip on my arm is like a vise. Her emotions are as tumultuous as a storm, regret paramount amongst them, but there's something else now there too.

My awareness centers on the tension in her muscles, the way her body presses against me with each breath, the subtle way that her hold on me changes. Her hand moves up my arm and then to my shoulder, her fingers trailing over my neck and raising the hairs on my skin. She exerts the slightest pressure to draw me closer, and my inhibitions shatter as I realize exactly how true it is.

I need her.

I can't think anymore, and I don't want to. I caress her face, tracing an invisible path across her cheek before moving in to kiss her. Her lips part as an invitation for more, and my soul ignites. Her hand clings to my arm like I'm her lifeline, her other hand raking through my hair. Every touch sends small charges through me, awakening feelings I thought were destroyed long ago.

She shifts her body so she's lying completely beneath me. I'm careful not to crush her with my weight, and I revel in her soft supple curves that yield against me, her sweet and wild scent, her strength. She's perfection.

The darkness surrounds us, absorbs all of my worries, overshadows everything else in the world except for her. So much uncertainty in this realm, but all I know right now is what she does to my heart.

"I've been waiting for decades for you to do that," she whispers. "But this seems like damned poor timing."

"You're not going to meet your end, Raleigh. I swear it." I brush back her hair from her neck, and she draws in her breath.

My fingers trace over her collarbone, my lips following to kiss her skin, and she releases her breath again as a sigh.

I've touched her like this before, but it's always been to check for wounds. Her fingers tremble as they start to unbutton my shirt, even though she's done it dozens of times to look for injuries. I follow the V-line of her shirt down until I caress the swell of her breast, and she arches against me. Desire sears through me like fire, and I can't remember how to breathe.

The sharp ding from the elevator sounds from the hallway outside the studio, and we both freeze.

I strain to hear any movement from outside, but the only things I can hear are the distant whir of the building's ventilation system and the soft swish of fabric against the wood floor as Raleigh shifts positions. I push up and off of her, taking her hand to help her up. We both sit still and listen, electricity and anticipation lingering between us like an unspoken promise.

"See?" she says, and there might be a smile on her lips. "Damned poor timing."

I squeeze her hand. "I would have to disagree."

"Another guardian? Or someone else?" she whispers. "I can't tell."

"I can't either." My senses are flooded with Raleigh and obscuring almost everything else.

She lets go of my hand, rising to a standing position and moving over to the light switches. I listen for a second more before getting up to join her in the small adjoining office. Raleigh's already frowning down at her security monitors by the time I get there, and I move to look over her shoulder at the various camera views — all of the building entryways, shots of the stairwells and rooftop, and the hallway outside the studio. We watch as the elevator doors slowly close, but the corridor is empty.

"An accidental stop on your floor perhaps," I muse. "Or do you think someone was scoping out your territory?"

She shrugs. "Could be the cleaning crews for the offices above."

We stay and watch the screen for another few minutes, but I can't see anything I'd consider suspicious, and my attention shifts to Raleigh rather than on the monitors. Her tawny locks are in disarray, her shirt falling off one shoulder. I reach out and slide it back in place, brushing back a strand of her hair and trailing my fingers over her skin.

Raleigh turns around to face me, her cheeks becoming rosy when she sees how close I am. She casts her gaze to the side in a way that's almost shy, and I take a step back and button my shirt again, wishing I didn't have to.

"So…" She clears her throat. "Are you going to try to talk to Hope? She should be out of school in fifteen minutes."

"That's the plan." I extend my hand, shooting her a crooked grin. "Mind giving me a ride?"

<hr />

Raleigh sprinkles *lumen* around school premises to distract the masses as she pulls into the student lot, but I doubt it will work. She and I are far too conspicuous on her Ducati, and she earns several bug-eyed stares from the boys walking toward their cars in the lot.

I dismount and take off my helmet. Right before we left Raleigh's studio, I'd called Hope and left her a message telling her to meet me in front of the school, and I scan the steady stream of students for her. Five minutes pass and still no sign of Hope despite the fact that her car is still here.

I try calling her again, but it goes directly to voicemail.

"I'm going in to find her. Mind waiting out here in case I miss her?"

Raleigh takes off her helmet too, shaking out her hair. "You're really going in there? High school is perilous," she teases.

I quirk an eyebrow. "I'm sure I will manage."

"Use the Pathicomm if you need me to rescue you," she says with a smile.

"How little confidence you have in me." I smile at her and start to walk away, but immediately turn back. Her eyes widen in surprise as I take her face in my hands and kiss her but then she sinks into me, grasping my arms and kissing me back. I break away from her long before I want to, flooded with emotions so sweet but also somewhat devastating.

My worries about her impending trial compound with the fact that things are different between us. Not that I wouldn't have done anything to save her before, but now my reasons are simply more clear.

"Be safe," I say very seriously.

"I'm not the one going into that hellhole." Her tone is light, her cheeks flushed. "Good luck."

I enter through the front doors of the school and immediately see what Raleigh means. It's like walking through a village that just experienced a raid, the students shouting to each other or throwing things back and forth as they run toward the exit. Papers and food wrappers fly to the ground in the wake of the mass exodus, and I narrowly dodge a football that whizzes by my head.

"All visitors must sign in at the front office," a surly voice says from behind me. A stubby thumb pokes me on the shoulder when I don't respond, and I turn around and find myself face-to-face with a rail-thin woman with pinched lips and watery eyes. My God, it's the 21st century female version of the viscount.

I don't have time for this, and I summon my *lumen* and spear her with a shot of energy. She blinks, the suspicion in her eyes abruptly gone.

"Yes," she says vaguely. "It is a lovely day."

"Do you know where I'd find Hope Gentry?"

She gives me a blank look, and I curse myself under my breath. I may have exerted too much of my power on this one.

"Hope Gentry…" Her eyes light up with recognition. "Oh, yes. Her locker is in the west hallway."

"Excellent. Thank you."

She blinks at me as though trying to figure out why she's talking to me, and I walk past before she can remember. I duck into an empty room and channel my energy into running, making it over to the west part of the school within seconds.

The only ones in the hallway are a couple that look like they're fused to one another and a girl with short brown hair that's juggling books by her locker. One book falls from her hands, and I speed over and pick it up.

"Ack!" She jumps and drops another one, and I reach down and catch it before it hits the ground. She gawks at me as I hand them back. "Um, thank you."

I suppress a grimace as she jams her books into her bag with no consideration for the bindings. It's a long shot, but I ask anyway, "I don't suppose you've seen Hope Gentry around here?"

Her eyes skate over my black suit and black dress shirt, and she gapes some more. "Are you her brother?"

I've been told I look older than nineteen, but to be mistaken for Davis? This girl obviously doesn't know Hope very well. I start to walk away.

"She said she was meeting you outside," she calls after me, and I stop. "You must have just missed her."

I puzzle over this information for a moment, finally figuring that Hope must have met up with Davis today. "Thank you," I say to the brunette, but out of distraction I slip into my old ways and give her a slight bow. Her jaw drops to the floor as I quickly make my departure.

I try calling Hope one more time as I exit the building, and this time she answers.

"Hey, I was just listening to your voicemail. I was about to call you." I hear music in the background and guess that she's already in Davis' car.

"Good, because we need to talk."

"I'm so sorry. Can it wait an hour? Davis and I have to go into the city to take care of some stuff because I just turned eighteen. Sounds very legal and exciting."

"Is Micah with you?"

There's a long silence on her end. My hand clenches around the phone, and I try to temper my frustration. This is going to cause her more pain, but in the grand scheme of things, I think Hope would agree that Micah's survival is also a big deal.

"Raleigh told you." Her tone is cautious now. "He's not with me, no. But he'll be back tonight. Why?"

"It can wait an hour. Call me when you're done with Davis." I take a deep breath and add, "Have fun, my dear."

"I'll try," she says more brightly. "Talk to you soon."

I jam my phone into my pocket and stalk over to the parking lot. But I come to an immediate stop when I see that Raleigh isn't at the motorcycle anymore.

"Raleigh," I think into the Pathicomm. *"Where are you?"*

The silence echoes in my head, my heart feeling like it slams into my throat when I see Raleigh's helmet. It's lying on the ground several meters from the Ducati, and I pick it up, grazing my hand over the new scratches on the enamel. My imagination concocts violent images that flash in my mind, of an ambush, a shadowy figure snatching Raleigh and tossing the helmet to the ground.

My eyes fix on a small splatter of blood next to the motorcycle, and my fears become real. I chase the trail, but it terminates several meters away.

"Raleigh!" I yell.

I spin around, my vision swimming as I scour my surroundings. The sun beats down on the asphalt, making everything falsely bright and distorted. All of the buses are gone now, the parking lot largely cleared except for a couple of stragglers that linger by the few remaining cars. They must have seen what happened here, must have seen *something*, but they carry out their conversations like everything is normal.

Everything feels wrong.

I rush over and ask the students if they saw Raleigh, but they stare back at me with dazed glances that are just as telling as any answer. Guardians took her, blanking out the memories of the witnesses just like I'd barely done to the hall monitor inside the school.

The keys are still in the ignition of the Ducati, and I get on and kick the motorcycle to life. I tear down the streets to the waterfront, the streets a blur and my mind on the brink of insanity by the time I get to Tricia's apartment building.

I leave the motorcycle on the street and speed inside, sprinting up the stairwell in a blur. I'm almost to Tricia's floor when I hear the voice in my head.

"Jonathan."

It's quick and desperate sounding and hardly more than a whisper, but I can tell that it's a male's voice. Whoever it is, he's using her Pathicomm to communicate with me.

"Who is this?" I demand.

"They took her."

I'm guessing this is someone on Tricia's team, very likely Raleigh's informant from the original incident at the warehouse. But I don't have time or the interest to ask who it is.

"Who took her? Where?"

"The guardians took her to trial early."

No. I'm out in the open air, but the world feels like it's closing in on me. This cannot be possible. Tricia is playing her games again to get the directorship. Only I know the truth – that this isn't a game, and it never was.

"Arete decreed it," the whisper adds.

Arete? My hopes lift slightly at this. *"Where is Raleigh?"* I repeat. *"And is she all right?"*

"She's all right, but she cannot speak to you. You have to hurry, Jonathan. They are about to convene."

I run back to Raleigh's motorcycle, the engine roaring and then purring as I start it up. *"Where is the trial being held?"*

"In the guardian warehouse where the incident occurred."

I'm left with only the weight of silence and my conflicting thoughts. Arete is involved, which must mean she had a change of heart. Still, if she does act, it will be for the greater good, not specifically to alter the course of Raleigh's fate in the trial.

For the sake of my own sanity, I force myself to concentrate on my physical surroundings. I speed through the side streets to avoid the city traffic, only the streets are full of high school kids walking home. I cut over through to one of the main avenues, but afternoon traffic is unusually thick. I tear up between the lanes, focusing on avoiding pedestrians. Trying to think only about the most direct route to Raleigh. Trying not to think about what she's going through at this very moment.

Trying not to think about any of the worst moments of my life because it's all about Raleigh this time. The horror screams through me despite my best efforts to keep it controlled. But I'm in control of nothing.

I hit the throttle and race the rest of the way to the guardian warehouse.

24

Micah

Everything feels like it's finally starting to come together, like I actually have things under control. A little ironic considering that we're all moving out tonight into unknown territory.

Ben's totally on board with the alliance and the plan to reestablish in Buffalo, and I told him I'd leave him with the Albany group for the afternoon so he can help them get ready. Right now he's crashed out on one of the couches in the lounge, exhausted from the travel that pushed him to the limits as a teleporter. Shandra is asleep on another one, and when Isabela approaches me, her voice so low that I have to strain to hear.

"Shandra and I will stay only as long as it takes for us to help the group settle in," she whispers. "I made a commitment to help Cael for a year."

"He told me," I whisper back. "But he didn't say that you'd be helping this group. Did he tell you to follow me here?"

"Yes." She lifts her shoulders in a shrug. "All part of his grand master plan, I suppose. Cael thinks through every move very carefully."

"Guess so. If he'd told me how bad things really were here, I would've had second thoughts." I add after a second, "He's a good leader."

She tilts her head slightly to the side. "You'll make a good leader, Micah. Shandra can see it in you, and I think Cael and Eli see it, too."

I blanch. "I'm not leading anything. I'm just helping out."

"You've brought everyone a new sense of purpose. Look at Ben and how he followed you here all the way from Alaska. It wasn't easy for him to do that, believe me. And Eli already looks to you for guidance."

Maybe there's a little bit of truth in that, but only in the sense of how I talked reason into Eli about some pretty basic stuff. "Ben followed me here because he's got misplaced hero-worship, and Eli's group has been in shambles for a week."

"You have a light within you that touches others."

She flashes a smile at me, but my answering smile is touched by the old cynical Micah. "Nope. Don't have any light in me. Fire maybe. I don't think I'm ready to be the leader of anything."

We're interrupted as Eli walks into the lounge with a cup of tea for Melanie. She's been working on new spells for the past two hours, and he sets the mug down on the floor next to her and comes over to me and Isabela.

"She senses a disturbance in energy in this realm," he says in a hushed voice, his attention shifting to Isabela. "Can you feel it?"

Isabela shakes her head, her eyes shadowed with concern. "No. That's well beyond my ability. I work more by sensing an energy disturbance in individuals."

I check my watch, and Eli notices. "Are you taking off?"

"Yeah, I'd better. I'll let you know what I find."

He furrows his brow. "Tomorrow's the last day of finals, and everyone will be moved out by the end of the day. We'll need to leave by then."

"Understood."

Ben comes back to life and drags himself off the couch, ambling over with a crooked smile on his face. "Hey, so before you go...."

I wonder what he's up to, but before I can ask, he pulls something from his jacket pocket and hands it to me.

"New and improved," he says proudly.

I weigh it in my hand. It looks and feels just like a phone.

"Better design than the bracelets. It's on a secure channel for use as a two-way comm if you need. It has a better range than the old ones, and if you accidentally activate it when you're too close, it won't shock you," he says. "I came up with the modifications myself."

"Nice." I stick it into my pocket. "I'll send you a location when I confirm the place in Buffalo." I give him a light hit on the shoulder. "You did good, Ben."

He grins at me, his face reddening a little at the compliment. "Ah, it was nothing. I like doing this sort of stuff."

"Here's your tech guy, right here," I say to Eli. "I'll see you guys later."

"Sounds good. Be careful out there," Eli calls out to me as I leave the lounge.

The two of them start talking about other gadgets Ben has up his sleeve, and I book out of the quad. It's just past three-forty in the afternoon when I hit the air, and I head straight for the address that Shandra gave me. It's an elementary school in the heart of the Bronx.

I walk past the front of the brick building as the bell rings and linger with some of the people waiting outside. The kids start pouring out of the doors, some of them heading off on bikes or walking home and others meeting up with their parents or older siblings. Nostalgia hits me hard because I used to wait for my younger brother to get out of school whenever my mom couldn't do it.

My mom, Eva Condie. The only one I've known my entire life. My nostalgia morphs to guilt before I walk inside, but I can't turn back now. I'm here, and I just gotta do this.

I look for a directory and find it in the first hallway. A bulletin board with photographs of all of the teachers, listed by name and grade. This is it. My heart races as I scan through the grades to find her name. But there's no Elizabeth Jakobs.

I know from experience that anyone who sees a stranger loitering around an elementary school is going to assume the worst, and I glance down the hallway in both directions to make sure no one is paying attention to me. I assumed that my mother worked here, that this is why Shandra gave me the address, but I was obviously wrong. Maybe she was one of the parents that was waiting to pick up her kid outside.

My stomach turns inside out. I never considered until now the possibility that she would have a family. But of course she would have started over after what happened with my father and me. She has a different life now. And I have no idea if I have any place in it.

"Excuse me. May I help you?"

Still tangled up in my thoughts, I turn to the source of the voice. A woman with dark brown hair and bright red lipstick gives me a friendly but cautious smile. She's wearing a suit, and I recognize her from the top of the directory. Her name is Ms. Jones, and she's the principal.

I push my hand through the tangled mess on top of my head. "Yes," I hear myself say. "I'm looking for my cousin. I think she works here." She frowns, and I add, "I haven't seen her in a really long time."

"Most of our staff is already gone for the day, but if she works here, I'd be happy to let her know you came by. Your cousin's name?" She looks me up and down, and I'm glad that I'd taken time at the dorms to wash my clothes.

"Elizabeth Jakobs."

"And your name is?" she prompts.

I feel like I'm one of the elementary school kids. "Micah. Micah Tokasz."

She holds up her index finger to tell me to wait, giving me the same friendly but cautious smile before walking away. My mouth goes dry as she steps into what looks like the front office. Several minutes pass, or maybe it just feels that way because my nerves are shot. I glance at the front doors, preparing to take flight in case the principal sends out security.

A woman steps out of the office, and I stare at her as she approaches me. Light brown hair pulled back into a long ponytail, intense blue eyes, heart-shaped face. She's dressed in scrubs like the school nurse and she looks young, like maybe in her early thirties. Way too young to be my mother.

The color drains from her face, and I can taste her fear like salt on my tongue. My throat dries up, and everything I'd planned on saying to her dies on the spot.

She doesn't smile. "Micah. It's been a long time."

～✕～

I sit across the booth from Elizabeth in the small corner cafe. My biological father hadn't ever talked about her, and sitting across from her right now feels like I'm living another person's life.

I remember this one day from high school, back when I was at Amherst High. There was this other kid in my class who was adopted, and I overheard him talking to his friends about how he found his birth mom. I was jealous at first, but think I eventually convinced myself I was happy I didn't have to go through all of that.

Elizabeth's eyes are downcast as she looks over the menu, and I don't want to be rude but can't stop staring. Her makeup is carefully done, heavy and almost like a mask. My initial impression of her sticks. She looks too young to be my mother, but maybe that has to do with whatever Isabela did to heal her.

I don't know what to call her, so I don't call her anything at all.

The server comes to bring out our drinks and take our orders. I take a sip of my water and hand the menu back to him without ordering anything.

"You're not getting anything? I thought teenagers are always hungry." She stops pouring creamer in her coffee and looks at me, dark blue eyes mirroring my own with curiosity. Some caution. A little bit of fear.

"I'm okay."

I take another drink of my water. She doesn't say anything more, and I sit and listen to the clinking of her spoon against her coffee cup.

"I'm sorry this is so difficult." She frowns. "I honestly never thought we'd ever meet."

"Difficult" doesn't even begin to describe it. I drop my gaze down to look at the table, willing myself to have low expectations. It doesn't work. Her hand stretches out on the table, and for a second I think she's reaching toward me but she grabs the pepper shaker instead. I imagined this would go differently, like when that kid in my school finally met his birth mom. He talked it up like it was the most amazing thing in the world, but maybe that was just his story-telling face. It was probably as awkward as hell.

She clears her throat. "I don't expect you to understand why I left you. But believe it or not, it would have been more dangerous for you if I hadn't."

Yeah, I get that, why my mother would have felt like she needed to go into hiding from the Impiorum. What I don't get is why she's been hiding out in New York City this entire time. I mean, if she was going to bail and run, why stay so close?

But I don't voice these questions. When Shandra gave me that piece of paper, it felt like a gift from God. But now my tongue is tied in knots, my doubts overwhelming everything else.

"Micah, you came to find me, not the other way around." She briefly shuts her eyes. "Sorry. That came out all wrong. I just meant, here we are after all this time. You must have some questions for me."

I nod. I do have so many questions, too many, but they all congeal into a giant lump. She waits for me, patiently, but I guess by the way she rubs her forehead that she's weary. Her directness throws me. I think I pictured her as being soft-spoken and sweet, and she's so unlike what I thought she'd be.

I finally get why this is awkward, why I'm so uncomfortable. It's because Elizabeth is totally the opposite of Eva Condie.

She takes a long drink of her coffee, the server arriving right at that moment with a bowl of soup and crackers. He asks me again if I want anything, and I shake my head, my stomach in a knot.

I'm suddenly aware of a rank smell from the direction of the kitchen, but Elizabeth is sipping her soup like she doesn't notice. I look around to see if anyone else does, but it's business as usual. One of the diners at the counter swivels on his stool to look at me, and my heart stops.

Jack. Jack Williamson, my old boss and mentor. My friend. But he's dead, his soul supposedly resting in the Sea of the Dead.

He pushes his hand through steely gray hair. "You going come to home soon, Micah? Because we need you back." His voice is a little rough, like he hasn't spoken in a while. He cocks an eyebrow at me, flashing me a smile, and I notice how white and perfectly straight his teeth are now.

I gawk at him, unable to respond. He was, or is, a ward of Asphodel. It's possible that they sent him back to this realm, but for him to show up here of all places? He's even dressed like he always was for work, in a suit and tie and dress shirt that's perfectly pressed.

"Why are you here?" I whisper.

Elizabeth's head whips up, her brow creasing. "Because you asked to speak with me."

Her tone is sharp, like she's reprimanding a bad dog or a smart-mouthed kid. Half my attention is still on Jack as he gets up from the stool and pushes himself away from the counter. That stench of death, what I picked up before, is definitely coming from him. His suit is a lot more wrinkled than I first thought, his hair thinner. I watch him out of the corner of my eye as he limps past our table, my skin crawling as I watch his transformation.

By the time he staggers out the door, he doesn't look like Jack at all.

"No, sorry," I say to her. "I just thought I saw…was just talking to myself."

"Fair enough." She sighs and puts her spoon down. "But while we're here, maybe you should use the time to ask me those questions."

"Okay." Even if I never see her again after this, I have to know, and I ask her what's been burning in my head the longest. "Did you ever try to find me?"

A grimace stretches her mouth. "No, but I thought about it. It was the hardest decision I've ever had to make, leaving both of you behind."

When I meet her gaze, I notice how some of her years finally show around her eyes. "Both of us? Me and who else? My *father?*"

"You and your brother."

What? Her words thunder through my head like an aftershock.

"A half-brother," she clarifies. "Born three years before you. His father and I divorced, and we had joint custody of him until we both remarried other people."

I have an older brother and discovered my mother, all in the same day. My head reels like I'm on a carnival ride. "What's his name? And is he like me?"

"His name is Christopher. And no, his father is completely human, not a..." She stops, her forehead creasing as she stares at me.

"He's not a Demon," I say. "I know what I am."

She tilts her head a little, like she's trying to focus on a spot inside me to see what makes me different from her. That's a totally different story that I don't know I'll ever get. How she got involved with my father and why she thought he was ever worth it.

So glad I didn't order anything to eat. I'm not hungry for anything but answers. "Do you know where he is?"

"I don't," she admits. "I stayed in contact with his father on and off for a while. But he cut off communications with me when I married your father. I tried to search for him a few years ago but couldn't find anything about him or my ex-husband."

Elizabeth tried to find my brother but she didn't try to find me. It hurts. Not gonna lie.

I watch as she plays with a sterling silver ring on her middle finger, turning it around and around. "Honestly, I think the Buffalo Impiorum found out and hunted him down," she says in a quiet voice.

Well, that's the answer to whether or not she knew about the evil demon organization. My mouth goes dry, and all the water in the world won't help it. "But you don't know for sure?"

She shakes her head. "I stopped looking. I didn't want the Impiorum to know I was searching."

My thoughts are like a cyclone. If the alliance can serve as a refuge for defectors, they can help others on the run from the Impiorum too. Cael kept on a couple of humans as part of the Alaska alliance, not just defectors.

This means I can help my brother. Assuming he's still alive.

Elizabeth hasn't touched her soup yet, and she doesn't look like she's going to. I shove back my chair, and she gazes up at me and blinks. "You look so much like your father."

"I'm nothing like him," I say firmly. "Do you want to know if he's alive or not? Christopher?" *My brother.*

She sips her coffee. "Too dangerous."

"It's dangerous," I agree, "assuming what you think happened to him actually happened. I'm heading to Buffalo. Do you want to come?"

Her cup lands on the saucer with a clatter. "What? I can't just up and leave. I have a life here. I have a husband."

It was impulsive of me to ask, and her response was instantaneous. I watch as her forehead creases, the hardness in her eyes becoming even more steely, and it's like she's twisting a knife in my gut. Despite how full the Condies made my childhood after they adopted me, I think that never knowing my biological mother always left a small part of me empty. But knowing she doesn't want anything to do with this — with me — just replaced that emptiness with a bleeding, jagged hole.

It's almost worse than thinking she was dead this whole time.

"I understand," I say even though I don't. I stand up, not wanting to ask any more questions. "It was nice to finally meet you."

Elizabeth stands up too, digging into her purse and throwing a ten down on the table. "When are you going?"

"What?"

"When are you going to Buffalo?" she repeats.

"Tonight."

She heads toward the exit without saying anything else, and I follow, not knowing why she bothered asking and not daring to hope. We'd walked here from the school, and she pauses on the sidewalk, looking up into the sky like the answers are up there in the clouds.

"I'll have to arrange to have a couple of days off of work. And figure out what to tell my husband," she says more to herself than to me, but then she gives me a pointed look. "I can come out in a couple of weeks to help you, but I won't be able to stay long."

"Really?" For a second I wonder if I heard her right, but she just gives me a tight smile. "That would be great."

She doesn't say anything to this, just looks up and down the street. "Where did you park your car? Or did you get here by other means?"

"I flew here," I admit.

"Oh?" She doesn't even blink. "Your father could do that too."

"If you don't want to drive the whole way to Buffalo, I can come back and...." I trail off, not knowing how that would work if I flew her back with me. When I fly with Hope, I usually hold her in my arms but the idea of doing that with my mother feels more awkward than the entire time we just spent at the restaurant.

She laughs and digs a pen and pad of sticky notes from her bag, and I can almost see a different, younger version of her. The woman that existed before she had to give up her sons and husband.

She scribbles down something and hands the sticky note to me. "My cell number. Call me when you get settled in there and are ready to do this." I take it from her, and she gives me a little grimace. "And thanks, but I'll take the train. I hated flying with your father. It always made me nauseous."

I nod. Just like how I felt when I used to make the jump with Jehoel. I look at the phone number and memorize it, and Elizabeth starts walking away.

"Thank you," I call out to her, and she stops and looks at me.

"For what?"

"For agreeing to talk to me. For telling me about Christopher and agreeing to help."

"It's nothing." She slips on her sunglasses, giving me a curt nod before turning away. "I owe you at least that much."

Elizabeth doesn't owe me anything, but I don't argue the point. She keeps walking, and I push my wings out and take to the sky.

25

Jonathan

The sentry sits as a silhouette against the sky, crouching on the roof of the warehouse like a gargoyle. Or perhaps like a harbinger of death.

I don't immediately recognize his brand of magic, but he's not a guardian or a demon. I get off of the Ducati and approach, my initial impression of him changing as I get a better look. If he is indeed a sentry, he's in the guise of a vagrant. Dirty hair, filthy clothes, taking occasional swigs from a bottle of Jack Daniels.

Every step that I try to take toward the warehouse makes me break out in a sweat, the compulsion to turn around almost irresistible. I look up at the drunkard, shielding my eyes against the sun.

"Let me through," I snarl. "Or I shall destroy you. I promise you."

He laughs and takes another drink, and the magic of his protective spell makes my feet drag against the gravel.

A magical being can always be countered in kind. I raise my hand and assault him with a shot of my *lumen*, and his facade ripples and shows me a glimpse of his true form. The ritualistic scars on his cheekbones stand out in contrast to his cleanly shaven face before he shifts back into his disguise. He's a warlock, and I'm betting that whatever's in the bottle in his hand isn't whiskey at all but part of his magic.

I take another step toward the warehouse but wobble on my legs. I grit my teeth and take another, losing my balance but managing to stay on my feet. A third step, and I fall to my knees.

All I can think about is Raleigh and how there's not enough magic in both worlds to keep me from getting through.

As though aware of all of the guardians converging upon one spot, Christianna's *clavis* is humming inside my jacket pocket. On impulse, I grab it, the energy's vibrations coursing through my arm as I stare up at the warlock. "You shall *Let. Me. Through.*"

I throw another strike with the *clavis* in hand, and the bottle in the warlock's hand explodes. Clear liquid rains down on the gravel, sizzling and frothing as it absorbs into the dirt beneath, and my feet feel bound to the spot as the warlock leaps down to the ground. He straightens from a slight crouch, his body broadening out from a scrawny frame to become barrel-chested. Grease and dirt fall away from his hair as it lengthens past his shoulders, and the glazed expression in his eyes hardens like flint, but they also hold respect.

"That key – it belongs to Arete. You're a ward of Asphodel?"

I flat out lie. "I am."

"And what is key to Arete?"

It sounds like a riddle, and I rack my brain for the answer. Something that any ward of Arete's should know.

I think of her last words to me, and I think I have it.

"Harmony."

The warlock inclines his head, and the strength immediately returns to my legs. I run to the door of the entrance, but my relief is short-lived as I process how I was granted entry. I assumed the warlock was part of the Chicago coalition, but his knowledge of Arete makes me think he might be a servant to the Praxidikai. Their presence here tonight could be very good or very bad.

Hope calls me on my phone just as I enter the building, but I ignore the call. This is the last place she should be.

My own hopes are at an all-time low when I step into the main room. The mood in here is murderous. I fight against a sea of guardians from the Buffalo and Chicago sectors to get near the front, some of my constituents jostling me and murmuring unkind things as I pass. They're all gathered in a circle around the middle, with the tribunal members making an arc of twelve in the very center.

Raleigh is dressed in royal blue from head-to-toe, standing on the exact spot where she shed Rowan's blood. The light from the high windows slices across half of her face, leaving her eyes masked in shadows. Her hands look as though they're bound behind her back by invisible restraints. Seeing her like this gives my system a shock, but I can't afford to wear my heart on my sleeve. Not now and not here. Not with Raleigh bearing the responsibility of what should have been mine.

I spot Tricia standing on the other side of the circle. She's also surrounded by guardians, and they're clinging to her like she's their salvation. Her gaze locks with mine before she looks away.

The magistrate steps forward from the shadows on the side of the room, and a hush falls over the crowd. She's wearing the long black formal robe for the proceedings, her dark hair pulled back in a severe manner from her face, her dark eyes gleaming as she crosses the slice of moonlight. Her face still displays the mark of youth, and I recognize her from the Chicago sector as being one of the elder guardians – an entire century older than me but forever trapped in a fifteen-year old body because of when she transformed.

"Raleigh Peyton, you are here to stand trial before your peers," the magistrate says in a clear, sweet voice. A good foot shorter than Raleigh and with her prim appearance, she's the antithesis to Raleigh. "Do you understand the charges against you?"

"Yes, magistrate." Her voice is tight, and she feels like a controlled tempest with anger and fear temporarily in check.

"Guardians from your sector were witness to you beheading Rowan O'Connelly eight days ago. Do you deny this?"

"No, I do not deny this."

"Do you claim your actions to be in self-defense?"

"My actions were in defense of our director," she replies, lifting her head high.

The magistrate's eyes bores into her. "Yes. Your director, Jonathan Draper. Rowan is obviously not here to speak for himself, but kindly explain to me why your director would require you to kill one of your own kind?"

"The challenge for directorship did not just come from one, as it should. Rowan and approximately thirty others unleashed a vicious attack against the director in an attempt to oust him."

"According to the incident report, Jonathan attacked Rowan first."

"That's not true," Raleigh states, her jaw working with anger. "It was obvious that Rowan and the other guardians were intent on destroying the director, not just removing him from the directorship. And it was Rowan that made the first move to do so."

"This is also contrary to the report," the magistrate says without a break in her composure.

"As of course it would be," Raleigh shoots back. "Did this report mention that Rowan kidnapped two demons and one innocent human that night? Jonathan and I originally came here that night to set matters straight only to find that Rowan had convened almost all guardians from this sector for the ambush I described."

The tribunal members exchange silent glances, and the magistrate frowns. Her gaze sweeps through the crowd, stopping at me.

Without breaking eye contact, she calls out, "Tricia Han. Enter the circle."

There's an immediate stirring of the crowd like the buzz in a disturbed hive. The guardians around Tricia part to let her through, whispering words of encouragement as if they're sending their greatest hero off to war. She walks to the center of the room to stand next to Raleigh, both of their postures laced with tension.

The magistrate's eyes are stony as she directs her attention on Tricia. "Are these allegations true? Were there two demons and a human present at this incident?"

"This is correct, magistrate," Tricia says smoothly. "Rowan took the demons into custody because he suspected they were the Impiorum's *Seraphim*. The human was being held captive by the two demons, and we were in the process of taking care of her when Jonathan appeared on the scene."

"Lies," Raleigh interjects. "The demons were innocent of what you claim."

"The *Seraphim* are malicious and don't know the meaning of innocence. Everyone knows their history," Tricia replies.

"They were far too young to be *Seraphim*, magistrate," Raleigh says respectfully. "And the girl was with one of them of her own accord."

Tricia barks a laugh. "The only reason someone would be with a demon is if he compelled her with his powers."

"That's not always the case," Raleigh retorts.

"Enough." The magistrate holds up her hand for silence, and I hold my breath as she looks at Raleigh with interest. Hope. Raleigh was thinking about Hope as the exception, and all it would take to expose her would be one telepathic guardian who picked up on her thought. Raleigh needs to redirect her efforts toward her defense. That Rowan was in the wrong and that she believed me to be destroyed.

The magistrate shifts her attention to Tricia, and I start breathing again. Tricia is spinning lies, and surely the magistrate will be able to pick up on it.

"The omission of this information from the report will be dealt with at a later date," the magistrate announces. One of the tribunal members acknowledges this before the magistrate turns her attention back to Tricia. "You were acting under Rowan's orders. Did he tell you what his intent was in convening all of the guardians at the time?"

"He was trying to make an example of the *Seraphim*."

"Not to make an example of Jonathan Draper?" the magistrate asks.

"Absolutely not." Tricia's tone is firm.

"What was the intent of the guardians that attacked Jonathan?"

"Forgive me, magistrate, but am I on trial, or is Raleigh Peyton?"

The magistrate arches her eyebrows. "You petitioned for this tribunal hearing. This does not make you exempt from questioning."

Tricia inclines her head. "I apologize, magistrate. Their intent was to defend Rowan from Jonathan's subversive and unsolicited attack."

"You lie," Raleigh hisses. Her eyes catch the light, blazing with anger as she whips around to face the other guardian. Tricia's lips curl back to bare her teeth, and the magistrate holds up a hand.

"Thank you. You may leave the circle, Tricia," the magistrate says in a sharp voice.

Tricia pivots on her heels, but she pauses to give Raleigh a steely glare. "Your love for your director is misplaced," she spits out.

"You wouldn't know it if love hit you in the face," I hear Raleigh mutter.

The magistrate ignores this exchange and says in a raised voice, "Jonathan Draper. Enter the circle."

The room becomes deathly quiet, the guardians an amalgam of emotions as they part to let me through. I'm surprised to learn that not all of my constituents hate me. Some of them fear for my life or perhaps fear for Raleigh's. A few of them incline their heads in deference, and one even dares to mutter a word of encouragement.

I take my place next to Raleigh, where I should have been all along.

"Magistrate," I bow respectfully.

"Spare me the niceties," she says briskly. "I need to understand this."

"Everything is as Raleigh described," I state.

She waves her hand as if swatting away my statement. "I'm sure Tricia's supporters would say otherwise. No, what I want to know is this." She takes a step closer to me, her eyes narrowed as they scrutinize me. "Why would Raleigh Peyton *kill* for you? Out of loyalty? Out of love?"

"Raleigh believed me to be destroyed," I reply. "The incident was indeed an ambush, and I was on the verge of being destroyed by many of whom are present today. I used the illusion of death only as a temporary cover so I could elude my attackers and rescue those Rowan had taken prisoner."

"I see." The magistrate's gaze becomes intense, but I meet it with calm. "Did your second-in-command not know of your ability to do this?"

"He told me of this ability once," Raleigh interjects. "But I failed to remember at the time."

The magistrate breaks her eye contact with me, her body language retreating. She's finished with asking me her line of questions, but that doesn't mean that I'm done defending Raleigh.

"Magistrate," I say hurriedly. "Raleigh was only acting to protect me in the most honorable manner. She has provided the most loyal service to me and the previous director for decades, and the fact that she mistook me for being destroyed is all on me. Not on her."

The magistrate remains still as I speak, but she does not look at me.

"Not true, magistrate," Raleigh says quietly. "My actions were in response to Rowan's attack, but they were my actions."

"Thank you, both of you. You may leave the circle, Jonathan."

I glance at Raleigh, but she faces straight ahead with her chin held high, and she refuses to look at me. My legs feel like lead, and I don't know how I make my way back to my position outside the circle. I don't know why Raleigh insists on shouldering this herself. The only thing I know with absolute certainty is that I want to fight the entire crowd to release her and to hell with the consequences. Only I can't.

The magistrate focuses on Raleigh, and all eyes land on the center of the circle.

"Raleigh Peyton, do you have anything else to say in your defense?"

"No, magistrate," she says quietly. "I have told you everything, and I have spoken the truth. I stand by my actions."

For the first time since I entered the building, Raleigh makes eye contact with me. I'm wound up as tightly as a bowstring, but for self-preservation, my emotions are locked away. I wish I could send her my thoughts right now, if only she still had her Pathicomm.

I think them anyhow.

I should be there instead of you.

She keeps looking at me, her expression controlled but her eyes fluid with emotion. We both wait for the verdict, separated from each other by a crowd but somehow together.

The magistrate holds out her hands to the sides, and the six other tribunal members step forward and form an interlocking circle around Raleigh. They communicate silently amongst themselves, only small fractions of Raleigh visible. It's obvious from the thunderous looks on the faces of some and the stiff stances of others that they're arguing. The tribunal members are not in accord, and watching them debate the fate of my friend is pure agony.

Gradually, the collective storm in the center of the room calms, and the circle breaks. The anticipation in the room heightens to excruciating levels, and the magistrate bows her head as though in prayer.

Raleigh looks straight ahead, and the magistrate lifts her head and addresses her.

"Raleigh Peyton, you confess to taking the life of a guardian. You confess that this act was not done in self-defense. We have no concrete evidence to back your claim that you or your director's existence was in danger. You have committed the ultimate crime against another of our kind, and you show no remorse for your actions.

"We therefore are in accord that you be sentenced to the ultimate death."

26

Jonathan

No. I will not let this be so.

But the tribunal's verdict has been delivered, and their judgment hangs in the air like a noose intent on strangling me.

All is not lost. It's what I told her, and I believed it at the time, but the magistrate's judgment flies in the face of everything. One of the tribunal members moves toward Raleigh, and I watch helplessly as she yields under his power and kneels. The guardians closest to Tricia raise their voices as a cheer, but there are others whose expressions look as stricken as I feel.

"*No!*" I shout. "I contest!"

I shove through the crowd to get down to the floor, but the guardians near the front grab my arms and push me back, forming a physical barrier so I can't get through. Raleigh lifts her head to look at me, and she gives me a serene expression that frightens me most of all.

A shout sounds from outside, heads turning to look at the exit just as the warlock guard crashes through the row of high windows of the warehouse. His body is crisscrossed with blood and hits the concrete floor with a sickening thud. The guardians scatter, the room filling with *lumen* as everyone draws out their powers, only there's nowhere for us to go.

I force my way to the center of the room. Raleigh's arms are still bound behind her back by invisible restraints, but in the chaos, her guard retreats to the circle of those protecting the magistrate. We move to stand next to each other, and I put my arm around her shoulders.

"Stay close to me," I say, drawing out my blade.

She nods, her eyes trained on the black panes of glass above us.

I feel the collective emotions invade the room before they do. The darkest sort of hate. Resentment and rage. Bloodlust. If this is the *Seraphim*, they'll have the advantage over us if we use our regular powers – just like when I fought the one at UB – and I shout for everyone to internalize their light. But nobody listens. The *Seraphim* jump in from the windows, their mixture of *deimos* and *lumen* consuming all the guardian power in its path. Raleigh cries out and falls into a crouch as she's hit, but her restraints break as they steal the magic that binds her. I grab her hand and pull her back up just as a chimera rushes us. Raleigh spins away from me, grabbing him by the hair and yanks his head back, and I swing my blade and slice cleanly through his neck.

"Don't use your destructive powers," I say to Raleigh when she's again by my side. "They'll swallow up your *lumen*."

"Understood," she says. She stands behind me, lightly bracing her back against mine as we both survey the situation.

There have to be fifty or more guardians in here, and I estimate twenty or even less of the *Seraphim*. The number is still surprising – the Impiorum demons have obviously been busy. Tricia slices through one closest to her with a short sword that I recognize as Raleigh's, and the rest of her followers take her lead in attacking with weapons and not *lumen*. The chimera closest to us falls to the ground with his head partially severed, and Raleigh leaps forward and pries the blade from his hand before resuming her position by me.

We have just a second to share a moment of camaraderie. Almost like the old days.

A half-dozen more of the *Seraphim* storm through the shattered windows, the room exploding into turmoil. One of them lands in front of me with a leer and hits me with a pulse of pure *deimos*. He's a regular Impiorum demon, not a chimera, and my *lumen* is so internalized that I take his hit full-force and stagger back into Raleigh. She swings around and charges the demon with her knife drawn and power blazing, but one of the *Seraphim* from the first wave lunges at her from the side. He towers over her, one of his hands closing around her wrist and the other one clamping around her neck. I hear him laugh as she swipes at him with her knife and misses.

He lifts Raleigh off the ground by her throat, her *lumen* weakening as the chimera takes it into himself, and I grab the demon standing in my way and break his neck with one sharp twist.

I charge forward, but another one tackles me. I jab my knife into his side, giving the hilt a quick yank, but the demon doesn't let go. He latches on, simultaneously digging his fingers and *deimos* into my arm. With half an eye on Raleigh, I bear down and blast him with as much *lumen* as I can muster.

I realize my mistake just as a chimera grabs me in a chokehold from behind. My power courses through me as hot as the adrenaline in my veins, and I'm suddenly ablaze with pain as he steals my life force. They're tag-teaming us, the Impiorum demons tearing down our defenses so the *Seraphim* can finish the job and destroy us.

Raleigh and I make eye contact, neither of us able to break free, and my fury rises to match her level of despair. I refuse to let her die at the hands of the tribunal or by these monsters. I refuse to let her die, period.

I'd left my knife buried in the demon that had attacked me, but the *clavis* is still vibrating within my jacket pocket. I grope for the stone, my fingers closing around the smooth part. It's hot to the touch, and I grit my teeth and jam one end into his arm. The pure power of Arete's *lumen* jolts through me like ice water, the chimera howling as his arm deadens and drops away from me.

I look around wildly for Raleigh. She's still fighting back but weakly, her skin white as a sheet as the chimera drags her to a growing stack of bodies. I grab the knife she'd been using from the blood-stained floor and give chase. I leap up, the chimera turning just as I bring down the blade and plant it squarely into his head.

"Jonathan," Raleigh gasps.

She stumbles toward me, and I take her hand and draw her close just as a blinding light flashes from across the room. One of the entire walls bursts into a glow, and the noise of the battle subsides as the guardians and demons alike shift their attention to the wall.

I can feel her *lumen* before I see her, and I know the guardians feel it too. They disperse and then tighten into small groups, poised to defend themselves against the *Seraphim* but also keeping an eye on her approach.

"What is it?" Raleigh whispers. She clutches my hand, a tremor in her fingers, and I slide my arm around her.

"Arete," I say with certainty.

The mother of all guardians appears like a vision through the light, her form a silhouette until the moment she steps through the gateway onto the floor. Her pure white hair and white robe stand out in contrast to the darkness in the room, her eyes ablaze with *lumen* as she takes in the scene. Her nose wrinkles, as if she isn't accustomed to the smell of mortals.

She didn't travel alone. The immortal demon Raphael strides through the gateway behind her, his taller form looming above Arete like a storm cloud. The doorway closes behind them with a resounding boom, Arete moving forward and Raphael remaining behind with his head of dark hair bowed as if in deference despite the fact that they're equals. Two halves of a whole, each with the power to mete out ultimate justice.

Arete surveys the battlefield with a glower, and guardians and demons alike lower their weapons in submission. The *Seraphim* are the only ones in the room that remain restless, looking around as though they're confused, and one of them charges the group of guardians that includes Tricia. Arete and Raphael simultaneously look over, and the chimera flies up into the air and hits the metal beams of the warehouse before falling back down to the floor. I hear Raleigh's sharp intake of breath as all of the *Seraphim* are struck down one by one.

The Impiorum demons watch in stunned silence at first, but then they raise their protests from where they stand.

"You have been unleashing these monsters into the human population. There are stakes here that you don't comprehend," Arete proclaims.

"You would kill your own children for it?" one of them challenges.

We may be on opposite sides, but the same question burns within me. Raphael and Arete could strip the *lumen* from the *Seraphim* without killing them. It had been part of my initial request to Arete, and while we'd been in the process of fighting off the *Seraphim* too, their actions don't make sense.

Raphael doesn't answer the demon who'd asked the question. Instead he bows his head as though in grief. Arete is the one to speak, her whisper with as much impact as thunder.

"The *lumen* and *deimos* oppose one another but they also balance each other. They are meant to be synergistic, but with the Impiorum's attempts to force together the guardian and demon lineages, they have created monsters."

Arete is the picture of grace and strength as she glides toward us. The guardian mother dismisses me without so much as a glance, but she extends her arm and places it on Raleigh's head.

"You, my child, are no monster. Your *lumen* is pure and perfect."

She smooths her hand over Raleigh's hair as if comforting a child, and I feel Raleigh's fear surge. Or it might be mine.

"I told you, Jonathan Drapier." The guardian's eyes don't leave Raleigh's face. "The forces will equilibrate and be in harmony once again. I must confess, I was the one that originally charged the Impiorum with merging the powers of light and darkness." She says it placidly, her hand dropping from Raleigh's hair and folding gracefully in front of her. "Unfortunately, their attempts have given us the equivalent of madmen. I shall ensure that this is done correctly this time."

Her words strike me in the heart, and I hear shocked murmurs all around. Arete is the mother of light, mother of us all. She is full of love and *lumen* and couldn't possibly be responsible for any of these dark schemes.

"Raleigh Peyton shall not be sentenced to the ultimate death. That particular type of end serves no purpose. She shall be given a new end. An end to serve us all." Arete's voice rises and echoes throughout the room. "I sentence thee, Raleigh Peyton, to be the first subject of the transformation of a guardian into a chimera. I have tried to infuse the demons with the *lumen* from the collective, but I believe the light must come from an actual soul. A good soul."

Raleigh eyes drop to the floor, refusing to look at me as Arete's proclamation travels through the room. The exclamations roll through the guardians like a wave, some fearful, some excited. Tricia's gaze seeks out mine, her expression satisfied. She'd wanted an out from being held accountable for the creation of a chimera, and this was it.

"No, Arete," I plead. "*Not this*. This will solve nothing. The Impiorum will only make more *Seraphim*, and the energy imbalance will only get worse. This is no way to achieve harmony."

Tricia speaks up as though I hadn't. "You'll show us how to make her into a chimera?"

Arete turns to her, her lips pressed together in displeasure. "I shall take her to Asphodel and do it myself. The threat of the *Seraphim* are gone now, and Raphael shall sentence to his eternal end any demon who attempts to create more. Raleigh shall serve as an example of our future."

Arete moves wordlessly to stand in front of me. It's the first time I've ever looked directly into her eyes, and I can see the tinge of madness lurking within. "You have something of mine, Jonathan Drapier. I require that it be returned."

I know what she wants, and my mind rebels but my hand moves without my will to retrieve the *clavis* from my pocket. She takes the stone back into her possession and floats away, and my throat constricts as Raleigh too succumbs to the guardian's power and falls in line by her side. Raphael steps over the destroyed bodies of the *Seraphim* to take his position on the other side of Raleigh, and the two immortals escort Raleigh to the gateway.

"Jonathan is right. The Impiorum will only make more of their monsters!" a guardian yells.

"How is giving her a new chance at life justice?" another voice shouts.

The room erupts into chaos, drowning out my voice as I call after Raleigh. I regain control of my body again and push through the crowd to get to her, but I'm too late.

She's gone. Without the *clavis*, I have no possible way to follow her.

27

Micah

West-bound. Back home and with the promise of a new life. First task is to find a place for the Albany group to set up a temporary home base, and I fly to Buffalo, my heart light and mind full of possibilities.

I head straight for the community center in the middle of the city. Troy's waiting for me in the back of the building in his workout clothes and guzzling from a water bottle. I'd called him from a campus phone at the University at Albany about an hour ago and he suggested we meet here.

I touch down silently behind him and clap him on the shoulder, and he spits out his drink.

"What the hell, dude?" He turns and tries to slug me in the chest, but I dodge it. There's a huge smile on his face. "Is that how you greet your best friend after being AWOL?"

I grin back at him. "Pretty much. It's good to see you. How've you been?"

"Me?" He shrugs. "The same. Oh, except I might actually get an A in math this semester. Hope told me you were in Alaska? How did everything work out?"

"Good. Learned a lot more than trig, that's for sure."

"Yeah?" His eyes shift around like he's afraid gang members are watching, and I notice for the first time that he's holding a flashlight. "Come in and tell me all about it."

He uses a set of keys to unlock the two locks on the heavy metal door, and I follow him inside. We start down the corridor, the beam of the flashlight sweeping over old fliers on the floor.

"What happened to this place? Zombie apocalypse?"

"AWOL for two months," he mutters under his breath. "They moved everything over to a new center. It's in a better part of the city instead of here in the ghetto, so a bunch of people protested because the poorer kids don't have anywhere to go now. Those people lost out. It's been all over the news for a while now, but you've been…" He trails off, looking sheepish.

"I've been caught up in my own crap for too long." I pause and give him a crooked smile. "Come to think about it, when *haven't* I been caught up in my own crap?"

"Pretty much never," he says with a straight face.

"Yeah, that's what I thought," I say a ruefully. "Sorry. You should find some normal friends."

"Shut up. Just tell me what you think about this place." He stops by a doorway and looks at me, and I can barely make out the crease on his forehead. "You said you needed something like a hideout, and I remembered my mom still had the keys even after she moved to working at the new center. It's scheduled for demolition in a couple of months, but it's the best I could do on short notice."

I peer into the room, which turns out to be a restaurant-grade kitchen. "It's great," I say honestly. "We don't need much. When I called you, I was wondering about one of your parents' properties in the city, but this is actually a lot better."

"Yeah. Their properties are all overpriced, undersized condos." He takes me through another doorway into a run-down gym and kicks at a ripped mat. "Though I'm glad you don't need much, because this is definitely not much," he adds, waving the flashlight around.

"It's got potential. We can make do with almost anything with enough space. In Alaska, we were in an old juvie detention center. The group in Albany used to take up a whole section of dorms at the university."

He cants his head to the side. "How did they pull that off? Taking up that much of a dorm without anyone noticing?"

"Magic. Witches, to be exact. There's some spell that they do that deters people from getting too close. Or it disorients people if they accidentally cross the boundaries." I smile a little as Troy's eyes grow huge. "Hey, you think this place has its own generator?"

"Witches. Real witches. Okay." He pushes his hand through his hair. "And I don't know about the generator, but we can check it out."

We look at everything, my confidence growing with each room we pass through. It has plenty of space, with old offices that could be divvied up for private rooms and plenty of communal areas too. It does have a generator, though I don't dare try to power it until this place is protected, and we'd have to figure out how to get the water supply back on. But those are just details. This feels like the right place for us.

"So, if you have witches and spells at your disposal to deter people, then wrecking crews and trespassers might not be a problem?" Troy says hopefully. We stop in the gym again and sit on one of the old mats. He turns off the flashlight, but we're not in total darkness because of the natural light from the row of high windows.

"Trespassers like us, you mean? If it turns out to be a problem, we'll find another place, but I honestly think this is great. Thanks, Troy." I add, "And thanks for spending time with Hope when I was gone."

"You don't need to thank me for that. She's my friend, too." He looks at me curiously. "So, does she know you'll be stationed here? Because she seemed to be under the impression that you'd be living in Albany."

"I haven't had a chance to tell her yet. Things changed." I frown. "Have things been okay here? The group back in Albany was hit hard by a pretty bad group of demons called mercenaries. Hope didn't seem like she'd heard of them, but we didn't have time to catch up on everything, either."

He winks. "I bet you caught up on the important stuff."

"Troy…" I roll my eyes. "I'm serious."

"Yeah, I know." His jaw sets in a grim line. "No, the latest news here are some bad dudes called *Seraph* or something. From what I've been able to piece together from what Jonathan and Hope talk about, they're demons but worse."

I automatically tense up at the mention of Jonathan's name, which is stupid because I know Hope has to have spent time with him. *Seraph….* An angel? The name rings a bell from a night a few months ago, during a disastrous hunt at the Griffis Sculpture Park. It's not quite the same as what I'd heard before, but it's close enough.

"How are they different? Did they say?"

"I think they have a little bit of guardian in them or something?"

"The *Seraphim*," I blurt out, suddenly remembering. "They're part-demon, part-guardian. That douche Samael Richter was one of them. There are more of them now?"

"Yeah, *Seraphim*. That's it. I was there when Jonathan broke the neck of one of them. There are definitely more."

The *Seraphim* are here, and they sound similar to what the alliance has been calling mercenaries. I wonder if they're one and the same.

"So Jonathan lets you come on their guardian missions, huh?"

"I didn't really give him the choice. I'm just there, like that pesky friend that tags along and won't take a hint." He shoots me a look. "It's all guardian stuff when they hang out, you know. She's all about you and always has been."

"I know," I say automatically. "I trust her. I just don't trust him."

"I agree that he's kind of an ass sometimes, but he'd never do anything to hurt Hope. And that includes coming between you and her."

"I know," I say again, but I don't think I do. I stand up, desperately needing to change the subject and now with the *Seraphim* weighing on my mind. "Hey, I'm going to call the guys in Albany real quick."

"Sure." He jumps up too and switches on his light. "I'm gonna see if there's anything left in the kitchen worth eating. I came here right after practice."

I take out the tracker device that Ben gave me and call him, but there's no answer. I'm about to hit the button again when Ben's voice comes in.

"Ninja to Darkwing. Acknowledge."

"What? This is Micah."

I hear him sigh. "I was using codenames. I thought it would be cooler. And safer."

"And I thought this line was secure."

"It is. Okay, so that was maybe not so cool, but please humor me next time?" His tone gets more serious. "Did you have any luck?"

"Yeah, I found a place," I say, looking around. "Need directions?"

"Are you there right now? Cuz I can pull your location off the tracker."

"I am. And you can? How can you do that if it's secure?"

"It's a secure *line* so no one else can but me," he says smugly. "Better design, remember?"

"Okay, sweet. What time you think you'll leave?"

"Bonecrusher says that if we heard from you, that we'll leave at twenty-oh-hundred hours."

I laugh. Bonecrusher must be Eli. "Okay, see you tonight. Darkwing out."

"Ninja out," Ben replies, sounding pleased.

I stick the tracker back into my pocket, shaking my head. Ben and Troy will probably get along great.

The bracelet tracker activates next, the one that's connected to Hope. I feel a directional tugging in my head as my *deimos* makes a connection to it, and I frown down at the leather and metal band around my wrist. She'd been so insistent about not using the tracker because she was afraid of bothering me, so either she's activating it by mistake, or something's wrong.

I deactivate it, but it goes off again.

Officially worried, I make a beeline for the kitchen, where I find Troy eating a handful of breakfast cereal straight of the box. "Hungry," he explains.

"Not judging. Hey, can I borrow your phone?" The breach in protocol nags at me a little. But I figure it's no different than if Troy and Hope call each other, which they probably do often enough.

He tosses me his cell, and I hit her number in his contacts.

"Troy!" she cries out without preface, and my heart sinks like a stone. She sounds panicky, upset.

"It's me," I say. "I'm with Troy in the city and saw you activated the tracker. What's wrong?"

"Oh! Micah." She sounds like she's running. "I'm in the city too. Do you have time to meet me? Tell Troy to come too if he can."

I hear a voice in the background murmur in displeasure, and it's like an echo of my own feelings as I recognize who it is. But this isn't a secure line, and I say quickly, "Yeah, we'll be right there."

Troy gives me a quizzical look as I pass the phone back to him. "Everything cool?"

"Don't know. But we have to go and meet Hope. She asked for you to come too. And she's with Jonathan." I stomp down the stab of jealousy that surfaces as I say it. Don't have time for that right now.

"Let's go," he says, already heading for the door. "I parked just down the street."

He takes out his car keys and tosses me the one to the community center. I stare at the heavy metal key before tucking it away in my pocket. The key to my new life here.

"You're the best, Troy. Don't know how to thank you for all of this."

"Whatever. I need a place to go for an escape now and then too." He holds up his keys and shakes them, and I see an identical key on his keyring. "Just make sure the witches let me in."

28

Micah

I wait for my head to ache in that telltale way, but it doesn't. If Jonathan's here with Hope, he's doing a good job of masking it.

A faded sign on the weedy lawn of the old rock church claims it's a designated historical landmark. If it's true, whoever's in charge hasn't been doing much with it because the rock is crumbling in spots, half of the stained-glass windows cracked and the others so dirty I can't tell what color they're supposed to be. This place looks like it's been neglected for decades.

Troy shoots me a funny look when I tell him to pull into the overgrown parking lot. "I think we should go. This place isn't open to the public."

That may be so, but the Mazda 6 and a bright red Ducati are parked in the dark shade of the trees.

"That's Hope's car over there." Troy perks up a little but slumps down in his seat again. "I'm getting a bad vibe from this place."

I thought the Mazda belonged to Davis when I saw it in their garage, but after being gone for so long, I guess I should get used to not assuming things. Still, I eye the bike one more time before reaching the door of the church. It must be Jonathan's because there aren't any other vehicles here, but it doesn't seem like his style.

I look at Troy, who's literally squirming in his seat. He's afraid of pretty much nothing, and I think I get why.

"There's some sort of a protective spell on this place," I guess. "That's why you don't want to be here. I can't feel Jonathan's presence either, and usually it's like someone scratching nails on a blackboard, believe me. Come on, you'll feel better once we're actually inside."

The lock is solid-looking, but the door swings open easily. We step inside the church, which is muted and dark except for a few streaks of evening sun that manage to seep in through cracks. Just as I thought, my head starts to ache even before my sights land on Jonathan.

Hope, Davis, and Jonathan are making their way single-file through one of the rows of dusty pews, Hope's expression brightening when she sees me. Davis looks scared out of his mind, his gaze fixed on the long black box tucked under Jonathan's arm.

Hope tries to squeeze past Jonathan, but he catches her hand. "Tell him. He needs to leave."

I stop in my tracks. Jonathan said it in a barely audible voice, but I heard him. Loud and clear.

"Dude, what's wrong?" Troy whispers from my side.

I don't answer, my sights locked on Jonathan. I know his comment was about me, and it makes a lifetime of resentment boil to the surface.

I've tried. I've tried to put my trust in Jonathan the way Hope did from day one. Without him, I might not have made it through my demon transformation. Without him, Hope wouldn't have had a mentor to help her through her own changes. But Jonathan also made that damned deal with the Praxidikai that ultimately bound me to Vahni, and now he wants Hope to tell me to go away.

She doesn't listen to him, instead yanking her hand away and climbing over the row of pews to get past. I should take comfort in that. What matters is how Hope feels, not what Jonathan thinks, and I need to put out of my head what he said to her. I should focus on what really matters and go to her, but a whisper in my head pins me to the spot.

The ire you feel is natural. Raphael split the demon and guardian lineages long ago, and the races became mortal enemies in your realm as a consequence...

Not now. This is no time for one of Vahni's history lessons. I grit my teeth, trying to shake the goddess out of my head. It's not her usual grating whisper, but it has to be her. Who else?

...now you have the chance to set things right.

"Not helpful," I snap, and Troy stares at me.

"Hope." Jonathan calls to her this time with urgency. "Tell him. And then we have to go."

My resentment twists into something darker, and I head up the row to Hope. Jonathan leaps over in one swift move to stand between us. As if he's protecting her. From *me.*

I growl, low and angry, ignoring the look of shock that flashes across Hope's face. I charge up the row, but Jonathan stands his ground, the expression in his eyes looks completely crazed. Troy calls me back, and Davis gets to his feet, his eyes shifting back and forth between me and Jonathan. But I ignore them too and run to close the distance between me and Jonathan. We have a score to settle. More than one.

I feel him summon his light, but Hope is right behind him and I don't dare do anything with her so close. His strike hits me before I can get out of way, and pain sears through my nerves like crackling white heat.

I push out my wings, swooping up to the high ceiling.

"Micah, wait!" Hope cries out. "Jonathan, what are you *doing?*"

He doesn't answer her, his eyes narrowing as he scans the ceiling for me, but my camouflage went into effect the moment I took to the air. Luckily my wings didn't explode into flames this time, either.

It is now in the demon's nature to hunt guardians...

I've never truly gone after a guardian before, the closest being when I've sparred with Jonathan or Hope in the past, but the shift into hunting mode happens easily. The pain in the center of my head subsides, my senses sharpening.

Compared to the usual feeling I get around guardians, this almost feels good.

Hope continues to call for me, Troy joining in now. But the monster in me is louder, egging me on to finish this with Jonathan. And maybe it's Vahni or maybe it's me.

The sensation in my head suddenly grows sharper, like my *deimos* is latching onto Jonathan's signature and pulling me in. Taking me down so I can finish this. He already threw the first shot at me in here, and my anger burns in me until it inflames for real. My wings burst into flame, and the three of them all look up at me at the same time, at the freak with the goddess power.

Jonathan messed up *my entire freaking life*.

I land in front of him and throw a punch, but I'm not camouflaged anymore, and he catches my fist in a hand full of crackling-white heat. My knees buckle as his light sends shocks of electricity up my spine.

I snarl at him. "You stay away from her. For your whole immortal life."

Vahni's *ignis* bursts from me, and I shove Jonathan back. He goes flying into a stack of pews, and the voice whispers encouragement in my head.

The races are mortal enemies now. Finish him off.

The command shocks me back into my senses.

No.… My blood might be boiling because of Jonathan, and Vahni might even be right in that this is what we've evolved to do. But ever since I found out what I was, I've been fighting off the temptation to feed, to hunt, to be an animal.

I refuse to give in to those instincts now.

My anger slowly recedes, my decision settling over me just enough to let the pain in my head dull. Jonathan rises from the pews and adopts a defensive position, eyeing me warily as he walks back over to Hope. The hyper-awareness I have of him feels strange, as though his signal isn't just below me but all around us.

Something's not right. I don't feel the urge to hunt him anymore, but there's something else here.

A high-pitched sound screams through the church, and I have just enough time to see the panic on Hope's face before the windows explode. I'm thrown into the rafters, pain shooting up my spine before I fall back down to the floor. I barely catch myself in a crouch, scanning for Hope in the mess and Jonathan doing the same as they run for cover from the showers of glass splinters. Davis follows them, but Troy heads in the other direction. He waves his arms wildly for them to come to the door, but they keep heading away.

I touch down next to them and try to pull Hope with me to the door, gesturing for Davis to come with us. He looks like he's saying something back, but my ears are still ringing from the blast.

"What are you waiting for? Let's get out of here!" I shout to equally deaf ears.

Hope shakes her head and points at Jonathan. He's running his hand over the wall, and when he looks at me, his eyes are full of dread. Whatever's coming, it's enough to rattle a five-hundred year old guardian, and my own panic slices through me as I look around for the source.

"Who's coming for us?" I yell. The buzzing in my ears isn't as bad anymore, and Jonathan must be able to hear me because he answers.

"Enemies."

His fingers seem to sink into the plaster, and I stare as the wall moves. It's a concealed door, and I get it when I glimpse the top of a stairwell. It's some sort of safehouse, probably the reason they were here in the first place.

But Troy is still on the other side of the church, and while he can handle himself in ordinary situations, I already know that this situation won't qualify.

"I gotta get Troy!"

Hope blanches but nods before letting go of my hand. If the bad dudes are coming for us, I can't let Troy face them alone. I grit my teeth and sprint for the door, knowing Jonathan will keep Hope and Davis safe. The admission is hard, but it's true.

And besides, I'll be gone for just a second.

A woman lands in front of me, her arm whipping through the air, and I feel the sting on my arm a fraction of a second later as something slices through my skin. She whips around at superhuman speed and swipes at me again, but this time I grab onto the long braid in her hair and throw her to the ground. She rolls with it and leaps over a row of pews to block me, a wicked double-edged blade braced in her hands. Whoever she is, she's definitely a guardian, and she's definitely pissed about something.

"You're coming with me, whether it be in pieces or whole," she yells. "You choose."

Not much of a choice. "I'll stay in one piece, thanks."

She smirks and comes for me again. My *deimos* feels like sludge, but the *ignis* jumps easily to my fingertips as fire. I catch the flash of surprise on her face even as she's swinging the blade at me, and I dodge the attack and flick the flames over to her. The tip of her braid ignites, and she shrieks and hurries to pat it out with her hands. It gives me time to note the closed church door and the fact that Troy is gone. I glance back and see five more guardians cornering Hope, Jonathan, and Davis by the wall. The secret passage is concealed again, and our way to the other door is blocked by a half dozen more guardians that are dropping into the church through the windows.

I don't know who these guardians are or why they're here, but I believe what Jonathan said about them being enemies. The small group rallies behind the one with the braid, and I catch the murderous glint in her eye. I'm guessing she's the leader. She cut me pretty deeply, and I clamp my hand over the wound as I sprint back over to the wall to help the others. I jump over a pew as one of the guardians races toward them, and Jonathan whips out a gleaming sword from the black case.

Geez. Guardians must really freaking love knives. This one is way too big and way too close to Hope for my comfort, and I cringe as Jonathan whips the sword in a sharp arc at the charging guardian. He clutches his arm and crumples to the floor, and I feel something reverberate through me like an aftershock of power.

I dash through the gap the fallen guardian leaves to stand by Hope's side.

"Hey. You okay?"

Her eyes grow wide. "I'm fine, but you're bleeding."

"It'll heal. Did you see where Troy —"

"Hold on." She frowns in concentration with her arms out in front of her, a burst of *deimos* striking one of the enemy guardians that's breaking away from the group. He flies back and hits the row of pews closest to us and tumbles heavily to the floor.

"Nice one," I say, eyeing the guardians. They're finally wising up and falling back slightly, congregating around the one with the braid. Three down, only about twenty more to go.

"Thanks," she gasps. "I didn't see where Troy went."

"I saw him run outside," Davis interjects. "I bet he got away. None of these assholes bothered using the door."

Davis seems weirdly accepting of all of this, but he's had a couple of months to adjust to the fact that his sister is partly like me and partly like Jonathan. We form a line of three, with me between Jonathan and Hope, and with Davis behind us and against the wall.

"So who are all of these douchebags, anyway?" I ask Hope.

Jonathan answers. "Guardians from my sector and from Chicago too."

"You said they were enemies," I say back. "What did you do to piss them off?"

"Quite a bit, as it turns out. But in this case, they are looking for you."

What? I stare at him to see if he's joking. But he has no reason to joke around with me, and he looks totally serious. Typical.

"For *me?*"

"If we survive this, I'll explain everything to you."

Jonathan's responsible for all of this. I knew it. If we survive this, I may kill him.

What the guardian with the braid said – that I was coming with her – it wasn't just a general threat then, but she really meant that she wanted me. But I can't mull over it anymore because the guardians are banded together now and moving toward us.

They're coming for *me*, but they don't know what they're getting. My senses sharpen, my pulse quickens, my sights hone in on the one with the braid like she's my prey. She bares her teeth back at me like I'm hers.

Demons are meant to hunt guardians.

Yeah, I hear you, Vahni. I'll make an exception for this one.

"Stay together!" Jonathan barks.

"Planned on it," I reply through my teeth.

We stand together and face the approaching swarm.

29

Jonathan

We may be cornered, but I'll be damned if they defeat us.

With Raleigh's sword in hand, it feels like she's fighting by my side. The design is something she came up with herself, and the metal is somehow able to conduct the energy of the wielder's *lumen*. It's one of a kind, like her.

"What was that explosion?" Micah sounds frustrated. "And why can't I use all of my powers to fight?"

"It's called a disrupter," I reply. "Be grateful that you can at least use some of your powers to fight, because I cannot." I add after a slight pause, "But evidently Hope can."

"Maybe it's because I have mixed powers," Hope suggests. "It still affected me. Can't use my light, only my *deimos*."

Micah puts his arm around her shoulders. "There has to be another way out of here," he grinds out. "Where does that door in the wall go?"

"Downstairs." I think of all of the weapons in the main chamber of Raleigh's sanctuary, but if we head down there, we'd risk the guardians getting hold of her stash. "No, the only way out of the building is through the doors or windows on this floor."

Davis slides out from behind us and stands by my side, but Hope and Micah are too focused on the approaching threat to notice.

"We need to do *something*!" he says.

Indeed we do. Including Tricia, I count twenty-three of them. The blast from the disrupter hadn't been as direct this time, and I can still sense their emotions. I read hesitation in most of them, pick up on the fear in some, and sense genuine remorse in a few. But they also smell of desperation. They're here because Tricia convinced them to come, not because they're convinced it's right.

"Hand him over, Jonathan," Tricia calls out in a velvety voice. "Or *she* will do just as well. You failed to mention that you had two chimera."

"Neither of them are on the table for negotiation."

"Why do they think you're a chimera?" I hear Hope whisper to Micah.

"No idea. Maybe we should ask Jonathan," Micah grumbles.

I ignore his accusatory glare, looking down at his hand instead. He's clenching and releasing it, small flames appearing at his fingertips before he kills them again. He may not be a chimera, but he brings powers from Asphodel to the mix. We may have our way out after all.

Tricia didn't bring her small army here to negotiate. They continue moving forward as a mass, and we can't move back because we're already literally up against the wall.

I stare down at Raleigh's sword, trying to recall what she told me about this one. The power in it is bound to the metal and can't be disrupted, and I can feel it reverberate through the blade like a gentle hum. I sweep my arm in a wide curve, and sure enough, a swath of *lumen* ripples and shimmers in the air between us and the guardians. It's weaker than if I would have done it myself, but maybe it'll be enough.

"Nice try," Tricia sneers. "But you're outnumbered and outgunned."

"Do they actually have guns?" Davis whispers.

"No, because bullets don't kill us," Hope whispers back.

"Yeah, and limbs don't grow back if you cut them off, huh?" Micah mutters.

"Limbs would in fact grow back," I murmur. "But a head would not."

Tricia gestures to the guardians, and they move in unison toward the last set of pews separating us. I glance at Micah, who's alternating between watching the approaching guardians and the ceiling, as though he can feel the *lumen* in the air. He's still playing with the fire in his hands.

"Ignite it," I tell him.

He frowns at me. "What?"

"The mirage that you can see in the air. Ignite it," I say urgently. "Trust me."

His expression closes off, his hand forming a fist and killing the fire. The guardians are almost upon us, and I absorb his incredulity, Hope's weariness, Davis' uncertainty. I raise Raleigh's sword in preparation for the mob's attack, not having the time to alter past events or my own desperation right now. If I could only plead to his sensibilities, maybe I could break through his armor.

"Micah, I turned you over to the guardians, yes," I say urgently. "But it was to protect Hope. Everything I have done is for her."

"I get that," he growls. "But *why?*"

It's too late. Too late to explain that my love for her is not as he thinks, too late to explain that his fire would use the *lumen* like fuel and give us a way out of the church. Tricia rushes first, and I step forward and engage her, sword to blade. The look in her eyes is dark and murderous, and I feel her fury in each strike. I deflect her in kind, half an eye on the rest of them. Hope stays next to Davis and repels the guardian advances with her *deimos*, and Micah throws fiery assaults at over a dozen guardians that target him. But they drive him back and away from Hope, until we're divided into three groups.

Divided. There was once a time that we stood together, back when I was Micah's mentor, but I split us up when I betrayed his trust.

Tricia increases the intensity of her attack, her body twisting and spinning before coming at me again with her blade. Metal strikes metal, and I deflect her.

"You won't win this," I snap. "Even if you destroy me and take Micah, you won't win the love of any of these guardians."

"They loved you once, but you lost all of them with your indifference."

Tricia throws her entire body into her next strike, her blade locking with the metal of Raleigh's sword. For a split-second, we stand eye-to-eye, and I see how remorseless she really is. She would lead all of the guardians to their ultimate ends if it meant her glory.

I grab her wrist and roll backward, bringing her with me and using the momentum of the roll to throw her. She flies over my head and hits the floor so hard that I hear the crack of her head on concrete. I jump up and hurry over to Micah first, grabbing the closest guardian by the collar and yanking him away. He swings around and swipes at me with a long dagger, but I duck and slice low and deep through his Achilles' tendon. He falls to the floor with a howl, his foot partially severed at the ankle. He'll be out of commission for a while, but the damage won't be permanent.

There's a pause in the melee, as if the others are looking around for Tricia. She's still on the floor but pushing herself to a crouch now, slowly and as though she's stunned, and I know we don't have much time.

I throw a weak ribbon of *lumen* into the air. And another. And a third. It's like coloring in a giant tapestry with a fine-tipped pen.

"Micah!" I call to him. "Hope shares your soul, but she shares my blood. That's why! Now please *ignite it.*"

He looks at me, his appearance macabre with blood streaking his face. But I think I see the understanding dawning on his expression. He may be a demon, but he's always fought for the same side as me, and in that flash of a moment, we connect with our single goal. Hope's always been the unifying force since day one.

With a roar, Micah shoves back his remaining attackers with his *deimos*. He pitches a fireball into the air like a baseball, and the *lumen* explodes into a flash of light and sends flames spiraling up to the ceiling.

"Head for the door!"

I run over to Hope and Davis, leaping over a female guardian in my way. I come down right behind her, sweeping the sword as I land and cleanly slicing off her right arm. Hope jumps back and clutches at Davis, but I grab her hand.

"No time." I shout. "We have to go!"

My eyes skate over her to make sure she's all right. She has dark circles under her eyes, her face drawn and pale, but she'll be okay. We run as fast as humanly possible toward the door, Micah catching up to us within a couple of strides. It's painfully slow running at human speed, but the burn that accumulates in my muscles and lungs also makes me feel alive.

The fire is like a cloud above us, steadily raining down sparks but not yet touching the floor of the church. Only a short stretch to go before we're out the door, and I twist around and summon all of my *lumen* that I can as I sweep the sword high in the air. The fire flashes, fanning out and finding even more fuel in the dusty and dry pews. Remorse and regret fill my heart to hear the guardians' screams as the fire leaps hungrily to consume them, but once they find their way through, they also shouldn't have permanent damage.

We're almost out. I'm almost there, Raleigh.

Davis yanks open the door and puts his hand on Hope's back to guide her through, but Micah isn't next to her anymore. He's standing near the growing front of the fire, and I can feel the shock jetting through him.

The woman steps out from the fire, hair ablaze. Blackened skin shows beneath her burnt clothes, one side of her face blistered and resembling melting wax.

Vahni. Micah thinks it's Vahni, but it's Tricia, and she's holding the disrupter.

She throws it straight at us, and it lands and rolls, stopping right at Hope's feet. I yell at her to kick it away, but she freezes, and my head echoes with a deafening boom. The sword falls out of my hands, all of the strength leaving my limbs. I feel someone cuff me on the back of my neck, and I drop down to the floor.

I see Hope through the growing darkness. She's lying next to me, her hands over her ears and her face trapped in a silent scream.

30

Jonathan

I've never prayed so hard for someone's safety as I much as I did for hers.

I rode into the night, the crescent moon and my own determination as my only guides back to the prison where Adrienne waited for me. This place essentially acted as my bleak home for the past year, the guards and other interrogators my surrogate family since my father was killed and then since Adrienne was taken from me. But no longer. Once I escaped with Adrienne and took her to Maman's house to reunite with Colette, we would be a real family. Forever.

The guard outside the main entrance to the prison cells stepped aside respectfully when I asked to enter. I placed my hand on his shoulder as though we were comrades.

"I'm here to relieve you of duty. Your services are no longer needed for the night."

His expression brightened at the prospect of leaving that dark place twenty minutes early. I waited impatiently until he was down the corridor before going inside, and it took all of my willpower to walk instead of run – to my wife and my future.

I entered the cell where I had left her, and she was lying on the bed as if in sleep. My hopes and heart flying, I knelt by her side and took her hand. "Wake up, my love. I have Colette," I whispered. "She is safe and waiting for us."

Adrienne didn't respond, and only then did I notice how shallow her breathing was. I took hold of her arms and gently shook her, and her eyes *opened. There was an unspeakable amount of pain in them, and a chill chased up my spine when she lifted her hand and I saw the empty vial.*

A touch of death, only this time more than just a touch.

I rested my head against her chest, and her heart still beat but weakly. She started to whisper something softly under her breath, and I recognized the words of a final prayer.

"Adrienne, what did they make you do?" I knelt by her side and took her face in my hands. "We are so close to being free. Stay with me."

Oh God, please help me. I need to find a way out.

⤙✦⤚

It's pitch black, and I struggle to see, struggle to hear. I lie on a cold stone floor, the chill seeping through my veins as I drift in and out of the abyss of unconsciousness.

I need to find a way out.

Look for the weak spot…

I struggle to open my eyes, squinting into the thin slice of artificial light that invades the prison cell. I can make out Adrienne lying down next to me, but something is wrong with my memory. She's no longer in the bed but lying still on the floor. I'm in a prison, yes, but not the rooms for the prisoners of nobility. And it's Hope who's lying here so motionless, not Adrienne.

My limbs feel like lead, and I push myself up and manage to crawl over to her. She's unconscious but breathing, and I say a silent prayer as I touch trembling fingers to her cheek. She's warm to the touch, and I let out a sigh of relief.

"Is she okay?"

The voice is pained, and it belongs to Micah. He's separated from us by a row of bars. Davis is sitting on the floor in one of the corners, looking dazed.

I don't answer. Hope's eyes move restlessly despite being closed, and I gently push back one of her eyelids. Her *lumen* shines

295

brightly from the darkness of her pupil, and I let her rest, not daring to disturb her by measuring her *deimos*. I look around, but there's nowhere more comfortable for her to lie. The cell is bare except for a toilet in the corner and a jug of water by the door.

"She will be fine," I finally say.

"That disrupter thing did this to her?" Micah asks, his voice shaky with anger. "I should have been right there with her. I should have taken the hit…"

"Stop." My tone is cutting. "You cannot blame yourself for this. It was Tricia's doing, not yours."

"Tricia is the messed-up guardian with the braid?"

"That would be her."

I get up and test the bars, my *lumen* feeling like molasses as soon as I make contact. There's something in here still deadening my powers, like the entire place is emitting the signal of the disrupter. I look around for anything that could be of use, but I've seen everything there is. We're in the equivalent of a tomb, with no windows and bare concrete walls. Raleigh's sword is obviously gone. The *clavis* is in Arete's possession now. The Pathicomm is still in place in my ear, but I have no allies to hear my thoughts.

"Don't suppose you have any more useful secrets locked up in my brain? Like something we could use to bust ourselves out of here?" Davis asks hopefully.

"Unfortunately not."

Something nags me from the back of my own mind as a possibility of escape. A thought or an idea… Or perhaps a prayer.

I walk to the back wall of the cell, inspecting the bricks with my hand. The stones are cold if not a little damp to the touch, the only light in the holding area coming from an old-fashioned lantern in the narrow space outside the cells. This tomb might as well be one more realm away from Asphodel.

I think back to when we'd been captured by Tricia and the others. My head had been in a fog when we were taken, and I vaguely recall that my body had been in restraints, but my waking thoughts had been full of a prayer.

God, please help me. I need to find a way out.

And a response.

Look for the weak spot in the wall. Look for a leak or a crack.

It wasn't a prayer at all. I tried to use the Pathicomm to communicate to Raleigh's informant, and he responded. I probe the brick wall, and Davis and Micah both give me curious looks.

"What are you doing?" Micah asks.

I brace my hand on one of the stones again, a slight sting hitting my hand. "If we could disrupt the magical field, we might be able to get out of here. We're underground, but we could get out through this wall."

"What?" He narrows his eyes. "How do you know this?"

"I was given information from a guardian on our way here. An informant of Raleigh's."

"And you actually trust this person? Guardian? Whatever?" Micah grumbles. "Because I wouldn't."

I keep testing the wall. "This informant was the one who told me what happened to Raleigh in the first place. And whether you trust this guardian or not is not relevant," I say.

"Why were those guardians looking for me anyway?" he retorts. At the church, we adopted the fight-first ask-later approach to everything, and I know I owe him answers to at least some of his questions now.

"They were hunting for a chimera," I say.

"That doesn't explain why they were looking for me, unless…." He trails off, his jaw tightening.

"Yes, unless," I confirm, "that they believed you were one."

I watch as the storm clouds his expression. "Why do I get the feeling that you were responsible for this?"

"They had reports of a chimera at UB. You were also sighted there that night. They demanded a name, and yes, I gave them yours." I stop there. I honestly don't care if he understands the details – that Raleigh had been in danger, and that I feared for Hope's safety. I take full responsibility for everything.

"You make way too many decisions for other people," he grumbles.

I incline my head. "I have no defense for that."

"That's it?" he huffs. "That's all you're going to say?"

"What would you like me to say?" I ask quietly.

He shoots me a furious look. "I don't know. But the thing that's killing me now is the fact that you're with Hope right now, and I'm not."

I meet his furious gaze with fire of my own, finally hitting my breaking point. "You are not the only one with something to lose, Micah," I say coldly. "Do not make that mistake in assuming that."

"Yeah? I lost my best friend, an entire group that I'm supposed to be leading, and my chance to find my brother that I didn't know existed up until now. What did you lose?"

"The person I love most."

He falters – I see something almost like compassion or perhaps empathy – but then he shuts down again. "What did you mean before when you said that Hope shares your blood? Because she's a guardian? Do you think that gives you some special sort of status or something? Because the actions of the guardians who put us in here pretty much speak to the opposite."

"No, not because she's a guardian. Hope and Davis are my descendants."

A heavy blanket of silence settles over the room, and Micah and Davis stare at me like I physically struck them.

"What?" Davis looks stunned. "No. Get out."

I puzzle over this for a moment, not knowing where I could possibly go. "Yes," I say simply.

"Wait. The safekeeper thing? Hope's visions?" Davis rubs his forehead. "How long have you known?"

"Since you were born. I keep track of everyone in my family. I just haven't made it a practice to…"

"Interfere?" Micah chimes in.

"...interact with any of my progeny, but in this case, Hope actually sought me out. Multiple times."

"Wow." Davis blinks. "Are there more of us?"

"No. You are the last of my line, unless you have children of your own someday."

"So what do I call you? Great-granddad?"

Despite everything, my lips quirk up in a brief smile. "You should call me Jonathan," I say. "Nothing has changed."

"Yeah, tell that to Hope when she wakes up," Micah says under his breath.

I sigh. "I plan to."

"Why haven't you said anything?" Davis' tone is curious but also laced with a little bitterness. "All this time, we thought we had no one left in the family. I mean, you know what happened to our parents."

"Yes," I say. "Unfortunately I do know. And I can offer you no simple answer, only that I thought it would be bad luck."

"Bad luck to tell people the truth?"

Raleigh made a similar judgment of my actions, and the regret hits me hard. "Call it superstition, but I thought... I thought that if you knew who I really was, you'd both meet with your deaths soon after. As has all of the family that I've let into my life."

The second confession is also met with silence, this time even heavier. The major exception to this pattern had been Colette, but that's because I had been the one to walk away from her.

"Oh," Davis says, running his hand through his hair. "Well, as far as superstitions go, that one might be justified."

Micah studies my face, understanding beginning to dawn in his eyes. "Hey, Jonathan?" he says, his tone still hostile but perhaps a hair less. "What did happen to Raleigh?"

"Arete took her to Asphodel." I quickly fill him in on the essential details from the trial, and his expression transitions from looking disgusted to puzzled. Guardians and demons plotting together, everything orchestrated by Arete. I agree that it's a terrible mix, and I'm not sure if I'll ever make sense of it either.

He's quiet for several moments as he digests everything. "The mother of all guardians, huh? I wouldn't have guessed it."

"Unless we get out of here, I will not be able to get her back. Even if we do get out of here, I no longer have a way to get to Asphodel."

"What about the key?" Davis chimes in. "The one from my mother's grave?"

"Arete took it back," I say.

"There has to be a way," Micah mutters.

An uneasy silence settles over the cells again, and I use the time to study Micah. I hadn't been able to before -- the church had been too chaotic for me to make more than a brief assessment. He's always come across to me as serious, more so than the typical teenager in this day and age, and I get the same impression from him now. He mentioned leading a group, which I know from experience is a heavy load to bear. And he'd also mentioned a brother.

"Who is this brother?" I ask.

"Nobody," he murmurs. "It's nothing. Just a pipe dream."

Hope stirs, and I lean over and check on her. She whimpers, as though she's fighting to come back from her own nightmares but can't quite make it. Her *lumen* had looked strong enough, but she's a chimera and needs to replenish her *deimos* as well.

That's really the thing, the crux of the problem. All this time, the guardians have been clamoring for a chimera as the perfect warrior, but with both forms of energy, they are twice as vulnerable.

"You can do it, Hope," I whisper. "Fight a little harder."

I need to fight harder, too. There has to be a way out of here and to Raleigh, and it can't just be a pipe dream.

31

Micah

I think I finally get it. Not everything, but I finally understand why Jonathan always put Hope first. Why I was inconsequential to him. Understanding doesn't mean automatic forgiveness or that I even need to like him. But the connection between him, Hope, and Davis is something I have to respect.

We've been trapped in the partial dark and full silence for what feels like forever. Davis is slouched against the wall, but I pace around the tiny cell. My nerves are shot as I wait for the slightest signs of Hope regaining consciousness. She's in the same position on the floor, only this time with her head resting on Jonathan's leg. I'm not sure if that's just an attempt to make her more comfortable or if the head-elevated approach applies to guardians with trauma. The fact of the matter is that we don't know what happened to her, and I'm worried about her being out for so much longer than the rest of us. I need to get her out of here so I can take her to Isabela.

The guardians stripped me of my phone-tracker that I could have used to send a signal to Ben. I'm still wearing the tracker bracelet, and it looks like Hope is too, but we have no way to communicate to anyone but ourselves. I keep waiting for a guard to show up or maybe our captor to rub it in our faces that we were caught. Someone. *Something.* But they know we're powerless, so there's no need for them to come down here and torment us more than they already are.

I even try talking to Vahni, and for the first time ever, I'm hoping I'll hear that gravelly, awful voice of hers.

Vahni, I'll come back, just like you wanted. Just let me cross through.

I don't go further than that, just in case she can actually hear me. I know I shouldn't barter with an immortal goddess. It's a crazy idea – to want to cross realms, but if Arete really has Raleigh, maybe I could save her and then we could save the others. It's a lot of maybes. Too many.

It kills me that I can't be with Hope right now. Jonathan's keeping a close eye on her, and I keep waiting for him to tell me if there's a change in her status, but he doesn't say anything.

"Jonathan," I hiss.

"What?" he says back.

I fiddle with the tracker on my wrist. "You said something before about disrupting the magical field? How would you do that?"

He treats me to one of his super long pauses, and I'm glad we're in separate cells because I want to throttle him for an answer.

"I have never done it before."

"Come on. Think," I say, desperate. "How could we do it?"

"I think we would have to do something akin to creating an electrical disturbance, only with magic," he says. "Which leaves us back with the original problem. We can't create a magical disturbance without magic."

"But assuming we could," I insist, "do you have enough energy to bust us out of here?"

"Assuming we could," he says firmly, "I will do everything it takes to bust us out of here."

"Good." I eye Hope's tracker. "See that bracelet on Hope's wrist? I need you to give it to me."

He doesn't move. "Why?"

I roll my eyes. "Look, I get it. I trust you about zero percent, but I'm trying to help you too. Can't you just give it to me?"

"I like to know what I'm getting into before I actually get into it," he says calmly.

We're wasting time talking when I could be testing out my theory, but I bite back my retort. I'd be the exact same way if our positions were reversed. Jehoel had never told me what the details of our plans were, and I always resented that about him.

"The bracelets are actually trackers. It magnifies *deimos* energy and is how we can find each other over greater distances than normal," I explain. "But this initial design was a little glitchy, so when the bracelets are activated right next to each other, they put out a lot of energy. I've done it once by accident… It kind of feels like an electrical shock."

He sits up ramrod straight. "So it might provide the interference that we need."

"Yeah, that's what I was thinking. Don't know if it'll work, but it's worth a shot."

"Agreed."

Jonathan unfastens Hope's tracker, Davis and I watching him silently from our side of the cell. He tosses it to me, and I hold one tracker in each hand and mentally brace myself for the worst. Electrical disturbance was an understatement. The last time I did this – Jehoel was just on the other side of a wall from me, and I'd accidentally activated mine – both of us had nearly gotten knocked out.

"Okay, so this might only cause a temporary magical short, so get ready to act right away," I say to Jonathan. I hold up the trackers, hoping to God that this works. "On three?"

He nods, and I count down quickly from three. I grimace, pressing on the metal pieces while Jonathan keeps his hands flat against the stone wall. I feel a jolt of energy tugging on my *deimos*, but it's weak at best and then fizzles.

"Crap." I drop Hope's tracker, making a fist with my other hand. "I was afraid of that."

"What?" Jonathan barks. "What happened?"

Nothing happened, which is exactly the problem. "We might need a direct connection to Hope. Forget about it."

"Forget about it? Why forget about it? We can't just give up," Davis protests. "You guys might be used to this kind of stuff, but I'm totally freaking out. We're locked up in some underground jail that probably no human knows about, and we haven't seen anyone for hours. They may just leave us here to starve to death. Or to eat each other."

"You watch too many movies," Jonathan says wryly. "Micah, let me try."

"It's supposed to connect to a *deimos*," I say doubtfully. "But you can try. Squeeze the metal part between your thumb and forefinger when I say."

I toss Hope's tracker back through the bars, and we both activate at the same time. This time, I feel absolutely nothing. I shake my head. Maybe the magic in here is too strong, but it's more likely that it isn't compatible between guardian and demon.

"Put the bracelet thing back on Hope and try it again," Davis says.

"It might hurt her," I explain. My heart twinges as I stare at her, lying on the concrete floor with her head on Jonathan's leg. "I don't know how hurt she is to begin with..."

"But if you need to connect to another *deimos*, hers is the only other one we've got," Davis says.

"Micah?" Hope lifts her head from Jonathan's leg, her movement tinged with pain and her voice groggy. But she's awake, and my heart leaps at the sound of her saying my name. I run over to the bars, ignoring the sting as I come into contact with them.

"I'm here. Are you okay?" I try to keep my voice steady, but my fist clenches around the iron bar. I feel the magical restraints worm through my skin, and I release it.

She groans, struggling to sit up, and Jonathan puts his hand on her shoulder. "Take it slow, my dear. You were out for a while. We're breaking out of here, and you'll need your strength."

She stops struggling but stays sitting, leaning against his arm. Her eyes sweep through the cell, her lips turning up in a small smile when she finds me.

"How do you feel?" Davis calls over.

"I'm okay. A little dizzy." She looks around, blinking. "Are we…in jail?"

"Pretty much," Davis says. "Nice, isn't it?"

"I heard some of what you said." She cradles her wrist. "Whatever you just did, it helped to wake me up. And it didn't hurt me."

Jonathan and I exchange hopeful glances. I'd felt something too, though it was weak.

"I don't want to risk it though," I say. "Not if you're not feeling one hundred percent. We'll try something else."

"Like what? If I've been out for so long, you guys must have exhausted all of your other ideas," she challenges. "You need two demons to make this tracker work. I heard you say that."

She must be feeling okay if she's arguing with me, and I give her a grim smile. "Yeah, but it might not work at all if the magic in here is suppressing everything, Plus there's only one demon in here."

She shoots me a withering look, taking the tracker bracelet from Jonathan. "But there's someone in here with a *deimos*. So let me try."

"No," I say.

"No," Jonathan echoes.

"You guys don't get it." She turns to Jonathan. "You can't protect me from everything. You aren't so removed from your humanity as you think. You can accept help now and then." She puts her arms around him and squeezes, and I see the surprise register on his face. "And I know you love Raleigh," she whispers, "so please let me help you get her back."

She releases him and gets to her feet, walking slowly but steadily over to the bars to face me. "Micah." She reaches for my hand, wincing a little when she comes into contact with the bars. "I tried to tell you this before you went to Alaska. I'm part of you, and you're part of me, and we have to do this together or not at all."

Her words hit me hard where it matters, right in the heart, and silence settles over both cells. Even Jonathan holds his tongue.

"I trust you, Micah," she says. "You have to trust me too."

She's right. I was mad at Jehoel for making decisions for both of us. I'm furious at Jonathan for the same reason. If I'm mad at Jonathan for making decisions for both of us, then how can I fault Hope for being mad at me for doing the same?

"You're absolutely right. We're a team. And I do trust you, Hope. Always have."

Her eyes widen, like she's surprised I gave in so quickly. But then her expression softens, and she links her fingers with mine. Her *deimos* may be weak right now, but she's so strong, stronger than anyone I know.

"On three?" she says.

"Yeah." I look into her stormy gray eyes and take a deep breath. "Brace yourself. One."

"Two," she says.

She keeps looking at me, and for a moment, the bars aren't there. My anxiety about Troy, about the Albany group, about my family and Elizabeth all fade into the background. For just this moment, Davis and Jonathan aren't watching us either. Right now the only thing in the world that matters is her and the fact that we're in this together. We always were.

Her grip tightens on my hand.

"Three," we say together.

I activate my tracker, and she does the same.

My sense of her *deimos* tears through my head like a scream. The fire rips out of my skin before I can stop it, and I hear Hope scream for real. Davis tackles me from behind and brings me down to the floor.

The pain subsides, the tracker connection now broken. I look up, desperately searching for Hope to make sure she's all right, but the fire is everywhere and I can't see anything but red.

"Jonathan, go!" I shout.

He doesn't respond, and I can't see past the blinding heat to help, but I think he must already be going because I hear the sound of something like an avalanche. I'm vaguely aware of Hope calling for me, and I crouch down and concentrate on drawing everything inside. But instead it gets much hotter, so much that I know I can't take it for much longer. I was wrong. I can't control Vahni's power like I thought I could, and now I'm going up in flames.

I open my eyes, surprised when I don't see fire. Not even a wisp of smoke. I'd succeeded in internalizing it, and Jehoel is standing in front of me, his face greenish and his smile wry.

"You?" I blurt out. "What are you doing here?"

"A signal like that was too hard to ignore. Might as well scream in my ear. I'm getting you out of here." He grabs hold of my arm, his grip like iron. The heat envelops me like a hellish cocoon before I can protest.

I rise to my feet, slowly. Jehoel is standing next to me, his body wracked by dry heaves as he leans against a wall. A jump from Alaska plus another one right afterward. He's gotta be hating it.

I look around, panic rising in my throat like bile. We're in a dark room, and it's just the two of us in here. He only took me and left everyone else behind.

"You have to go back and get the others," I choke out. "Please."

His brow furrows. "The hybrid and human only. But not the guardian."

I don't know the exact history between Jehoel and Jonathan, but it doesn't matter. This is non-negotiable.

"Bring out all of us, and then we're even."

"Fine," he says with a shrug. I watch, incredulous, as he fades away in a blast of heat. I expected him to put up a bigger fight than that.

God, I hate how he always does that. It must be the easiest way out of having to deal with stuff, to just disappear in the equivalent of a puff of smoke. And I don't even know where I am. I'm in a cluttered, square room that has papers all over the floor. I pick up one of them and hold it up to the light from the window so I can see what it says.

I laugh out loud.

I'm still grinning when Jehoel returns with the others. He immediately steps away from Davis, who braces his hands on his knees and pukes. Hope and Jonathan are both covered in rubble and dirt, as though they'd been tunneling their way out of the tomb. She clings to his arm, looking as white as a sheet.

"It's the effect of the teleporting," I reassure them. "You'll feel better in a minute."

"I remember," Hope says, gaining a little more color in her cheeks even as she says it. She detaches herself from Jonathan and rushes over to me, giving Jehoel a meaningful if not totally friendly look. It surprises me to think it, but she's probably made the jump with him before. After all, Hope's the one who initially approached Jehoel and introduced him to me that night from hell at UB. Hope trusted him to help me, which is the entire reason I placed my trust in him too.

I hug her close to me, the fact that we're together right now the greatest reminder of how far I've come. I guess I forgot about the beginning somewhere along the way.

My arms still around Hope, I nod at Jehoel. "Thank you," I say.

He adjusts his glasses in that familiar gesture, looking uncomfortable. "Despite my dislike for that one," his gaze slants over to Jonathan, "I would have felt slightly guilty leaving them buried under the ground."

He's trying to be funny in his strange way, but I want him to understand. "Well, it says a lot that you came in the first place. And then you brought me exactly where I need to be," I persist. "How did you know?"

His hand goes to the bridge of his glasses. "Cael spoke with Eli earlier today." A trace of a smile touches his mouth as he adds, "Don't worry. It was via a secure channel. Eli mentioned how you instructed them on better protocols."

"I wouldn't call it protocol, just a common sense reminder." But I see what he's trying to really say. I'd gotten into countless arguments with Jehoel over the right way to do things when we worked together in Alaska. I think it was his way of testing me and my convictions, so I'd be able to find my own way.

"Sorry, but I don't get it," Hope says from my side. "Why are you happy that he brought you here of all places?"

"Because this is the old community center, which is where I told the alliance to meet me. This is where I need to be." I say to Jehoel, "This was your idea all along, wasn't it? You wanted me to lead them."

"Ultimately it was Cael's plan. I told him of your great leadership potential, and when the raid happened in Albany, he was convinced him that you were the natural choice to lead them."

"But I'm the one who has to make the decision to do it."

"As you say." He inclines his head, and when he lifts it again, there's no reservations, no guardedness, only respect. "Micah, what you want to do now is ultimately up to you. The alliance is a brotherhood, and if you decide to stay active in it, that's up to you too. If not, then I'll wish you well and leave."

I turn away, needing time to mull this over, time that we don't have. I'd told the Albany group that I would help them relocate, but I'd been treating it as an assignment from Cael. Isabela had even made some comment as to how Eli and the others responded to me, but she probably knew about Cael's plan too.

No, this has to be my decision. And I think I know what it's going to be.

Jonathan approaches us. "Forgive me, but I need to be somewhere else right now. Thank you for your assistance," he says stiffly to Jehoel. "Though we were on our way to freedom when you found us."

Jehoel flattens his mouth into a line. "True," he says back. "As long as you acknowledge that your way to freedom was through twenty feet of dirt and rock."

"Wait," Hope interjects, ignoring Jehoel. "How are we going to get to Asphodel?"

"I'm going to have to find another ward of Asphodel and convince him or her to take me. You," he adds pointedly, "shall stay here."

She rolls her eyes. "Aren't wards difficult to find?"

He gives her a wry smile. "Yes, but I don't exactly have another option."

"Hold on." I interrupt this time, my eyes fixed on Jehoel. "That night at UB. You had the *clavis* that belonged to Raphael. Where is it? I could use it to get through."

"I threw it into the gateway before it closed," Jehoel admits.

"Why would you do that?" Davis blurts out. He looks just as pale as Hope does, but at least he's not green anymore.

"Same reason that I hid the location of the *clavis* within your mind," Jonathan says. "Because no one would ever get to it."

"Within whose mind? Davis?" Hope stares at him.

"You're not the only one with superpowers, sis. I'm like a keeper of secrets." Out of the corner of my eye, I see Jonathan trying to catch Davis' eye with a silent plea, but Davis ignores him. "Just ask Jonathan. He's the one who gave us all of these powers, in a matter of speaking."

"What do you mean?"Hope sputters. "Jonathan?"

Jonathan turns his attention to her, his expression enigmatic. "I promise I will explain everything to you, my dear. I owe you that and so much more."

We all have secrets and we all have weaknesses. I look at Jehoel, who's standing off to the side like a casual and somewhat amused observer. But still, he came to my rescue without question. Hope is my unfailing source of strength, true to her name, and Davis isn't kidding about superpowers. I walk away, not envious of Jonathan having to extract himself from that entire mess. If only he would have come clean with her from the beginning, he'd have a lot less explaining to do now.

His words resonate in my ears. Owing her that and so much more.

Owing Vahni.

A ward of Asphodel.

There's a way to put the nightmares to rest, if only you open your eyes and really see.

"Micah, what's up?" Davis asks. "You look like you have an idea."

"Give me a sec." I shove my hand through my hair and walk into the hallway so I can get away from the talking.

The nightmares and the visions haven't gotten better since I came to Buffalo, they've been getting worse. Vahni's expecting me. She wants me to return home. She knows Arete is up to no good. That's why she's been appearing to me, not because she wants to kill me. She could have done that a million times by now.

I stare down at my hands, at the clear part of my palm because of the mark that never forms anymore. I was relieved when I found out I couldn't make the mark and open the portal to the other realm, but it wouldn't make sense for Vahni to take away my power to open the doorway if she wants me to come back.

Unless I don't need the mark to get through.

I can help Jonathan get through too. I'll do that much for him. Because of Hope and because of everything he's done for her. Okay, and also because of the things he's done for me too. He was my original mentor. He helped me through my final transformation into a full demon. More importantly, he's helped Hope in ways that I simply couldn't. I peek into the room, taking in Jonathan's hallowed appearance, the pain in his eyes, and I think I know why he looks so tortured. The guy's in love with Raleigh.

I'm going back to Asphodel. To help him get her back.

I walk back into the room, a grin on my face, and everyone looks at me like I've officially lost my mind.

"I'm a ward of Asphodel. I can take you."

Stunned silence meets my announcement. Jonathan recovers first and says quietly, "But the demon *clavis* has been lost."

"I'm pretty sure I don't need a key. If you want to get into Asphodel, I'm your ticket."

Jehoel approaches me, his brow creased in concern. "Micah, may we speak?" He takes my arm and leads me to the corner without waiting for my answer. "Why are you doing this?" he demands. "You have an entire alliance group coming here that's relying on you."

"I know that." It's an admission that I'm finally willing to make. "I'll come back and help them."

"And if you don't come back?"

"He will," Hope says, sounding confident but also horrified at the notion. "They both will."

I walk over to her, feeling her tense up as I put my arm around her. She looks to the door, Jehoel and Jonathan already advancing as we all hear the footsteps sound from the hallway. It's from a good distance away, and it sounds like someone running.

"Wait," I say. "Let me check it out."

I open the door and poke my head out, looking into same hallway that Troy had given me a tour of before all of this craziness went down. And it's Troy that comes around the corner, his jaw dropping when he sees me.

"Micah!" He sprints down the rest of the way, giving me the equivalent of a tackle hug before noticing everyone else behind me. "How did you get away?"

"Long story, but it involves a teleporter and disrupting a magical field. How did you get away? And how are you here?"

"I hid and tried to follow you after they took you, but I lost you. I figured I'd wait here for that Albany group to show up and ask them for help getting you back." He grins. "But now I guess I don't have to."

"You'd do that?"

"Told you, buddy. I'm in this for the long haul."

"We'll all help," Davis chimes in.

I look from him to Hope and Troy, and then to Jonathan and Jehoel. After everything the guardians put us through, I know we could all use a break to replenish our energy. Davis is still a little greenish but is still willing to help, Hope covered with dirt and debris but with a look of optimistic determination on her face that matches Troy's. Jonathan looks haunted but equally resolute in what he has to do. Even Jehoel is still here when he could have just left, and I know that despite our differences, I belong to the brotherhood just like he does. We may have taken a beating, but we're like an unstoppable force, all of us in this together.

You shall return home to me, one way or another.

"Jehoel, if I take Jonathan to Asphodel, will you stay and wait for the Albany group until I get back? They're going to need some help settling in."

He inclines his head. "Of course. Until you get back."

"Troy, you too," I say. Jehoel raises his eyebrows, and I add, "Troy is part of the brotherhood too."

Troy barks a laugh. "Sweet. Honorary demon status. I'm totally cool with that."

"I'm coming with you," Hope says when I turn to her.

"If she goes, I go," Davis insists, and she reaches out to him.

"Hope, you got hit hard," I protest. "There's a woman who's traveling with the alliance that can heal you."

Her cheeks redden. "She can do it when I get back. I'm not letting you do this without me."

"You're a chimera. Given Arete's agenda, I think you should stay as far away from Arete as possible," Jonathan says.

"I'm coming too," she says firmly.

I step up to her and look into her eyes. They're full of determination and trust, and they aren't stormy anymore. She reaches up and touches my face and says in a softer tone, "I'm not letting you leave without me this time."

"Hope, are you absolutely sure? I've been to Asphodel before. It's not an easy journey."

She gives me a small smile. "It's never been an easy journey for us, Micah. But we're in this together."

I pull her close, loving the feel of her next to me and knowing she's right. So many times in the past year that I've wished I could take her away from everything – that we could leave all of our problems and obligations behind. But I've never been able to do that, no matter how far I've run.

I just never dreamed that I'd be taking Hope away with me to Asphodel.

The acceptance of what I'm about to do gels in my head, and I can almost feel Vahni's approval as her presence links up with my awareness. She wins this round and she knows it, and her voice enters my head and sends a fiery chill up my spine.

Let me guide you home.

32

Jonathan

It's like we're marching into war, and everybody's emotions flood me all at once. Excitement. Determination. Fear. Love.

We're two blocks away from the community center, and Micah tells us to stand guard and get ready. He paces the alley, testing the outside wall of the building and trying to decipher whatever instructions he's receiving from the goddess Vahni. Davis is a bundle of nervous energy, and he directs it into organizing the supplies that he and Troy were able to throw together from the community center's pantry. He and Hope speak in the softest of whispers as though conspiring with plans of their own.

I look at Hope, who's eating peanut butter straight out of jar with a spoon. Out of the four of us, she's the only one who feels calm, but I can't hold back any of my misgivings any longer.

"Exactly how many times do you need to die before you learn your lesson?" I say to her.

Hope stops whispering and passes the jar to Davis. "Don't hold back, Jonathan. What are you really trying to say?" She plants her hands on her hips, her chin set in an equally stubborn stance.

"Asphodel is not for the weak of heart."

"Not a problem then," Hope says, patting her chest. "My heart doesn't beat."

"Not a problem for me either," Davis chimes in. "Even though mine still does."

"Have you ever been there?" Hope shoots me a sidelong glance, some of her anxiety finally leaching through.

"Only once." I blow out a breath. "And it was enough. I don't like the fact that you're both putting yourself at risk for me."

She gives me a smile that's both sweet and stubborn. "We're not putting ourselves at risk for you. Davis is obviously going because of me. And I'm going because of Micah and Raleigh, and okay, maybe a tiny bit because of you."

Despite everything, I smile a little. But our banter dies off as Micah's fist strikes the outer brick wall. He's several meters away and ignoring all of us, his concentration fierce as though he's trying to crumble the brick to dust.

"What is he doing?" Hope whispers.

"He's looking for a way in. Guardian portals usually show up of their own accord, but I have never seen one appear due to sheer will of a ward," I explain.

We stand and wait, Davis and Hope passing a water bottle back and forth between them. She offers one to me, and I take it. We were imprisoned for at least a day, and I don't realize how thirsty I am until the water hits my throat.

Hope reaches for my hand and squeezes it, her confidence flowing into me upon the physical contact. "Raleigh's going to be all right, Jonathan," she says in a quiet voice.

"And if she's not?" The very thought hurts my heart.

"She's still okay," Micah says without looking at us.

I hate that I have to turn to him for help and now for answers too, but my pride can be damned right now. "How can you be so sure?"

He grimaces, touching his hand to his forehead. "Because Vahni says we still have time."

The wave of relief that rides through me is almost overwhelming, but there's still the matter of bargaining with

Arete once we get there. Vahni is supposed to be the impartial one of the three ruling members of the Praxidikai, and from what Micah says, it appears that she's in disagreement with Arete. Impartial or not, I hope that both of these things wind up stacking up in Raleigh's favor.

"Is she speaking to you?" Hope asks. She starts walking toward him, and I pick up on his emotions, tightly wound and desperately hanging onto control. I feel his control slip, and then his fear.

"Hope, get back!" I warn, but it's a second too late.

Fire roars up the wall from the ground, rapidly ascending the bricks like angry fingers. Hope stops and throws her hands in front of her face to protect herself from the heat, but Micah doesn't move. He stares at the fire with his head slightly cocked, watching as a hellish doorway to the other realm carves its way into the wall.

"Stay back. I need to clear the way through," he calls.

He closes his eyes, his lips moving silently as if speaking a prayer. I'm abruptly flooded with his intense feelings of anguish. I've been there, and I know. He's going to sacrifice himself, but I can't let him do this.

I call to him and start running just as the fire engulfs Micah from head to toe. His howl echoes in the alleyway, Hope wailing his name as she sprints toward him. I hear Davis mutter a curse from behind me, but I'm already sprinting forward to catch her. She kicks at me as my arms encircle her, Davis taking hold of her arm and yelling at her to calm down. She keeps throwing out punches and kicks, a flicker of her *deimos* spearing me in her attempts to get free. I close my eyes and bear the brunt of her desperation and anguish, and I hold her tightly until her efforts to twist free become weaker, until the tears are pouring down her cheeks. I hand her a handkerchief, and she clutches it, finally still except for the sobs that rack her body as we stand and watch him burn.

As soon as it starts, it stops. The fire is gone from the brick wall, the archway a red glow in the alley. Micah staggers back, his head down as the flames are drawn into his body with an audible suction of air and heat. The smoke clears in the next second, and he slowly turns to look at us.

"No," Hope chokes. My arms fall away from her, and her hand rises toward him. "Micah..."

"Holy hell," Davis mutters.

Micah's body is half-burnt to ash, his hair blackened and brittle, his skin charred and peeling. I'd seen Vahni once, long ago, and it's as though Micah is a partial reincarnation of the fire goddess. He lifts his hand in front of his face, a guttural gasp uttering from his throat as he sees his own skin. Without a word or a look in our direction, he turns away from us and walks into the gateway.

"No!" Hope screams, a stronger pulse of *deimos* tearing out of her. It's small but stuns me long enough for her to twist out of my grasp. She starts running toward the red glow, but she's too late. Micah's already gone.

"Hope! Wait!" I give chase, but she puts on a burst of speed, and my heart feels like a chunk of ice when the flash of auburn disappears into the gateway.

Adrienne. Colette. I lost them both, but I won't lose Hope. And I won't lose Raleigh.

My thoughts are determined, my will twice as much as I chase them into the gateway. There's a brief sting of heat, but it dissipates almost immediately, and I find myself choking on an acrid-smelling mist instead.

"Hope? Micah?"

The mist is so thick that I can't see my hand in front of me, the ground crunching under my feet with something that feels like bone. Davis stumbles into the space next to me and curses.

"What the hell just happened? Where are we?" He trails off, gulping as his foot hits a patch of something disturbingly crunchy.

318

"I had to take the heat of the fire to clear the gateway." Micah's voice sounds like it's coming through an old speaker. I hear lighter footsteps crunching on the ground and then a sharp intake of breath.

"Micah," Hope cries. "You…You're…"

"I'll be okay, sweetie. I'm already healing," he rasps. "Come on. We made it through, but we still have a ways to go."

I step quickly though the ever-thickening mist toward his voice, my hand finding his shoulder. "You do not need to do this," I say gravely.

"I know." His voice is a fraction clearer this time. "But you're important to Hope, and she's important to me."

The mist becomes unbearably thick and pungent, and I hear Davis gag from behind me.

"Help him." Micah's voice starts to fade. "We're crossing over…."

I'd made the journey to Asphodel once before, and I still remember the terrible sensation as we'd crossed over. My chest feels like it's bound in iron bands, the heat from the mist stinging my eyes and nose. But I force myself to take in a deep breath, and the pain lessens. I do it again, and it's almost bearable.

I find Davis, putting my hand on his back and trying to transfer to him as much calm as I can. He stiffens, and I feel his guard go up and repel me.

"Breathe," I tell him. "I promise it'll be easier on you if you do."

"Micah?" Hope sounds like she's speaking through a tunnel, and for the first time since we set out on this journey, I sense how afraid she really is. "Don't let go of me."

"Never again," I hear Micah tell her.

We walk for miles, the air hot and sky bright despite the twin suns sitting low on the pink horizon. Miles of craggy black rock, sand, and twisted trees flank the right side of the path. The sea extends out as far as I can see on our left, the greenish water angry and spraying us as we make our way down the slippery black stone. The way is narrow, just wide enough for two, and Micah and Hope take the lead, the sunlight glinting off Hope's auburn hair and transforming it to fire. Davis walks with me and looks at the landscape in awe and disbelief.

The sea crashes down on the surf and sprays us, and Davis wipes his hand across his cheek with a grimace. "Are we on a different planet?"

"No, we are still on Earth." I shoot him a sideways glance. "A different realm."

"Seriously?" He walks a few more steps before breaking the silence. "I don't get how this could still be on Earth. How have scientists not discovered it yet?"

"It's an alternate realm," I say. "They wouldn't be able to find it."

"But how does that work?" he persists. "So if I'm standing on a street corner in my so-called realm, does that mean there's someone from a different world standing in the same space?"

"Generally not. This place is all subterranean, just like in the myths of the underworld."

Davis looks out towards the suns, utterly baffled, and I add, "The suns are just an illusion. They're essentially a metaphor for the powers of guardian and demon."

"The suns are *metaphors*?" Davis sputters.

"There are a lot of illusions here," Micah says without looking back at us.

Micah's appearance is slowly improving, seeming to heal as we walk. His skin is cracked but doesn't look like burnt paper anymore, and his hair is slowly transforming from the charred strands back to blond. Hope walks hand in hand with him as though nothing is different, and they talk to each other in quiet voices. Now and then Micah will laugh out loud at something she says.

Hope. The common denominator. She's important to Micah, and she's important to me, and the simplicity of his statement from earlier astonishes me. But it shouldn't. The equation has always been that simple. Hope is the reason that I agreed to ever meet Micah, why I saved his life once. But I also betrayed him for the same reason - twice - when I gave him up to the Praxidikai and then again to the guardians.

For some reason, the weight of what I've done feels much heavier here, in the stark landscape of this realm. The scenery shifts, a sheer black cliff growing out of the low craggy rocks on our right, and Hope and Micah pause to look up at its trajectory. She puts her arm around him, tenderly as though she's afraid of hurting him.

Hope may have been my reason for my actions, but they were my actions and mine alone.

"Micah, I'm sorry." They both turn around to face me, and I'm filled with even greater remorse to see him close up. His eyes are bloodshot, his skin ashy in some places and scaly in others. He's been healing, but not as quickly as he would if he were sleeping.

"I'm sorry," I repeat. "For all I have made you endure. If I hadn't bartered with the Praxidikai —"

Micah barks a humorless laugh. "I would have done the exact same thing to you if it meant saving Hope. Besides, if you hadn't handed me over to the guardians, we wouldn't have been able to cross over and show everyone this awesome realm." He looks at me steadily. "Can't exactly change the past, am I right?"

"What are you guys talking about?" Hope interjects. She scrutinizes my face then looks at Micah's. "Is there something I should know?"

I wait for him to tell her everything, willing to receive the brunt of Hope's wrath when he does. But Micah simply shrugs before turning away. "It's nothing. Come on, let's keep going forward."

I stare after them as they make their way down the never-ending path. I'd expected more of a fight from him, or at the very least for him to tell Hope more about how I'd turned him over to the guardians. I may be too accustomed to the reactionary style of other guardians, and I'm surprised that he seems like he's moved past this.

I frown down at the black rock, same as it was when I was here centuries ago. Going forward. It's something that I don't do very well at all.

The suns sink as low as the horizon before making their ascent again. There is never pure darkness in Asphodel, not even from the demons. The two races that live here don't war with each other nearly as much as we do in our realm. Christianna even told me how much she'd grown to prefer the constant peace dictated by the Praxidikai over the unrest of the realm of Earth.

I survey the barren rocks and cliffs, the lifeless sea that's also one of Vahni's illusions, and know that I could never thrive here.

"Micah, is Vahni still speaking to you?" I call ahead.

He shakes his head. "No, but she knows we're close." Hope murmurs something in a low voice, and he shrugs. "I can just tell."

I glance at my watch, but the hands are still. The scenery shifts again after an unspecified time, the green waters quieting and the cliffs growing even taller. I spot an outgrowth of the black rock far ahead of us, but as we get closer, the shape of the rock becomes more defined. A human form, but it's not on the rock. It looks like a man, and he's standing in the sand just beyond where the path ends.

"Who's that?" Hope whispers. "The welcoming committee?"

"I'm not sure, but let me do the talking," Micah replies.

No one argues, and we continue forward. The figure turns around as we get closer, and Micah makes a choking sound.

"Jack...."

The man is in a gray business suit, his hair also a steely gray. His head is bowed, and when he looks up, he looks like Jack Williamson, the former district attorney of Buffalo, only his skin is mottled and wrinkled like something dead that's been left on the surf too long.

Micah's surprise is intense and hits me like a shockwave. I know from Hope that Micah did an internship for Jack and that they were close. I also know that it would be a mistake to think that this thing is really the former D.A.

"Hello, Micah." His voice is as coarse and gritty as the sand, his hand sinewy as he lifts it in greeting. His gaze is cloudy as it slowly takes in the rest of us.

"Is it really you?" Micah asks, suspicion mixing with his shock.

Jack's lips lift in a brief smile, sea water dripping out from two of his bottom teeth. "It is me. My physical form is irrelevant, temporary, as it was when you knew me up on the surface."

"No." Micah shakes his head. "You had a life there, and a family. They're still back there and very *not* temporary."

"You're Arete's ward," I interject as the realization hits me. "Micah, he is not to be trusted."

My comment bounces off Micah, who's completely taken in by Jack. The ward turns to me, his eyes a milky green just like the sea, before dismissing me.

"You may pass through, ward of Vahni," he says to Micah, "but these others have not been summoned."

"They're with me," Micah says, his tone more confident than he feels.

"Regardless, the Praxidikai has only summoned one today, and so I may only call one Victis," he proclaims. Sand falls from a crack in his neck and trickles down to his feet at a disturbing rate.

Hope exchanges alarmed glances with Davis, and I step toward Micah. His eyes are slightly less red but still reveal the pain he's in.

323

"We're in this predicament because of me," I say. "I should be the one to go."

Micah frowns. "We're here because Vahni wants me to be here. We'll both go."

"One Victis," Jack repeats, the sea water and sand mixing at his feet to form a black sludge. "Only one will see the Praxidikai today."

"I don't need the Victis to get up there," Micah says, but he sounds less sure of himself.

"You cannot fly that high on demon wings, ward of Vahni. The Victis will ultimately decide."

Jack faces the cliffs, letting out an unearthly sounding series of low notes, and the terrible song bounces off the rocks and echoes into the sky. I scan the cliffs until I see it, the black shadow that dances against the rocks like a passenger pigeon of death. It's been centuries since I visited Asphodel, but the sort of dread inspired by the Victis isn't something I would ever forget. The Victis playing by the cliffs is made of despair in its purest form, of all of the poison that humanity carries with it.

Hope looks back and forth between us, her face pale. "What does he mean, the Victis will decide?"

"He means it'll choose me because I'm the ward," Micah says simply, throwing me a stubborn glance.

He takes Hope's hands, the emotions from the two overshadowing what I can feel from the Victis. Micah leans down to whisper something into her ear, and she turns her head and kisses him.

"Whoa," Davis murmurs from next to me. "Are you seeing what I'm seeing?"

Micah's hair moves like the water churning in the ocean, only it brightens instead of darkens, the charred strands springing back to life. The cracks and scales in his skin fade and transform to be smooth again. He's like a phoenix springing back from the ashes, and it's somehow because of Hope. I can feel her bittersweet emotions, her strength intermingled with her desperation that he's leaving her yet again.

I can't change the past, but I can change this.

Before they can separate, I step forward to the edge of the path and concentrate my thoughts on the Victis. I don't call up my old memories this time, just focus on what's at stake in the here and now.

I think only about Raleigh. The way she's so strong but also so vulnerable. The way she laughs. The way she makes the lightness in me come out and make all of my darkness fade to the background. The way I'd felt the first time we kissed and how I don't want it to be our last.

The Victis stops its dance. Its shadow hovers in the air as though making a decision. If it takes me, it will feed off my energy and twist my good thoughts into pure poison. It's what these creatures live for.

Choose me.

33

Micah

She isn't the reason I'm choosing to go up the cliffs. She's the reason I'm making sure I come back.

Ever since I took the heat from the gateway, my bones have been brittle, my skin like paper, every breath I draw feeling like an inferno in my lungs, but when Hope kisses me, the fire cools. Her lips are sweet, her touch on my skin igniting my power to heal. She helps me become whole again, in this place of all places.

The air around us becomes as cold as a northern wind. I dismiss it as being part of the healing process until I remember. The Victis are colder than death.

I break away from Hope, and her gaze roams over my face like it's the first time she's ever seen me, her fingers lifting to touch my cheek. She gives me a small smile. "Be careful."

"Always."

Hope moves to stand by her brother and clings to him like she's afraid they might get swept away. I walk out to the edge of the rocks next to Jonathan. He stares at the Victis with fierce concentration, like he's trying to will it to do something.

"I'll get her back," I say to him. I'm going to have to pit two immortals against each other to get Raleigh back, but Vahni wants me here, and that knowledge gives me confidence.

Here goes. The Victis sways back and forth in the shadows of the cliffs, as if it's watching us, and I stand determined and face it. A chill pierces my heart as I remember the last time one of these things took me up the cliffs. Teleporting is cake compared to traveling with one of these things. It screams over from the cliffs like a bullet, and I hear Hope's gasp and Davis' curse as it approaches the end of the rocks in a streak of darkness.

It envelops itself around Jonathan.

"No!" I shout. "*Take me!*"

It's no use. I watch helplessly as Jonathan's shrouded and bound, as his expression reflects back the horror inflicted by the phantom. And then he's gone into the sky.

It should have been me. Jack said I was the one who was summoned. I push out my wings, but Hope runs over to me and catches hold of my arm before I can take flight.

"Jack said you can't fly that high!" she protests. "Right, Jack?"

The gatekeeper Jack is facing the sea now, like he's still listening but has nothing more to say. Even though my human connection to him may be gone, he was my mentor in real life, and I'll never forget his lessons from when I was his intern. He taught me how to negotiate. He showed me how important it was to take risks when something was worth fighting for.

If he's a ward of Arete, he wasn't sent here to help me. But I know Jack. He's waiting for me to come to my own conclusions.

"He said I can't fly that high on my demon wings, but I think he was hinting that I could make it with Vahni's power. She helped me get down from the cliffs last time I was here."

"Are you sure?"

I glance to Jack as he starts walking toward the green sea, like his job is done here. When he was the D.A., he always did that to signal that he was done with the conversation, walking away whether the conversation was still going or not.

"Yeah, I'm sure." I see how stricken her expression is, and I squeeze her hand. "Jonathan can't face them alone."

"Exactly why I need to come too."

"And me," Davis adds.

I look back and forth between her and Davis, torn by indecision.

"He's our last living relative," Davis says firmly. "We're coming."

Hope draws away from me and stares at him, her mouth open. "What did you say?"

"Jonathan's like our great granddad multiplied by a factor of eight. It's the truth, baby sister."

"I…I can't even…."

I tune them out for the moment. If I'm going to help Jonathan, I have to go now. I look up into the sky, barely able to make out the shadow of the Victis beneath the layer of clouds. The home of the Praxidikai is even higher than that. I can kid myself all I want and tell myself that it's an illusion, but it's still an illusion I'm going to have to get through.

I'm whole again thanks to Hope, and I take a deep breath to steel myself. Vahni's power inflames within my veins, and I coax it further until flames burst out of my shoulder blades. Hope and Davis stop talking and stare at me as I stretch out pure wings of fire. The power sits comfortably on me now, and I know it's mine. I'm strong enough to do this.

I hold out my hands. "Let's go."

With their hands firmly in my grasp, I jet straight into the sky. We soar higher and higher, the twin suns rising with us, and I expect the air to become thinner, but it doesn't.

The Praxidikai might have given me no choice but to take Vahni's power. But this time I choose to use it.

You shape your own destiny, Micah, despite your worst fears that you cannot.

⤳

The gates are closed when we get there.

"Watch your step," I tell them. Hope nods, swiping her hair out of her eyes and looking behind us. Davis cranes his head up and gapes.

There's a sheer drop-off of a cliff behind us, the pair of massive stone doors set within the 50-foot tall walls straight in front of us. The clouds that represent the collective energy of light and darkness swirls high in the sky just above the wall, but the Victis and Jonathan are nowhere to be seen.

I walk up to the door and hesitate, trying to remember how Christiana had gotten in last time. Secret knock? Regular knock? Or had she just walked in? I'm still deliberating when the massive stone slabs slowly swing open. The stench of death wafts out at us, and my heart clenches like a fist. Asphodel is the place where souls go to rest, not bodies.

Hope slips her hand into mine, and I squeeze it. No turning back now.

I lead us through the doorway, throwing out my senses but detecting nothing except for the smell of decay.

The last time I'd been here, I'd walked through an otherworldly forest of silvery trees and grass. This time the black stone path still leads to the temple of the Praxidikai, but the way is lined by what looks like a small city. The buildings look ancient, like something I would have seen in history books about ancient Greco-Roman times, only when we walk past the first one, it has modern-looking elements like doors and fixtures. The second one we pass looks like a fossil of a house, dust and rubble around the base and interior, as though it got bombed.

"Who lives in these houses?" Davis asks.

"Don't know." I shrug. "They weren't here last time I came here."

"I can't believe you were ever here," Hope whispers.

They're just part of that illusion that Jonathan was talking about. Vahni's domain lies just beneath us, and the city is a mirage that separates us from the Underworld. It's a convincing illusion, with details down to a spider web shining in a streak of light from the rising suns.

There's no signs of life here though, not so much as an ant in sight. I look up and down the main stone path, rows of houses and narrower paths branching off from the main one. This whole place is like a ghost town, and if Jonathan's here, I can't sense him at all. I just hope we don't run into any actual dead people.

We pass by another house that has spatters of dark paint on the stone. Butterflies swarm in my gut as I stare at the pattern, and Hope's hand tightens in mine as she sees it too. It's blood, not paint.

She swallows hard. "Should we check out if he's inside?"

I glance down at her. She's a little pale, but she's poised as though she's ready to open the door and march in to face whatever's waiting for us. Given that we're standing over an entire sea of souls from dead people, it could be anything.

"Hey." I nudge her with my elbow, and she breaks her concentration from the house to look up at me. We haven't had much time to breathe since I came back, and I need to tell her.

"I love you."

The look in her eyes softens. "Love you too."

Davis clears his throat from behind us, and Hope blushes. "Feeling left out, Davis? Sorry. Love you too, big brother."

I laugh a little, the tension of the moment broken until I turn back and look at the door. There's a smudge that dulls the shine of the brass door handle, and I step closer and see that it's blood in the shape of a fingerprint. My eyes transfix on the whorls and grooves as they fill up with fresh blood, and I stiffen, a hiss caught in the back of my throat.

"Step back for a second, 'kay?"

Hope lets go of my hand, and I wait until she's next to Davis. I reach for the doorknob, turning it gingerly and avoiding the blood. The door creaks open slowly, and I steel myself to see Vahni or some other horror.

But it's worse.

"Lina," I choke out.

You came home.

My heart leaps into my throat as my dead sister steps out onto the stone path and closes the door behind her. She isn't drowning like in my dream, but she's just as I remembered in life. Her eyes are bright and vibrant, her face breaking into a warm smile when she sees me.

The nightmares that Vahni sent me couldn't have prepared me for this. It's like Lina's walking out of her old apartment and on her way to work, her blouse and skirt freshly pressed and hair perfectly curled with every strand in place. I haven't seen my sister since the night she died, and I never thought I'd see her again.

"If you stay, we can see each other all the time," she says, her dimples deepening.

Oh my God. I don't know how many times I've thought about what I'd say to her if I could just have the chance. How deeply sorry I am that she died so young. How much I miss her every day. I always thought that if I had the opportunity, I'd ask her if she was at peace. If she could find it in her heart or soul to ever forgive me.

That last one is too much to ask. Way too much, and all of the words I want to say dry up in my throat like dust.

"You don't need to say anything, Micah. She said you would come. I'm just so happy you're home." She takes my hand, and my senses flood with the scent of the lotion she always used.

Home. It's the word that Vahni had kept using to talk about this place. And that's twice now that Lina had responded to me as if I'd spoken my thoughts out loud. I back away, but Lina's grip on my hand becomes amazingly strong.

"Come inside," she coos. "I can't wait for you to meet everyone, Micah."

Her smile. It's too wide and unnatural, and her tone isn't like Lina at all. Lina was fiery, full of cuss words and while she had a sense of humor, she wasn't all smiley and sweet like this.

"Feels weird to hear you say my name," I manage to say.

A frown creases her brow, but it vanishes as she lets loose with a tinkly laugh. Her teeth are unnaturally white. "Oh, Micah. You'll get used to me talking to you again."

That wasn't the point, and the real Lina would know. She always used to call me Mikey. Both of my sisters did, and Lina especially would do it on purpose to embarrass me when I had friends over to the house.

But the compulsion to follow her is strong, the pull toward the house almost irresistible. She pushes open the door, and that same stench of death assaults me, only it's even thicker this time. My hand flies up to cover my mouth and nose, but Lina just grins at me.

I need to breathe, but the smell is too much… I can't. I use what feels like a superhuman effort on my part and yank my hand out of her grip. As soon as I break away from her, the hold she has on me is broken too.

"You're not Lina," I growl.

Hope and Davis. In my shock, I'd forgotten about them. I turn my head and see them standing with a man and a woman about four or five houses away. The woman has long brown hair and the same slim build as Hope, and the man is about Davis' height and has his hand on Davis' shoulder. I catch a glimpse of Hope's face, and when I see her tears, I think I know who these people are supposed to be.

Hope steps into the woman's embrace, and Davis starts toward the house with the man.

"Get away from them!" I yell. "They're not really your parents!"

Lina lunges for my arm and catches it, her grin twisting into a leer as my legs seize up. Her teeth aren't white at all. They're yellow and turning brown as I watch, the whites of her eyes darkening to a yellowish-gray. The skin of her neck prickles like gooseflesh, and I fight back the urge to puke as hundreds of little black needles worm through and poke out. She shakes her head, the needles bursting into bloody feathers.

"You can't leave," she hisses. She narrows her eyes at me, dark pupils expanding to fill her whole eye.

She's a harpy. My sister is a freaking harpy, and I stand there and gawk at her until something or someone grabs onto my calf. I kick at it, and the harpy wobbles but throws out her feathered arms to catch her balance. It's her foot that's latched on to me with talons, the skin of her leg dried out and shaping itself into scales before my eyes.

I shoot a wild glance over at Hope and Davis. Their parents stand next to each other, hunched together and horribly misshapen. They're changing into some sort of creature too, one that's more furry than feathery and probably complete with claws. I shout for them to run but they're already on it. I watch with a mixture of panic and relief as Davis shoves the beast back and pulls Hope away.

I'm still held captive by my sister. But she's not really my sister, and I think about that indisputable fact as I scream in my head for Vahni.

"Vahni! You wanted me to come home, and I'm here!"

I was not the one to summon you.

The goddess' voice grates through my consciousness, but her words don't make any sense. She had been the one who called for me, but before I can think it through, her presence emerges, filling everything in the air like a smoke that creeps over my skin. I feel her essence in my blood like a rush of energy and heat, and then I see her.

She steps out through one of the houses between me and the others, beautiful and monstrous at once. Blood-red eyes fix on me and blaze with fury at the sight of the harpy — at least I hope it's because of the harpy. Vahni's face contorts with anger, her charred skin lined with angry veins like a roadmap to Hell. She looks like she's been waging her own wars here.

She undergoes her own transformation, shafts of fire-colored feathers rapidly piercing through her skin and bursting like flames before she takes off into the sky. The harpy lets go of me and takes off with a shriek, and I shield my eyes against the suns that are now high and watch it pursue Vahni. A crunch sounds from the rooftop of the house next to me, the two-headed griffin that was in the guise of Hope's parents leaping into the air and extending its own wings. Vahni looks like an angel of death as she soars higher and higher, dipping and twisting as she leads the harpy away, and the griffin rumbles then roars as it gives chase. The air fills with unearthly cries, balls of fire lighting up the sky like the sunset.

I really hope this is all just a really bad dream, but judging from the sharp sting of my leg, it's not. Hope stumbles into me just as I turn around to find her.

"We have to get Jonathan and get out of here!" she cries.

Her face is tear-streaked and ghostly white. While I'm not going to argue with that plan, I take the time to look her over. "Are you okay?"

She laughs, and it's not a happy-sounding one. "I just saw my parents turn into a monster. What do you think?"

"I think Arete has a sick sense of hospitality. And they weren't really your parents."

"I know." She swipes at her cheeks. "If I ever get to meet Arete, I'm going to kick her ass. Davis was able to break us free from them. Somehow."

"I have this weird thing I can do thanks to our great-grandpa." He shrugs. "I'm still trying to figure it out."

I take Hope's hand, she grabs onto Davis', and we run together toward the temple. The buildings crumble apart as we pass, like whatever power is holding them together is dying or at least diverted. A loud boom sounds from above in the sky, and the house on our right explodes into dust and debris.

"This is where our souls go when we die? This place *sucks!*" Davis shouts.

Not gonna argue with that one either.

We reach the bottom of the stairs to the temple, and Davis and Hope pause to catch their breath and gape up at it. The building is black rock like the path leading to it, rising from the cliffs and set against the dark clouds. We start climbing up the cracked, stone steps, but it feels like I'm walking through sand. My head grows heavier, forcing me to look down at my feet. A piece of the rock slides out from under my feet, and I stumble and keep climbing. I don't remember it being this hard the last time I was here, and from the sound of Davis' huffing and puffing, I'm not the only one having a hard time.

We should have been there by now, but when I drag my head to look up, the temple is just as far away as it was.

"Another illusion?" Hope pants from next to me.

"Arete's tricks," I agree. "She's trying to tire us out."

"It's working," Davis gasps, resting his hands on his knees.

"We have to keep going. Keep your head up and look at the top," Hope says after a long moment. "Remember that this isn't real."

Arete's illusions might only be tricks, but the puncture wounds in my leg is evidence that we could get hurt here. Or even die.

The thought shakes me to the core, and I fight to keep my head up and keep climbing. Hope was right about looking up, and we trudge our way to the top of the steps within minutes, Davis gasping for breath and Hope blowing out hers in a hiss.

Arete's standing just inside the entrance of the temple, and I let loose a low growl when I see what she's done.

She's dressed in her long white robe, flanked on both sides by Raleigh and Jonathan. Raleigh's in a long white dress too, but

Jonathan's still in his usual black suit, and they're holding onto Arete's hands like they're a paper doll chain. I take in the vacant look in Raleigh's eyes and in Jonathan's too, and my heart grows heavy.

"You are finally home, Micah." Arete's voice is quiet, but her words hit me hard.

"You?" I stare at her. "It was *you* that wanted me back? I thought it was Vahni."

She doesn't answer, and my mind whirls with the shock of the realization. Arete was the one who messed with my head back home, who made the Hope-corpse appear in the woods. Made Jack appear in that diner when I was with my mother. Told me to kill Jonathan.

Arete made Lina and Hope and Davis' parents appear just now. Toyed with our emotions by creating those visions of the people we loved. Turned them into monsters.

My heart twists with hate, my mind searching for an explanation. I don't understand why she would bother doing all of that. So she could make Raleigh into a chimera and have me here to watch? It doesn't make sense.

Hope's hand tightens on mine as Arete turns an interested eye in her direction. The immortal guardian smiles at us, and I bristle.

The sounds of the battle between Vahni and the monsters continues behind us. Vahni, the only one who could possibly help us now. Arete glides toward us, Jonathan and Raleigh stepping in unison with her until we're face to face.

Three against three. Arete may have tricked me, but I won't let her win.

34

Jonathan

*A*drienne was on the verge of breathing her last breath, and I would do anything to save her.

I just didn't know how.

She lay in my arms, her cheeks spotted with the faintest pink. Her body was weary from the struggle, and when I touched her face, her eyes fluttered open for a second before closing again. My heart filled with fear, and I whispered her name.

"Can you tell me? What did they do to you?"

"The viscount found me..." she slurred. "The touch of death."

"No." I could not bear to hear any more. I gently lifted her eyelid, saw how dilated her pupil was, and I knew she had taken too much. There was an antidote for the poison, but I would have to leave her again to find the components of it. But she was so weak, as if she was on the verge of letting the fire in her soul go out.

"Colette," Adrienne whispered. "Protect her. You must use this to get out of here." She lifted her hand and placed it in mine, and I had a vial of the poison in my palm.

"I will get both of us out of here. I promise you." My voice shook, and I gathered her up in my arms and walked with her toward the door. We'd played the game for long enough, and I was getting her out of this God-forsaken place. "Just please, hold on until I can get you some help."

"Stop. It is too late for me." She reached up and touched my face with trembling fingers. "Jonathan, my love. Please. Forgive me..."

Her lips trembled, and her arm fell to her chest. She rasped a shaky breath, and she didn't take another.

"Adrienne, No!" I sank to the floor with her in my arms. The expression in her eyes was vacant, and I knew she was gone.

I stared down at her face as it became slick with tears, and I realized that they were from me. She deserved so much better, but she chose me and she chose to spend her days with me working in the depths of hell. She was like a light that extinguished the darkness of those around her. Even in a place like this, she was able to ease pain and misery instead of creating it. I would trade places with her in a heartbeat, only her heart remained silent, and mine hurt with the deepest sort of ache and regret. But then I cradled her to my chest, and I felt the slightest stirring from deep within her as I remembered her words from earlier.

"Do not let your abilities define you. Trust in yourself."

The vial burned in my palm. She wanted me to use it to feign my own death, so I could be free of this place. But Adrienne's words from happier times echoed in my head, and in that moment, I knew what I needed to do instead.

My gift of being able to bend wills and manipulate emotions never made sense to me. In the interrogation rooms, I could have been an instrument of the devil. But Adrienne taught me to help them and not harm. She taught me how to love.

The answer was so simple.

I placed my hand on her chest, searching deep within me for not just the emotions but for the power to harness them. All of the moments we'd spent together flashed before my eyes like I was the one that was dying. Hiding in secret and laughing together. Daring to talk about our dreams. Watching her walk through the doors of the old church with the single wild rose. The ecstasy of finally being with her on our wedding night.

A torrent of energy flowed through me, exhilarating in its intensity but draining at the same time. Adrienne drew in a rattling breath as I took *my last. My lips mouthed the words of Adrienne's final prayer, the fingers of cold death seeping into me.*

This was it. This was the end for me, but I would embrace it if it meant her salvation.

✥

Raleigh stands no more than a meter away from me, but I cannot reach her. We're both bound and silenced by Arete's magic, the guardian having imprisoned me the moment the Victis delivered me to her. Raleigh's eyes show her despair, and I don't need the Pathicomm to be able to read what she's saying.

You shouldn't have come.

There's no way I wouldn't have.

The house of the Praxidikai is stark and cold, absent of the immortal guardians or demons of Asphodel normally in attendance. The one other time I was here, this place had been alive with the direct descendants of Arete and Raphael. Today only the towering alabaster pillars of the temple stand as our witnesses.

Until Hope, Davis, and Micah walk up to the temple.

My mind screams all of the warnings that I can't make my lips say. That I can't believe that they would all place themselves in such peril. That they need to turn back. I try to communicate this to them with a look, but Micah only glowers at Arete. Davis sweeps a hand through his hair and gawks at the inside of the temple. Hope stares back at me with a stubborn set to her jaw. Her eyes are puffy and red like she's been crying, and the sight makes me livid.

"Choose who it will be. You or Raleigh Peyton." Arete leans close, my neck breaking out into gooseflesh at the feel of her whisper against my ear. The muscles in my throat loosen as she releases my ability to speak.

"Arete, great protector of light, I beg of you," I say with appropriate decorum. "You took an oath to uphold the collective. You cannot destroy all who depend upon you."

"You shall not be destroyed." Her lips pull back in a frightening smile. "Your *lumen* shall live on within Micah."

"What?" Micah pales. He takes a step back, his expression frozen.

Arete touches her left temple in a deliberate gesture, and the alabaster pillars by the doorway rapidly shift, grinding on the marble floor to form a barrier in front of the entrance. She gives him a beneficent smile before continuing.

"Raphael and I are directly descended from a single race, but in splitting from our ancestors, we made each lineage weaker. Guardians are limited in not ever being able to develop new powers or abilities. Demons must constantly feed off souls to survive."

I can't quite believe my ears. "You sought to create chimera to remedy this?"

"The Impiorum chimera have so far been a great disappointment. Their versions of the *Seraphim* are temperamental and volatile." She draws herself up to her full height, as if annoyed that I questioned her. "Their creation was a mistake."

Micah frowns. "So you're going to make the same mistake all over again with me?"

"No. You are a perfect blend of *deimos* and *ignis* – the power of fire and life that you received from Vahni." Arete stretches her hands out to him. "I originally thought I could merge the darkness and light into one being, but in seeing you, Micah, I now believe the *ignis* is the key to holding it all together." Her eyes gleam. "All you need is the *lumen* from a guardian, and you will be as our ancestors once were. In harmony."

"That time that *thing* appeared in the forest?" he says in a low, dangerous voice. "The 'chosen one' message that it sent me? That was you?"

She nods once, ignoring the threat in his tone.

"I'm not going to be your guinea pig," Micah replies. "None of us are."

She tilts her head at him, as though puzzled. "You would deny yourself of this honor? You would be the first to begin this harmonious way of life. The races will war no more. Tell me Micah, when is the last time you fed on souls?"

Micah's expression remains stony as I wonder the same thing. I can't recall him going out to feed since we were imprisoned, and from the jumble of his emotions right now, I'm guessing that Arete's comment struck a chord of truth with him. But even if there was a potential to create a demon that wouldn't feed on human souls, this is not the way to achieve it.

Hope and Micah – and his entire alliance group – already represent the solution in their choice to not feed, but she doesn't see it.

"Arete," I interject. "You allowed Raphael to create and destroy all of those demons. You would kill more guardians now in your quest for 'harmony' between lineages? You cannot destroy all of this life. You took an oath to protect it."

"Yes, what about all of the current guardians and demons that are alive now?" Hope demands.

The corners of her mouth turn down in displeasure at being addressed in this way. "It is for the good of the whole. Guardians and demons shall *all* live within Asphodel once more. And in peace."

Hope's look of horror mirrors my own feelings. Arete was right about guardians not being able to evolve – she's the prime example of this if she thinks we can revert back to a way of life that's two millennia old.

"But what of the humans in the other realm?" I protest. "Without guardians, there would be no way for their souls to come to rest."

"The reason demons originally escaped to the surface is because they required a life source and found it within the humans. With this way, we would no longer need humans," Arete waves her hand as though the entire issue is a mere annoyance. "That species would no longer be our concern."

"This is totally insane," Micah growls. "I bet Vahni isn't on board with any of this, which is why you're attacking her out there, right?"

He exchanges a quick glance with me. Micah's assessment is dead on. In being in Asphodel for so long, Arete has lost her connection to others aside from those in her small circle. Not to mention her sense of humanity. If she sees humans as a power source and nothing else, it makes her no better than the very worst of the soul-sucking type of Impiorum demons I've battled for centuries.

"And what of Raphael?" I challenge. "The Praxidikai are a tribunal of three. He cannot possibly be in support of this."

"Raphael he has no choice but to back my campaign."

Davis blurts out, "I don't know who you are, but you seem pretty ignorant of all the good you could do with your power instead of evil."

Arete's temper finally flares, and she glowers at Davis as though she'll evaporate him on the spot. Thankfully she turns to me instead, a storm in her eyes.

"I await your answer," she says, her impatience leaking through. "You or Raleigh?"

"I cannot in good conscience answer this."

"Then I will choose for you." Arete draws herself up to her full height, looking stately and menacing at the same time. She glides toward Raleigh, and Micah pushes Hope and Davis back behind him before charging forward. His hand springs to life with fire, but Arete whips around to face him, eyes narrowed and fingers touching her left temple. He cringes as his *ignis* is extinguished, his fist encased in what looks like black molten rock. The floor beneath his feet liquefies, and Micah sinks into it ankle-deep before it solidifies back into marble.

Hope curses loudly. "We won't let you do this."

Arete's eyes shift to Hope. "A bold statement coming from a chimera. You embody the weaknesses of both lines."

"I'm not weak," Hope says between her teeth. She links hands with Davis, and he looks down at his sister.

"Do it," he whispers. He closes his eyes in concentration, and I feel his emotions pour from him, vivid and desperate.

A door slowly opening.

Hope.

Lying on the bathroom floor.

Hair matted to her forehead with sweat or maybe blood.

Not moving. Lifeless.

He relives that same worst moment of finding Hope that he showed me at the cemetery, and I think he must be doing it to help Hope feed. Sure enough, Hope's *deimos* spikes in strength as she draws off his negative energy, and he wavers on his feet but remains standing. They must have prepared for this possibility before, perhaps when we were back in the alley. Despite the direness of our situation, I feel my heart fill with pride.

Hope lets go of his hand and rushes full-speed at Arete. The immortal guardian touches her temple, and *lumen* pulses toward Hope with the force of a supersonic blast. Hope cries out but sprints through it, and it's Arete's turn to exclaim in dismay when Hope grabs her arm and latches onto the immortal's *lumen*. Even when she was a human, Hope's strength was always in being able to drawing out the negativity of others, and Arete has a lot to give. I fight against the invisible restraints as Hope tugs with all of her might on Arete's power, and feel the bindings give just a little.

Arete strikes Hope across the face with her other arm, the force of the physical hit sending Hope skidding across the floor. A snarl rips out of Micah's throat, and he pounds his fist against the floor with the strength of a wrecking ball. The marble cracks but doesn't release him, and he brings his arm down again in an attempt to free his legs.

Hope scrambles to her feet and throws her hands out in front of her, sending bullets of her *deimos* toward Arete. A current of heat streaks through the chamber, and Raphael appears next to Arete, absorbing the impact of the assault. Hope's fear spikes, and I keep straining against Arete's bindings. They give a little more. Almost there. Almost free.

"What is this intrusion?" He glowers at us one by one, his expression leveling when he sees Micah. "Only my son has permission to be here."

"Sorry, but I'm not your son," Micah snaps.

Raphael's temper flares at the insolence, and he takes a step toward him, his expression dark. But then it clears, and he looks up to the blocked entrance.

"*Arete!*"

The pillars blocking the entrance grind apart, and Vahni stalks through, her voice echoing in my mind like the aftermath of thunder. She's like a firestorm, her blood-red feathers shedding like embers from a fire, her eyes alight with fury. Her presence is both magnificent and terrifying.

"Vahni," Arete says with derision. "You were already outvoted in this matter."

"*We do not act unless we act as three.*"

My world feels twisted and distorted from the way I knew it, and the fact that we're in a different realm right now is only one of the reasons. These three members of the Praxidikai are supposed to represent justice, supposed to protect the forces that sustain all life. But the chamber reeks of distrust, and I can't possibly fathom how they could ever mete out justice when they don't even trust one another.

Vahni moves to stand in front of Micah, shedding the last of her fiery feathers so she's back in her female form. She places ashen hands on either side of Micah's face, and he suppresses a shudder of revulsion but bears it. The marble floor shimmers like liquid mercury, rising to push Micah's feet out of its hold before it solidifies beneath him once more.

They stand like this for what feels like an eternity, Vahni with her eyes closed but with a sharp awareness of the others that even I can feel, and Micah frowning deeply in concentration.

Vahni's eyes fly open as they separate from each other, and Micah bows his head. His emotions are locked away, unreadable to me, his gaze even averted from Hope's desperate one.

"*Micah Tokasz is my ward,*" Vahni declares. "*If any transformation is to occur today, I will conduct it myself.*"

Her blood-red gaze flits toward Micah and then back to Arete, as if daring the guardian to challenge her on this matter. Hope lets out a small sound of despair, but Micah doesn't react, as though Vahni had somehow drugged him into acquiescence.

The weight is heavy within my heart as I struggle to understand. Vahni may be bonded to Micah as his master, and she may have some semblance of connection to him. But that doesn't mean she has any better of a connection to any of us or any of the humans. Despite wanting to do things on her own terms, Vahni would apparently still go along with this horrendous plan because of Arete and Raphael.

Micah lifts his head to look at me, his gaze direct and probing. I know that he doesn't dare use his telepathy in this company, but he seems to be trying to tell me something else. Something that he's broadcasting with his emotions.

Confidence. Hope. Trust. He's trusting me to do the right thing, only we're stonewalled right now and I don't know what that is.

"Very well," Arete says in a clipped tone. She pivots around and grabs Raleigh, her patience at her limit. "My original plan was to use you. You are perhaps too emotional, but you were pure of heart in life and as such your *lumen* is strong."

"No!" I object.

Arete ignores me, and Raleigh takes one pained step forward, having been released from her bindings. She sinks to her knees before Arete, her outward demeanor brave, but her inner heartbreak as real and as true as Raleigh is herself. Arete is wrong. Raleigh isn't too emotional. She's my center, my balance, and she achieves her own harmony by being passionate about everything she does.

"Not her!" I shout. "*Take me! I choose me!*"

"Jonathan, don't! Please!" Raleigh cries out.

Arete hesitates, and Vahni steps up to me, ash trailing behind her. She smells like a mixture of burnt driftwood and the sea, and my senses fill up with her until I can't breathe. Her hands cradle my face in her hands.

I close my eyes and try to accept this. Try to prepare myself for the inevitable, for what I asked for, for her to strip me of my *lumen* and destroy me.

Half a millennium was longer than anyone should have to walk on the earth, and I always thought I would welcome this moment with open arms. I'm leaving behind my legacy in Hope and Davis. They'll always have each other, and she'll have Micah. And if my soul will be part of him, she'll always have part of me too. But there is still no way to be ready for this. For the end.

I can't read Vahni's emotions, but when I look at her again, I can see the satisfaction in her eyes.

"*This one is pure and strong as well,*" she declares.

I seek out Raleigh, who's still next to Arete but no longer in her grasp. I try to smile at her but falter, my heart fracturing at the sight of her tears. If I could have another five hundred years, I would take it and make up for the past fifty.

No, there is no possible way to prepare for this at all, and I'm definitely not prepared for the images to flash in my mind. They're Vahni's memories, and they show me Asphodel as it once was, with beautiful gardens instead of the stark and treacherous landscape. Arete is saying something to Raleigh and the others, but I can't hear them. I can only hear Vahni.

"The triangle's trust was broken long ago. Arete is my daughter, and I cannot act against her, but my ward has chosen you to be the one."

Micah chose me to fix things here? To destroy Arete? I suppose this is only fitting considering all of the choices I've made upon his behalf. But exactly how could I defeat an Eternal?

"Only an Eternal can replace another. I will grant you the power of an Eternal if your intentions are true."

I stare into Vahni's ancient gaze, and it's like peering straight into the pits of Hell.

"What would happen to Arete?" I ask.

"She would be as you are now."

"What would happen to me?"

"If you accept this path, you will become one of us." Her eyes sear through my consciousness. *"We have the power to choose, Jonathan Drapier. Do you choose to accept this fate? Are your intentions true?"* she repeats.

To become an Eternal. I never intended to live forever. I've spent the past five hundred years trying to come to terms with my past life. I tried to use my daughter to make up for my failed life with Adrienne, but that ended in heartache for both of us. I attempted to distance myself from my entire bloodline, but Hope insisted on entering my life and staying with me, through thick and thin. Everyone I've ever loved stayed true to me, with the exception of Adrienne.

I died waiting for all of my sins to wash away, but they never did.

When I woke up, Adrienne was gone, and I heard her voice in the corridor. My vision was blurry, my balance off, but I shuffled over to the door and listened.

"He is dead?" It was Adrienne, and my heart leapt in my chest at the sound of her voice, but then I heard the viscount's slick and oily reply.

"Yes. You have done well, madame, to catch the traitor for us, and you shall be rewarded."

"The only reward I require at this point is what we agreed upon. That my sisters and I can leave the province without persecution. I did everything you asked of me…"

I stumbled back from the door, my hands covering my ears as though it would block out the pain. Adrienne was working as a spy for the viscount? I refused to believe it, yet her words rang of truth and created a fissure in my heart. This would explain why she had unrestricted access to the prison. This would explain why she never wanted to leave.

She wasn't ever a damsel in distress. She wasn't a bored noblewoman looking for entertainment in the prisons. She betrayed me.

All of our conversations about our hopes and dreams for the future. Her caresses and kisses. My heart fissured as I considered that these were also fake. But she'd tried to get me to kill Cyril. And she told me about our daughter and made me leave to ensure that Colette was safe.

Adrienne had been coerced, undoubtedly, but this was no comfort to me at all. If I could ever forgive her as she asked me to, it was because she had used me to save our daughter from this madness.

Hope and Davis may be my last remaining links to my past, but they're not like my wife from so long ago. They're solid and true. They're as much my family as I have ever had, and they're worth fighting for because of who they are.

"Yes," I say out loud. "My intentions are true."

"*I see this too, Jonathan Drapier.*"

Vahni throws back her head and gives an unearthly cry, and a tempest of heat rushes through the pillars and fills the chamber. Arete throws Raphael a look of alarm, but he only bows his head and steps back, as if in acceptance of his sister's fate. Arete rushes toward Vahni, screaming at the goddess to stop as the hurricane of energy swirls around us. But she's too late.

This is no ordinary wind — it's a fury of emotions. Of not just unrest but also peace. Sadness mixed with strength. Gratitude and acceptance. A beam of light brightens a spot in the air in front of Hope, and she stares up at it in wonder. Davis moves to join her, and they both reach their hands up to touch the glow that radiates pure love. Micah does the same, a single tear running down his cheek as he touches a ray of light granting him forgiveness.

These are all of the souls from the Sea of the Dead, and I know that Sarah Gentry and Micah's sister must be amongst them. I'm filled with strength and a sense of peace as one of them touches me too.

Colette.

My sense of my daughter tears away from me as Vahni erupts into flames. Arete is almost upon us when Vahni channels the fire of the Underworld into me. My nerves scream in pain, and so do I. My intentions must have not been true after all, because I pray for release and none comes.

Vahni lets go of me, and I fall to my knees and burn.

My hands brace against the marble floor, my reflection gaping back at me. The heat lingers in my body like it's burning every remaining link that I have to my old life, but I'm whole as I was before. I lift my head, my vision blood-red as though I'm seeing through Vahni's consciousness.

I barely hear Arete's screams. Vahni stands by a pillar, and she has Raphael in her embrace as he watches the Victis take his sister away.

But I can't find Raleigh.

I wade through my fading agony to find her, my gaze landing on Hope and Davis. My blood and my last remaining legacy. I was wrong to think it was a legacy of darkness. Their spirits are as bright as the suns in the sky, and I know in this moment that they'll go on to do great things. Not because of some prescribed Fate or because of the legacy they were born into, but because they choose to. I reach out and beckon to Davis. I have one more thing to tell him. The only secret I have left.

"Jonathan!"

I search the temple to locate her. Raleigh is running toward me, tears flowing down her cheeks and her heart on her sleeve as it should be. I watch her lips mouth the words to me.

She says that she loves me. I'm ultimately here right now because of who she is, and because I love her too.

Two weeks later

Micah

My heart is in my throat as I touch down in the shadow of the house. It's Thursday night, and the entire family will be home for Mom's traditional dinner.

I can already hear the chatter from inside. My dad talking to my younger brother Nick about his last track and field competition, my kid sister Dani asking my mom for more milk, my mom asking if everyone has enough to eat. Lina never missed a week of Mom's Thursday night dinners, and her absence makes a wave of nostalgia ride through me to think about her. But this time I don't let it bring me down because I can still feel her in my heart. I'd been too angry about her death to remember that she's been with me this entire time.

Lina was my big sister and my best friend, and she was a huge part of my life. I was six years old when the Condies adopted me, and Lina helped me get through some hard times back then. She helped me heal all over again two weeks ago when her soul came to me in Asphodel. I felt her energy after Vahni released the souls from the Sea of the Dead, and she was vibrant and a little sassy.

I love you, Mikey. But you need to be with them, not here with me. They love us, and they need you.

I walk into the house, and Mom sees me first. Her fork drops to her plate with a clatter, and Dani cranes her neck to see. Her big brown eyes grow huge as she jumps off her chair and runs to me with curls flying. A tentative smile appears on Nick's face, but he stays at the table, his eyes straying from me to our dad.

Dad pushes his chair back from the table and stands. His hair is a little grayer, the lines in his face a lot deeper, his posture stiff as he frowns at me. He lost his daughter, and then I ran away right after that without even so much as a goodbye. I'll always feel the remorse over that, but I know exactly what I have to tell them now.

"Micah," Mom chokes out. "Where on earth have you been?"

Dani tackles me, and I put my arms around her. "I'm so sorry that I left the way I did. Jack left me an assignment before he died."

I see the shock in Dad's expression as my words sink in. It's a stretch of the truth, though Jack was originally the one to coordinate my initial visit to see the Praxidikai. But Dad and Jack had been old friends – just one more person that he lost in all of this mess.

The story is necessary. Right before she died, Lina figured out that I wasn't quite human and was pretty close to finding out what I really am, but I don't think the rest of my family is ready for it. Nick is eleven and Dani just barely turned seven, and maybe I'll tell my siblings my secret someday. But my parents might never be ready.

"So where have you been?" Dad demands.

"I was in Alaska helping to establish a youth group. They all had the same backgrounds as me." I hug Dani a little bit more, not elaborating on the details because both she and Nick are here, but I know my parents understand. They know how many scars I had from my biological father when I came to them.

"Couldn't you have told us before you left? Or called?" Mom's voice is hoarse, full of the hurt that I caused her.

"If it was Jack, Micah didn't have a choice." Dad walks over to me, still putting off an angry vibe. He looks me in the eye. "Did you succeed?"

"Yeah, I did." I steel myself to say the rest. "I didn't have a choice about being able to call when I was there, but I did have a choice in whether or not I did it in the first place. I chose to go."

He stares at me for a long moment, and I wait for him to give me the final word as to whether I should stay or go. Mom holds her breath, and Nick and Dani stare at Dad like they're bracing themselves for an explosion. Dad's gone the rounds with me before, about some things that have been serious and others that haven't, and it's always been to protect the family.

"Sounds like a worthy assignment," he finally says.

"It was," I reply. "Totally worth it."

"Come have some of your mother's dinner and tell us about it then," he says in a gruff voice. He puts his hand on my shoulder and steers me toward the table. "And don't make your mother worry about you like that ever again."

We're not quite at complete forgiveness yet, but it's a lot more than I hoped for. I pull one of the extra chairs over from the kitchen so I can sit next to Dani, and Nick intercepts me with a grin.

He punches me hard in the arm. "Dork."

I shove him back. "Loser."

It feels good to finally be back. With my family.

⌒メ⌒

A sharp tap on the door wakes me from a dreamless sleep, and I bolt up, not remembering where I am.

"Mom? Dad?"

I'd fallen asleep at my parents house, but now I remember I'd come back to the alliance stronghold after waking up on their couch. I look around at my room, fighting off the grogginess and disorientation. It's been a long time since I felt a sense of permanence with any place, but the Buffalo stronghold is my home for a while, for maybe a long time.

We divvied up the quarters two weeks ago, and I took one of the bigger rooms. I've been working on and off to make it the equivalent of a studio apartment. It's sparsely furnished because all of my old stuff was destroyed in the apartment fire, but most of the guys here have even less than I do or nothing at all because of the *Seraphim* raid. We're all pretty good here at making do with what we have.

The knock sounds again, and I check the clock. 4:52 a.m. Man, I hope nothing major is wrong.

I drag myself out of bed and stumble to the door. When I open it, Elizabeth is standing in the hallway with damp hair and her bag in hand.

"Sorry to wake you up." Her mouth presses into a line as she takes in my messy hair and rumpled t-shirt. "My train leaves early, so I need to get going."

For the past three nights, she's been staying in one of the rooms we're designating for new recruits. She told me last night she was leaving early, but I guess I didn't expect to fall asleep tonight. But now – I'm not sure if I should shake her hand or hug her goodbye. It still feels like the equivalent of a sea is between us, maybe a slightly smaller one than the ocean from when we first met. But even after spending two whole days scouring records for my half-brother and with her staying here, Elizabeth and I aren't close.

"Thanks for everything."

She fiddles with the silver ring on her finger. "I wish we would have found out something different. I think…I think you might have liked Christopher."

"I bet I would have. And I'm sorry you had to find out like that." I hate how empty my words sound. Or maybe my words make me feel empty because they remind me that I have one more person to grieve.

We found out that Christopher used to live here in Buffalo like she thought, but that he died four years ago. He'd been seventeen and a minor, and someone had taken elaborate measures to cover it all up. No news press, no obituary, no missing person's report even though he basically just dropped off the face of the earth one day. Raleigh had been able to use her resources to help us finally unearth the truth.

"Here, I want you to have this." Elizabeth takes the silver ring off of her middle finger and holds it out to me. "It belonged to my father." She slants me a look. "Your grandfather. I always thought I might give it to one of my sons one day."

I take it from her, a lump in my throat that I can't explain.

She smiles a little and starts to turn away but hesitates. "Micah? I need to tell you something."

Here we go. My defenses immediately go up. She's going to tell me that she wished she could have given the ring to Christopher instead of me. Or that finding out he died was too much for her and that she doesn't think I should contact her again.

Her cheeks color. "When I first saw you at the school... I was afraid of you."

"Because I look a lot like my father," I say flatly.

"Yes."

Her reply knocks me down inside, and I swallow hard. "I'm sorry I remind you of him."

She says quickly. "Micah, no, you don't understand. He wasn't a bad person when I knew him."

"Just so you know," I interrupt. "There's probably nothing you could ever say to me that would redeem him in my eyes."

"That's not why I mentioned it." She drops her bags and walks up to me, lifting her hand to rest against my shoulder. "I'm proud of you. I mean, look at what you're doing here." She gestures at the walls around her. "You're building this entire place here to help others like you. I'm proud of you and the person you've become, but I can't take any credit for it. Your adoptive family gave you such a good life, but even if they hadn't, I think you would have still wound up here."

I still have that lump in my throat but for different reasons. She puts her arms around me and gives me a gentle hug, and when she steps back, her eyes are tearless but bright.

"You can meet the Condies if you want to sometime," I say. "My other family. My mom is from Italy and makes amazing food if you want to ever join us for dinner."

Elizabeth blinks in surprise, and I hope I didn't cross any line I shouldn't have. But she just wipes at her eyes and nods. "All right. A little weird maybe, but I think I might like that."

It's weird, yeah, but I think Mom will be okay with it. And I shouldn't feel any sort of weirdness for thinking of Eva as my mom, because that's what she is.

Elizabeth picks up her bag again. "How long does it take you to fly between Albany and Buffalo again?"

"About an hour."

She gives me a tentative smile. "Want to get some ice cream or something after school sometime next week?" she asks. "You can bring Hope with you. I haven't met her yet, and I'd like to. But only if that's something you both want."

"I'll see what day is good for her," I say. Today is definitely not a good day, and apprehension spikes through me to think about what Hope and I are doing later.

"All right. Let me know. I'd better catch that train." She starts down the hallway, and I shake myself out of my stupor and call after her.

"Oh, Elizabeth? Sorry, but you can't leave that way."

Her back stiffens, and she turns around, reluctantly. "Dammit. You're going to make that teleporter of yours take me out of here again, aren't you?"

"It's either me flying you out or Ben teleporting you."

"Fine." She sighs and tilts her head to look up at the ceiling, her eyes squeezed shut. I start to ask if she's okay, and she holds

356

up a finger. "Give me a sec. I'm deliberating which is the lesser of two evils."

"I'd go for flying, personally," I say lightly.

She sighs again and cringes. "You're really going to make me do this, huh?" she asks. "Your own mother?"

"Sorry," I repeat, smiling back. "It's alliance protocol."

The entire day crawls until the moment I have to leave, and then I suddenly wish I had more time to get ready. Crazy that I barely helped to save the entire city from the *Seraphim*, but I'm a nervous wreck about this.

I pull up to Hope's house on the Triumph, letting the engine idle as I calm my nerves. Davis' car is parked out on the driveway instead of in the garage, shining as though he just had it washed and waxed. He opens the front door when I ring the bell and steps back to scrutinize me and my tux.

"Come on in, Micah. She's in her room." He watches as I put my backpack down and take out the small florist's box. "God, I remember doing this." He clears his throat. "Please don't do what I did with my date after prom."

"Seriously, Davis!" Hope walks into the foyer. "You did not just say that."

She glares at him, and I soak in the sight of her. She looks gorgeous in her dress and with her hair done up, but it's the slight flush in her cheeks and the way she looks at me that makes my heart speed up to unnatural proportions. She once told me this wasn't a big deal to her, but that was before, when my life was completely unsettled. Life is still a little crazy, but I think we're both feeling more solid now.

I take her hand and put on her corsage, and Davis whips out his phone and starts taking pictures while I try to ignore him and the million things that are awkward about this moment.

"You're so beautiful," I whisper to her.

She blushes hard-core. "So are you."

Her fingers tremble as she fastens a flower onto my lapel, her concentration fierce despite Davis continuing to snap pictures. "Look over here, sis," he says cheerily. "Sorry, but Dad would want me to get these pics."

"Yeah, and Dad would use his nice camera and make us pose a billion times, so thanks at least for not doing that." She crosses her eyes and gives him a silly grin, and Davis laughs. We spend the next ten minutes doing ridiculous poses and one serious one, and then it's time to go.

"We're having a late dinner with the alliance after prom," I remind Davis. "I promise I'll take good care of her."

He sticks his phone in his back pocket, his smile disappearing as he steps forward and shakes my hand. "I know you will, Micah." He turns to Hope, hesitating a little before he adds, "Seriously, though. Dad and Mom would have loved seeing you do the whole prom thing. And with a guy that's willing to literally go to Hell and back with you."

Hope's face breaks out in a smile, and she lets go of my hand and throws her arms around Davis in a hug. "Thanks, big brother," she whispers. "For taking that same journey with me."

"Yeah, well. That's what family is for, right?" he says gruffly, but his eyes are misty. "Hey, Micah. The helmet will mess up Hope's hair, so why don't you take my car? You guys might have these amazing healing skills, but I have no desire to have anyone's head crack open."

He tosses me his keys, and I catch them and catch Hope's shrug out of the corner of my eye at the same time. She'd actually asked me to fly us there, but I don't mention this little fact to Davis because after the cliffs of Asphodel, I doubt he'd go for that either. He stands on the front porch and waves as we get into his car, and we wave back. I see the tears in Hope's eyes before she looks out the window, and search around for a tissue. If Jonathan were taking her tonight instead of me, he'd probably hand her one of his black handkerchiefs.

We don't talk about Jonathan much these days, but I know Hope thinks about him a lot.

He's still in Asphodel with Vahni. The goddess doesn't appear in this realm anymore as apparitions, and I sleep easier these days. Those apparitions, the voices, the nightmares I had before were all from Arete. Vahni is pretty quiet these days, but now and then I can sense her, and once she actually spoke to me.

The Eternal has chosen to come back.

Given that Arete isn't in the equation anymore, I assumed she meant Jonathan and not Arete. I also assumed she meant come back to this realm. It's what I've told Hope anyway, because I know she's worried.

Hope rests her hand on my leg, and I lift up her hand and press it to my lips. Her skin is so warm – more than usual tonight – and her smile makes all of the butterflies in my stomach break loose. I brake at the next stop sign, looking over my shoulder to make sure no one's behind us before leaning over to her.

"What are you doing?" she whispers.

I don't answer. I kiss her instead, almost running my fingers through her hair but remembering at the last second not to mess it up. I caress the curve of her neck and run my palm over her bare shoulder, kissing her until the inevitable honk of a car sounds from behind us. Hope breaks it off, giving me a smile that makes me feel like I do when I'm flying a little too high, and I take a deep breath and start driving again.

In Asphodel, her kiss had helped me heal, and I think it's because the powers that make both of us possible agree. She and I are in this together. Not because of fates or some prophecy, but because we choose to be.

The prom is at a place called Salvatore's Italian Gardens, and I stay off the freeway and take the side streets to get there. Hope slips her hand into mine, her thumb rubbing against my palm and driving me a little bit crazy in all of the good ways. She was the one to insist that we go separately instead of with Troy, Sylvia, and our other friends, and I'm glad for it.

"So, about dinner later," she prompts. "Are you sure I'm not overdressed?"

"Probably, but so am I." I smile at her. "Besides, it's kind of a big deal, you know? Formal dress for formally inducting you into the alliance."

"It's just so much it hasn't totally sunk in yet." She looks down at our linked hands. "I didn't use to belong to anything, but now I'll be part of this plus I'll be part of Raleigh's constituency."

"It's still Jonathan's constituency," I correct.

Hope sighs. "That's what Raleigh keeps saying too. But he's part of the Praxidikai now, and Davis told me that would be a conflict of interest. Though him staying director might be a good thing since you're director of the alliance."

"Davis might be right, but wait until Jonathan comes back to see for sure." I wait for her response, but she's looking straight ahead. "And I'm not a director," I correct her.

A faint smile touches her profile. "Whatever, head leader of demons. The title doesn't matter. It's what you do that counts."

What I do. I don't want to think about the alliance right now, but it's pretty much a constant in my life because there's still a lot to do. Working on the physical set-up of the community center and organizing our efforts. Scouting locally – we want to bring in defectors from as far as Chicago, but we're going to start by scouting here. Making sure all of the guys are part of things – Ben finally admitted to me that he never finished high school, and he'll be going to one of the schools in the city and can help out there.

"I haven't even met all of them yet." Her hand tightens on mine. "What if they don't want me to join?"

"There's no way they wouldn't." I wink at her. "And I'm not just saying that because I'm the head leader of demons."

When we get to street with Salvatore's, the parking lot is jammed. Everything started a half hour ago, but there are still a few limos and cars making their way to the front. I turn on my signal to make the turn, but Hope reaches over and flips the signal off. "Keep going straight."

I glance at her, surprised. Troy and the rest of our friends are waiting for us in there, and my phone is going crazy with notifications. I turn it off and ask, "What are we doing?"

She tucks a stray hair behind her ear and gives me a small smile. "I just want you for a minute before we go into that crowd. We were going to fly in before my dear brother got other ideas for us, so take me flying."

"Good idea."

I pull into the parking lot next door to Salvatore's and get out, Hope stepping out of her side before I can walk over and open the door for her. I close the distance between us, sliding my hand around her waist and pulling her close, and she wraps her arms around my neck and tilts her chin to look up at me.

"I missed doing this with you."

My *deimos* erupts, my wings knowing my intentions and ready to bring us into the sky. But I kiss her first, lingering over the feel of her lips moving with mine. She presses herself closer to me, our kiss becoming slower, hungrier, more devastating. My senses fill with her, of the faint sweet scent of her mixed with the flowers, of the softness and warmth of her lips, and of her strength. I missed flying with her too, but I'm pretty sure I missed doing this with her much more.

Her arms tighten around me, and she suddenly breaks off the kiss and laughs. I look around, half-dazed. We're about fifty feet up in the air, with a bird's-eye view of Salvatore's.

"So," she says, and when I look back at her, her eyes are full of desire. "You *are* the perfect being."

I roll my eyes. "That's not exactly what Arete said, and even if she had, I wouldn't believe it."

Hope's eyes glint with mischief. "Are you sure no one can see us right now?"

"Yeah. Why?"

She leans in and kisses me again, her lips parting and one of her hands tangling through my hair. My grip tightens on her waist, and I take the kiss deeper as I simultaneously take us up, spiraling higher and higher until it feels like we're on top of the world. She breaks off the kiss with a gasp, and I hug her tightly to me as we look down at our city. The sun is low and starting its descent over Buffalo, a siren sounding in the distance and the sounds of music floating up to us. It's so different than my life in Alaska. It's full of activity and full of life, and it's better.

I rest my forehead against Hope's. "Thank you," I say.

"For what?" she whispers.

"For believing in me." I look into her eyes, my heart filling with more gratitude than I know I'll ever be able to express. "Your light balances out my darkness."

She smiles and holds onto me a little tighter. "Yours too."

"Not even," I retort. "I don't have any light in me. Just darkness."

"But that's not true." Her gaze searches my face. "Micah, do you remember when you told me right when you came back from Alaska? That you figured out how to live without hurting anyone?"

"You're using my own words against me?" I tease.

"Yup," she says firmly. "You were able to do that because of the light you've had in you this whole time. I'm not talking about the *deimos* or the *ignis* or whatever those things are. Just the fact that you're you."

"After all we just went through, I feel a little selfish now," I admit. "There's a lot of things I want to make sure I have time for besides alliance stuff. College. Life." I let us start to float to the ground, holding her close to me. "You."

She shakes her head. "It is perfectly forgivable to have selfish desires in other aspects of our lives, especially when it comes to those we love."

It sounds like she's reciting a speech, and I puzzle over it for a second before I get it. "Did Jonathan tell you that?"

"Yeah," she admits, and there's a little bit of sadness in her voice. "Though ironically, what he did was probably the most selfless thing I've ever seen."

"He's coming back," I reassure her. "There's no way he wouldn't. He has too much to come back to."

"Maybe you're right." She sighs. "I just worry. That place can get under your skin. Look what happened to Arete."

"Yeah, but he's strong enough to not go insane like Arete."

She leans away from me and gives me a small smile as we almost touch down. I don't know what she's thinking about, but I'm guessing Jonathan, and I'm a little surprised to be thinking about him too. Despite everything from our past, I don't feel any bad blood toward him or toward Jehoel either. Not anymore.

"Oh, please keep us in the air," she says, looking down at the parking lot in surprise. "I don't want to go in just yet."

"Anything you want."

I take us higher until we're suspended in space a few hundred feet above the building. The garden staff opens the doors to the outside to let the music filter into the air, and I twirl Hope slowly around in our very first dance. We went through so much to be here, and we have so much more to look forward to. Given who we are, the future is bound to come along with some craziness, but with Hope by my side, I know we can conquer whatever comes our way. Even if it means harpies and two-headed griffins.

"Just so you know," Hope says with deliberate nonchalance. "You're going to be great as leader of the alliance."

"Why? Because I'm a perfect being?"

"Exactly." She laughs, and I grin at her, knowing that no matter what, it's going to be okay.

"I really, really love you," I tell her.

She rests her head against my shoulder and sighs. "I love you too, Micah. Always."

Epilogue

Jonathan

*A*drienne orchestrated a scheme in which I was supposed to die. I listened to her conversation with the viscount from my cell, not believing my ears when I heard her ask him for the freedom of her sisters and herself in exchange for my death.

I raged inside, but a small part of me clung to the hope that maybe she hadn't meant for me to die. That she meant for my death to be a ruse, as hers was. That we could get out of this prison for good. But for the girl I loved to do this to me – I didn't know if I could ever forgive her, let alone trust her again.

I shouldn't have been standing there in the first place. I had died and come back somehow, and my horror and disbelief began to be overshadowed by emotions I didn't understand. Grief. Terror. Smugness. It was as though the feelings were flowing from Adrienne and the viscount and spearing me straight in the heart. My hand went over my chest, sure that Adrienne's betrayal would cause it to stop beating. But my heart was already still.

None of this was possible.

"One last thing that you should know," I heard Adrienne say. "Your interrogator Jonathan Drapier was loyal to the crown. He was never part of the Huguenots."

I gripped the door handle and forced myself to listen.

"Your betrayal has gone far enough," the viscount sneered.

"I…I do not understand," Adrienne stammered.

"Your father greatly prides his relationship with the House of Valois, and when I told him about you and your sisters' involvement with the opposition, it troubled him greatly." He paused to let these facts soak in, and I heard Adrienne draw in her breath.

"You were not to speak of any of this to him! That was the arrangement."

He continued as though she hadn't responded. "He couldn't fathom why you were associating with the Huguenots until I spoke to him one day about your visits to the prisons." I could almost make out the viscount's smirk from where I stood, and I knew that the smugness I felt was coming from him. "I was not completely convinced by your initial story. A bored aristocrat that was fascinated with death? I was as curious about this as he was until we discovered that we shared a mutual acquaintance. Jonathan Drapier."

"No." Her whisper was horror-struck.

"I must thank you for helping to rid the prisons of the traitor, but your attempt to fake Jonathan Drapier's death backfired," he said in a snide tone. "I checked on your former love, and he is truly and actually dead."

"You lie!" Adrienne hissed.

She made a strangled sound that was comprised of half-sorrow, half-rage. I heard the scuff of footsteps, a shot of a pistol, and then her cry of pain.

I was still reeling but had heard enough, and I broke myself out of my stupor and ran into the corridor where Adrienne lay. The viscount backed away from me, his face draining of color as if he was looking at a ghost. I saw the blood soaking through the bodice of Adrienne's dress, and I was upon him. It took me mere seconds and no physical effort whatsoever to grab him and the pistol that he already had drawn.

I could have killed him, but something stopped me. Not his terror – I had felt the terror of others so often within these walls that I was desensitized to it. It was something greater than that. I looked past the dread in the viscount's eyes and straight into his soul, and I knew that despite his deplorable actions, he was not completely lost.

A lightness of being overcame me, and I felt it depart me like a burst of pure energy and travel over to the viscount. He stared at me with a glassy, stunned expression, and then turned to see Adrienne's body on the floor. His face contorted with horror as though just realizing what he'd done, and he sank to his knees and wept. I was done with him. Vengeance had no place in my actions toward men, and they never did, not even when Adrienne asked me to kill Cyril.

I looked at Adrienne too, and my heart was like deadweight.

She was bleeding profusely, and I saw the position of the wound and knew she would not survive. I brushed back her hair, and she opened her eyes and saw me. Relief mixed with her pain, and there was sorrow too. She lifted her hand and pressed her palm against my chest, but my heart no longer beat for her to feel.

"My love. What have you done?" Her voice quivered. "You should not have come back for me. I have made a mess of things."

"You speak nonsense," I whispered back. "I could never leave you in that prison cell."

It was the truth. Even though she had betrayed me, I understood now why she did it. She tried to save everyone — her sisters, Colette, me — but her efforts had been thwarted by the viscount. I had tried to do the same by somehow giving her the energy from my soul, but my efforts weren't enough to save her either.

I held her in my arms as she slowly slipped away from me. We said a few more words to one another, and I didn't know how I did it, but something about my physical touch eased her pain. Eventually she was too weak to talk, but I felt the peace in her heart before she died.

I carried her out of the prison, having little memory of how I managed it, only that I was somehow able to run faster than any steed. I took her back to the church where we were married and dug a grave for her by a stand of trees. My tears flowed as I laid her to rest, and I grieved for the brief happiness that we shared and the life we would never have.

Except there was one last remaining light for me. When I was done burying my wife and my heart, I walked away and went to Colette.

I open my eyes, and Vahni nods knowingly.

"You forgave Adrienne. And you eventually forgave yourself."

"Yes," I say simply. My empathic abilities have been both a curse and a blessing, as they've forced me to relive the emotions of that day. Forgiveness was the only way to prevent myself from going mad.

"That was ultimately Arete's downfall," Vahni replies to my unspoken thoughts. *"Arete never forgave herself for agreeing to split the guardian and demon lineages. She blamed herself for the conflict that arose between her children and sought to turn back time instead of moving forward."*

Vahni walks with me through the gardens of Asphodel next to the temple of the Praxidikai. The place is vibrant with energy, the guardians and demons back from where Vahni had hidden them away from Arete in the Underworld. Now they work to restore the beauty of their home.

"Will she ever return?" I ask Vahni.

"Arete's soul resides in the Sea of the Dead, and there she shall remain."

It's not the first time I've asked Vahni about Arete, but she's never answered me before. I know she grieves over her lost daughter and has expressed guilt for not removing Arete from power sooner than she had, but I sense that the healing of Asphodel reflects Vahni's healing as well.

Time moves at a different pace here, and I don't know exactly how long I've been away from the living realm. But I've been here long enough to understand this place better. Micah once said that the twin suns were a metaphor, and the same applies to this entire realm. With Arete's madness had come suffering and ultimately ruin, and while the gardens are far from the lush place they once were, they're well on their way to recovering from the centuries of hardship.

Raphael appears in the gardens in a sudden swath of heat and darkness, his mood close to jubilant. He bows to Vahni and then to myself.

"*Welcome back, my son.*" Vahni's voice resonates in our thoughts in as warm a tone as she's ever used. "*You succeeded.*"

He holds up the obelisk-shaped object, the twin to the keys for the guardian gateway. I'd told him what Jehoel had said about pitching the demon *clavis* into the gateway before it was destroyed, and he left in search of it either weeks or months ago.

"It was as you described," he says to me. He still feels sorrow over the loss of his sister, and he can't bring himself to directly address me as anything in particular. "I had to search nearly all of the possible gateways, but I finally located it within a tomb in Italy."

Except for the one original demon key that Vahni keeps in the Underworld, Arete had destroyed the rest of the demon *claves* after a bitter feud between herself and her brother. Raphael has been without a ward ever since, but this means he can finally appoint one.

As it turns out, Raphael isn't nearly as much of an ass as I'd thought. He's bound as I am to protect the energy of the collective, which includes both light and darkness.

"*Have you thought of whom you will appoint as a ward?*" Vahni asks him. "*You have not chosen yet, I see.*"

"What about Micah?" I suggest.

"*Micah is my ward,*" Vahni interjects. "*He cannot serve both me and Raphael.*"

"The ward will be of my own choosing." Raphael's tone is one of disdain, but his emotions are more on the side of joyous.

He and Vahni engage in a conversation about the global state of affairs with the Impiorum, and I listen but also reflect upon the local state of affairs of my former guardian constituency. Tricia was called to stand before the tribunal and found guilty of perjury, conspiracy, and endangerment of human and guardian life. With Tricia's influence gone, over three-quarters of the Buffalo constituency stepped forth and confessed to the tribunal what really happened, and Raleigh was exonerated of all charges.

She stepped in as my natural successor, but I don't know if she intends to stay in that position. She never wanted it, but things may be different now.

A lot of things will be different after I return.

One of the guardians of Asphodel glides forward, coming to a stop in front of me and bowing low. She holds out something in outstretched hands, and I accept the offering and bow back.

"Jonathan Drapier, eternal protector of light –" the guardian begins.

"It's just Jonathan Draper now," I say. "I am impressed by your workmanship. Thank you."

The guardian looks at me, shock reverberating through her because of my lack of decorum. After multiple millennia of serving Arete, I probably come across as quite a shock.

But I won't be staying. I need to move forward. As if she senses my intentions, Vahni faces me, and for the briefest of moments, shows me her true form. Her blackened skin heals so it's smooth and almost translucent despite still being dark, and her hair lengthens and shines blue-black in the glow of the temple. The red of her eyes clears, and she gazes at me with warmth as she smiles.

"Farewell, Jonathan. Return to us soon."

This is part of the arrangement, and the omniscient goddess already knows that I'll uphold my obligation. I suppose I'll eventually need to choose a new ward too, though Arete's former wards – twenty-nine of them in total – are under my direction and dispersed throughout the living realm.

I have to make one last stop before I leave this realm, and I head for the green sea at the bottom of the cliffs. I find Jack Williamson walking back and forth in the surf, as he's been doing since the day he escorted Micah, Hope, Davis, and Raleigh back through to the realm of the living. He hasn't come up to the temple like the other wards, and I haven't forced him to do so.

I approach him, and he looks up, a current of dread riding through him before he bows down on one knee.

"Father of guardians and protector of light. How may I assist you?" he asks with great solemnity.

"Stand up, Jack."

He obeys, and I place my hand over his heart.

I release you.

Jack's eyes close, his physical form shuddering as his soul releases and begins its ascent up the cliffs. The life he lived in Buffalo as the D.A. was only one of over a hundred that Jack attempted, and he clings to his sorrows from each one of those lives. But now he'll join his loved ones in the Sea of the Dead. I watch his departure, glad that he's not transported by misery or the sorrow of the Victis but via my power and with a sense of well-deserved peace.

I retrieve his *clavis* from the sand, reflecting upon the fact that we really need to do something about those Victis when I get back. I'll have to petition the other two Eternals to release their souls as well.

The harmony in Asphodel is restored, at least for now. I can go home again.

Stepping out into the living realm is like being released from an eternity of sensory deprivation. The air is hot and thick with the humidity of summer. The scent of freshly mowed grass is so vivid that it makes me dizzy. Even in the fading light of dusk, the colors are more vivid here than in Asphodel.

Hope's pacing back and forth within the small grove in her back yard as though looking for something she lost. She doesn't know yet why she felt such a strong compulsion to be here, but

I'd sent to her subconscious the approximate location of the gateway before I crossed over.

Her jaw drops when I step out from the trees.

"Jonathan!"

She runs to me, and I extend my arms out to embrace her. She ducks and punches me in the chest instead, and I stagger back a step.

"Ouch." I place my hand over my heart in mock pain. "Was I gone for that long?"

"Were you gone for..." She repeats, her eyes shining with anger and unshed tears. "You were gone for almost the entire summer, Jonathan. How could you not know that?"

I look at her closely. I'm by no means as omniscient as Vahni is, but I can tell just from a visual inspection that aside from being furious with me, she appears to be doing well. Strong. Centered. She peers back at me as though trying to determine if I'm any different.

"It's still me," I assure her.

"Yeah, except you're an Eternal now. Raleigh filled me in on the history of the Praxidikai when you were gone." There's something in her tone that's inexplicably sad, and the smile that she finally gives me is hesitant. "You're just here for a visit, aren't you?"

"No, I'm here to stay."

"Really?" Her expressions brightens. "But how is that possible?"

"Vahni and Raphael agree that we cannot lose touch with our senses of humanity. Ultimately, we decided the Praxidikai would benefit most if we remain connected with the realm of mortals."

She frowns. "Isn't that what wards are supposed to be for?"

"In part, yes. But ultimately I believe this contributed to Arete's downfall. She never once left Asphodel, not until Raleigh's trial. Raphael often ventures into this realm, and so does Vahni on occasion."

"Kind of like the Greek gods, huh?" A mischievous smile plays on her lips. "Yeah, well. If there's anyone who's in touch with everything in this realm, it's you."

I cock an eyebrow. "Joke all you wish, but I'm quite modern compared to Raphael and the ancient goddess of the Underworld."

"I bet you are." Her tone changes to become more serious. "I'm happy you're back. And I bet Raleigh is too."

"I haven't seen her," I admit. "I came here first."

Her jaw drops for the second time. "Oh, but you *have* to see her! She'll probably punch you even harder than I did if you don't."

"I will go to her," I assure her. "I wanted to give you this first."

I draw out from beneath my jacket what the Asphodel guardian had presented to me before I left, and Hope's eyes widen almost comically.

"Is that what I think it is?"

"I haven't perfected my mind-reading abilities yet, so I don't know what you think it is," I quip. "But yes. It is for you."

The knife was made in the fires of the Underworld to my specifications. Its artistically-serrated blade is much like the one I'd taken from an Impiorum adversary long ago, only instead of the hilt being made of Raphael's demon *clavis,* the black obelisk shape is Christianna's old *clavis.* It's a reincarnation of the knife that started it all, the one that I once carried and that Hope used against the Impiorum demons on the fateful day that she transformed.

"It's mine," I clarify. "Technically I'm supposed to choose a ward and bind them to me in service, but I already have twenty-nine wards in this world. Twenty-eight," I correct myself, thinking of Jack.

"You want me to have it?" She shakes her head. "Does that make me your ward?"

"No. But you can use it to communicate with me whenever you wish," I explain. "Or use it to cross realms."

She blanches. "No offense, but I think I'll pass on that second one. But the fact that it's a knife? Are you expecting another battle?"

"No, but one can never be too prepared. Every guardian needs a good knife." I take in her incredulous expression and smile. "Consider it a belated graduation present. Or a family heirloom, if you will."

"Family heirloom. Wow." She enunciates the single syllable and finally reaches for it, her hand closing around the *clavis*. I close my eyes as I'm speared by a sense of her spirit. So much strength and love in one soul. It's true that Hope possessing the key won't automatically make her my ward – I have no desire to bind anyone else to me in service, least of all someone I love.

"Thank you," she says solemnly. She looks like she wants to say more but holds back.

"You are wondering why I didn't tell you sooner that we were related?" I guess.

Her eyes narrow in suspicion. "I thought you couldn't read minds."

"I said I hadn't perfected those abilities yet," I reply. "To answer the question, would it have changed anything for you if I told you?"

She leans against a tree and stares at the knife as she mulls this over. Dusk is fading into darkness now, and the lights on the main floor of her house flicker on. I can hear Davis calling for her, and Hope gestures for me to come. We head for her house, the only sounds being the soft snaps of twigs and local street traffic as she mulls over my question.

"Honestly? It probably wouldn't have changed much," she answers.

"And I was under the misconception that it would have changed everything," I confess. "Do you remember the story I told you about Colette?"

"I do." She stops in her tracks as I wait for her to form her own conclusions, and the realization slowly settles over her expression. "She was your daughter, wasn't she? You had to leave her."

"Yes. In retrospect, I regret not telling her what I really was," I admit. "I think she might have accepted it, but I always thought there was a good chance she wouldn't. She was terribly headstrong."

"Huh, I wonder where she got that from?" Hope slips her arm into mine, and we continue walking to her house. "Will you tell me more about them someday? Your family when you were human?"

"Yes, of course. I owe both you and Davis your family history." I escort her to her back porch and smile down at her. She and Colette are similar in that they're both headstrong and true – but as soon as I think it, I know I'm through making comparisons between the past and the present. Hope is unique, and I'm grateful that I have her lifetime to know her better.

I finally give her that embrace, briefly pressing my lips to her forehead before letting her go. "I'll see you soon, but right now I have to take care of another very important thing."

"Yes, you do." She squeezes me back as Davis throws open the door to the outside.

"Oh, there you are. I've been looking for you!" he exclaims to Hope. He stops short and gawks at me. "Great-granddad! You're back! Nice suit."

"Hello, Davis." I brush my hand over one of the sleeves. "Thank you. They made it for me in Asphodel."

"No way." Hope peers at me more closely in the light from the house. "Is it *dark gray* instead of black?"

"Indeed," I say to my progeny with mock sternness. "But no making fun of your great-granddad."

The old rock church is a skeleton of rubble and ash now, but the *sanctuarium* magic itself lingers in the space like a lost soul. No fire crews had come to put out the fire that Micah and I had started – ironically enough, they'd been repelled from the site by the protective magic.

My own story began in a church much like this one five centuries ago, and perhaps it's only fitting that I face my new beginning in a similar setting. I'd spoken the truth to Hope earlier when I said I was still me. I feel much as I had before, with a couple of major exceptions.

It's dark, and I pick my way through the debris that used to be Raleigh's sanctuary until I touch one of the partially standing walls. The *sanctuarium* magic funnels through my fingertips and threads its way into my *lumen*, and I breathe in as I receive a sense of the building's energy. The church has a long history, and some of what it retains is negative – the hostility and bitterness that filled this place on its last day standing – but much of the energy is peaceful.

I depart the premises, having everything I need. I never did have a chance to replace my car, but I head into the city by foot, connecting with the rooftops and running until I reach Raleigh's studio. She's there right now, her presence like a beacon to me, and I internalize my own signature to keep it hidden before dropping into the stairwell from the roof.

I hesitate and listen from the stairwell door that opens to the studio's floor. Judging from the sound of Raleigh's footsteps and feel of her *lumen,* she's practicing her swordplay with one of her remarkable swords. I walk out onto her floor, and her footsteps silence. With an eye on the camera at the end of the hall, I head toward the door.

It opens before I can knock, and Raleigh stands before me in a purple tunic and with her emotions in a messy knot. Her face is shiny, her hair swept back with a purple headband, and her sword still drawn. She's beautiful to her core, and I don't think I ever really looked at her in the way that she deserves until now.

Her eyes gleam with angry tears. "Is that all you're going to do? Stand there and stare at me?" she demands.

"Absolutely not." I step up to her, half an eye on the sword, and I kiss her.

I breathe her in, taste her, revel in her. Her kiss sends a delicious burn through me, and I pull her closer as she clutches at my arm. Her sword drops to the floor with a clatter as she pulls me into the studio, and I kick the door shut, my fingers threading through the silk of her hair. She tugs me with her across the room, and we land in a giant pile of cushions on the floor.

I momentarily lose the capacity to think as a confusing mix of emotions bursts from her. Most paramount amongst them is the fact that she's furious with me.

"I've been a fool," I say.

She draws in and releases a deep breath. "Oh no. What have you done now?"

Her emotions are roiling, and I can see the conflict in the green of her eyes. I draw upon the feeling of peace from her old sanctuary and trace my fingers over her forehead. "I'm so sorry I hurt you," I say.

She gasps, and her hand snaps up to grab my wrist. "Don't you dare," she snaps.

"Raleigh…" I keep my voice steady. "You're the last being on this earth that I ever want to hurt."

"Oh, Jonathan. You're right. You're a fool." She pushes me back and sits up, and I sit up to face her on the mountain of cushions. I'm hit with my own confusion as she jumps up and paces the room and then surprise as I really see her studio for the first time. She transformed it into a rough approximation of her old sanctuary, but right now the softness and peace of the physical surroundings are in direct contrast to her mood.

Her eyes flash at me. "It's perfectly normal to feel things. You can't fix the way I *feel*. Nothing is that simple."

"We do this all of the time, Raleigh," I say slowly. "You do it too, when you need ease someone's pain."

"Yes," she huffs. "When we're on rescue missions. But not in our real relationships with people. If you're going to be with me, you need to let my emotions be mine and not what happens to suit you. I mean, really. Do you think Cupid shot me with an arrow to make me fall in love with you?"

My heart leaps to hear it, but Raleigh whirls away from me before I can answer. I jump up and catch her hand, and her temper flares as she grabs onto my arm and steps back into me to throw me. I fly halfway across the studio before landing on my feet, and when I flip back around, she's standing in a defensive pose, ready to spar with me like she has hundreds of times. But never before with furious tears brimming in her eyes.

"Light on or off?" I ask.

"On."

"Magic or no?"

"Leave your magic in Asphodel," she orders.

"Weapons?"

"Not if you want to keep your head."

She charges at me at full-speed, and I leap into the air, twisting myself mid-air so I'm upside-down. When I see the blur of purple, I reach down to catch her arms, but she dodges me, and I land in the middle of a table with lit candles.

Raleigh stands across the room from me. "You've always relied too much on your empath abilities, and it's probably even worse now that you're an Eternal," she says. "Your powers magnify to ridiculous proportions when you're one of the Praxidikai, don't they?"

I don't respond to this. Instead I tap out the candles so they won't serve as fuel for another sanctuary fire.

"Also, about that safekeeper power?" she accuses. "I hope to God that whatever secret you planted in Davis' mind in Asphodel doesn't completely fry his brain when you try to release it."

I don't argue with any of this. Raleigh needs to work through her anger and pain, without the help of my empathic abilities.

She starts prowling across the room. "You should have let it be me!" she cries. "You could never get past Adrienne and everything that happened in your mortal life, and now you'll have to endure all of that for eternity. Why didn't you let it be *me?*"

I doubt she can see me with all of the tears coursing down her cheeks, and that plus her words push me to the limit. For once I take the offensive, running in a circle around the room toward her. She darts away, and I pinpoint the flash of purple before catapulting myself off one of the mirrored walls. My trajectory is strategic, and we fall straight into the middle of the pillows on the floor. She kicks her leg in an attempt to throw me, but she can't produce enough force without bracing against a hard surface.

"Sparring session is over," I declare. "I have something important to tell you, so please stop fighting and listen to me."

Raleigh stops struggling, and she flops back into the cushions with her hair fanning out like a mane. Her chest gradually rises and falls at a slower rate, her fury eventually decreasing with each breath she takes.

"First of all, I moved past Adrienne and my mortal life a long time ago. Just because I use those memories does not mean that I am trapped in them," I inform her. "And about me almost using my empath abilities, circumstances have not been kind to you and I, Raleigh." I soften my tone as I brush a strand of hair from her face. "Maybe I just wanted things to be simple for once, but you're right. I've drawn upon the emotions of others for so long that I temporarily lost touch with mine."

She's very still now, her hands still braced against me but without making a move to get away.

"What I told Davis wasn't a safekeeper secret," I confess. "When I was transforming in the temple, I had a moment when I couldn't find you. I had no idea what was going to happen next."

"That must be the most understated description of that entire day." She clamps her mouth shut when I shoot her a look. "Sorry. I'm listening."

"Davis was supposed to tell you that I would return to you, no matter what, to build us a new sanctuary."

"Us?" Her breath catches as the meaning sinks in. Joint sanctuaries aren't unheard of, but they are very rare. It's equivalent to sharing the deepest sort of guardian bond.

"Yes. Us," I repeat.

Her grip goes from bracing against me to clutching at my arms. "Davis didn't tell me," she says quietly. "Maybe he thought he had to go through excessive brain trauma before he could release that information to me."

"Undoubtedly," I retort. I'm waiting for her serious response, but she's still tensed up beneath me like she's waiting for something else.

I sit up and take her hand. "Raleigh, I love you. Not because of an arrow from Cupid or because we're old friends. You are unlike anyone I've ever known, and I just…" I search for an explanation. "I cannot explain why. I just do."

"That's pretty much how it works." She sits up too. "I love you too. Despite how much I want to kill you sometimes."

I chuckle. "I wouldn't have it any other way."

"Good." She smiles and looks down in a gesture tempered with shyness. "If I may suggest, could we make our sanctuary here? It's already our space because the only ones who ever come here anymore are you and me."

I nod and get to my feet, pulling her to a standing position and leading her to the side of the room. I touch the mirrored walls, and the *sanctuarium* magic that I took from the rock church bursts from my fingertips and radiates through the air. The mirrors reflect the unearthly glow for a second before the magic sinks into the walls, the floor, the ceiling. Into us.

"Done."

"It really is, isn't it?" She shakes her head, gazing at me as though she's in awe of this. "What you ask me to do for you sometimes…I swear, it's pure madness."

I grin at her. "After five hundred years of this life, I'm not completely sane."

We head up to the rooftop and sit next to each other on the ledge so we can see our city. For once in a very long time, I don't feel the unrest in the souls below, and the quiet is a welcome change. I don't know what the future holds for the guardians or demons of this realm, or even necessarily for myself and Raleigh. But I do know that she owns my heart, and that's enough for now.

Raleigh watches the moon ascend, and I watch the city lights below. She bumps her shoulder into mine, her expression impish when I look at her.

"So?" she asks. "The night is full of possibilities. What do you want to do now, my Eternal one?"

I smile at her. "Make up for lost time."

Five hundred years is a long time to hang onto all of those memories, even if some of them have served a purpose. And as my mouth descends upon hers for a kiss and as she slides her arms around me, I feel the heaviest memories release.

It's time for me to make new ones.

For Eternity

deimos

lumen   ignis

soul

ACKNOWLEDGMENTS

Writing this story has been a long and wonderful journey. I couldn't have made it to the other realm and back without the encouragement, guidance, advice, and inspiration of these people:

The Demon Horde, my street team, for their loyalty and undying support despite the fact that I put their beloved characters through Hell. Laura H. for her harpy-sharp proofreader eyes and for unconditionally loving her demon boy. Megan P., for her amazing writer twin skills, historical knowledge, and deliberately hilarious critiques. Elaine V., Tasha S., Rosalyn E., Erin S., for their brilliant suggestions, daily encouragement, and sticker parades. Betsy B. and Shandra N. F., for sticking with me and my characters from book one to eternity. Elise L., for being my round-the-clock consultant on French customs and language. Janice P., for constantly cracking the whip and being evermore the evil queen. Colby P. and Chris C., for going above and beyond minion requirements and also supplying duct tape so I could keep my life together. The Hypnic Jerks, especially J.T., who served as the real-life inspiration for Jehoel minus the scars. Mary Jo T., for insisting that Jonathan be the man, and Kimber K., for insisting that Micah always be the one. Stephanie Varella and Eric Balfour of Off the Grid Entertainment, for taking a chance on my story and bringing my characters to that mysterious realm known as Hollywood. All of the lovely bloggers and reviewers that do so much to help my books find new readers. My sweet family most of all, for putting up with my insanity. And the Mythology cast – Hope, Micah, and Jonathan – for helping me banish my own demons.

To all of my readers. Thank you for making my stories matter.

ABOUT THE AUTHOR

Helen Boswell loved to get lost in the pages of a story from the time she could sound out the words. She credits her dad, an avid fiction reader (and at 79 years old, arguably her oldest fan of her Young Adult novels), with encouraging her to read everything on his shelves from the time she was a teenager. An author of both urban fantasy and contemporary romance, she loves to read and write characters that come to life with their beauty, flaws, and all.

Find out more about Helen and her books at www.helenboswell.com.

CPSIA information can be obtained at www.ICGtesting.com
Printed in the USA
BVOW05s1133050815

411985BV00008B/37/P